"She has a skill for creating characters mired in problems as thick as coal sludge but making them sympathetic enough to hold an audience . . . a rich, textured story woven with complex moods and mistakes . . . well-crafted."  —*Palm Beach Post*

"As she did in her acclaimed debut, O'Dell displays a marvelous gift for serving up eccentric, believable characters and vividly captures the bleakness and harshness of coal-mining country . . . Captivating."
—*Library Journal*

"O'Dell is an accomplished writer; assured and perceptive, she is especially good with quick dialogue that captures the anger and disappointment these characters carry."  —*Pittsburgh Post-Gazette*

### Praise for *Back Roads*

A Main Selection of the Book-of-the-Month Club

"An intense story of family, frailty and dysfunction, set in the coal-mining towns of western Pennsylvania . . . captivatingly told."
—*Chicago Tribune*

"Tense . . . involving . . . deftly captures the voice of a teenage boy who's in trouble."  —*The New York Times Book Review*

"Outrageously unconventional . . . a very funny book."
—*The Baltimore Sun*

"In Harley, O'Dell has created a hero who's heartbreakingly believable; like Holden Caulfield, he uses caustic humor to hide his pain. Readers will care very much about him and his future, if indeed he has one."  —*St. Petersburg Times*

Also by Tawni O'Dell

*Back Roads*

# TAWNI O'DELL

# COAL RUN

NEW AMERICAN LIBRARY

New American Library
Published by New American Library, a division of
Penguin Group (USA) Inc., 375 Hudson Street,
New York, New York 10014, USA
Penguin Group (Canada), 10 Alcorn Avenue, Toronto,
Ontario M4V 3B2, Canada (a division of Pearson Penguin Canada Inc.)
Penguin Books Ltd., 80 Strand, London WC2R 0RL, England
Penguin Ireland, 25 St. Stephen's Green, Dublin 2,
Ireland (a division of Penguin Books Ltd.)
Penguin Group (Australia), 250 Camberwell Road, Camberwell, Victoria 3124,
Australia (a division of Pearson Australia Group Pty. Ltd.)
Penguin Books India Pvt. Ltd., 11 Community Centre, Panchsheel Park,
New Delhi - 110 017, India
Penguin Group (NZ), cnr Airborne and Rosedale Roads, Albany,
Auckland 1310, New Zealand (a division of Pearson New Zealand Ltd.)
Penguin Books (South Africa) (Pty.) Ltd., 24 Sturdee Avenue,
Rosebank, Johannesburg 2196, South Africa

Penguin Books Ltd., Registered Offices: 80 Strand, London WC2R 0RL, England

Published by New American Library, a division of Penguin Group (USA) Inc. Previously published in a
Viking edition.

First New American Library Printing, June 2005


Copyright © Tawni O'Dell, 2004
Readers Guide copyright © Penguin Group (USA) Inc., 2005
All rights reserved

NEW AMERICAN LIBRARY and logo are trademarks of Penguin Group (USA) Inc.

New American Library Trade Paperback ISBN: 0-451-21512-5

The Library of Congress has cataloged the hardcover edition of this title as follows:

O'Dell, Tawni.
Coal Run / Tawni O'Dell.
     p.   cm.
1.  Coal mines and mining—Fiction.   2.  Ukrainian Americans—Fiction.
3.  Football players—Fiction.   4.  Family violence—Fiction.   5.  Wife
abuse—Fiction.   6.  Revenge—Fiction.   I.  Title.
PS3565.D428C93  2004
813'.54—dc22      2003062645

*For my grandparents,*
*Naomi Rebecca and the late H. E. Burkett,*
*whose love for each other*
*and their patch of Pennsylvania*
*inspires and sustains me always.*

# J&P COAL COMPANY MINE NO. 9

*March 14, 1967*

## A MEMORY

THE DAY GERTIE BLEW, I WATCHED MY FATHER LEAVE FOR WORK like I did every morning. It was called morning by the men who worked that shift, but to me it was still night, black and cold and silent except for the far-off rumble of the coke ovens as their doors were thrown open and the infernos inside them roared. I could see them clearly from my bedroom window, strung across a distant hillside, the mouths glowing red, then going dark in a steady rhythm like the blinking of a hundred fiery eyes watching our valley.

I didn't know exactly what it was that woke me. Maybe the squeak of the mattress springs as he got out of bed in the room next door, or his muffled voice along with my mother's as they said their good-byes, or the sound of his steel-toed safety shoes pacing the kitchen floor while he waited for the coffee to brew.

Whatever it was, it had the power to pluck me from my bed and send me stumbling half asleep across the cold, bare floor in my bare feet where I waited at the window to watch him cross our front yard along with the dozens of other men crossing their front yards carrying silver lunch pails the size of toolboxes, their mouths already solemnly working the plugs of tobacco they chewed to lubricate their throats against the gritty coal dust.

They didn't converge in a sudden stream the way they used to when my mother was my age and watched her father and the other men leave the three-room, soot-coated houses in the discarded company town a few miles down the railroad line from here. These days they left one at a time, but still together, in a synchronized solitude.

I always waved at him when he stopped at the car door and looked up at my window, and he always gave me a nod with a scolding half smile that said I should be in bed but what Mom didn't know wouldn't hurt her. It was our secret, one we shared man to man.

It wasn't until the last taillight on the last car or pickup truck winked out of sight around the bend in the road that I went back to bed, but never back to sleep.

I stopped by my bookshelf that my dad had built out of two-by-fours and proudly scanned my small but growing library of alphabet and number books, books about trucks and trains, Little Golden Books and Dr. Seuss books, and a book of Mother Goose nursery rhymes that had belonged to my mother.

At the very end of the row was the copy of *Wonders of Nature* that Santa had left under the tree for me that past Christmas. I took it back to bed with me every morning, along with my flashlight, crawled under my covers, turned to the page about prairie dogs and the diagram of the elaborate underground maze where they lived, and let my mind journey to the place where my dad went every day to do his job.

I didn't know that much about it because my dad and the other miners never talked about their work; they only talked about their fear of losing it. What I did know, I had learned from my mother, who explained to me once that he worked underground in tunnels where he dug coal that was very important to everyone. It gave us energy. It made steel to build buildings. Without coal America would come to a screeching halt.

The part about working underground in tunnels made the biggest impact on me, even bigger than the thought of a colossal shriek of brakes heard around the country and everyone and everything ceasing to move until my dad, and Grandpa, and Uncle Kenny, and Val next door, and my best buddy Steve's dad, and my teacher Miss Finch's boyfriend, and Jess Raynor's dad—who everybody called "Chimp" because one of the other miners once said he'd rather shoot coal with a monkey than be partnered up with Clive Raynor—all went back in the mines and dug some more coal.

The tunnels were what bothered me. I knew certain animals lived underground. Groundhogs and moles and snakes. But I couldn't picture men down there.

The first time I came across the picture of the prairie-dog town was the Christmas morning I got the book. I walked over to my dad, who was sitting in his favorite chair smoking a cigarette, drinking a cup of coffee, and casting glances I didn't understand at my mother, who was sitting on the couch with her bare legs curled up underneath her bathrobe and a short, shiny pink nightgown Santa had brought for her lying across her lap.

He was wearing a bathrobe, too, a gray one over a pair of gray pajamas. The only time I ever saw him wear pajamas was Christmas morning and once when he had the flu and my mom made him miss a day of work. They didn't suit him. He wore them uncomfortably, almost in an embarrassed way, as if he was trying to pull off a disguise.

I stood in front of him holding my new book while he finished looking at Mom through a few wisps of smoke left hanging in the air after the last puff off his cigarette.

I opened the book to the page with the prairie-dog town and asked him if that was what a mine looked like.

He took the book from me and studied it in the serious way he approached all books and all questions, then looked at me with his hooded, brittle blue eyes that were two sparks of startling color in a man otherwise lacking all color.

Sometimes when I watched him in the evening, washing up after work in my mother's green-and-yellow kitchen, stripped to the waist, his arms in black sink water up to his elbows, I thought of him as a person who had been cut out of a black-and-white photo and unknowingly pasted into the real world, and, like the subjects in a black-and- white photo, he seemed to have more clarity to him than people with lots of color.

He was pale skin, black hair, gray stubble, gray work pants, black coal dirt, gray cigarette smoke climbing from between his fingers or his lips, and a blue-gray tattoo etched beneath the dark hair on his hard left forearm, of a glaring man with a bushy mustache nailed to a cross the way Jesus was in church. The man was ugly and frightening but eerily fascinating to me, especially when my dad took me on his lap and traced his outline in his skin and repeated the word "Stalin."

"It's very much close to this," he replied in his broken English. "Except this. See."

At the sound of his command, my sister, Jolene, got up from the play tea set she was arranging on the floor and toddled over to see the book, too, her dozens of new dress-up bracelets and necklaces made of plastic gold and silver beads clicking against each other as she walked.

Dad pointed to the many escape routes the prairie dogs had made from their underground world to the world on top.

"We don't have this," he told us. "We have one way in and one way out."

I had my *Wonders of Nature* book with me at the kitchen table when Gertie blew. I was leafing through its pages while I was eating a late breakfast and might have even been looking at the prairie dogs and thinking of my dad at the precise moment when he would have turned his head toward the roar of the fireball before he was incinerated. Or maybe he never saw it coming. Maybe he was buried instantly by tons of earth without warning. Maybe his bones were broken, his organs crushed, his senses obliterated, his existence erased before he had a chance to understand what was happening. But I doubt it.

He had been a miner his entire adult life, and, like all miners, he understood the language of the coal face. Crackles, hisses, sighs, pops, squeaks, creaks, groans, gurgles—each noise meant something to them: a methane leak that could be ignited, an underground water source that could flood a shaft, a weak section of ceiling that was about to cave in. In response to the slightest tap of a shovel, the wall spoke back to them. I'm sure when it found itself about to be destroyed, it shuddered and screamed in a way they all recognized.

I was in afternoon kindergarten, so I got to spend my mornings at home. I was concentrating on a bowl of Alpha-Bits cereal, trying to spell my name with the sugary letters, being frustrated by the lack of a V. Jolene was in her high chair drawing a picture with her big-girl spoon in the applesauce she had spread all over her tray. She had a cold, and Mom was sneaking up behind her with a bottle of red cough syrup and a teaspoon.

The explosion came first, an enormous underground thunder that shook our house and shattered our windows in a spectacular musical instant with a sound like a million glass bells ringing all at once.

Mom dropped her teaspoon, and it hit the table, where the vibrations bounced it across the Formica leaving a trail of bright red drops like a nosebleed. Her face went ashen as all around us cupboard doors sprang open and dishes fell out, pictures jumped off walls, canned goods tumbled off shelves and rolled across the floor.

Then all movement and all sound ended as abruptly as it had begun. An absolute quiet filled the room that was every bit as loud as the explosion. It made my ears ring, and I clapped my hands over them protectively, somehow understanding that the silence was even worse.

Jolene began to cry. Mom didn't notice. She stared straight ahead at the wall where Dad's most prized possession had hung for my entire life: a portrait of a glowering king with a mustache that drooped to his chin, wearing regal silks and a simple hammered metal crown that looked like a child might have fashioned it out of an old can and some cheap birthstones. It was the only object he had been able to salvage from the remains of his family's farm in Ukraine after the war.

SUPREME SOVEREIGN VOLODYMYR THE GREAT, the little gold plaque at the bottom of the frame read.

"Supreme sovereign of what?" Val asked my mom once.

"Our kitchen," she told him.

Now the portrait lay facedown in the midst of a scattering of glass shards.

I waited to see what Mom's reaction would be. Volodymyr was sacred to Dad, and so was the massive gold frame he had bought with his first paycheck working in the Illinois coalfields years before he came east to Pennsylvania. Her eyes didn't leave the wall, and I realized she wasn't looking at anything. She was paralyzed with fear, waiting for something else.

None of us had ever heard the sound before, but when it finally came, we instinctively knew it meant death. It was a low, moaning wail that rose to a shriek, eerily human yet inhumanly immense, as if the earth itself were crying out in pain.

Mom's eyes filled with tears, and her mouth began to move. I couldn't hear her voice over the scream of the siren, but I could read her lips. She didn't say Dad's name or the name of anyone else she knew working the morning shift. She simply said, "The men."

Before I knew what was happening, she reached out and grabbed me, knocking over my chair. She hoisted Jolene onto her hip and dragged me along behind her by my arm. We went running out the front door, stepping over toppled furniture and crunching through broken window glass spread all over the carpet.

One by one the women of Coal Run joined us. Women I knew well. Women I hardly knew at all. Women my mom liked. Women she didn't like. Old and young. Fat and thin. Pretty and plain. Some pregnant, some not. Some in housedresses, some wearing jeans and cotton blouses like my mom.

They dashed out of their homes and stopped suddenly as if an invisible door had been slammed shut in front of them. They clutched the shoulders and arms of their children or breakfast dishes they had been washing or laundry they had been folding.

They all stared in the same direction, at a spot two miles distant, impossible to see from our homes, but now it was marked by a thin cloud of black smoke seeping lazily across the blue sky. I searched the tilted faces, and for a moment, all their surface differences were stripped away and they were nothing but the daughters and sisters and wives and mothers of miners.

One woman screamed like a girl in a scary movie. One woman groaned and collapsed to the ground. But these were the only signs of hysteria. The rest rushed with shell-shocked responsibility back inside their toppling homes and came out again with their car keys and purses.

Our next-door neighbor Maxine went running for her car. Val was her son. He had dropped out of high school this past year to start working in Gertie. She shouted at my mom to come with her. Mom ignored her and started running.

Down the side of the road we flew, her grip on my arm like a tourniquet. My legs couldn't keep up with hers. I fell, and she yanked me up. I fell again, and she yanked harder and screamed at me to get up. Jolene sobbed from the pain of being jostled against Mom's hip.

I started crying, too. All around us the world was crumbling. Sections of the road sagged. Halves of houses sank into the ground. I watched a dog disappear with a solitary yelp, his paws scrabbling uselessly at the ground as the weight of the doghouse he was chained to pulled him down. I thought the world was coming to an end. I couldn't know that acres of mine tunnels were collapsing beneath the town.

Mom ignored everything and kept running. Soon I became aware of cars and trucks driving past us. Just a few at first. Then a steady stream. Like blood cells through an artery, they came rumbling up from side roads and back roads, bouncing across fields and crashing through woods. The pickup-truck beds were filled with kids and dogs and old people holding on to gun racks for balance.

Some of the drivers slowed down and shouted at Mom to get in, but she didn't seem to hear or care. We ran the whole way.

By the time we neared Gertie, we were the only ones on the road anymore. Hundreds of people had passed by us in a matter of minutes, but now the roars of the engines and the shouting were gone. I could hear birds chirping and distant dogs barking to each other, along with the sound of Mom's labored breathing and Jolene's quiet, frightened sobs and the blood pounding in my own head. I was in a state of near delirium from exhaustion and the pain in my shoulder where Mom gripped me, and I no longer felt the ground beneath my feet. I seemed to be floating. The only thing real to me was the fierce little glitters of quartz in the road as Mom continued pulling me along.

I fell a final time about a quarter mile from the complex. Gertie was at the top of a hill, like all the other deep shaft mines around here. It loomed at the end of a packed dirt and gravel road, looking like an enclosed village inhabited by a race of people who traveled by chutes and ladders and conveyor belts.

Mom wrapped an arm around my chest and dragged me the rest of the way. My knees were scraped raw, and the skin where she had gripped my arm while we ran had turned purple. Her knuckles were white. Her ponytail had come loose, and her pale gold hair, now dark with sweat, was plastered to the sides of her face. Her bare feet were bloody. She hadn't been wearing shoes when the siren sounded.

She released me and put Jolene down, then bent over, coughing. The air was hard to breathe here. It had a charred stench to it, like a hundred moms had burned a hundred dinners and refused to open a window.

Emergency vehicles from all over the county had arrived a while ago. Ambulances, fire trucks, police cars, and the cars and trucks of regular people had all been hastily abandoned at strange angles with the doors left open.

Some people stumbled blindly, calling out names. Others walked around with uncertain purpose, their eyes searching, lips mouthing names they couldn't bring themselves to say out loud yet. The rest stood in stiff, silent, immovable rows, like an orchard in winter.

My mom headed off determinedly, as if she knew of a destination that was worth arriving at, but the only destination I saw was the hillside, and despite having felt the explosion under my feet and hearing the shriek of the siren and seeing the commotion going on all around me, it was hard to believe anything bad had happened inside that hill. It didn't look any different than any other hill.

Where was proof of a catastrophe? I didn't see anything that resembled the aftermath of explosions I'd seen on TV. No leaping flames. No organized heroics by men in uniforms and badges hauling people to safety. The miners on the outside, the police and firefighters, were gathered in big impenetrable knots of grave discussion.

A sick feeling started in the pit of my stomach as the soft weight of Jolene's hand snuck into mine.

There were plenty of men around and lots of equipment and machines meant for digging. Why wasn't anyone doing anything? Why wasn't anyone saying anything?

The gray wooden faces in the orchard began taking on the identities of people I knew. Kids from school. Neighbors. My teacher, Miss Finch, whose boyfriend worked with Dad. Big Dr. Ed, with his dark crew cut and stance like a conquering warlord, who had prescribed the red cough syrup for Jolene yesterday. The lady who drove my school bus. The lady who worked behind the ice cream counter at the Valley Dairy.

I saw my best buddy, Steve, being dragged through the crowd by his mom. I saw the glint of her wedding band on her dirty hand clutching his dirty forearm. He saw me. His eyes were raw from crying.

"Is your dad working?" he shouted at me, his voice high-pitched and shaky. "My dad's working," he said.

I saw our next-door neighbor, Maxine. She was standing on her tiptoes, looking all around her. Suddenly she started pushing her way through people, and I watched her find Val.

Val did everything I aspired to do when I was full-grown. He drove too fast, threw horseshoe ringers, ate Twinkies for breakfast, bagged two bucks every season, wore the same dirty clothes day after day. He could belch the Pledge of Allegiance and throw a football through a tire swing from fifty feet away.

When he wasn't working in the mines, he lived in a backyard world of beer, rock-and-roll anthems, and puddles of motor-oil iridescence. He was always working on his truck, or working on the garage he was building to put the truck in, or working on the description of the girl who was going to sit in the truck when it was running smoothly again. I was his helper. My job was to find the tool he requested in the midst of the dozens of tools spread all over the driveway that led to nowhere, since the garage wasn't finished yet.

Maxine ran to him and threw her arms around his neck. Her weight dragged his head down, and her own head cracked against his helmet. She touched him all over his filthy work clothes, and cupped his blackened face in her hands, and kissed him again and again. I heard her sobs of joy. They should have made me feel good, but they were ugly-sounding things.

I headed toward him, pulling Jolene along behind me. Val would have an answer for me. He'd be able to tell me why everyone was here but no one was doing anything. He had an answer for everything. Not the kind of answers my father gave me that were well thought out and took into account all the knowledge he had accumulated over a lifetime. Val's answers were instantaneous proclamations based on the inconceivability of an alternative.

"Why's the sky blue?" I asked him once.

"'Cause it would look pretty stupid if it was purple," he replied.

We arrived at his side, and I called up to him. He didn't notice us at first; then he finally glanced at me and Jolene, and our presence began to register on his face. I saw a terrible sadness there. It took me a moment to recognize the expression. I'd never seen Val look sad. He got pissed a lot. Anger was his emotion of choice when dealing with tragedy or misfortune. Not rage, but a sort of resigned aggravation that once again life had dealt someone an unfair blow and there was nothing anyone could do about it except swear and have a beer and think about something else.

"Is my dad okay?" I asked him.

I waited for him to say, "It would be pretty stupid if he wasn't."

He knelt in front of me, something he never did. My dad was always crouching down to my level to explain things to me, almost as if he thought we were equals, but Val liked being taller than me. It might have been because he wasn't tall compared to a lot of the other miners.

He clutched me by both arms, and the pain in my shoulder made me jerk away from him, but he held fast. I started to cry. It was the last thing I wanted to do in front of him.

"You be strong for your mom," he said.

"Why?" I screamed the word at him.

"You just do it. Okay?"

I dropped my eyes to the ground. A pair of bare feet appeared in my line of vision. They were filthy and spattered with blood. A few of the pretty pink toenails were cracked. One was ripped off. My mom's feet. She and Dad were going to Miss Finch's wedding tomorrow. She was going to wear high-heeled shoes with her toes sticking out. The night before she had shown my dad a bottle of pink nail polish and a bottle of red, and he had picked pink.

"What's going on, Val?" I heard my mom say.

They began talking in quiet voices, with my mom staring intensely at Val and Val staring intensely at her ruined feet, about what was being done and what wasn't being done and why. Val told her we were waiting for a drill bit to be driven down from Somerset and a rig to be driven up from West Virginia. We didn't have anything here that could drill deep enough. Mom wanted to know why they were drilling instead of trying to go through the mouth. I lost track of the details then except for the numbers. The men were working Left 12. Two miles from the portal. Five hundred feet under the ground. Val said trying to estimate their whereabouts underground and drilling from the top was the only way.

"I don't understand," my mom finally said.

She lifted her hands up and covered her face. When she pulled them away again, tears had cut streaks of white through the dirt on her cheeks, but her voice stayed steady and calm.

"What are you saying?"

"It's gone, Mrs. Zoschenko." Val paused and made a strange noise like he was gulping for air. "The shaft. It's gone. It's collapsed. The whole thing."

I heard my dad's voice in my head: one way in, one way out.

I waited to see what my mom would do next. It seemed to me that everyone was watching her. She was the sister, the daughter, and the wife of a miner, and, because of me, it was assumed she would be the mother of one, too. Her brother and her father were also working the morning shift in Left 12 along with her husband.

She sat down in the middle of the dirt the same way I'd seen Jolene plop down in the yard about a hundred times while she was learning to walk. When Mom hit the ground, Jolene crawled into her lap. There was nothing on Mom's face. Nothing in her eyes.

She held out one hand like she was waiting for someone to help her up. I walked over to her and took her hand and held it in my own the way I'd seen knights in storybooks kneel and hold a queen's hand.

"Did you wave good-bye to your dad this morning?" she asked me.

I nodded.

"Good," she said.

She pulled me down into her lap along with Jolene.

"We're going to pray," she said.

"Pray for what?" Jolene whispered to me.

"The men," I whispered back.

I clasped my hands together and closed my eyes. I prayed with all my might that my dad was still alive. A couple days later, I would hear my mom praying behind a closed bathroom door that he had died instantly.

# SUNDAY

# ONE

I FINISH MY BEER, CRUSH THE CAN OUT OF HABIT, AND TOSS IT onto the floor of my truck, where it hits the other cans with a small clang. From where I'm parked, a sparkling stream of piss seems to be coming directly from the filthy blue roof of a yellow, pink-shuttered plastic playhouse, as if the structure itself is filled with liquid and has suddenly sprung a precise and artful leak.

I keep a watch on it as I take another bite of my ham-salad sandwich from the Valley Dairy and reach over to the glove compartment where I keep Vicodin and my revolver. I take out the pills and a folded piece of paper. An old high-school football team photo that Art, the owner of Brownie's bar, took down from his wall of fame next to the men's room and gave to me and a road map fall out, along with a can of shaving cream and a folder filled with car accident reports.

The piece of paper is a fax from the state parole board. I open it and flatten it out on the seat beside me.

Reese Raynor's grainy, black-and-white face stares up at me with the stale eyes of someone who thinks he's always being told something he already knows. His teeth are clamped shut, his top lip drawn back in a smirking snarl that I would probably find cartoonish in its attempt to intimidate if I didn't know him personally.

He has changed amazingly little during eighteen years in prison. Except for a paunchiness around his jowls and the loss of some of his hair, he could be the same kid I went to school with.

Beneath his mug shot is the standard information on the parolee, his crime, his sentence. The only item I care about is the release date and time: Tuesday, March 12, 8:00 A.M. Today is Sunday. It's 1:16 P.M., and I'm late picking up Jolene to go to Zo Craig's funeral.

Next I glance at our old team photo in a needless exercise of confirmation: 1980 Centresburg Flames. AA District Champions. One game shy of a state title. Myself in the front row: I. Zoschenko, cocaptain. Reese in the back row, on the far end, with his stare like two grimy nickels. Beside him his twin brother, Jess, the other cocaptain, his eyes glazed with the determined numbness of someone forced to share a bus seat with a ticking bomb.

A few weeks after the photo was taken, Reese was kicked off the team. Most of the guys couldn't believe he lasted as long as he did. He rarely attended practice. He never opened a playbook. He stalked off in disgust each time Coach Deets wheeled the blackboard into the locker room. For Reese every defensive play began and ended with the simple wisdom "A crippled man cannot score."

But Deets let all that slide. He would've let Genghis Khan play for us if he could block, and Reese could block. He had no finesse or speed, and a very limited understanding of the rules and objectives of the game, but no one could get past him.

What finally made Deets give him the boot was his performance off the field. The day after a game—even the games we won—members of the opposing team would find the headlights on their trucks bashed in, or all the windows on their houses blackened with dog shit, or a younger sister deposited on the front yard, drunk and deflowered.

Deets would have tolerated that, too, but the other teams had a problem with it.

I put the photo back in the glove compartment and unfold my deputy's map: a highly detailed blowup of the county. I've traced what I think will be Reese's path, highlighting all the bars along the way and making a looping detour near Altoona to accommodate a trip to The Tail Pipe, a favored strip joint in the area.

I'm assuming he'll head to Jess's house. He doesn't get along with his parents, and the rest of his family in the area is made up of sisters who are married to men who won't let him come near their homes. He and Jess were the oldest and the only boys in Chimp Raynor's tribe of pale, lip-licking girls with dark stares like cloaks who never spoke unless spoken to and never walked down the middle of a hallway. The two brothers were the meat of the family; the girls were the drippings.

My job has brought me to the home of one of the sisters. She's married with kids now. Her mother is on the premises as well, the ominous incubator of Jess and Reese. She's hiding in the gunshot-riddled Buick in the driveway.

I get out of my truck and close the door softly, trying to be quiet, and take a few careful steps up the driveway, but my boots crunch over the windshield glass sprayed everywhere. As the pisser comes into view, he turns to look at me but keeps himself aimed in the same direction, continuing to make an impressive arc over his wife's peacock green gazing ball and her lawn goose prematurely dressed for Easter in a bunny costume they're already selling out at the mall.

I see his gun leaning against the playhouse where he put it while his hands are otherwise occupied. A Winchester twelve-gauge. Chuck, our dispatcher, didn't say anything about its being a shotgun, but his wife probably didn't think to specify when she called. I reach into my pocket for a roll of Certs and pop one in my mouth to mask the scent of beer.

The man's face doesn't register any definable emotion or even recognition upon seeing me, but he raises a hand in greeting.

The gesture causes him to lurch slightly to one side as he's drying up to a trickle, and the goose and ball get spattered. I glance toward the front window of the house and see Bethany Raynor, now Bethany Blystone, and her two little girls peering through the curtains. She turns livid when she sees her goose get hit.

I take a few more steps toward him, passing by the car. Inside, his mother-in-law is hunkered down as far as she can go on the floor.

There are fragments of glass in her teased, gray hair that look almost decorative when she cranes her neck up toward me out of the shadows and a plank of daylight falls across her face. The seat above her has been ripped open by the shotgun blasts.

"Are you all right?" I ask her.

She's trembling, but she's remarkably calm considering the circumstances. Forty-five years of marriage to Chimp have probably taught her to dole out hysteria sparingly. She manages to nod, then whispers to me, "Why are you all dressed up?"

She works at the Kwik-Fill on the north side of Centresburg where I buy my gas, and she always sees me in a deputy's shirt.

"Funeral," I whisper back.

"Zo Craig's?" she asks.

I nod.

"I saw her obituary in the paper," she goes on. "It was almost as big as Elizabeth Taylor's."

"I'm pretty sure Elizabeth Taylor is still alive."

"Oh, you know who I mean. The other one."

I look in Rick's direction again. He has a slight sway to him now.

"Right," I say. "I loved that movie she did. You know the one."

She nods again.

"Jess did Zo's mowing. Did you know that? She has a real nice John Deere tractor. He loves that tractor."

"I better go talk to Rick," I tell her. "You stay put."

I take a deep breath and start walking toward him. There's a strong smell of wet dirt beneath the acrid carbide smell still lingering around his gun and the stench of alcohol wafting off him. I'm not close enough to smell yet, but I swear I can see it hanging around him the way heat in the summertime makes the air ripple.

The dirt smell makes me think about Zo's impending funeral and the freshly dug plot that's waiting for her in the J&P cemetery next to her long-dead husband, one of the ninety-seven men who died in Gertie.

"How ya doing, Rick?" I call out amiably.

He fixes a glassy stare on me.

I move closer but still keep a fair distance away from him so I don't panic him. I have two objectives at this point: get hold of the shotgun and save the lawn ornaments from any future urination.

I motion at him to move toward me.

"Why don't you bring it over here, Rick? Your kids play around there, don't they?"

He's staring at me trying to place me, not in the present but in the past where most of us like to keep each other now that we've seen the future.

He finally drops his gaze and looks forlornly at the puddle he created next to an overturned doll stroller with a stuffed animal strapped inside it.

With his back toward me, I move quickly to the playhouse and pick up the shotgun.

He doesn't turn around. He raises his head and stares at the land behind his house beyond his yard.

The morning rain has stopped, and the sun is trying to make its presence known by shining dimly behind the wall of gray clouds that meets the rim of lavender-smudged hills with the finality of a lid. The weather's been pretty good lately. It's a shame it couldn't have been a little drier today. I know that wherever Zo's practical soul is right now, it will be upset over the thought of all the good shoes that are going to get caked with mud and the time spent cleaning them afterward.

"Ivan? Ivan Z?" Rick asks unsteadily, turning around to face me.

"Yeah, Rick. It's me."

A smile ticks briefly at the corners of his mouth like a small spasm.

"I heard you was back, but I didn't really believe it. Working for Jack, huh? How's it going?"

"Okay. How's it going with you?"

We both glance at his house, where the two little girls are still pressed against the window, but Bethany has disappeared. Their stares dart back and forth between their dad and me and the car with the shattered windshield where their grandmother is hiding. It occurs to me that they might not know if she's living or dead.

"They're closing Lorelei," Rick announces.

He stands in the middle of the yard and somehow manages to look uncomfortably stiff even though everything about him, from his dick hanging out of his jeans to his arms hanging at his sides to the drunken slackness of his unshaven cheeks, is limp.

"So I heard."

"I only got called back nine months ago. I was out of work for almost a year before that."

I hear the front door open and see Bethany, out of the corner of my eye, head for the car. She opens the door, and a sob catches in her throat. Her mother stumbles out, and they wrap their arms around each other. Rick watches them.

"There's only Marvella left now," he says, "and it's all longwall."

He shakes his head.

"I don't want to do it again. I can't do it again. Being unemployed."

The two women are crying. He notices and points accusingly at them.

"My mother-in-law has a steady job. She's been working at that goddamned Kwik-Fill since the beginning of time. She used to sell Slim Jims to Ben Fucking Franklin."

We watch the women help each other into the house. Bethany shoots him another scathing look, this time directed at his exposed manhood.

"And then there's Chimp. Worst miner ever lived. And he ends up working longer than anybody. Gets full retirement. Now he's even collecting black-lung benefits when nobody else can get them, and he doesn't even have it. You know he doesn't have it. He's got that shit you get from smoking all the time. What's it called? Empha-seeming?"

"Emphysema."

"Yeah. That's it. I swear, if he fell into a pile of shit, he'd come up with a golden turd in his mouth."

I think back to high school and the few times I visited Jess at home. He and his family lived in a peeling, sagging shell of a farmhouse with a pack of spittle-flinging dogs roaming in and out of the propped-open front door and had a yard covered with so much junk it looked like the house had vomited its contents.

If there were such things as golden turds, Chimp obviously didn't know what to do with them once he found them.

"Is that why you tried to kill your mother-in-law?" I ask him, getting back to the topic at hand. "Career envy?"

"I didn't try and kill her," he says.

He takes a few wobbling steps toward me, then stops suddenly like the ground has been yanked away.

"I was shooting at the car," he says once he finds his balance again. "I didn't want her to leave. That's all. I knew she was going to drive straight back to her house and call every goddamned old lady in the tristate area and tell them what a loser I am. What a goddamned fucking loser I am!" He screams it to the heavens.

The effort makes his knees buckle, and he drops onto the muddy grass. Once he hits, he starts crying. I don't know if it's out of misery or because he got caught in his zipper. He puts himself back in his pants and brings his hands up to cover his face, knocking off his company ball cap with J&P COAL stitched in frayed, faded gold across the front. Losing his hat makes him cry harder.

I squat down in front of him, and my bad knee sings out in pain. It's been almost twenty years and six operations since my accident. I can walk pretty well, but I will never again be able to squat; however, something in my mind and body won't allow this fact to register, and I'm still constantly attempting it the same way my mother continues to make mincemeat pies for Christmas every year, even though my dad was the only one in our family who liked them.

I put my hands on Rick's shoulders. He stops sobbing for a moment, and understanding briefly skates across his dull gaze.

"You gonna arrest me?" he asks.

"I'm going to take your gun for a while. Do you have any more in the house?"

"Two rifles."

"I'm going to take those, too."

I brace his shotgun against the ground and use it as a crutch to help me get back to a standing position.

"Why don't you just stay here for a minute?" I instruct him, needlessly.

He's already fallen over, sprawled out on his stomach, with his eyes closed, mumbling to himself. I head for the house and knock on the front door.

Bethany answers. She's not happy to see me even though she's the one who called and asked me to come here.

She stares at me, courteously defiant. She's put on about sixty pounds of flesh and attitude since high school.

I try picturing her young self without the extra weight, with her hair feathered like Farrah's, wearing Chic jeans instead of the orange stretch pants she's wearing now, worn shiny at the knees, along with a voluminous thigh-length sweatshirt created by retailers for the sole purpose of concealing various types of female physical hell.

"How's your mother?" I ask.

"She's fine. A little shaken up is all. She's lying down."

"Your husband says he wasn't trying to kill her. He was trying to prevent her from leaving."

"Yeah," she says. "I told her to just sit down and let him cool off, but she had a hair appointment. Now she's missed it anyway."

Behind her is a room that belongs to a woman who doesn't put housekeeping high on her list of things to do. Toys, laundry, stacks of unopened mail, dirty dishes, and miscellaneous fragments of day-to-day life surround the two little girls sitting in a patch of cleared carpet watching TV and eating Mootown Snackers. They dip their pretzel sticks into their portions of cheese spread at the exact same moment and bring them hypnotically to their mouths.

"Has he ever done anything like this before?" I ask her.

"No."

"Violent outbursts of any kind? Toward you? Toward the children?"

"He throws things at the TV sometimes, but he don't hit us."

"Does he drink a lot?"

"Not more than anybody else."

Her stare doesn't waver.

"Are you going to arrest him?" she asks me.

"Do you want me to?"

"That's a strange question."

"I'm off duty, and I have a headache," I explain.

"You want an aspirin?"

"No, thanks."

She drops her eyes away from mine for the first time and looks down at my jeans and mud-caked Caterpillar work boots, then takes in my black dress shirt, black sport jacket, and the tie I borrowed from Dr. Ed that he pulled out of a filing-cabinet drawer and tossed to me while telling me not to worry about the stain. It wasn't blood, it was gravy, and no one would notice it because it blends in well with the pattern of migrating ducks.

"Why didn't they send an on-duty deputy?" she asks suspiciously.

"I was easier to find. Look, if your mother wants to press charges, I'll be happy to take him back to town with me."

"He did commit a crime, didn't he?"

"Well, yes. Shooting at a person with a twelve-gauge shotgun is always considered a crime in the state of Pennsylvania, even if the person shot at is the perpetrator's mother-in-law. Unless of course it's mother-in-law season," I add, smiling.

She doesn't smile back.

"Okay," I try another tack. "Here's what will happen if I arrest him: I'll take him to jail. He'll stay there until he's arraigned, and then you're going to have to drive into town and post bond and give him a ride back home. Even if your mother doesn't want to press charges, the state will. You won't have to testify because you're his wife, but your mother will. She'll have to take time off work to do it. She could end up having to take off several days, maybe even a week, without pay. If you retain your own attorney, you're looking at thousands of dollars. At the very least, you're going to end up paying a considerable fine and court costs. He might get jail time, which will go on his permanent record and make it difficult for him to find future employment once he's released."

"We can't afford that," she answers.

I nod.

"How about for now I'll just take the guns? He said he has a couple rifles."

She doesn't hesitate. She leaves the room immediately, wanting to get this all over with. On her way past the girls, she nudges one in the kidneys with her foot and tells her to go load the dishwasher.

She returns quickly, carrying two rifles: another Winchester and a Remington .30-06, the same make and model Val used to hunt with.

I take the Remington and raise it to shoulder height like I always do when I'm around one. This one has a nice high-powered scope. I look into it, aiming through the front window at Rick, passed out in a muddy yard next to a goose dressed like a rabbit.

I start aiming at things in the house. Pictures on the walls. Empty beer cans on the coffee table. I come to a stationary exercise bike in a corner draped with towels and T-shirts and Christmas twinkle lights.

Bethany Blystone is staring at me with embarrassed rage. I slowly lower the gun and clear my throat.

"You used to be a Raynor, didn't you?"

She walks to the front door. I sense I'm supposed to follow. She holds open the door.

"I'm still a Raynor. That don't change just because my name did."

"Are you aware that Reese is being released on Tuesday?"

She says nothing.

"Have you had any contact with him recently?"

"Why do you want to know?"

"I'd like to keep an eye on him so I can help out if he encounters any difficulties making the transition to life outside prison."

"You mean you want to harass him?"

"Something like that."

I step outside, and she stands in the doorway staring at me uncertainly. A shadow of her former skinny, frightened self passes over her, the self that used to live in the same house with Reese.

"He'll go to Jess," she announces, and shuts the door on me.

Back at my truck, I unlock my footlocker and put Rick's guns inside with a half dozen others.

I grab a blanket and go check on him a final time. He's unconscious, but he's on his stomach so he won't choke to death if he throws up. I cover him. I don't know how long he'll be out here.

The little girl who was nudged in the kidneys comes walking over. She's not wearing a coat or shoes. She has a football with her and a Sharpie permanent marker in her hand.

"He's fine," I assure her.

She doesn't even glance at him.

"You should go in the house before you catch cold," I tell her.

She holds out the ball and marker to me.

"Mom wants to know if you'd give us your autograph. She says it would mean a lot to Dad."

The request is delivered as two separate statements. There's no asking involved.

I take the ball from her and take the lid off the marker.

"You got any stickers?" she asks me.

"What?"

"Stickers," she repeats. "Dr. Ed always brings stickers."

"Does Dr. Ed come here a lot?" I ask.

"When Daddy loses his job, he gives us our shots here instead of us going there. I don't know why."

I know why, but I don't explain to her that when Daddy loses his job, he also loses his benefits. Dr. Ed won't accept lack of an insurance card or any other reason people give him for not bringing their kids in for their vaccinations. If they won't come to him, he goes to them.

I finish signing the ball and hand it to the girl. She puts it up against her face. At first I think she does it so she can read it, but it's because she wants to smell the ink.

I search my pockets for something to give her. I wish I had something pretty, but all I come up with is the half-eaten roll of Certs and the rabbit's foot Val made for me before he left for Vietnam. I give her the mints.

She takes them and gives me a shrug. There's gratitude in the jerk of her shoulders. It's enough. I know that this girl could never say thanks. It would imply that I had done something for her.

I get back in my truck and watch her trudge over to the doll stroller. I'm going to wait until she's safely back inside the house, even though I'm not sure exactly how safe that is.

In the meantime I finish eating my sandwich while reading the bumper stickers people and local businesses have given me over the past eight months since I've been back that I have plastered on my dashboard: OLD HUNTERS NEVER MISS, THEY JUST LOSE THEIR BANG. McCREADY SEPTIC SYSTEMS: THIS JOB SUCKS. MY WIFE, YES. MY DOG, MAYBE. MY GUN, NEVER. WELDERS HAVE THE HOTTEST RODS. PUFF N' SNUFF FOR ALL YOUR TOBACCO NEEDS. DIAL 911: MAKE A COP COME.

One is from the Salt Lick Motel. The word "Salt" has been worn away completely. In my boredom I've peeled away some of the other letters. It now reads LICK M— —E—. My six-year-old nephew, Eb, gets a real kick out of this.

# TWO

WHEN I WAS A KID, A TRIP TO CENTRESBURG WAS AS MOMENTOUS as a journey to see the Great Wall of China or the Taj Mahal. In some ways it was more exciting and enviable than traveling overseas to exotic locales, because those places didn't impress the people who lived in Coal Run. It wasn't that they hadn't heard about them or didn't appreciate their significance; it was simply that they had no need to go there and we were a community ruled by need.

Need as a noun, not as a verb. Needing to have something was never reason enough to get it. Having a need usually was.

The one exception to this rule in my family, the only time we were allowed to blatantly want something frivolous aside from the annual circling of toys in the Sears Christmas catalog, was when we went to Centresburg.

The riches of Woolworth's five-and-dime store were able to tempt even my widowed mother, a woman who spent her nights hunched over a box of coupons, a grocery list, and newspaper sale flyers with the concentration of a general studying maps and reports from the front.

The display windows were a carnival of things no one needed: ruby-red wineglasses, bolts of glittering silver rickrack, thermos-size bottles of pink perfume with names like Moonbeam Mist and Starfire spelled across them in gilt letters, bowls of shiny, grim goldfish—all of it could be seen from the municipal lot where Mom parked the car after circling the block for fifteen minutes waiting for a space to open up inside it because she had never learned how to parallel-park on the street.

Jolene and I were allowed to spend fifty cents and share a bag of the salty yellow popcorn sold at the lunch counter. After giving us our dollar and an extra quarter for the popcorn, Mom would instantly disappear down the stairs to the mysterious lower level known as House Wares.

I always headed straight for the baseball cards or the Hot Wheels. Jolene was always torn between the pet section, where she had become deeply involved with a peanut-butter-colored hamster she called Peanut Butter, and the jewelry counter, where she would stand with her tiny hands and nose pressed up against the glass staring at the colorful rows of fake birthstone rings that sparkled fiercely in the store light but turned a uniform shade of dirty-ice gray if they were worn anywhere else.

She couldn't afford to buy anything at either location and usually settled for a pack of sequins from the notions department that she took home and poured out into the square of sunlight that appeared in the middle of our living room carpet between the hours of two and four in the afternoon and entertained herself by flicking them around with her stubby toddler fingers and watching them shimmer.

She never got the hamster, but she would eventually own a pink-eyed white rabbit a boyfriend presented to her one Easter. She would go on to own a museum's worth of Woolworth's jewelry, most of it from male admirers, some of it from Mom. I was the one who finally bought her the birthstone ring. Green for May.

I did it one day, out of the blue, during one of our trips to the store. I was watching her stare at the ring like she always did, and I realized that when I first started watching her do this, her face was pressed up against the side of the glass and her eyes were level with the ring and now she was tall enough to look down at it from the top of the counter.

Maybe she didn't need that ring. Maybe she would never need it, but in my mind she had earned it, and since I was the person who recognized this, I felt the need to give it to her.

Centresburg hasn't changed much since Jolene and I were kids, except when we were kids, everything functioned. The buildings and structures are all still here some thirty years later, but the reasons behind them are long gone.

The twin stacks of Franklin Tires belched clouds of chalk-blue smoke that hung in the air like they'd been drawn there. Jolene and I used to find shapes in them: a cow, a car, a big head, a castle, an alligator. We always knew when we drove by the stacks again on our way out of town that the object would still be there. Those clouds never moved or shifted like the white clouds God made.

Idling train engines rumbled in the rail yards waiting for their cars to be loaded. If we happened to be sitting next to them at the red light at the corner of Union and Seventh Streets when the tipples opened, the rain of coal was so deafening it drowned out the sound of the radio and always made Mom jump, and Jolene and I would laugh.

Packard Mining Equipment had a fleet of flatbeds always coming and going carrying gigantic drill bits and colossal cogs and gear wheels I used to imagine were going to be dragged up the beanstalk to fix the giant's clock. A constant melodic clanging came from the plant, accompanied by hisses of steam. Long after I was home again, lying in bed at night, I'd hear that sound playing in my head. I'd fall asleep to it.

I drive quickly down the corridor of shuttered warehouses and heaps of scrap metal.

To the left sits Franklin's smokeless smokestacks. To the right sits the silent, burned-out shell of Packard. A fire raged through it a couple years after it closed, gutting it and scorching the red brick to the color of spoiled beef.

At the rail yards, rust-streaked coal cars sit beneath the disintegrating metal mouths of giant loading tipples waiting for a final run that's never going to happen.

Alongside it is the faded billboard: WELCOME TO CENTRESBURG. WE'RE IN THE MIDDLE OF IT ALL.

I've never been exactly sure what we're in the middle of. Certainly not the state. We're in the southwestern quarter. We're not in the center of the county or even the township.

Jolene's youngest son, Eb, is convinced it means we're in the middle of the universe and stands by that belief even when his middle brother, Harrison, explains to him there can't be a middle to something that doesn't have finite boundaries. Harrison thinks it means we're in the middle of a bunch of crap.

There's no denying the amount of crap, but not far from these crumbling carcasses stretched out in their shadows is a thriving thoroughfare whose fast-food restaurants and convenience stores lead like yellow brick to the local Oz: the county's biggest Blockbuster and Super Wal-Mart.

Behind it a new development of tidy, bright, white Monopoly-marker houses dots a backfilled hillside that used to be a moonscape of strip mining.

It's an odd kind of depression and a purely blue-collar American one, from what I know of poverty in other countries, past and present, that my father was always quick to point out to me on television news shows and in books and newspapers when I was little.

No one's starving here; on the contrary, many are fat. No one's lacking material goods; everyone has clothing, a place to live, a TV to watch, and a car to drive.

Most people have been able to find a way to make a living since most of the mines closed and Franklin went under, too. There's a small United Can & Container plant twenty miles west of town. There's a branch of a state university about thirty miles in the opposite direction that requires a small army of secretaries, food-service workers, janitors, and groundskeepers. There's the hospital. There's a new juvenile-detention center that provided a lot of construction jobs while it was being built; now it has a full-time staff of thirty-five. There's

Sheriff Jack's car dealership. There are stores and offices and restaurants to work in.

But despite all this, there's still deprivation in the air. It's something my father predicted years before it happened.

My mom told me once about a conversation she had with him not long before he was killed. He brought up the inevitable extinction of the coal-mining industry, which was a pretty radical discussion to have with a woman whose family had been tied to the Pennsylvania coalfields since the time of the Molly Maguires. But the signs were already there, and the future was laid out fairly clearly to anybody who wanted to see it. Environmental concerns, cleaner fuel alternatives, cheaper steel imports, labor disputes, and the undeniable fact of nature that the coal we had the technology to reach would eventually run out all pointed in only one direction. My mom knew it as well as anyone.

What struck Mom the most about their conversation was that Dad didn't focus on what the loss of all these jobs would mean to a family's pocketbook. He wasn't overly concerned about tables without food on them or Christmas trees without gifts under them or children without shoes on their feet.

Times had changed since Mom's great-great-great-grandfather first took a pickax and a shovel and was dropped down a hole to dig coal. The work itself hadn't changed that much. Or the dangers. But the world outside supposedly had. It was a kinder, gentler America now, according to my dad. There was the union. If that failed, hopefully there were other jobs to be had. If that failed, there was unemployment compensation. There was welfare.

No one would starve: This was a very important point with my father, that he kept making over and over again by pounding his fist on the armrest of his favorite chair and flashing his fierce blue stare, but it wasn't the most important point, and as he was a man who had faced starvation himself and who had lost his mother and sisters to it, Mom thought it should be. His main concern was spirit, she told me. His fear was a poverty of purpose.

"You can have all the food and toys and even all the bombs," he told my mom while they shared one of their last nights together, "but no man can protect himself against uselessness."

I take side streets to Jolene's house. She moved to Centresburg the same year I moved to Florida. She only had Josh then. Now she's the mother of three boys and the wife of no one and seems equally pleased with both situations.

She's a career waitress, not only in the sense that she's been doing it long enough to consider it a career but in that she has always seen it as a career option to be taken just as seriously as being a teacher or an astronaut. If asked what they do for a living, the other women who wait tables with her will reply, "I work as a waitress." Jolene will proclaim, "I am a waitress."

I was disappointed in her for a lot of years. I thought she could've done more with her life. When she got pregnant with Josh right out of high school and made it clear that she had no intention of marrying his unemployed, soon-to-enlist, nineteen-year-old father because, as she put it fondly and accurately, "We have a great time messing around together, but I can't imagine depending on him for anything more than a boner and a pizza," I thought she should've had an abortion.

Once she decided to have Josh, I thought she should've been one of those very pretty, very noble unwed mothers I used to watch on *ABC Afterschool Specials* who somehow managed to find good, affordable child care for her baby while she worked two jobs to put herself through college and still found time to do volunteer work at the old-folks' home and bake cookies for her older brother, who was away at Penn State on a football scholarship driving a new sports car that a grateful alum gave him after his team won the Sugar Bowl in '83.

When she got pregnant with Harrison, I thought she should have had an abortion. She was still young. She could still do something with her life. Josh was seven now. He was in school all day. One kid wasn't so much of a burden, but two was a lot. Maybe she could still go to college. Maybe she could still get married, but not to Harrison's dad, since he was a one-night stand in a Red Roof Inn and she had forgotten to get his phone number. And his last name. And money for the room.

Once she decided to have Harrison, I thought she should've been a slightly older, very pretty, very noble unwed mother of two, who has a full-time job as a waitress and takes night classes while still finding time to bake cookies for her brother, who was now living in Florida killing bugs for a living, drinking for a hobby, and limping around on a leg with a synthetic knee.

When she got pregnant with Eb, I picked up the phone in the office trailer of Perez Pest Control at the end of our workday and called her while my boss, Mr. Perez, and his son, Ernesto, looked on, grinning at me while passing her letter back and forth between them, pausing to appreciatively eye her feminine handwriting on the pale pink stationery and to smell the hint of perfume that clung to it. I told her to marry the guy. Whoever he was. Marry him, for God's sake.

After an ominous silence—ominous because Jolene is never caught without an instant counterremark to a command—she said to me, "You haven't called me in eight years, and the first time you decide to take the time out of your incredibly busy, bug-killing, ESPN-watching, hanging-out-at-Hooters day and pick up a phone and spend a few bucks to talk to your only sister, it's to tell me how to live my life?"

"Yes," I said, then thought better of it. "I mean, no. I mean, I'm not really paying for it. I'm calling on the company phone."

She made a small indignant huff before she steamrolled on.

"A life that you have made clear you have absolutely no interest in? When I call you and you miraculously happen to answer your phone and I start to tell you about me or Mom or the kids, I know you're watching TV or you're doing one of your stupid crossword puzzles and you're not listening to anything I say."

"What?" I asked her.

"You're going to give me advice? You? A guy who ran away from home because he broke his leg and couldn't play football anymore. Boo hoo! A guy who's never come home for a single visit and never calls and never writes and never says thank you for the tons of cookies I make for him—his favorite, pecan tassies, which are a major pain in the ass to make because you have to put the dough in all those tiny little tassie cups and then spoon the melted butter and brown sugar in and then put the pecans on top, and it takes hours. Hours!

"And whenever Mom or I try to come visit you, you always find some lame excuse for us not to come, like you're suddenly moving or you're sick or you're having your apartment fumigated, and I want to go to Florida! Damn you! I look great in a bikini. Women who look great in bikinis should get free trips to Florida constantly. As a matter of fact, that should be the criterion for being allowed to take a trip to Florida. It shouldn't have anything to do with, 'Can you afford it?' It should be all about, 'Does anyone want to see you in a bikini?' I have a brother who lives in Florida, and I look great in a bikini. With that combination I should be spending half my life in Florida.

"Do you know Josh is twelve years old now and he's never shaken Mickey Mouse's hand or paw or whatever you call it? What do you call it? Is it a hand or a paw? Do mice have paws?"

"They have feet."

"But he wears gloves."

"He gets dressed in the dark."

Another silence. Then, "I'm not going to marry Randy Craig. He's a nice guy, but I already have enough laundry to do."

She hung up, and I hung up, too. Ernesto and his father continued smiling grandly. I told them that she wasn't getting married, and some money exchanged hands.

I didn't bother telling them the details of the conversation, except for her belief that women who look great in bikinis should get free trips to Florida. They agreed wholeheartedly.

Mr. Perez broke out a bottle of rum and a bottle of Coke, and we set about drinking Cuba Libres and thinking up various fund-raisers that could pay for the free trips until Mrs. Perez called and Mr. Perez left happily to be with the woman he loved and Ernesto and I were left to continue drinking until Ernesto's wife called and he left to be with the woman he was afraid of. I ended up calling Jolene back and thanking her for the cookies.

She came to Florida when Eb was one and a half and was sure her body had sufficiently returned to looking great in a bikini. She drove down by herself with the three boys and never talked about the trip except to announce after they arrived that they weren't going to talk about it.

Josh was a teenager by then and wouldn't be caught dead shaking Mickey Mouse's hand or paw or foot or whatever it was, so Harrison did it after waiting in line for two hours in 102-degree heat.

Afterward we got to spend another hour at the nearest air-conditioned first-aid station with twenty other sunstroke victims, being offered water, orange juice, and Dumbo-shaped cookies by tan, pretty girls in short, bright yellow, health-professional smocks. If they had served beer, it would have been my favorite spot in the whole park.

Eb came down with a bad cold after being refrigerated so soon after being simmered in his own body fluids for most of the day. Harrison got an ear infection from the swimming pool in my apartment complex. Josh got a bad sunburn and developed a crush on the cute blond transvestite who lived two doors down from me. Harrison said he was bored every day.

All the summers since then, Jolene's taken the boys to Lake Erie.

The trip wasn't a total disaster, though. After seeing her again after all those years and seeing her boys, too, I realized I wanted back some of the role of big brother that I had purposely thrown away when I left. I didn't want all of it back. I just wanted the part where I checked up on them and made sure they were doing okay, so I started calling her instead of always waiting for her to call me.

For Jolene's part, she stopped trying to convince me to come home again. I can't say why exactly. It couldn't have been because she saw I was happy and doing well, because I wasn't. It couldn't have been because she saw that I had found a place where I was better off, because I hadn't.

I think it might have been as simple as her needing to see firsthand how I was living to understand how serious I was about staying away. She finally realized that knowing the reason I left wasn't the same as understanding why I couldn't come back. My mom always knew the difference. She never once asked me when I was coming home.

A few more years passed. The cookies kept coming. Photos of the boys kept coming. Strangely enough, once Jolene stopped bugging me about coming home, I started to consider it. Then one day I received a newspaper clipping, sent anonymously, with no return address, and home became all I could think about.

It was one of those pieces about violent crimes in rural areas that periodically ran in the city newspapers. Reese was always the highlight of these stories, and, despite the fact that he committed his crime almost twenty years ago, he was the centerpiece in this one, too. It seems the story of the Coal Run redneck who beat his wife into a coma in front of their three-year-old son and then, after serving only two years of his six-year sentence, beat a fellow inmate to death and was sentenced to fifteen more years holds timeless appeal for the local crime reporters.

In a sidebar Reese's impending release date one year later was mentioned, along with a quote from Laurel County's sheriff, Jack Townsend, who said, "If he chooses to come back here to live, there's nothing we can do about it. Coal Run is his home. We'll just have to hope he's learned his lesson."

In the margin, written in black pen, was a question for me: "What are you going to do?"

I couldn't figure out who sent it to me, and I still don't know. Whoever it was would have had to know my address in Florida and, more important, my tie to Reese, and no one knows my tie to Reese.

I couldn't get the question out of my mind.

I park my truck in front of Jolene's house and honk the horn. She lives in a quiet neighborhood made up of a collection of small, working-class houses. Some are clapboard. Some are brick. Some sided in white or gray aluminum.

Hers is a rosy one with white gingerbread trim and an old-fashioned front-porch swing. It's in good condition, because there are about a dozen men on her street who'd do anything to be close to her, including painting her eaves, cleaning her gutters, trimming her hedges, and shoveling her sidewalk in winter. Fortunately, the women like being near her, too, and let their men do it.

Her front door opens, and Jolene steps outside carrying her purse and a folded garbage bag. Her heels click across the porch floorboards. She's halfway down the front walk when she stops suddenly and calls out to me, "I have six black dresses. They're all low-cut or have fringe. Except this one."

She spreads out her arms and turns around once. Her fingerfuls and armloads of rings and bracelets clink and twinkle as she twirls. She's wearing a very short, very tight, black dress.

"It's very nice," I say.

"You don't like it."

"I said it's nice."

"What's wrong with it?"

"Nothing."

"It's an angora blend."

"It's great."

"Wait. I'm having second thoughts."

"Shit," I say.

"I love it, but it is a little short. People might think it's inappropriate."

She looks down at her legs. Like a child or a dog, Jolene's sense of wrongdoing depends solely on how others react to her and has nothing to do with listening to her own conscience, since this part of her is always telling her to do whatever she wants.

"I haven't been to a funeral in a long time. What will other people be wearing?"

"Funeral attire."

"What does that mean, exactly?"

"I don't know."

"What will Zo be wearing?"

"Zo? Zo is the corpse."

"I know. What will she be wearing?"

"How the hell would I know?"

"You're the one who found her."

"That doesn't mean I get to dress her."

"Who does?"

"I don't know."

"What was she wearing when you found her?"

"Stop it, Jolene. Would you just shut up and get in the truck?"

I don't tell Jolene, but I remember exactly what Zo was wearing the day I found her stretched out on her couch waiting for me to pick her up and take her grocery shopping: a tiny, cotton-haired woman dressed in navy polyester pants and a matching vest over a striped blouse, a tan raincoat, and the kind of clear plastic rain kerchief that folds up into a perfect little triangle and slips unseen into an old lady's big white pocketbook.

Jolene starts digging through her own purse the minute she climbs into my truck. I glimpse lipsticks, hair clips, a packet of Dr. Scholl's corn pads, a pink satin bra, rolls of LifeSavers, a Fisher-Price pirate holding a sword between his teeth, nail polish, gum wrappers, an old campaign button that reads CLINTON FOR PRESIDENT. INHALE IN '96, an undeveloped roll of film, her name pin from Valley Dairy, a construction-paper valentine, men's phone numbers—with and without names—scribbled on everything from dollar bills to the backs of labels ripped from beer bottles, and a pair of pantyhose.

She stops searching when she finds a twist tie. She sets it on the seat beside her and glances in my direction.

"Nice tie," she snickers.

"It was the best I could do on short notice."

"You should have borrowed the one Eb offered you."

"It had Scooby-Doo on it."

"Ducks are better?"

"By the way, what kind of six-year-old has a collection of neckties?"

"He likes them. They make him feel dressed up."

She shakes out the bag and starts picking trash off the floor. She holds up a beer can in front of my face.

"You're going to get fired," she tells me.

"I can't. It would violate Jack's religion. He's a Penn State alum."

She picks up a can of shaving cream and shakes it to see if it's empty. Satisfied that it is, she puts it in the bag.

"So you're not taking Eb?" I ask her.

"He's too little to take to his grandma's funeral. Josh offered to go, but I needed him to stay home and watch Eb. Harrison refused to go because she's no relation of his. That's the way he put it."

"Nice," I grunt.

"Sometimes I can't believe the mouth on Harrison, and he's only eleven. We had another fight today. We fight all the time lately."

"What was the fight about?"

"I'm not sure, exactly. As I was leaving, he said, 'Even a hooker doesn't try to pick up men at a funeral.'"

"What did you say?"

"I said, 'Yes, a hooker would.'"

"I think you missed the point."

"I got the point. He thinks I'm obsessed with men, but the truth is, I hardly ever date. He knows that. When do I have the time to meet anyone? And where am I going to meet him? And frankly, who's left for me to date?"

"There's some guys out at Safe Haven on life support."

"Very funny."

I sympathize with Harrison. I know what it's like to have a pretty, unmarried mother and then to arrive at an age yourself where you start to be interested in girls and you realize the guys sniffing around your mom are thinking the same thoughts about her that you're thinking about your Farrah Fawcett poster. If your mom responds favorably to their thoughts, you're not sure if you should be happy for her, or protective of her, or angry at her, or repulsed by her. I was doubly cursed. Eventually Jolene came of age, and I had a pretty sister, too.

The best and worst of male intentions were constantly pulling in and out of our driveway: my mom shunning most of their advances, Jolene accepting most of their advances, but neither one of them the least bit attainable.

She picks up a hunting knife I confiscated from three kids last night who were in the process of slashing the tires on another kid's pickup because he stole one of their girlfriends. I explained to them that girlfriends can be lured, enticed, manipulated, duped, dazzled, misled, and bought, but they can't be stolen. Then I showed them how to throw the knife into a tree and get it to stick. None of them knew how to do it. Kids don't develop life skills anymore. None of them could belch the Pledge of Allegiance either.

She opens the glove compartment to put the knife inside and finds Reese's mug shot.

"Reese Raynor is getting out of jail?" she says. "I thought they threw away the key."

She brings the fax close to her face. I have the irrational urge to swipe it away from her for fear just the image of him could inflict some kind of bodily harm.

"God, that was so long ago. Let's see, that was your senior year. You'd already signed with the Bears. Your accident happened right around the same time," she ends slowly, and looks over at me with her eyes narrowed into slits of blue.

"Why do you have this?" she asks.

"It's part of my job."

"Since when do you care about anything that's part of your job?"

I try to take it from her, but she holds it out of my reach.

"I never understood any of that," she goes on. "Crystal was such a quiet little thing. No one even knew she was dating Reese, and then one day—bam—she's pregnant and marrying him and didn't even finish high school. Reese Raynor. How could anybody have sex with Reese Raynor? Jess I can understand. He was cute."

"They're identical twins," I remind her.

"Only when they're together. When you see them apart, they don't look anything alike."

She sets the picture on the seat between us and goes back to cleaning up my mess. I glance down at his face. She's right. He doesn't look like Jess. She's always pointing out something nobody needs to know until she points it out, and then you wonder how you got through life so far without realizing it yourself.

# THREE

THE PINK-AND-GOLD MEMORIAL ROOM AT LYLE'S FUNERAL HOME is packed, and I'm happy for Zo. I knew she'd been hoping for a big turnout when her time finally came. It was always the first thing she mentioned when she told me about the latest funeral she had been to. "People were standing," was her highest praise.

People are standing at her service. All the seats are filled. I can't stand for long periods of time because of my knee, but I'm not concerned. Jolene only has to pause for a moment in the back of the room and cast her gaze searchingly over the sea of folding-chair mourners for men to start shifting and rising. Within a matter of minutes, we're seated.

During twenty-five years as administrators of Safe Haven, an eighty-bed convalescent and elder-care home on the outskirts of Centresburg, Zo and my mother have been directly and indirectly involved with the families of just about everybody who lives around here. Apparently most of them felt that Zo was worth paying final respects to.

The fact that my mother didn't is a social faux pas that won't be easily forgiven by some people, but anyone who knows my mother also knows she isn't acting out of disrespect; she's simply being true to her pragmatic nature. She's a great celebrator of life and life in the hereafter; death is a distraction from both and serves no purpose in her mind, so she won't waste her time on it. Not even two hours for a funeral.

She also doesn't put much stock in what she refers to as "religious events," which includes anything that takes place in a church or involves a minister.

She used to be a churchgoer. She attended Coal Run's Methodist church her whole life; then she married Dad and started going to the nearest Ukrainian Catholic church in Union City with him. It was a dark, cramped, wooden place clouded with incense and Slavic chanting. The services were excruciatingly long, because the sermons were delivered twice: first in Ukrainian, then in a begrudging English. Even in the height of summer, no one could crack a window, because some ancient, hollow-eyed woman in a threadbare sweater with famine and war carved in her face would totter over and close it.

After Dad was killed, Mom stopped going. A lot of people whispered behind her back that she had strayed from God, but I knew better. She wouldn't have anything to do with either church, yet she still read her Bible, still made us say our bedtime prayers, still scolded Val whenever he took the Lord's name in vain. She hadn't stopped believing in God's existence the way I had. She had just stopped believing that she owed him anything.

Zo's casket sits in front of a wall of dusty pink satin curtains trimmed in gold fringe beneath a chandelier dripping glass tears.

She would have been happy with the surroundings. Even though her own home was decorated simply, she had a secret love for the flamboyant. She loved Las Vegas. She was always telling Jolene how she envied the glitter gels young girls could smear on their faces, hair, and bodies these days. She never went to work without wearing one of her big fake gemstone pins on her polyester suit-jacket lapel. She had six that I knew of: a ladybug, a frog, a red motorcycle, an American flag, the initial Z, and a watering can.

As I stare at the gaudiness surrounding her now, every detail of the room where she took her last breath comes rushing at me: the yarn diamonds of an orange, green, and yellow afghan hung over the back of the couch; a gold-fringed pink satin souvenir throw pillow with a flaking silk screen of a Vegas slot machine on it; piles of *Reader's Digest* and *Better Homes and Gardens* magazines stacked on the coffee table; her black leather Bible lying on a side table with the red ribbon bookmark always marking a different place in the solid shininess of the copper-edged pages; the framed photograph of her dead husband standing on the back of an out-of-tune upright piano between her son Randy's high-school senior photo and a shadowy, bedroom-eyed portrait of Christ.

Nothing in her living room ever changed from the time I was a child until now, except for the eventual arrival of a color TV set and the reluctant replacing of the couch and carpeting due to wear and tear.

Jolene and I used to spend a lot of time there, along with a lot of other kids. Zo was the founder of a relief society for the widows and children of the Gertie miners. She lived alone with Randy—the miracle baby that she wasn't able to conceive until she was almost forty—in a big, three-story brick farmhouse originally owned by her well-to-do grandfather. Her doors were kept open for any woman who needed a baby-sitter or advice or simply someone to talk to.

She used her own money to establish the financial-aid fund. She had a bit from an inheritance. Her mother had been the only child of the head cashier of Centresburg's First National Bank. His wife died when Zo's mother was a baby, and his life centered on his daughter from then on. He had high hopes for her to marry well when she grew up and spared no expense to make sure it would happen by sending her to an exclusive girls' school in Philadelphia with the wish that she'd meet and mingle with the right class of boy. He was understandably upset when she came back home from school one summer and fell in love with a miner.

But his new son-in-law won him over, and long before he died, he gave Zo's parents the house on two hundred acres of land to live in and another large parcel of property that Zo would eventually use as the site of Safe Haven. When her grandfather did die, Zo's parents inherited a nice sum of money, too.

The farmhouse was far from a mansion, but it was a palace compared to the three-room company houses the other miners lived in. Zo's father shared his good fortune and treated the place like communal company property. During the booming coal-town days when Zo was a child, it was always filled with miners and their families. When she was a grown woman and raising her own child, it was still filled, but this time only with the families.

Not even the sound or the smell changed over the years. The loud, solemn ticking of her grandfather's grandfather clock and the scent of lemon-fresh Pledge are the first things I remember from the first time I stepped through her door over thirty years ago and the last things I remember as I stepped out two days ago after calling the coroner and picking up her arthritic fist, dangling over the side of the couch, clutching a coupon for twenty cents off Ziploc sandwich bags, and placing it on the small hill of her chest, where it lay with the other one like two jagged lumps of broken clay. I had been fifteen minutes late picking her up to go grocery shopping.

Directly in front of the casket is Zo's son, Randy—Ebbie's father—sitting in the first row with his wife and two legitimate children.

According to Jolene, she and Eb haven't seen him for about two years. He lives in Maryland and works for a company that sells medical supplies to hospitals. In any given year, Jolene can tell how well the bedpan market did by the price of the Christmas present he sends to Eb.

He moved out of state when Eb was a baby to try to find a job after Franklin Tires closed. Jolene says he used to come and visit them a lot, even though it was a six-hour drive, but then he got married and the visiting stopped. It had nothing to do with his wife, he assured Jolene. He was just busy at work, and it had suddenly occurred to him that the drive was too long.

Jolene was upset for a while, not for herself but for Eb. She said Randy really seemed to like him, and she could already see the attachment forming. If he had met the wifey just a year later, the bond might have been too strong to break.

I know that's the main reason she didn't bring Eb today. Not because she didn't want him to see his grandma dead, but because she didn't want him to see his dad so alive.

I glance around the room. Some people are looking at me like they know who I am, and most of them do. Some are looking at me like they know me personally, and most of them don't. Some are looking at me like they're trying to figure out who I am and once they do, they'll be forced to ask someone if I am who they think I am. Some are looking at me like they already understand the difference between knowing who I am and who I was. Others will figure this out later. To some the difference won't matter. Others will be happy about it or depressed as hell.

Regardless, at some point today, I will be at least a fleeting thought in the mind of everyone in attendance at Zo Craig's funeral, and I can't help feeling that she knew this and wanted it.

"Who is that?" Jolene whispers in my ear.

She has her neck craned, looking toward the back of the room. There's someone standing inside the door leaning against the wall. His clothes are ragged. He's dirty and unshaven, his presence a vulgar violation against the pink-flocked wallpaper, like finding a cigarette butt in a little girl's jewelry box.

I can't stop staring at him. Something about him bothers me, besides his lack of respect for an old lady's funeral. He's wearing a Cuban military cap, the kind Fidel Castro wears and the kind Mr. Perez wore during his youth. He has the brim pulled down low enough to hide his eyes. Long, dark hair grazes the shoulders of his fatigue-green jacket. One leg in torn camouflage pants ends in a scuffed leather army boot. The other ends in a heavy black shoe.

"Who is that?" Jolene asks again. "Do you think Zo knew him? He looks like he just crawled out of a jungle."

"Jesus," I say out loud.

A dozen pairs of outraged eyes turn on me.

"Sorry," I say, and begin to stand up without realizing it.

"Where are you going?" Jolene asks.

I don't answer her. I make my way slowly down the aisle. The closer I get, the more certain I am that it's him, even though everything about him is wrong.

He would never attend a funeral poorly dressed. I went to the mass burial of the Gertie miners with him. Mom let me ride in his truck. I remember hesitating at the passenger-side door and staring at him in his dark blue suit and tie and hard-soled shoes and bare head with no ball cap. His hands glowed raw and pink from the scrubbing he had given them, and he smelled like his mom's Dove soap. I wasn't sure it was him until he leaned over and belched, "Get the hell in the truck."

He would have never let his hair grow long. Fag hair, he would've called it. Sissy hair. Pussy hair.

And why would he come back to a place he had avoided for over thirty years to attend the funeral of a woman he didn't know? He didn't come back for his own mother's funeral.

His hand rests against one of his legs with the palm turned out and a cigarette held loosely between two fingers. I get a sick feeling in my gut that quickly turns to a restrained excitement as I realize the reason for the two different shoes. He has a fake leg. It's the proof I need.

My mind reels back to the day Maxine opened her mailbox and received the news from the Department of Defense. She crumpled to her knees and began to sob before she even opened the envelope.

It was near dinnertime, and Steve and I were playing in my front yard. My mom was on the front porch with Jolene, snapping the ends off string beans and dropping them into a big blue bowl of cold water. She went rushing over to Maxine, with Jolene running along behind her. Maxine held the envelope out to her. We could see her hand was shaking. Mom took it and opened it and pulled out the letter. She read it silently with her lips moving. Then she burst into tears, too.

Soon they were hugging and kissing each other and crying even harder. I didn't get it at all. It was Steve who finally said, "I think they're crying 'cause they're happy."

Maxine looked up at us and waved the letter in the air. Her tears had made her mascara run and streaked her face black the way the soot had stuck to my mom's tears the day Gertie blew.

"Val's coming home!" she cried. "He's hurt, but he's coming home!"

Val's coming home. I had waited three years to hear those words. They became my mantra. I chanted them in my head every night before I fell asleep. I said them to my mom at the breakfast table, and she'd smile and nod. I repeated them to myself in time to the ticking of the clock on my classroom wall as I labored through the endless schooldays. I told Dr. Ed, and he gave me a bag of red lollipops to give to Val when he came home; red was his favorite when he was a kid.

My mom helped me make a banner. I wrote the news on the sidewalk with a piece of bony: VAL'S COMING HOME.

But he never did.

He leans forward a little off the wall and tilts his head up enough so I can see his eyes.

I know I must be grinning from ear to ear. I want to hug him, but I know that's out of the question. His only forms of physical affection were handshakes, head rubs, and shoves. I'm too big for a head rub, but in my heart, I'm still too little for a handshake. I think about shoving him, but then I decide that might not be the greatest thing to do to a guy with one leg. I try not to think about his missing leg, everything leading up to it, and everything after it.

I can't think of a single thing to say to him.

"Hey," I finally blurt out. "How have you been?"

He slowly brings the cigarette to his lips and looks right at me. His stare is impenetrable, his eyes full of conviction yet somehow vacant, like the eyes in portraits of saints and sovereigns and dead war heroes.

"You mean recently? Or for the past thirty-some years?" he asks me in a much deeper, raspier voice than the one I remember, but I have to remind myself that he was still a child the last time I saw him, not much older than Josh.

To me he was always an adult. He did a man's job and made a man's paycheck and had a man's responsibilities. He didn't have a wife or even a steady girlfriend, but he had his mom to take care of, and a truck.

"Recently," I suggest.

He blows a cloud of smoke into the funeral home and squints through it, his attention drawn briefly to Jolene the way it would be drawn to a shiny new quarter in a handful of oxidized change. She begins to smile at him. For Jolene smiling at men is a reflex action, like braking for children on bicycles. Apparently a thought interferes with her instincts, because this smile doesn't fully materialize.

She turns her head to face forward again, gets her compact out of her purse, and holds the mirror to her face to check her makeup.

"I feel like shit," he says.

He doesn't look down at his missing leg, and neither do I, but I assume this is what he's referring to.

"Would you like my chair?" I ask him.

"Would you like my hat?" he asks me.

"Why would I want your hat?"

"Why would I want your chair?"

I search his eyes for any sign of recognition. It seems like he remembers me. He's talking to me like he does, or is he just putting up with me because I'm talking to him?

"Do you remember me?" I blurt out.

"You're Rado Zoschenko's kid," he says without looking at me.

"That's pretty good," I say, smiling. "Remembering who I am. After all these years. I mean, the last time you saw me, I was a little kid. I was six."

"I've seen you since then."

"You have? Where?"

"When you broke your leg, it was in every sports section of every newspaper and on every sports segment of every TV news show."

"How'd you know it was me?"

"Well, let's see," he begins, still not looking at me. "I suppose it would have been pretty stupid for me to think the Ivan Zoschenko from Coal Run, PA—population five twenty-three—that I used to live next door to and who would have been the same age as this football player and now that he was grown up looked a helluva lot like his father would be you."

"I get the point," I say, nodding, my smile having turned into an idiot's grin by now.

"I've also had a subscription to the local piece-of-crap newspaper all these years, and there were a couple years there where you couldn't open the thing without seeing a picture of you holding a football and running across a field like a bull with your head down."

One of my hands instinctively jumps to my throat. I never ran with my head down. Deets's punishment for that was to make you practice with barbed wire wrapped around your neck. He called it a Barbie Choker.

I'm about to correct Val and tell him he was wrong—he never saw a picture of me with my head down—when he adds, "Zo made me do it."

"Do what?"

"Subscribe to the paper."

Zo made him do it? I couldn't imagine anybody making him do anything, and certainly not an old lady who he hadn't seen for over thirty years. I didn't even know he knew Zo.

"How did she make you get a subscription to a newspaper?"

"Same way she got me to come to her funeral. She said please."

Emotions I thought I had successfully buried start churning inside me again. The delight I originally felt over seeing him again is slowly replaced by the sting of betrayal.

He never wrote to me when he was in Vietnam. He never answered one of my letters. He promised he would. He promised he'd come back, and he never did, not even for a visit, not even after we all knew he was back in America, first in a VA hospital in Maryland and then somewhere in Ohio. His mom was never sure where. He didn't communicate with her, he never asked about anyone; he just sent money sometimes. All this time I'd been telling myself he had an excuse. It turns out he didn't have any. He had been spying on us.

"You knew everything that was going on back here, but you never came back?"

He says nothing.

"Why would you bother reading about a place you didn't care about anymore?"

Still nothing.

"How did you know Zo?"

He finally looks at me with those same calm yet troubling eyes, his stare giving off a kind of stagnant serenity.

"I've learned to deal with friendly people the way you deal with bears. If you stand real still and don't make any noise, sometimes they'll just sniff you and go away. I guess that's not going to work with you."

He takes a final puff off his cigarette, then stubs it out on his artificial leg through a tear in the fabric of his camouflage pants.

"Tell your sister she's not fooling anyone with that powdering-her-nose routine. I know she's watching me in her mirror. You can tell her I'm flattered. It'll make her day."

He pushes himself off the wall and begins limping away.

I start to follow him.

"Where are you going?"

"You always were a pain in the ass, and you still are. Asking a million questions all the time. Running around with that big fucking book with the animals on the cover. What was it called? *Natural Wonders?*"

"*Wonders of Nature.*"

"Yeah. That was it. Whatever happened to that book?"

"I don't know. My mom probably gave it to a used-book sale somewhere along the way."

At the mention of my mother, he pauses in his progress, then continues in a more determined way. I want to follow him. My reasons are purely selfish. I find I'm not as interested in knowing what he's been doing as I am in wanting to know if he remembers anything we used to do together. Does he remember any of the things he taught me: how to change a spark plug, how to throw a football, how to shoot a gun?

I was only six years old the one time he let me go hunting with him. My mother would have sent me to my room for the rest of my life if she had known.

I don't think Val would have let me near a gun at such a young age either, but I think he felt it was his responsibility to teach me, since my dad couldn't do it and he had already found out he was going to have to go fight in Vietnam so he had to do it right away. He showed me how to start a lawn mower and ride a two-wheeler, too.

He helped me hold the gun when we spotted the deer. He wrapped his arms around me from behind and crooked his finger over my finger over the trigger, then instructed me in a whisper to wait until the deer looked me in the eye before I killed her. To do it any other way was cheating.

I looked through the scope and tried to meet the deer's eyes like he told me to. I was far enough away that to her I couldn't have been more than a tiny upright figure with a black stick held strangely in my paws, or more than likely I wasn't an image at all, just a deadly scent. But I felt she was looking across the small dip of a valley separating us, through the screen of leafless trees where I hid, into the scope, down the scope, and right into my eyes, and there we stood, eyeball to eyeball, hard human blue eyes searching startled soft velvet black ones.

Thinking about her froze me, but thinking about me ignited her. She turned and began to bound away. I tried to go ahead and shoot her even though I knew it was too late. There was a deafening boom and a kick from the gun that would have sent me sprawling onto the ground if Val hadn't been braced behind me.

The sound made the deer run faster. Her tail flickered in and out of the trees like a white flame until it disappeared completely.

Frustrated tears stung my eyes. I waited for Val to laugh or lecture, but he didn't do either. He took the gun from me and leaned it against a tree while he lit a cigarette.

"What's wrong?" he asked.

"I missed," I said, trying to keep my voice from cracking.

"You know why?"

"Because I'm a bad shot."

"You're not any kind of a shot yet," he grunted.

"Because I was too slow?"

"Because you didn't want to kill her."

"What do you mean?"

He picked up the gun and started walking.

"I mean don't ever try and kill something unless you really want to kill it."

"Why?"

He stopped walking and looked down at me. I remember the cigarette flicking up and down in his teenage mouth when he spoke.

"Because it would be pretty stupid to kill something you didn't want to kill, wouldn't it?"

Now I watch him walk out the front door of the funeral home and decide it would be pretty stupid to follow a man who doesn't want to be followed.

I feel a sharp pain in my finger and jerk my hand out of my pocket. I'd been rubbing the rabbit's foot he made for me and slipped into my hand the day he left for basic training.

A perfect drop of bright red blood beads on my fingertip. The fur and flesh are long gone. All that's left now are bones and claws.

I need a drink. I'm not embarrassed or apologetic about the craving. Needing a drink isn't any worse than needing to collect Beanie Babies. I'd rather be a drunk than a moron.

I leave my truck behind at the funeral home and head down the street on foot. I'm going to catch hell from Jolene for leaving, but I don't care.

It took me a long time to get used to the fact that Val had been sent away to fight in a war. I adapted to the idea, but I never accepted it.

Next I adapted to the news that Val had lost his leg. I changed my plans for us. I knew he wouldn't be able to hunt anymore or take the long walks through the woods he used to love. I knew he wouldn't be able to stand over his truck's engine or probably slide underneath it either. He wouldn't be able to jump up off the couch all of a sudden when the Steelers scored a touchdown or play horseshoes or play catch. I knew he wouldn't be strolling on a Saturday morning from his backyard down to the mailbox, singing the chorus to a Foghat or an Allman Brothers tune, to get the mail before his mom so he could hand it to her, and it would be smeared with oily black fingerprints, and she'd scream at him, and he'd come out the back door grinning at me. I knew he wouldn't be able to do all the repair jobs he'd been doing for my mom since my dad died. I knew there was a good chance his fantasy girl would never go for a ride in his truck or have anything to do with him at all now that he was going to be a one-legged freak. I didn't know if he'd even be able to drive his truck anymore.

I came up with other things for us to do. Board games. Crossword puzzles. Watching TV. I thought maybe he could still throw a football or a horseshoe but do it sitting down.

I was prepared for him to come home in his altered state, but he never did. I even eventually adapted to that.

Now I guess I'm supposed to adapt to the fact that we have somehow miraculously found ourselves together in the same town again after all these years and he doesn't seem the least bit interested in hanging out with me. I could pursue him, but I don't know where he's staying or for how long. I don't even know anyone in town who might know.

There are six bars in town. Brownie's is my favorite. It's a dark lane of a bar with a sputtering Miller Genuine Draft sign hanging in the only window. It's named after the owner's dead dog, who wasn't dead at the time he opened the bar. He has a photo of the ginger-colored mutt tacked onto the wall next to the men's room, amid an impressive collage of magazine pictures of naked women and yellowed newspaper clippings of me breaking tackles.

I prefer Brownie's to other bars because the clientele is composed of career drinkers. There's none of the false camaraderie or violent outbursts or slobbering confessions of amateurs to deal with. Only the silent, steady, earnest consumption of alcohol by men who drink not because they think their lives turned out poorly but because they turned out exactly the way they thought they would.

I also like it because I'm largely ignored. In every other bar in town, I'm mounted behind smudge-free glass in galloping, ball-clutching glory, my past more relevant than my present and all my current failures, misdeeds, and shortcomings neatly excused, forgiven, and overlooked for the simple fact that I used to be very good at sports. Harrison calls the phenomenon O-Jayfication.

I walk past the post office, then past the somber stone face of the First National Bank built by Stan Jack—the J of J&P Coal—back when the area was producing more raw tonnage per miner than any other coalfield in Pennsylvania. It still houses the bank's officers and three yawning tellers who busy themselves counting and recounting the money in their drawers and balancing their own checkbooks. Their customers' banking is done at the ATM machines out at the mall.

Next to Brownie's is the abandoned Woolworth's building. The display windows are boarded up with plywood. The big blue block capital letters spelling out the store's name have faded to silver shadows that can only be seen when the light isn't too weak or too bright.

The three buildings form a sort of condensed history of the town. First National. Woolworth's. Brownie's. Boomtown. Shutdown. Remnants.

By the time I reach the bar, my knee is throbbing. It's been bothering me ever since I squatted in Ricky Blystone's front yard.

For the most part, my injury doesn't usually interfere with my job.

In theory, being a deputy should require a certain level of physical fitness and the ability to break into a sprint if needed, but the reality is, we spend most of our time sitting behind a desk, in a car, in an amazing variety of uncomfortable chairs and benches while we wait in hospitals, prisons, courtrooms, people's living rooms, auto-repair shops, churches, restaurants, bars, and anywhere else where an individual's rage, stupidity, carelessness, or the combination of all three finally brings him to rest.

Dr. Ed gives me prescription painkillers on the sly so nothing shows up on my insurance records that could alert anyone to a problem with my leg. According to my sheriff's-department physicals, I don't have a problem.

The falsified records are necessary but ultimately unimportant. Anyone who wants to challenge my physical capabilities can do it easily enough by digging up any of the old newspaper and magazine articles that ran when I broke my leg.

PENN STATE ALL-STAR PINNED UNDER MINING EQUIPMENT. BEARS LOSE PROMISING BACK. FREAK ACCIDENT CRUSHES ZOSCHENKO'S LEG, CAREER. JOE PA PAYS HOSPITAL VISIT. DITKA ON THE LOSS OF IVAN Z.: "A SAD DAY FOR FANS OF THE RUNNING GAME."

But everyone who knows me can't imagine why anyone would have a problem with my being a deputy, so they don't think there's anything wrong with a little white lie. To the greater statewide law-enforcement community, I'm simply a deputy in a no-crime county whose competence is vouched for on the local level, and there's never been a reason to question that competence.

As for the local level itself, Jack Townsend, Laurel County's sheriff for the past thirty-five years, estimates he won around fifty-thousand during my four years playing Nittany ball. One of those wins came in the last three seconds of a game against Miami when we were seventeen-point underdogs. I took a swing pass on third and long and ran fifty-seven yards for a touchdown. That game alone put the down payment on his hunting camp in Sinnemahoning, some of the best fly-fishing in the world.

It was Jack who convinced me to come work for him. We ran into each other at the State Store this past summer right after I came back. We were both buying the same bottle of whiskey for ourselves and the same pink wine in a box for the same woman. He had been widowed two years earlier and was only on his second date with Jolene, but it would be his next to last. She was about to discover that men in their sixties fall asleep around nine o'clock every night.

I take my usual seat at the end of the bar and join the assembly-line drinking. Soon I don't care that Val thinks I used to run with my head down or that I walked out on Zo's funeral or that Reese Raynor is days within my grasp and I'm not nearly as excited about it as I thought I was going to be.

On my way back to the bar after my second leak, I stop to look for Reese in any of the newspaper clippings chronicling my fame that are interspersed in the pieces of naked women. The photos have been taped up haphazardly, at strange angles, with many of the women's heads covered over by other women's breasts, legs, crotch shots, and asses. The result is a patchwork of dismembered female parts, which is all a man drinking at Brownie's is in any condition to handle. Just a part. Not a whole female.

I don't find Reese, but I find Jess. He's in a picture with Deets, who's standing on the sidelines in his cheap, shiny, gray polyester game-day pants and his silver-gray team jacket with red flames leaping up his back. He's a wide, solid stump of a man, bald because he shaved his head at the beginning of every season to prove he wasn't easily embarrassed, so the first time he slammed into the locker room during halftime to tell us we were embarrassing the hell out of him, he could point to his head and scream, "And I'm not a man who's easily embarrassed!" His arms are folded across his barrel chest, and he's glaring pop-eyed while shouting at Jess.

Jess was Deets's other star player. He had almost been my equal. He had speed, strength, intelligence, desire, but he also had fear. He didn't like to get hit. He didn't like to hit back.

Deets tried to torture the fear out of him. He used to make him rush the concrete wall at the back of the school. He'd make him take a three-point stance and then time him with his stopwatch to make sure he sprinted the distance to the wall, where he slammed into it full force with his shoulder.

One time I watched him hit head-on and knock himself unconscious for a couple seconds. I saw the bruises on him in the locker room the next day. I saw the way he could barely move in school. But he'd do it all night long if Deets told him to and never complain about it, yet when it came time for a game, he still flinched every time he took the ball in his hands. He still took the path of least resistance every time, even if it meant losing yards.

I let my eyes wander over the rest of the wall. I linger over a pair of long legs in red stiletto heels covering the last few paragraphs of the account of my career-ending accident. The headline reads: DISASTER STRIKES AGAIN AT GERTIE. Of all the countless articles written about me in newspapers and magazines, my local paper was the only one to make no mention of me, my crushed leg, or football in the headline and the only one to print a photo of the abandoned mine and make it five times the size of the one they printed of me shaking hands with Mike Ditka after I signed my contract with the Bears.

I've gone over the night of my accident hundreds of times in my head, trying to figure out why I went to Gertie that night. I had been there often enough during my childhood after the explosion. There was nothing to stop us from going, except warnings from our mothers. The buildings were abandoned but unlocked. The shafts were all left open. J&P never bothered closing its mines with anything more than word of mouth.

Kids went there on dares to look for ghosts and morbid souvenirs, or to climb up, jump off of, crawl into, and hide under things they weren't supposed to go near. Some just went out of curiosity. The empty complex could be seen clearly across the valley from the Coal Run junkyard. It sat gutted and forbidding against the lush hillside, tempting and frightening at the same time, like an old castle or the stripped gray skull of some colossal monster.

I went for the same reasons everyone else did, but there was something more that drew me there, something unpleasant but irresistible, the same thing that forced me to go look at a dead kitten on the side of the road instead of turning away as soon as I glimpsed a swarm of flies around it from a distance. Knowing it was dead wasn't enough; I had to see the small, mangled body.

Gertie haunted me, not just because it spoke of death but because it also whispered disturbing truths about life.

From the moment it blew, everyone talked about—but never outwardly accused—the new continuous miners: large, steel-toothed cutting machines that ripped the coal directly from the face and dumped it onto conveyor belts that led to shuttle cars on the tracks.

The miners had been against them from the start. They used to gather in our kitchen and talk in deep rumbles about the loss of jobs and the new dangers involved.

Not only would the machines put many of them out of work, since one continuous miner could rip more coal from a face than twenty human miners with chain cutters could, but they made more coal dust and left more cracks in the ceilings where methane could escape into the air, creating a lethal combination for the smallest spark to ignite.

J&P told the union they were exaggerating the safety issue.

The union backed off. There had been a lengthy strike only two years earlier that had turned violent and left one miner badly injured and another one in jail. No one wanted to go through that again, plus no one was sure of the legality of striking because your company wanted to update its equipment and improve its output. It was fine to fight for better wages, benefits, and safer working conditions, but what were the chances of winning a fight against progress?

One of the machines had started working in Left 12 three weeks before the explosion.

As a kid I didn't fully understand my feelings. I only knew that Gertie made me feel the same way I felt when I learned about slavery in school, or what happened to the Indians. I had nothing to do with any of it as an individual, yet I was part of a bigger, ongoing whole that had done terrible things to large amounts of people in the name of progress and greed.

Gertie made me feel ashamed because I was a part of us, and we had allowed something terrible to happen to us.

The night of my accident, I had been wallowing in shame for two solid weeks. I had been drunk the entire time, ever since I saw the news story about Crystal and went to see her in the hospital.

She had been flown to Conemaugh. Her injuries were raw and new. The places on her body where she had been beaten by Reese with a baseball bat were a gleaming shade of black-purple. She looked like she had been burned in a fire.

I close my eyes against the memory and make my way back to the bar, where Art, the owner and bartender, has another Jack Daniel's waiting for me.

The front door creaks open as I take a seat. I know it's Jolene by the way a dozen pairs of eyes slowly blink at her from the smoky gloom. Women rarely come into this bar, and never on a Sunday. If they're looking for a husband, they send a kid in to get him.

She walks, unconcerned, across the sticky, beer-stained floor, the click of her heels echoing off the wood-paneled walls. A few of the men drop their stares back into their beers, but most of them keep their sloppy gazes helplessly pinned to her.

She slides onto the stool next to me and doesn't say anything.

Art reaches out to refill my draft. Jolene asks for Tequila Rose. He squints at her, making his dark eyes disappear into the folds of his fat face.

"It's that pink shit," I explain to him.

"Oh, yeah." He nods. "We don't have drinks that come in colors."

"How about a Tequila Sunrise?" she says.

"How about tequila?" he suggests.

"Give her a beer," I tell him.

"Is it time for the funeral?" I ask her.

"You missed the funeral."

"I mean the burial."

"You missed that, too. I hitched a ride with someone else."

"With Randy?"

"Randy?" she scoffs.

She thanks Art for the beer and takes a drink. It leaves a little line of foam across her upper lip.

"He hasn't seen Ebbie in two years, and there he was only a couple miles away from him and he told me he didn't even have time to stop by and say hi. No, it wasn't Randy."

"So how is Randy?" I ask her.

"His hair is thinning, and he's put on some weight, but on the positive side, he's developed good posture."

"Here's to good posture," I say, holding out my glass.

She clinks hers against mine.

"He said to tell you he felt bad you had to be the one who found Zo, and he wanted to thank you for driving her around and running errands for her and all the other help you gave her after her first heart attack.

"He also said he appreciates me taking care of all Zo's stuff. He said Marcy really appreciates it, too. I told him I'm not doing it for him or the wifey. I'm doing it for Zo, who specifically asked me to do it."

She takes another gulp of beer.

"Why do you think she asked me? I could kill her for asking me. It's going to be so much work. There's no reason why Randy and Marcy can't do it. Marcy doesn't even have a job."

"She asked me to go through all her paperwork," I remind her. "Randy should definitely be the one doing that. Not me."

"We're suckers," she sighs.

"Here's to suckers."

We clink glasses again.

"So who was the guy you were talking to?"

"What guy?"

"The one at the funeral. The one you were grinning at like he was some leggy brunette in a harem-girl costume."

"Val. Our old next-door neighbor."

Her eyes grow big over the rim of her beer mug.

"I knew it. I knew it. Does Mom know he's back in town? She had a real soft spot for him. She still does, as far as I know."

"We didn't get around to talking about Mom."

"What did he say about me?"

"How do you know he said anything about you?"

She gives me a glance that says we both know it was a stupid question.

"He said he knew you were looking at him in your mirror and that I could tell you he was flattered, but I have to tell you I sensed a lot of sarcasm when he said it."

"Oh, no. He was serious," she tells me, nodding her head. "He knew about the mirror, huh? I wonder if that's because he was a soldier?"

"Oh, yeah. That must be it. I'm sure the Vietcong did a lot of spying on American troops with compacts."

"He's not bad-looking in a grungy, broke, and pissed-off sort of way."

"Are you kidding me? Do you know how old he is?"

"I don't care. I dated Jack."

She takes another gulp of beer, and this time I have to reach out and wipe the foam off her upper lip with my thumb.

"I don't see you dating him anymore."

"I didn't stop because he was old."

"Yes, you did. You stopped because he kept falling asleep because he was old."

"I stopped because he kept falling asleep while I was talking to him."

The phone behind the bar rings. Art answers. He hands the receiver to me.

"What are you up to?" Dr. Ed asks.

"You're calling me at a bar. What do you think I'm up to?"

"I need a favor. I'm going out to Jess Raynor's place. I just got a panicked call from Bobbie. She was close to hysterical. Their youngest hurt himself, and she wants me to come take a look at him."

"Why didn't she take him to the hospital?"

"I asked her the same thing. She said she didn't want to, and that was that."

"Why wouldn't she want to?"

"The only reason I can come up with is, he didn't fall and she doesn't want anyone at a hospital to figure that out, because they're obligated to report anything suspicious."

"Suspicious how? You think Jess Raynor is beating his kids? I can't believe that."

"Why not?"

"Because I know Jess. He wouldn't do that."

"How well do you know him? When's the last time you talked to him?"

"About twenty years ago."

There's silence on the other end.

Finally he says, "Okay, well, I hope you'll understand if I decide not to take your opinion on this too seriously. I'd like someone to come along with me, just in case Jess is on another one of his benders."

"What kind of benders?"

"Drunken ones where he goes off into the woods behind his house with his rifle and takes potshots at anything that moves in his yard."

"Are you kidding me?"

"No, I'm not kidding you. He lost his job about a year ago. Things are pretty bad out there."

"I'm off duty."

"I don't want you there in an official capacity. I want you there as someone who could deal with Jess while I'm dealing with Danny."

"But you're saying I could get shot at?"

I hear a heavy sigh.

"Meet me there," he commands, and hangs up.

I give the phone back to Art and drop a few crumpled bills on the bar.

"I'm meeting Dr. Ed at Jess and Bobbie Raynor's place," I tell Jolene.

"I'll come with you."

"I don't think it's a good idea."

She downs the rest of her beer and slides off her stool. She starts walking toward the door.

"Bobbie's one of my friends. And Gary is one of Harrison's friends."

"Has Bobbie ever told you that Jess beats any of their kids?"

"No. Jess would never do that."

"Has she ever told you that Jess shoots around their house?"

"That's ridiculous."

"Has she ever told you that she had a major crush on me in high school?"

She utters a laugh as she stops at the door. She opens it and stands in silhouette against the rectangle of gray daylight.

"She told me she had sex with you once in the backseat of her grandmother's car. She said it was a great way to spend three minutes in a Buick. You mean that crush?"

# FOUR

JESS AND BOBBIE RAYNOR LIVE ON A STRETCH OF UNPAVED ROAD that looks like the claw end of a gigantic hammer has been dragged back and forth across it. Their house is the only one for two miles in either direction. It's small, sided in faded yellow and trimmed in peeling brown, with a rusted railing running up the front steps.

The garage door is closed, and the lower half has been pulverized. Jagged boards hang loosely. Splintered wood is scattered everywhere. A Dodge Ram pickup truck is parked nearby, half off the driveway, with pieces of wood sticking out of the grille like whiskers.

A pair of beagles start howling from the tops of their doghouses as soon as we come within view. Tire tracks lead from the driveway right up to the front door. They cut across the grass in a series of indefinable patterns. I park on the road behind Dr. Ed's old orange Impala.

His squat, heavyset bulk is standing in the middle of the yard with the permanence and proprietary air of a rhino. He's holding his tackle box that he uses to carry medical supplies instead of fishhooks, and he's wearing a pair of baggy brown slacks and a wrinkled brown shirt that adds to the rhino effect.

Jolene gets out of the truck and starts walking across the ripped-up yard, stepping over pieces of garage door. Thanks to her many pageant years spent picking her way across muddy fairgrounds, torn-up football fields, and rutted speedways, she can walk gracefully in high heels through just about anything. Unfortunately, this is not a marketable skill.

I look around the place, and I'm depressed as hell. Back in school Jess and I were friendly with each other but never what I'd call friends. We couldn't be. Deets fostered a competitive hostility between us. Even though we were part of a team striving toward a common goal of victory, we craved and coveted his praise and attention, and he encouraged it.

Yet at the same time, I admired Jess. It was a stronger feeling for me than any affection I felt toward guys I considered my friends. There was nothing fuzzy or sentimental about it. It was a hard, uncompromising feeling that had little to do with who he was or what he was but was based purely on what he could do.

I knew Jess didn't have any big plans after graduation. He had worked Marvella with his dad as a summer job and talked about putting in for a full-time shift. In our yearbooks under future plans he wrote, "Travel to Alaska to hunt grizzlies. Come back home and go to work."

I tried convincing him once he was making a mistake tying his future to the mines. Even then the few remaining mines in the area were on the verge of closing or being updated with longwall machines that did the work of a hundred miners with a crew of five. The coal that was accessible had been depleted, and the technology to go deeper hadn't been invented.

Colleges were going to recruit him, I explained to him in the locker room one night when we both had to stay late after practice—Jess so he could ram the concrete wall, me so I could run bleachers, because I missed a hole on third and four during Saturday's game that would've got us a first down inside the twenty.

I remember staring at the fresh violet bruises on his upper arm and shoulder. They covered his skin completely and with a disturbing, fitting beauty, almost as if the bruised flesh were his true color and he was beginning to emerge from his pale-skinned cocoon, shoulder first.

"College can be your escape," I told him.

He reached for his locker door with his good arm and gingerly hung his practice jersey on a hook.

"Escape from what?" he asked me.

We were Deets's chosen ones, the sole inhabitants of his torture-filled, glory-filled kingdom. We shared the same fears and objectives, and, like men under fire or orphaned siblings, we depended on each other even though we knew we were completely alone.

I wanted better for him, not better than what I had but definitely better than this.

I join Jolene and Dr. Ed. He turns and looks at me with twinkling blue eyes cushioned in crinkled crow's-feet. His forehead is furrowed with grandfatherly concern beneath a snow-white crew cut that makes his skull appear soft and furry. He looks deceptively cuddly and harmless, the way a sleeping tiger does.

"I hope your theories are wrong about Jess. I've already had to deal with one drunk shooter today, and I'm not even working," I tell him.

"Who was the shooter?"

"Rick Blystone."

"What was he shooting?"

"He lost his job."

"Right." He nods. "Lorelei's closing. She was a deaf-mute, you know?"

"Who?"

"Lorelei Jack. Stan's aunt."

He studies the steep, heavily wooded land behind the house where Jess may be hiding, then tilts his head back like he's about to sniff the air.

"That's two Raynor families in one day," he comments. "You think that's a coincidence, or do you think there's some family tension going on that's pushing everybody over the edge?"

"Are you talking about Reese?"

He darts a quick glance in my direction.

"I don't know, am I?"

"How do you know he's getting out?"

"Do you know how many Raynor children I treat in my practice? Twenty-three," he replies to his own question, and starts off toward the house with the tackle box swinging at his side. "I know more about their family than they do."

Bobbie's waiting at the door for us. She's clutching a wad of blood-soaked paper towels in her hands. Her face is lined with worry, and her eyes are raw and red from crying.

"Dr. Ed," she chokes.

"Calm down," he says to her.

"I can't stop the bleeding. It just won't stop. His nose is swollen up like an egg. And he keeps passing out." She gasps at this, and fresh tears start streaming down her cheeks.

"Calm down," Dr. Ed says again.

He guides her back into the house. Jolene bravely tries to follow, but her own eyes have already welled up with tears, and she looks pale.

"Go wait in the truck," I tell her.

"I want to help."

"Go wait in the truck," I tell her more forcefully.

"Okay," she says. "But you come get me if you need me."

"I will."

The family room is admirably neat for a woman with four kids. It's decorated in the fake country style dictated by women's magazines whose urban editors can afford Shaker furniture and hand-painted farm-animal plates to be used for display instead of dinner. Bobbie can't, but she's done her best to uphold the image on Jess's income.

There are doilies and dried-flower wreaths and ceramic chickens. She has ruffled eyelet curtains, pillows upholstered in gingham, and a video cabinet shaped like a barn. The wallpaper is pale blue with tiny green apples.

On one of the walls is a smiling Sears family portrait of Bobbie, Jess, and their four children, all of them color-coordinated and temporarily united by their individual desires to be perceived as united. Next to it is a photo of a man in camouflage hunting gear smiling for the camera. He has his rifle in one hand, and the other is holding a cap against his chest like he's about to start singing the national anthem.

Hanging on a chain from a corner of the frame is one of Gertie's identification tags. Now they have plastic punch-out tokens, but back then they were brass. Each man had a number for the day. The tags were left at the cage entrance as a record of who was inside. They were recycled from shift to shift, but the company made an exception after the explosion and let the families of the dead miners keep the tags, the way a football team retires a jersey. For a lot of us, it was what we had instead of a body.

The man in the photo was Bobbie's dad. Chimp didn't show up for work that day. He was home with a hangover.

I follow Bobbie and Dr. Ed into the kitchen. Danny is on the floor, slumped against a wall, covered up in a Winnie-the-Pooh blanket with blue satin trim. His nose is badly swollen. The skin is stretched taut and has already turned a greasy shade of purplish gray. His eyes are open and glazed.

Bobbie claps her hands to her mouth as she enters the room, and tears spill over them like she's finding him in this condition for the very first time.

I feel sick to my stomach. During my time as a football player, I've seen my share of nasty injuries, and during the four months I've been working as a deputy, I've seen some pretty ugly stuff, too, but this is the first time I'm seeing a little kid who looks like someone punched him in the face. I can't believe Jess could do this.

Dr. Ed washes his hands at the sink. He kneels down and murmurs something to Danny as he gently tilts back his head and pushes at his eyelids with his thumbs. Danny suddenly comes to life, whipping his head back and forth, sending a spray of blood in all directions out of his nose.

Bobbie falls to the floor and tries to calm him, but he pushes her hands away, crying.

"What happened?" Dr. Ed asks her.

"He ran into a wall." She bites her lip.

"Don't lie to me, Bobbie," Dr. Ed warns.

"He did. He was running real fast with the girls. They were chasing each other, and he wasn't watching where he was going, and he smashed right into the wall."

She looks over at a space on the kitchen wall, then back to Dr. Ed with hope in her eyes, as if the fact that there was a wall there confirmed her story.

"Did he hit his head on anything when he fell back?"

"The floor."

"I want to take him to the hospital," Dr. Ed says, wiping blood from his own face.

"No, I don't want to do that."

"He might have a head injury."

"I don't want any trouble. I don't want Jess to know."

"You don't want Jess to know what? That his son smashed into a wall and needs to go to the hospital? What's going on here, Bobbie? Did Jess do this?"

She stands up and backs away from him, crossing her arms tightly over her chest.

"No," she says to the floor.

"Where is he?"

"He went for a walk."

"We can ask Danny what happened, and the girls."

She looks up and meets his eyes. The first spark of anger is in hers.

"They'll tell you the same thing I told you."

"Damn it, Bobbie!" Dr. Ed shouts at her. "What the hell is going on with you? You're not stupid. Don't you love your kids?"

"Yes, I love my kids!" she shouts back at him. "Of course, I love my kids. Don't you ask me that. I love Jess, too."

"That's the stupidest thing I ever heard."

"It's not stupid to love my husband. I don't want him to be mad."

"Mad?" Dr. Ed's face begins to turn red. Even the skin on his scalp beneath his white crew cut turns rosy. The tips of his ears are almost scarlet. "Mad? You want to see mad? I'm going to show you mad!

"Ivan?" he says. "Does she want to see me get mad?"

"I don't think so."

Bobbie makes eye contact with me for the first time since I've arrived. Unlike Bethany Blystone, she looks remarkably the same to me as I remember her in high school. She even still has the same short boy's haircut. I'm not usually crazy about short hair on women, but she can pull it off because her face is so pretty. It's an angel's face with a snub nose and round cheeks, big wide hazel eyes, and full lips that were always fixed in a bored, alluring pout or a sly, lazy smile. The hair is pretty, too, a dark coppery brown that used to shine in the sunlight streaming through a study-hall window like a freshly minted penny.

Our senior year of high school, one of the guys on the team threw a costume party at Halloween. Bobbie went as Pat Benatar, in a skintight cat suit with stiletto-heeled black leather boots and a chain-link belt hung with silver lightning bolts Jess made for her in metal shop. That costume is what led to our romp in the backseat of her grandmother's car.

I couldn't get her out of my mind. I knew she was dating Jess, but I didn't care. I didn't want her as a girlfriend. I just wanted to get my hands on her body.

I knew she had an after-school job every day but Thursday. That was the day she drove her grandmother to the beauty shop in Centresburg in her grandmother's car and did her homework while she waited for her. I'd seen her sitting in the front window of the shop with a textbook in her lap on my way home from practice.

I stopped one day and asked her if she wanted to go for a ride while she waited. She's the one who suggested we take her grandmother's car instead of my pickup. Afterward I realized it was because she was intending to do me just as much as I was intending to do her, and she knew the big backseat of the Buick would give us more room.

She wasn't like any other girl I had screwed up to that point. She didn't have a single hang-up about sex. She laughed and screamed and talked dirty. She wanted to be completely naked. No messing around with shirts and bras tangled around her neck and panties hanging off an ankle. She didn't care if I loved her or if I even wanted to date her. She made no demands except she wanted to be on top. Her legs clamping my hips were like a sprung trap.

That was the beginning and end of it. I never had an opportunity to see her alone again. Every time I saw her in school, she was with a friend or Jess. I stopped seeing her and her grandma's car at the beauty shop.

I wasn't going to call her. She was Jess's girl. Having sex with her was okay as long as he didn't know and she didn't care, but actively pursuing her would have been an overt declaration of war, and I wasn't willing to take it that far. Bobbie was a great place to visit, but I didn't want to live there.

I had never paid much attention to her and Jess as a couple before, but after we did it, I started watching them talk to each other at her locker. There was something about the way she looked at him that bothered me. I couldn't put my finger on it at first. It was a dopey look, a sort of embarrassed look, one completely out of character for the girl who had unzipped my pants before I could even get my hand under her shirt. She'd get flushed and smile guiltily at him like he was handing her a present she didn't think she deserved but wasn't about to turn down.

One day I stopped her in the hall. She smiled at me, but there was none of the sensual shame in it that she gave Jess.

"So what's really going on with you and Raynor?" I asked casually.

"Nothing you'd understand," she said.

"What are you doing here?" she asks me now, her voice turning icy. "I know you're a deputy now. Jolene told me you moved back."

She turns around to Dr. Ed, her anger deepening along with her paranoia.

"He can't just barge in here without saying who he is," she says furiously to Dr. Ed. "This is my home. You tricked me. You brought a cop with you."

"I'm off duty," I tell her.

"Get out!" she yells at me.

"Enough, Bobbie. That's it," Dr. Ed tells her from the sink where he's washing up. "I'm taking Danny to my office. I can treat him there. He can stay overnight. You can stay, too. If he seems well enough to come home, you can take him tomorrow. Otherwise he goes to the hospital. You're not going to jeopardize his health in order to protect Jess's cowardly ass."

"He's not a coward. He's not."

She starts to cry.

"Don't defend him. By defending him you're every bit as bad as he is."

"He didn't do anything."

"Where are the rest of the kids?" he asks her while he towels off his hands.

"I sent the girls to their room. Gary's at a friend's house."

"Get the girls and the keys to the truck. I don't want to leave him a vehicle if he's drunk."

He bends down and gathers up Danny in his arms. Bobbie puts his blanket over him and fusses with it, trying to tuck the blue-satin-trimmed edges beneath Dr. Ed's arms before she leaves to get her daughters. The boy jerks away from her again.

"You're not going to report this?" I ask as soon as she's gone.

"First of all, I'm not exactly sure what I'd be reporting, and second of all, Crystal used to call the cops on Reese before he finally caved in her skull," he says as we pass back through the family room.

"You don't have to put it that way."

"It's the truth. Calling the cops is not always the best way to handle something. You know that. Did you arrest Rick Blystone this morning?"

"No."

Danny shifts in Dr. Ed's arms. He's wide awake now and staring calmly at Dr. Ed's face. He looks a lot like Jess, except he has his mom's reddish brown hair.

We stop at the front door, and he looks down at the boy.

"Hey, Danny."

"Hi, Dr. Ed."

"What happened to your nose?"

"I hit the wall," he says automatically.

"Someone tell you to say that?"

"No."

"You want to go to my office and get some stickers?"

"Where's Dad?"

"He's not here right now. Do you want to see him?"

He tries to sit up in Dr. Ed's arms and look around.

"Where's Mom?" he asks, starting to panic.

"She's coming."

I open the front door, take a step outside, and freeze.

Jess has stumbled into the front yard, lurching and listing to one side like something rabid. He's dragging his rifle behind him and carrying the plastic rings from a six-pack, with one can of beer left dangling from them. A chew of tobacco swells his lower lip like a bee sting. He comes to a stop and stands, swaying, staring out at the road and my truck. I don't see Jolene in it.

Bobbie comes up behind Dr. Ed with a little girl in either hand. They all practically run into me. We stand perfectly still and silent in the doorway.

"Get back where he won't see you," I tell them.

I start down the steps.

"Hey, Jess. How's it going?" I call out.

He leans forward, squinting at me from beneath the bill of a J&P ball cap patched in several places with silver duct tape.

"Well, well, well. If it ain't the great Ivan Z," he says, finally, slowly straightening up and swinging his gun over his shoulder. "I heard you were back gimping around."

I smile at him and hold out my hand, walking around him so he turns his back to the house.

"I remember when the whole county used to get a hard-on when somebody said your name," he says, smiling back at me.

"The county used to get a hard-on for you, too," I remind him. "It just wasn't quite as big as mine."

He slowly lowers his last beer to the ground, takes my hand, and pumps it. He has the crushing grip I remember all miners having from my youth. The size or age or overall physical condition of the man didn't matter. They all had the same brute hand strength and forearms like rock.

"Now look at you. You're a public servant. You work for me. And you're not even a real cop. Just a deputy. And you wouldn't even be that with your bum leg if it wasn't for Jack. You're lucky he loves Penn State football so much. He'd probably pay you money just to stand in a corner."

"That's what I do most of the time."

Jolene is right. He doesn't look like Reese when Reese isn't standing next to him. They have the same features, but the intent behind the faces is so different they hardly resemble each other.

Reese was a confronter. A reactor, not a thinker. A destructive force. He couldn't walk down a hall without kicking a locker. He couldn't stand next to someone without shoving. He couldn't complete a sentence without a threat in it. He couldn't walk away from a tackle; he had to be pried off the other player like bark peeled from a tree. The way he stood, the way he smelled, the way he opened a book, the way he brought a fork to his mouth were all menacing.

Jess was an avoider. He was subdued and controlled and talked in a rumbling, unhurried half whisper that should have made people ask him to speak up but always made them fall silent, lean forward, and listen closer instead, like he was letting them in on a secret. Everything he did seemed to have an unspoken apology behind it, but not the kind with guilt attached, the kind a well-meaning neighbor might offer if he heard that your truck was going to need a transmission overhaul.

Despite Jess's smart-ass words and the alcohol clouding his eyes, I can still see the guy I knew in high school. I can't find the guy responsible for the bloody little kid in Dr. Ed's arms.

"So what the hell are you doing here?"

"How have you been?" I ask him, instead of answering such a loaded question.

"Okay, how about you?"

"Not too bad. How's your family?"

"Good. Bobbie's great. Did you see her? She's in the house with the kids."

"Yeah, I saw her," I say slowly.

I feel like we're talking about entirely different situations.

"How's your brother?" I ask him. "I hear he'll finally be getting out, if he can keep from killing anyone for the next forty-eight hours."

Jess freezes for a moment, not just physically; I can tell that his thought processes have come to a grinding halt as well.

"Yeah," he says slowly, his smile vanishing. "He's getting out on Tuesday."

"Tuesday?"

"Yeah, Tuesday."

"Is he coming here?"

"What's it to you?"

"I'm just curious."

He considers my question. I watch the inner workings of his mind show on the outer workings of his face. He's trying to decide if there's a reason not to be honest with me. His slowness comes from the booze. Jess isn't stupid.

"Yeah," he finally answers me. "He's coming here. You got a problem with that?"

"I couldn't be happier," I say in all seriousness.

He lets his gun slide down his arm and starts absentmindedly tapping the butt of it against his mud-caked boot.

"You got the safety on that?" I ask him.

He spits a brown stream close to my boot.

"Safety?" he repeats the word like it might be in Spanish. "Safety?" he says again, smiling crookedly, and pointing the gun at my crotch.

Behind him I see Dr. Ed edging out the door carrying Danny.

"Please put the gun down, Jess."

"What if I won't? You gonna arrest me?"

"No. It's your gun. Your land."

He aims it at my head.

"Come on, Jess. I won't arrest you, but if you keep this up, I might have to shoot you."

"Shoot me?" he hoots over the scope. "Shoot me? You don't even have a gun on you."

"I have one in my truck. Don't make me walk over there and get it. I've had a hard day. I just want to get back to Brownie's and watch some TV. There's a Chuck Norris movie on tonight."

"Which one?"

"I think it's the one where the Russians invade Florida."

He makes a loud suck on his tobacco.

"Your dad was a Russian, right? I mean something like a Russian. A Ukie. Right?"

"Yeah." I bristle. "And your dad was a man, right? Or something like a man. A chimp. Right?"

He takes a quick step forward and jabs the gun barrel into my stomach.

Fear spreads through my chest like a spray of ice water. His finger on the trigger twitches. If he pulls it, he will blow a hole through my gut.

He yanks the gun back and jabs it again, harder this time. I stare down at the sleek black barrel. A Browning Autoloader .22. He leans toward me over the gun connecting us now like a shared limb.

"You got a problem with my dad?" he says in a low voice.

I glance back at the house and see Bobbie with a little girl in each hand standing in the doorway behind Dr. Ed.

"Jess!" Jolene cries out.

He jerks with surprise and turns toward her voice, swinging the gun away from me. She's getting out of my truck, waving and smiling.

Dr. Ed takes advantage of the distraction and starts across the yard, carrying Danny, with the intent of a tank. Bobbie and the girls follow him with their heads down.

"Bobbie," Jess calls out to her, sheer worry in his voice. "What's going on?"

He's too drunk to process the amount of action occurring in different directions. He looks from his wife to Dr. Ed to me to Jolene, who's taking mincing steps across the torn-up yard.

"Hi, Jess," Jolene calls to him. "How are you?"

Doors slam, the engine revs, tires spin on gravel. He's confused, but not enough. He glances at Dr. Ed's car and back to Jolene again, who keeps walking toward him, still smiling and waving.

"What's going on? Bobbie!" he shouts again. "Where are you going? Where are you taking the kids?"

He turns to me, terror clouding his face.

"What's wrong with Danny? Why's the doctor here? Where are they going?"

"Bobbie!" he cries out a final time, sounding like a wounded animal. "Don't leave. Don't take the kids."

He raises his rifle and aims it at the tires on Dr. Ed's car.

"Jess!" Jolene screams.

He looks her way. She bends down, grabs the hem of her dress, pulls it up over her head, and tosses it into the yard.

He watches her, stunned stupid, and slowly lowers the gun.

I pick up one of the broken boards from the garage door and hit him across the back of the head. He falls to his knees, then flat on his face.

Dr. Ed pulls out.

Jolene looks down at her bra and panties. I know she's checking to see if they match.

# FIVE

SAFE HAVEN'S PARKING LOT IS ALMOST EMPTY WHEN I PULL IN around nine. Visiting hours are over, but my mom's car is still here, and two others.

I park far away from everyone else, roll down my window, and take a deep breath. The home's about two miles downwind from Franklin Tires. Years after its closing, the subtle reek of chemicals and burned rubber still lingers, as if the air has been permanently saturated like a rag and the sky might burst into flames if someone lit a cigarette nearby.

I dig into my pocket for my Certs, then remember giving my last roll to the Blystone girl.

I get my toothbrush and toothpaste out of the gym bag I keep in the back of my truck, give my teeth a vigorous scrub, spit onto the black-top, and breathe into my hand to check my breath.

I spent the evening at Brownie's after I dropped off Jolene. I was right about the Chuck Norris movie. It was an old one where the Russians invade Florida. Landed right on the beach and nobody noticed. The movie didn't really explain how this was able to happen, but it seemed to imply they were successful because it was dark.

The front doors of the home are still unlocked, but I don't see any-one in the reception area.

I pause for a moment before I go in. To this day, hospitals or any building related to health care gives me a queasy feeling. I can't walk into one without remembering all my surgeries, all my months of rehab, and all the pain.

Since the time I started playing JV football in junior high, it's hard for me to recall a single day where I didn't experience some kind of pain, whether it be as minor as sore muscles or a bloody nose after a hard day's practice or the bruised ribs, mild concussion, and two broken fingers that were the most serious injuries during my career.

I suffered less in college than I did in high school. Joe Pa worked us hard, but he took care of us. To him, football was a noble sport and the men who played it were prized athletes. To Deets, football was a brawl with a winner and a loser and the boys who played it were either winners or losers.

I've often wondered what Deets would have thought of the current generation of pampered millionaires playing his precious game if he had lived to see it: quarterbacks running off to get their pinkies x-rayed, linemen getting hooked up to IVs during halftime because they feel dehydrated, backs heading for the sidelines to avoid getting hit when they might have been able to eke out another half yard if they'd stayed in-bounds. Deets called that particular move "pussyfooting," and the punishment for doing it in a game was having the soles of your feet rubbed raw with sandpaper at the next practice.

But Deets didn't care what he did to us, because he wasn't preparing us to go any further. He didn't believe we were training for a possible lucrative career. We weren't on a road to fame and fortune. I don't even think he saw it as a sport. To him, playing high-school football was simply the most important thing we would ever do in our lives.

I open the door and walk inside. Even tonight my body tenses in remembrance of the night of my accident. That pain was like nothing I'd ever experienced before. It wasn't just a feeling but a presence, like a flaming blanket thrown over me. It couldn't be contained solely in the area where it originated and had spread to every inch of my body. Even then it was still expanding, searching for ways to escape the confinement of my skin. I was sure I could actually see my flesh pulse with it.

The gear that fell on me was heavy—heavy enough to easily crush all the bones and cartilage in my knee—but after I regained consciousness, I was able to push it off me in one of those agony-fueled adrenaline rushes that enable a mother to push a car off her trapped child or one dying soldier to carry another dying one to safety.

I had managed to drive myself to Gertie despite how drunk I was, but I forgot about my car's being there after the accident happened. It wouldn't have mattered anyway, since I wouldn't have been able to drive. I dragged myself instead for a half mile down the same dirt- and gravel-packed road my mother once dragged me up going in the opposite direction.

The moon was bright and full that night and had the effect of a spotlight. I could see clearly within a few feet of me in every direction; then the rest of the world fell away into inky country darkness.

I stopped to rest once, on the verge of passing out, and tried to prop myself into a sitting position, which proved to be impossible. I glanced behind me and saw a trail of dark stains on the road leading up to me. They turned out to be smears of my own blood, but for one homesick moment filled with fear and love, I was sure they were the bloody footprints of a miner's wife.

I continued and made it to the main road before passing out. I was found by a truck driver around 2:00 A.M. He checked my driver's license in my wallet. He knew who I was, and it turned out he also knew my mother. He got me to the hospital faster than any ambulance could have on those particular roads.

I vaguely remember my mother's pale face hovering over me, her hair pulled back in the same ponytail she was wearing the day my dad died, trying hard not to look in my eyes, searching for a doctor's eyes instead.

"Is he going to be okay?" she kept repeating.

Her voice and stare were equally glassy. Her hand rose and fell uselessly, like she was mechanically conducting an absent band; she couldn't decide if she could risk touching me or if she should already give me up as she'd already had to give up the others.

I take a handful of the hard candy sitting in a basket on the reception desk and start peeling off wrappers and popping pieces into my mouth on the way to my mom's office. I hope she's there and I don't have to go searching for her in patients' rooms.

The lights in the building have been dimmed, and many of the residents have already dropped off to sleep, with and without chemical aid. Small, pearlized Jesus Christ night-lights extend down the baseboards of the hallway like a glowing elfin army lined up for maneuvers. I watch them for a moment, until I'm convinced they're moving.

When I look up and see this woman coming at me, I think she must be a drunken hallucination, too.

At first I only see parts. Brownie's wall come to life. A mile of leg in a dove gray suit with a short swingy skirt and high-heeled black patent-leather pumps. A mass of dark curls. Lips with a natural raw redness to them, like she's been chewing on them nervously or she just got done eating a cherry popsicle. Amber eyes the same golden shade of brown as Mr. Perez's smuggled Havana Club rum.

She's in a hurry and has the kind of harried, distracted air about her that makes men look tired but makes women look combative.

She stops and stares at me like I'm a simple undertaking she understands thoroughly but might still give her trouble anyway.

"The great Ivan Z," she states without any show of emotion—good or bad—and without emphasizing "the great" in any way.

Hearing it makes me think about some of the old miners whose real names I can't even remember anymore. They've always gone by nicknames and still do even though the reasons behind them were lost a long time ago: Hairy Riley, who's bald as a cue ball; Smiley Lawson, who's practically toothless; Happy Jenks, who's hacking and gasping and slowly suffocating in Centresburg Hospital hooked up to a respirator and definitely not happy.

She extends her hand.

"Your mother and I were just talking about you."

I take the hand. Another part. It's cool and dry. The skin soft but the grip firm. Slender fingers. No rings. Nails unpolished, clean pink with rounded white tips like moon slivers.

"Huh?" I respond brilliantly.

"Your mother and I," she repeats slowly, exaggerating every word like I might be hard of hearing or English might not be my native language, "we were just talking about you."

"Yeah?"

"I'm on a fund-raising committee for the hospital. We're holding a silent auction tomorrow night to raise money for the new children's ward. Your mother suggested that maybe you could donate a signed football to auction off?"

"She did?"

"Yes. I was thinking that maybe you could donate a little more. How about dinner?"

Her question blindsides me. For a moment I just stare at her blankly. It's been a long time since a woman propositioned me. They used to do it so frequently that one of my roommates stole a number dispenser from the deli at a grocery store and installed it in our apartment outside my bedroom door. After a party I'd have girls showing up outside my classes, at my parked car, outside the locker room, in bars, in front of Old Main, every one of them waving paper numbers at me. That all ended when my career did.

"Dinner? Sure. Anytime."

"Great."

She smiles. Every nerve ending in my body fires. I made her smile. I've pleased her. She's pleased that she's going to dine with me. Shit, where can I take her? Eat'nPark? The Ponderosa? The Valley Dairy?

I need to think of someplace that demands a dress. A slinky dress. A short, tight, slinky dress.

"Then we'll auction off a dinner with the great Ivan Z, the award-winning, all-star, whatever-you-call-it, football-star guy."

"Huh?"

"Can you still throw a football?"

"What?"

"Can you still throw a football?"

"I . . . uh, I never threw a football. I mean, I don't mean I never threw one. I did. I can. I mean, it wasn't my position. To throw a football. I ran with it."

"Oh. Right."

She looks bewildered, but I detect a slight smile. I get the feeling the innocent confusion might be an act, maybe part of a joke, but I can't figure out why she'd want to torment me.

"Did you ever kick it?"

"No."

"Oh, well," she sighs. "I thought that might be fun for the man who bids on you. For you to throw a football to him or even kick it to him, but if that's not what you did . . ." She tucks her lower lip under her top teeth and bites it. "I suppose it would be difficult for you to run with it now." She glances at my knee. "Maybe you could just cradle it tenderly in your arms while you tell him some amazing football story, like the time you won the Daisy Bowl."

"You mean the Rose Bowl? We won the Sugar Bowl."

"Great. Just as long as you won some kind of bowl."

"You mean you want me to have dinner with someone else?" I manage to ask. "You want to auction off a dinner with me?"

"Yes."

"Like a bachelor auction?"

"Oh, a woman bidding on you. That's interesting. I hadn't thought of that."

I should be welcoming death right about now, or at least exiting quickly, but I'm a man, and although male pride and the male ego can be damaged and even destroyed in extreme circumstances, the male desire to be in the presence of a woman he finds extraordinary can't be tampered with.

Even if it's the last thing I ever get to ask her, I have to know who she is.

"Who are you?" I ask.

She smiles radiantly, but there's still a touch of mischief in it, as if she knows someone is standing behind me making faces.

"I'm sorry. I never introduced myself. I'm Chastity. Chastity Morrison. Dr. Morrison. That's why I'm here. I was checking on a patient."

"You're a Dr. Chastity?"

"I know. It's not the greatest name to be saddled with, unless you're a pilgrim or a stripper. What can I say? My mom was a Cher fanatic."

"But your name is Chastity."

She sighs again.

"What were you doing in the seventies? I'm named after her daughter."

"Right."

"Didn't you watch *Sonny & Cher?*"

"Not really."

She shakes her head and glances at her watch. She's about to leave.

"Do you know what Chastity means?" I ask her.

"No, I don't," she says, opening her eyes wide with mock admiration for the impressive explanation she's expecting me to deliver. "I'm a surgeon who somehow managed to graduate with honors from Carnegie-Mellon and put herself through medical school without knowing the definitions of simple words. Do you know what Ivan means?"

"It's really pronounced Ee-*von*. It's Russian for John."

"Do you know what John means?"

"A man who hires a prostitute?"

Her smile returns.

"A toilet?" I try again.

"God is gracious," she says.

"No it doesn't."

"Yes it does."

"It does not."

"Yes it does."

"No it doesn't."

"Okay. All right. You win. Monosyllabic, arrested sense of humor, immature. You've certainly done wonders to help debunk the stereotype of a dumb jock."

She delivers the insult with another one of her wry but radiant smiles.

"Yeah, well."

"So do we have a deal?"

"Sure. What do I have to do?"

"Nothing. I'll contact you after you've been sold. Can you still donate an autographed football, too?"

She doesn't wait for a response from me, or maybe I nodded.

"Just give the ball to your mom. Or even two balls. Actually, I'll take as many balls as you can give me."

With that she walks right past me, down the hall, and out the door.

I continue on to my mom's office after I manage to tear my eyes away from the place in space where her legs and the rest of her body disappeared into the black night.

I find my mom sitting behind her huge slab of a dark wood desk signing forms and looking very magisterial in her tan tweed suit with a pair of glasses perched on her nose and her hair pulled back in a knot. She's never worn makeup except for special occasions. My father didn't like her to. He said it was an affront to nature, like spray-painting a swan.

On all sides she's surrounded by shelves crammed full of books, papers, and dozens of trinkets, knickknacks, and framed photos residents have left for her after they passed on.

"Why didn't we watch *The Sonny & Cher Show?*" I ask her as I take a seat in one of the chairs in front of her desk where the loved ones of Safe Haven's internees have all sat in the past, racked with guilt or relief or a combination of both as they signed the crisp, blue-bordered white document with the home's seal of an eagle returning to her nest at the top.

"Jolene and I did," she answers me. "Jolene would have never missed an episode. To this day she could probably describe every one of Cher's gowns. You didn't like it. You didn't like the fact that Cher was taller than Sonny."

I slide back in the chair, extend my legs, and rub at my tired eyes.

"God, I was so enlightened."

"You were a child," she says, still busily writing. "Any particular reason why you wanted to know about Sonny and Cher?"

"How could I have missed Dr. Chastity? Why didn't you tell me about her?"

"What was I supposed to tell you?" she asks, smiling down at her hand traveling over the papers. "There's an attractive female surgeon at the hospital? You should run over there and try and have sex with her?"

"Yes."

"I'm your mother. It's not my place to help you find women to sleep with. It's my place to help you find a woman to marry and have children with, but since you have no interest in doing that, and since I happen to like Chastity, I wasn't about to introduce you."

"I think I was insulted somewhere in there."

"So how was the funeral?" she asks. "Were people standing?"

"Yes," I say, remembering Val leaning against the pink flocked wallpaper.

She finally stops writing, takes off her glasses, and gives me a maternal once-over that makes me instinctively straighten up in my chair.

"How are you?" she asks. "You look awful."

"How awful?"

"Pretty awful. But maybe I'm the only one who sees it. Sometimes

I wonder. Jack obviously doesn't see it. Even Zo refused to believe you have a drinking problem."

"She also refused to believe Liberace was gay."

She doesn't smile at this, but, to my relief, she decides not to pursue the subject of my drinking. She sticks with Liberace.

"I wonder who Zo left all those albums to. She must have fifty of them. I hope it's not me."

"So where's she from?"

"Who?"

"Dr. Chastity Morrison."

"Clearfield."

"Clearfield?" I cry.

"Yes, Clearfield. What's so shocking about that?"

"I don't know. I guess I just assumed she had to come from someplace exciting and interesting."

"Why?"

"Because she's exciting and interesting."

"Maybe you've underestimated Clearfield. You come from Coal Run, by the way."

"Yeah, I know. A ghost town. Now, that's appropriate."

She ignores my beginning descent into self-pity.

"Are you giving her a ball?" she asks.

"I'm giving her a lot of balls and a dinner, too."

"You're having dinner with her?"

"No, she's auctioning me off."

Mom laughs.

"It's not funny."

"I didn't think she'd have dinner with you. I'm pretty sure she's engaged."

"Engaged? No. I refuse to believe it. She wasn't wearing a ring."

"So? We had a crisis in water therapy today." She quickly changes the subject in order to distract me. "One of our patients fell out of the harness. Fell. She wasn't dropped. But it just so happened her daughter was here. She called her lawyer that very minute. It was Mike. He didn't want to make any problems for me. I felt bad for him."

"How can you possibly ever feel bad for Mike?"

"He's a decent man. I know you take a dim view of his profession on the whole, but some lawyers serve a worthwhile purpose."

"So do certain poisons."

Mom gets up from her big leather-studded wing chair, the one that used to sit behind Zo's grandfather's desk at First National. Zo didn't want it for her office. She was a small woman and felt dwarfed by it. The first time she took a seat in it and saw her reflection in the window, she scowled and said it looked like a bird had flown over and shit her there.

My mother gives the back of the chair a swat, a reflex action from all her years living in a mining town. She could never walk past a couch or an easy chair without slapping it to see how much coal dust rose out of it, to gauge how soon she needed to vacuum again.

If her intention was to get my mind off Chastity, it worked. My dislike for Mike Muchmore is a fairly all-consuming emotion that takes up most of my thought processes whenever I'm reminded of it. He defended Reese, but even without that onerous distinction, I'm pretty sure I'd still hate him.

He was able to get the attempted-murder charge against Reese dropped because no premeditation or malice aforethought could be proved. I remember reading the term in the local newspaper the day after the verdict was delivered. "Malice aforethought": big words the reporter had to look up in a crime reference dictionary after he looked up the term "voluntary manslaughter."

Maybe Reese's actions weren't premeditated as defined by the law, but that was only because his desire to inflict harm was such a natural part of his composition that forethought wasn't necessary. Does a disease plan to kill or only thrive in its host?

It didn't matter. Muchmore, his first year out of law school paying his dues as a public defender, knew exactly how to work the jury.

He grew up in Centresburg and was well acquainted with the stubborn pride of people around here when they were faced with something they didn't understand. Asking for help was equivalent to admitting you were stupid, so we never asked. We either figured it out on our own or decided to either hate the subject and have nothing to do with it or blindly embrace it and hope we weren't making a big mistake.

The prosecutor for the state's attorney's office grew up in a nice suburb of Philly and didn't know a bony pile from a hill of gravel.

I attended every day of the trial. I had just had my first of ten knee operations and was on crutches and wearing a complicated metal brace that looked like a compact version of the Jaws of Life, but I refused to miss a single minute.

Every day Muchmore threw a ton of legal terms and legal bull at the jury, and I watched the process, the subtle changes in their expressions and the varying levels of understanding, hostility, curiosity, desire to do what was right and desire to do what was least embarrassing wavering in their eyes. I saw them start to be overwhelmed, saw the window of opportunity for them to decide to believe or not believe, saw them appraising Muchmore not as a litigator but as the son of Gene Muchmore, a well-to-do local businessman who donated the land free and clear near Coal Run that became the J&P cemetery, where the miners are buried who died in Gertie. If it hadn't been for Gene, no one knows where they might have ended up. The town wasn't prepared. A community rarely has to bury almost half its population in one day.

I saw them begin to look at Reese not as a criminal but as one of the Raynors. Everyone knew a Raynor. Chimp came from a family of ten and had six of his own. Very few people could say something good about a Raynor, but they were a part of our landscape.

Crystal was not. She was too small and alone to make an impact. Her family had moved here when she was already a teen. She was an only child, her mother from a town in West Virginia, her father from Ohio. He never got his hands dirty. He worked behind a desk for a company near Pittsburgh that sold light fixtures. They weren't even present for the trial. They both moved away, leaving Crystal for dead in a state hospital where she received worse treatment than Reese did in jail.

No one was there to stand up for her. And her son was already gone from here. Adopted by an out-of-state family, their identity sealed by the court for his own safety, considering the ferocity of his father's crime against his mother.

I saw the window close. I watched them decide to listen to Muchmore.

The jury agreed with him that Reese meant to hurt Crystal and maybe even meant to kill her once he got started, but he didn't plan it. The baseball bat he brought home with him that day hadn't been purchased as a murder weapon but as a gift for his son. The cashier who sold it to him testified that he told her he was buying it for the boy. No one seemed to care that he was only three.

Reese got six years and would've been out in three except he beat a fellow prisoner to death in what his new public defender argued was self-defense. He was sentenced to another fifteen.

"Did you stop by for a reason or just to make me worry about you?" Mom asks me.

I search for the source of her voice. She's standing in front of one of her shelves looking at a framed photograph.

"Actually, I was more worried about you."

She looks over at me with surprise showing on her face and the beginnings of mild protest in her eyes.

Her face isn't just pretty; it's beautiful in a solemn, superbly crafted way that sometimes goes unappreciated by people around here for the same reason they wouldn't care to own a bust chiseled by a Renaissance sculptor but fill their houses with Precious Moments figurines.

Age hasn't harmed her dramatically because of her superior architecture. Her features are softer now, sanded by time, but still a pleasure to view. Her blond hair has faded to white, but she still wears it long and loose like a girl when she's not working.

Yet age has visited. Up close her skin is a delicate meshwork of lines and wrinkles, like she's made entirely of tissue paper that's been crumpled, then carefully smoothed out again.

"Worried about me? Why?"

I ease myself up out of the chair and walk over to her.

"Today was Zo's funeral," I remind her.

She picks up a photo of Zo off the shelf and stares at it.

I'm struck by how alone she is. Having Jolene and her three grandsons and a lifetime of suitors and friends and a job where she is always surrounded by people has done nothing to reduce her solitariness. It hasn't affected her in a bad way. It's not hard and impenetrable like a wall. It's more of a mist that shrouds her just enough that no one can ever quite find her.

"I know," she says. "I'm going to miss her. Zo and I saw each other every single day. We talked about everything. She was my alter ego."

She smiles to herself over some memory she isn't going to share.

"It's going to be hard for a while. It's going to be like having all the mirrors in my house broken and not being able to look at myself to see how I'm doing."

I put my hand on her shoulder.

"I'm sorry, Mom. You were okay until I opened my big mouth. I didn't mean to make you feel worse."

"No, it's okay. I'm fine," she insists, shaking her head at me. "Zo had a good life. A long life. It was her time. She knew that, and she was okay with it."

I believe that, too. From the time I came back, I feared she was on her way out, but she didn't seem afraid at all.

She had always been petite, but her presence was always the largest in a room, so her physical size often went unnoticed. When I saw her again after sixteen years away, I was startled by how small and frail she had become, even though her mental faculties and energy level hadn't been diminished at all.

During the last couple months, layers and layers of her fell away and she became smaller and smaller, seeming to curl up and retreat on herself the way a perennial flower does in fall in preparation for its winter sleep.

The last embrace I received from her was the week before she died. We had just finished having a cup of coffee and a piece of her spice cake at the kitchen table.

She made me promise to be the first one to go through her papers and put everything in order before handing them over to Randy. She was concerned that if he was the one who tackled the filing cabinet first and saw the bursting, disorganized drawers, he'd consider the task too daunting and never do it.

I promised her. Before I left, she gave me a quick hug that felt like the soft, papery flutter of a butterfly hitting against my chest, and I knew she didn't have much time left. She had completed the full circle of her life, returning at the end to what she had been at the beginning: a beating pulse inside the insignificance of a human body.

"Have you given any more thought to that house I showed you in town?" Mom asks suddenly, changing the subject again, this time for her own sake.

"What am I going to do with a house?"

"Live in it?"

"Very funny. Did Jolene say something to you? Does she want me to move out?"

"Move out?" Mom laughs. "You never moved in. You sleep on her couch a couple nights a week and come by for dinner when you feel like it."

"See, she did say something."

"She didn't say anything," she says, her voice turning into a scold.

"Jolene is thrilled to have you back, and so are her boys. I'm just saying, for your own sake, I don't understand why you don't want to find a place of your own to live in. You have a job. You have a steady paycheck. Everyone's glad you're back."

"What does that mean?" I interrupt her. "Everyone's glad I'm back?"

"Just what I said. Everyone's glad to have you back home again. You're a hero in this town."

"I was a hero."

"Once a hero, always a hero."

"Are you familiar with the term 'fallen hero'?"

She frowns at me.

"Are you familiar with the term 'pain in the ass'?"

"You've definitely been talking to Jolene."

"So you're not staying?"

"I don't know. I can't imagine staying. What would I do here?"

"What are you doing now?"

"That's what I mean."

"You want to go back to Florida?"

"I didn't say that."

"You want to go somewhere else?"

"I didn't say that either. Can we drop this?"

She nods and goes back to staring at the photo in her hands.

"Don't feel bad," I tell her.

"I feel bad for myself, but I don't feel bad for her. She got to finish her life."

I know she's thinking of my dad and how his was extinguished in the middle.

"You're thinking about Dad." I say my thoughts out loud. "You're thinking you wish I could have known him."

She looks up for a moment and puts one hand briefly against the side of my neck.

"No, I was thinking I wish he could have known you."

I leave her staring at the picture of Zo in her polyester summer pantsuit of dandruff-shampoo blue clustered inside the pink silk lining of Liberace's cape. He has his arms spread out behind her like a vampire or a protective Mother Goose.

Moments later she would march across the Las Vegas hotel lobby, armed with her big white pocketbook and rural determination to develop film for under two dollars.

On my way out, I stop by Crystal's room. Her roommate passed away last week after a long bout with cancer. The bed has remained empty. The nurses told me that Crystal seemed sad, but I'm skeptical. Detecting any emotion in her is next to impossible, although I have no doubt that she still feels things.

She's awake, staring at the end of another black day.

"Hi, Crystal," I say softly.

She can't turn her head. She can't move anything below her chin. On a good day, she's been known to swallow, but never enough to move food or liquid down her throat. She's fed through a tube. She eliminates through a tube. She can only hear through one ear. She doesn't see at all. One of the blows to the back of her head destroyed the vision center in her brain.

I try to visit her once a week. I'm doing my best to make up for lost time: the time she's been lying in this bed without me caring and the time I should have spent with her before this happened.

My mom has asked me about my devotion to her, and I made up a story about us being good friends in high school. She didn't buy it for a second. She knows better than anyone that the great Ivan Z didn't have close relationships with mousy girls several years his junior. I didn't even have close relationships with the guys who were supposed to be my best buddies and the girls that I dated. They were just people I hung out with; I never formed serious attachments.

My mom doesn't pry, though. It's a fairly remarkable quality in a mother, especially when it's not done because she's too self-absorbed to care or because she genuinely lacks interest. She will ask me about anything once. No subject is taboo. But if I tell her I don't want to talk about it, she won't press me.

For most of my life, it's been great, but lately I almost wish she'd nag at me and force me to talk to her, yet when she starts, I always stop her. I'm afraid she's going to convince me to make a decision I might regret or one I might not. Right now I can't decide which would be worse.

I sit down on the bed next to Crystal. Her emaciated body makes a small, angular hump beneath the hospital sheet, like a bundle of sticks. I pick up an unresponsive hand. It lies motionless on top of my palm, and I stare at it with the same repulsed compassion I'd give a broken bony bat.

"Who'd you get the flowers from?" I ask as I notice a browning bouquet of carnations and chrysanthemums I don't remember bringing her. "Don't tell me I've got competition."

I notice two more dried-up arrangements sitting on her nightstand. I find a card in one. They're condolence flowers for her dead roommate. I pick up all three vases, pitch the flowers in the garbage can, and go empty the murky water into the bathroom sink. Then I toss the vases in the garbage can, too, enjoying the sound of the glass cracking.

"I don't have anything for you," I tell her, walking back to the bed. "This was sort of an unplanned visit. I just happened to be in the neighborhood."

Her eyes stare blankly ahead, but I see the tip of her tongue move slightly inside her mouth. It's one of the few movements she makes. It means either nothing or everything.

I grab her plastic water pitcher and pour a small amount of water into a paper cup. I dip a finger in, then run it lightly over her chapped lips. I take a little more water and dab it around her forehead and neck. She always feels too warm to me.

"You're wearing my favorite nightgown," I tell her.

It's good to talk. She can hear. She's alive, and she can hear. No one knows for sure how much she understands, but the sound of a human voice must bring her some comfort. It lets her know that she's not alone, that she is connected to something outside herself. I talk to her, I suppose, for the same reason people talk to babies still in the womb.

"I saw a nightgown at the mall I want to get for you," I go on. "It's pink like this one, but it's a nice soft material and it doesn't have any scratchy lace."

I reach out and touch the lace around her neck. It's not stiff and scratchy anymore. It's been washed so many times.

She's facing her colored-glass animals displayed on the bookcase I set up next to her bed. She can't see them, but I describe them to her.

The state hospital she was in before moving here didn't allow personal effects, so she had nothing when she arrived, while the rest of the residents are usually coming from their homes and bring plenty of their belongings with them.

The sterility of her side of the room bothered me. I never knew her that well, but I remembered she had a shirt covered in fake sparkly gems and a necklace she used to wear all the time: a tiny, tarnished gold cage in the shape of a ball with colored jewel chips trapped inside it.

I was thinking about the necklace one day right after I started working for Jack, while I was standing in a small, dirty kitchen with Chad, one of the other deputies, reading rights to a guy we were arresting for the forty-odd TV sets, VCRs, and CD players he had spent the past couple days trying to sell out of the back of his van in a Burger King parking lot. He had been fairly adept at breaking into people's homes and stealing the stuff, but once he had it, he didn't know what to do with it. He explained to us that this had always been one of his worst shortcomings: He never thought ahead.

His kitchen was void of color except for a set of shot glasses clustered on the windowsill above the sink. Each one was a different vivid jewel tone. They were pretty and ugly at the same time and reminded me of Crystal's necklace and how she wouldn't take it off even after I convinced her to take off everything else.

The next day I saw a set of prancing glass horses at the Hallmark store at the mall, colored ruby red, emerald green, and cobalt blue. I've added dozens more animals over the past months, but the horses are still my favorites.

I pick up the red one. No one on the staff will dust them for fear of breaking one. I yank my shirt out of my jeans and polish it.

"I have my eye on this rooster," I tell her. "He's beautiful. About six inches tall. His tail looks like a psychedelic water fountain."

I pick up the blue horse next.

"He's out at that new Italian restaurant I told you about. Marcella's. It has a cigar shop attached to it that also sells gifts and chocolates."

I pick up the green one.

"We'll put him here on the top shelf where the sunlight will hit his tail. Every time a nurse or an aide comes in, she'll tell you how beautiful he looks. I can't afford him right now, but we have plenty of time to get him."

I give her a resolute smile. Her injuries are permanent but will not shorten her life.

The horses are done. I decide to leave the rest for my next visit. Most of the glass is from me, except for a collection of fancy bottles from Mom and Zo and a tiny pink ballerina from the family of her former roommate.

She doesn't have any family of her own except for the parents who moved away.

She was moved here about twelve years ago. Even my mom and Zo don't know who's paying for her care. Her benefactor has chosen to remain anonymous and pays the hefty monthly bill with certified checks through a bank in Harrisburg.

I crouch down next to her and kiss her flaccid cheek. It smells and tastes of a light, sweet sweat and a slight bitterness I'm convinced comes from a buildup of different medications that have begun exuding from her pores. There's nothing unpleasant about her person, but the bed has the damp, unclean odor of an overused dishrag no matter how often the mattress is turned and the bedclothes are changed.

"He's getting out Tuesday," I whisper against her good ear.

I've spent a lot of time discussing my plans with her about how I should get revenge against Reese. Most of the plans range from fantastic to comical and would be much better suited for the likes of James Bond or Bugs Bunny to carry out than for me. Now that Reese is about to be released, it's becoming more and more obvious to me that, as much as I hate him and as repulsive as I find him, I'd rather talk about dropping an anvil on his head than actually do it.

I think about hunting with Val. Did I miss shooting that deer because I was slow, a bad shot, or a coward? Or was Val right? Did I fail because I was trying to kill something I really didn't want to kill? I think I really want to kill Reese, but I guess I won't know for sure until I look him in the eye.

"I'm going to take care of it," I tell her. "Then I guess I should probably leave again. There's not really much of a reason for me to stay after it's done."

I wait to see if the tongue flickers. When it doesn't, I take it to be a sign that she might not agree.

# MONDAY

# SIX

I DIDN'T KNOW ABOUT THE KIND OF LIFE CRYSTAL WAS LIVING with Reese while it was happening, and I wouldn't have cared. She had disappeared from my thoughts years earlier with the same unthinking ease as a pair of old cleats did.

She was brought back one night when I was hanging out with some teammates at the Rathskeller during my last month before leaving for Bears spring training. It was a loud, crowded, rowdy bar, and there, like everywhere we went on Penn State's campus, we were treated like gods and paid for nothing.

I was sitting at the end of the bar on a stool, with a girl on my lap who was giving me a hand job. I was trying to convince her to get down on the floor and give me a blow job. She wasn't drunk enough yet and kept giggling and saying, "Let's go somewhere private," and I kept telling her I could get any woman to give me one in private but if she did it in the bar, she'd be special.

A buddy called out to me. I looked in his direction and saw him waving a hand above the sea of people as he made his way toward me.

"Hey, Z," he called again. "You're from that little shithole town, Coal Run, right? You guys are all over the fucking news tonight. Some redneck beat his wife to death with a baseball bat."

He pointed behind him at the TV hanging above the bar. I couldn't hear anything, but I immediately recognized my hometown behind the reporter.

It was spring, and the countryside surrounding State College was a vista of rolling hills and green velvet forests and a soft turquoise sky that looked rubbed on. But a hundred miles west, the sky was the color of old bones and the trees hadn't bloomed yet. The bare, gray maples and elms behind Coal Run were topped with tight red buds. From a distance they tinged the hillsides a sore dark pink.

The reporter was standing in front of a park where I had played hundreds of times as a kid. The grass was three feet tall now. The picnic benches were overturned. The rusted, outdated gray metal playground equipment looked like torture devices compared to the bright plastic padded jumbles of tubes and suspension bridges in the backyards around here.

Fifty yards beyond it all, in the midst of a strip-mining desert, loomed a colossal surface-mining shovel as tall as a twenty-story building, its monstrous mouth poised inside the TV screen above the reporter's head, looking ready to bite it off.

The reporter's lips moved silently. Behind him was a tarnished brass plaque embedded in a concrete stump. I had run my fingers over the raised lettering so many times as a kid that I knew it by touch as well as by sight. I closed my eyes in the din of the bar and tried to push aside the fog in my brain brought about by beer, and pot, and a girl's hand working diligently inside my pants until I finally felt the words tingle my fingertips like a blind man reading Braille: THIS PARK DONATED BY THE J&P COAL COMPANY.

I got up from my stool, knocking the girl onto the floor, and began walking toward the TV as the image flashed to a little white house with a birdbath in the front yard and a doe lawn ornament standing guard over a fawn.

More flashes. More images. State-police and sheriff's-department vehicles parked all over the road. An ambulance with strobing lights. The body being removed from the little white house. A shot of the interior with an ominously large bloodstain on the carpet.

Sheriff Jack brushing off reporters. Much younger than he is now, but the face already beginning to sag, the carefully groomed hair already beginning to gray, the eyes already receding into a calm, dark indifference most people will choose to see as wisdom.

I plowed my way through the crowd of people and came to rest directly beneath the TV set as the screen showed a shell-shocked three-year-old boy being carried out the door over a deputy's shoulder, eyes like the blackened windows of a fire-ravaged building, desperately sucking his thumb.

I knew the boy. I had seen him once, walking down a street in Centresburg holding his mom's hand. I was afraid she might remember me, so I turned down a different street.

The memory changes suddenly, viciously. I'm no longer standing in the bar watching the events unfold on TV. I'm there. I'm here. I can feel the spring chill that I missed when I first moved to Florida. Now my body has adapted to all those years of heat, and I can never get warm.

The air is misty but country-pure. It smells like earth and trees. The hills rise up behind the house in gray and purple and pink, all the colors of a bruise.

They are mountains, but the word seems too impressive for them now. They're no longer jagged or spectacular, although they were in their youth. The word "foothills" seems demeaning, implying they are merely part of something bigger, a servant to the larger mountains beyond them.

I don't know what to call them. My mind can't grapple with simple ideas. I look down and see my hands covered in blood. My boots and the cuffs of my jeans are spattered with it. My varsity jacket is soaked.

The police have gone, but they left a body behind lying on the cold ground.

I start to walk toward her. As I approach, I see another man coming from the opposite direction. I'm in Coal Run, but he's an ocean and several continents away, walking across what remains of his family's farm.

The land beneath his feet is barren and broken into cold, hard brown pieces. The house behind him has been burned to the ground.

The barn has been spared but stripped of anything useful and emptied of everything edible. He steps over the clumsily slaughtered carcasses of the few cows and pigs the family owned and stops a few feet away from the body.

He's terrified to look at it too closely for fear it may be one of his younger sisters. He already knows they're dead, but he was hoping they had escaped the rape and necrophilia.

It's impossible to know who did it: the Germans, the Soviets, his own countrymen turned savage by starvation and fear. He doesn't know who to hate anymore, which is as crippling as not knowing who to love. He crosses himself three times and kneels.

It isn't his sister. He looks up and sees me and motions for me to join him. I walk over and look down.

It's Crystal, splayed out white and naked on the bare ground, looking exactly the way she did the day I laid her out on my sweatshirt in the woods and fucked her. Her body is like a child's: undefined hips, breasts the shape and size of peach halves. The tiny, tarnished cage filled with dim, colorful stones hangs around her throat.

Even in death, her eyes show trust. She was frightened and unsure when I seduced her, but she believed in me. She believed all the garbage I told her. When I pushed inside her, she felt love, while I only felt pussy.

The man stares up at me from where he kneels next to her body. I know him, but we have never met.

"Did you do this?" my young father asks me.

I jerk awake with my heart thudding loudly in my chest. I'm not sure where I am. I look around to get my bearings.

I'm in my truck. I never left Safe Haven's parking lot. I've been covered up with a blanket. My mother's doing. My keys are missing from my pocket. Also her doing. They'll be waiting for me at the front desk.

I push up to a sitting position. I'm breathing heavily, and I'm drenched with sweat. I find my bottle. My hand is shaking. I try to remember how much I drank last night before I started on this one. It's about half empty. I hold it up in the morning light, tilting it this way and that, measuring the contents and gauging the severity of my impending hangover. I can work.

Bodies start to surface in the murk of my mind like they're bobbing to the top of a black sea. How many was I responsible for yesterday? Crystal? Did I kill Crystal? Did I leave her in her front yard?

I left Jess unconscious in his front yard. I left Rick passed out in his front yard. Did I leave Jolene in her front yard? Yes, but she was standing and she was very conscious. She was upset. Not as much at Jess for hitting his son or Bobbie for protecting him, but more at me for confronting Jess without a gun when he had one.

It takes me a few minutes to be able to separate memories and dreams and reality. A lot of what happened to me yesterday seems like a dream—seeing Val again, seeing Jess again, seeing Chastity for the first time—while the dream feels so real I'm almost afraid to look outside my truck for fear I'll see a girl's dead body and the ghostly stare of my twenty-year-old father.

I've never even seen a picture of him at that age, but I know exactly what he looked like. He would have been much thinner than he was when I knew him, almost emaciated from his years of near starvation. His hair would have been raven black, without any of the strands of silver that were beginning to appear the year before he died. His eyes would have been the same sparks of color, their decadent presence unexpected and remarkable in the hard, sober face, like finding a lost diamond ring glittering on the side of the road. The Magadan *nakolka* of the Stalin crucifix would have been fresh, sharp, and blue.

I make myself get out of the truck. The lot is half full already, but there's no one around.

I keep a couple clean shirts in the back of my truck for these kinds of mornings along with deodorant and a plastic bag full of Wet-Naps I've collected from barbecued-rib nights at the Ponderosa.

I walk over to Safe Haven and retrieve my keys from the receptionist at the front desk. Once I'm back at my truck, I turn on the engine and get the heat working, then strip off my jacket and shirt and walk around to the back of my truck, bare-chested, rubbing my arms in the cold. After a good scrubbing with a Wet-Nap, I pick out the least wrinkled of my shirts: tan with brown-and-gold keystone-shaped patches on the shoulders proclaiming me to be a member of the Laurel County Sheriff's Department.

Back inside the truck, I dry-swallow two Vicodin, take my badge out of the glove compartment, pin it to my shirt, and snap my revolver into my belt holster. I'm on my way to see Sheriff Jack.

I make one stop en route. I need real coffee this morning, not the stuff we have at work.

When we were kids, the Valley Dairy only sold ice cream. It was made with fresh milk from a local dairy farm. There were pictures of cows on the walls and gingham curtains on the windows and polished silver milk cans standing in the corners.

The place always seemed to do well, but the farm went under and the family had to sell. The new owners decided to expand it into a restaurant. They bought two deep fryers and a dozen high chairs, ordered some place mats for kids to color on and red plastic plates, put in some booths and had a slick laminated menu made, but kept the barnyard decor.

I survey the breakfast crowd. The waitresses move in and out among the booths and tables with the precision and wiggle of fluorescent-stained microbes on a glass slide. Their uniforms are an alarming orange, the same shade as the cheese in the grilled cheese sandwich pictured in the menus.

Jolene's working the counter in back. It's filled with men in all colors of dirty ball caps who work at a plant outside town where they're shredding old tires to mix into asphalt. The process is supposed to make the blacktop last longer. She's walking up and down the line with a coffeepot, smiling and making small talk.

She spots me, and the smile disappears. I guess I wasn't imagining her little lecture last night. It may have been more. It may have been a fight. I may have started it by yelling at her instead of thanking her for saving my life. I'm all for women's rights and equality in the workplace and all that stuff, but I draw the line at heroic stripping.

I start making my way to the counter. She moves to the end of the line of tire shredders to wait on a new customer. I slow down and come to a stop as she nears him.

It's Val. There's no question about it. He looks exactly the same as he did at Zo's funeral yesterday, right down to the cigarette hanging from one corner of his mouth and Castro's hat.

Jolene darts a questioning look in my direction. I shrug my shoulders and nod.

"Welcome to the Valley Dairy," she says to him, sweetly.

He's staring out the window. He takes his time turning his head toward her, then tilts it back so he can see her from beneath the brim of his cap.

"Have you ever been here before?" she asks him.

"No, but I think I can figure it out," he replies.

He takes a long drag off his cigarette and studies her as she reaches beneath the counter to get a menu.

"Weren't you Miss Slag Heap 1982?" he asks her.

She seriously considers his question for a moment. I know she's wondering if there could have been a local pageant that she missed.

I walk over and sit two tire shredders away from him.

"I was Miss Mountain Laurel," she replies. "Miss Teen Centresburg, Centresburg's Junior Miss, Laurel County Fair's Pine Princess, Miss Bucks County Mall, Miss Centresburg Mall, Miss November in a Keystone Auto Parts calendar, Miss Centresburg Speedway, and Miss Pennsylvania."

"Jesus," he says.

"I was also queen of a lot of things. Do you want coffee?"

"Yeah."

She hands him the menu and slides a cup and saucer in front of him.

"Miss Pennsylvania," he says thoughtfully, putting his cigarette on the edge of an ashtray. "That's a big one. You win anything good?"

"A car," she answers, busily plunking down containers of cream and sugar packets in front of him.

He makes a low whistle.

"What kind?"

"A powder blue Mustang convertible."

"What else?"

"A mink coat."

"Real mink?"

"Yes."

"What else?"

"Let's see. Five hundred dollars' worth of Maybelline makeup. Two hundred dollars' worth of Hawaiian Tropic products. Three Catalina swimsuits. A fourteen-karat gold, handcrafted 'Miss Pennsylvania' diamond necklace."

"Anything else?" he asks, brushing aside all the creams and sugars and reaching for the black coffee.

"A sterling silver, limited-edition Mickey Mouse watch. Oh, and a trip."

"To where?"

"Las Vegas."

"What hotel?"

"The Flamingo."

He takes a long swallow of his coffee, then settles his unsettling gaze on her, watching her with a condescending admiration, as if he finds her stupidity to be an act of bravery.

"Did you get a single prize that wasn't symbolic of something wrong with this country?" he asks Jolene.

"I got ten pair of shoes."

He barks a laugh. The tire shredders shift uncomfortably. It doesn't bother her at all.

"Weren't you at Zo's funeral?" she asks him.

"Briefly," he says.

"How do you know her?"

"How do you know her?"

"My son is her grandson."

"That would mean you fucked Randy. Was that more or less dehumanizing than being Miss America?"

"I wasn't Miss America," she replies angrily. "I was Miss Pennsylvania, and even if I had won, I wouldn't have been Miss America. I would have been Miss U.S.A."

He leans across the counter until the brim of his hat almost brushes her chin.

"Why didn't you win?"

"I was disqualified."

"No shit. For what?"

"I got pregnant."

"You were Miss Pennsylvania with your whole perfect little beauty-pageant future in front of you and you got pregnant?"

"I didn't do it on purpose."

She truly didn't believe they would take back her crown. She thought they would excuse the pregnancy because it had been an accident.

"What's the difference between this and falling down a flight of stairs and breaking my leg?" she argued with the officials when they came to our house for the final confrontation.

He picks up his cigarette and slips it back in his mouth.

"Hell, I'd give two pair of shoes to hear that story."

The tire shredders begin to shoot dirty looks in his direction. They don't approve of the way he's talking to her, but none of them seem anxious to challenge him.

"Do you want to hear our breakfast specials?" she asks.

"I want a burger."

"At eight in the morning?"

"You got a problem with that?"

She glances behind her at the plates of eggs and pancakes staying warm beneath the orange heat lamps.

"No. Okay, you want a burger. We have—"

"Don't," he interrupts her. "Don't tell me about your Caribbean Burger and your Tom Turkey Burger and your Alaskan Pipeline Burger. I want you to fry the piss out of a ground-beef patty and stick it inside a bun. A plain bun. Not sourdough or whole wheat or fucking poppy seed. I want the kind of bun we serve to our convicts and public-school children."

"Do you want fries with that?" she asks when he's finished.

He keeps staring at her for a moment.

"No," he says. "Forget it."

He starts to get up from the stool. His movements are awkward and jerky. He's been without a leg for over thirty years now. I always assumed he would've adjusted to it okay. As a kid I pictured him drinking a couple beers and uttering a string of swear words over his misfortune, but that would've been the end of it. Val would've never felt any self-pity or bitterness. He would've conquered the problem. He'd be one of those amputees who could run a marathon on crutches if he wanted to. I imagined it wrong.

He digs in a pocket for some change and puts it on the counter to pay for the coffee, then starts limping past the men seated on the stools. He doesn't really drag the fake leg; it's more like the rest of his body coerces it.

He stops when he gets to me.

"So what are you now?" he asks, the cigarette jerking up and down between his lips. "A forest ranger?"

I try to answer him, but no words come.

"He's a Laurel County deputy," Jolene answers for me.

"Your mother must be proud," he says.

He reaches across the counter and takes one of Jolene's hands in his, turns it over, and lifts it up like he means to kiss her palm, then presses two dimes into it and squeezes her fingers shut around them.

"Are you gonna let that guy talk to your sister like that?" a voice at my side asks me.

I look over at Jolene, who's staring out the door after Val and clutching the tip in an upraised fist like she's about to argue a point.

"Yes," I hear myself reply.

She catches my eye. I smile at her. She smiles back.

"He definitely remembers us," I tell her.

My reflexes aren't what they used to be, or I would've followed Val out into the parking lot and tried to talk to him. It's not until he's gone that I realize I still don't know anything about his friendship with Zo or where he's staying or for how long. I wanted to tell him he should go see my mom.

My stomach isn't ready for food yet, but I'm feeling a lot better. I take my coffee to go.

I park my truck in front of the sheriff's department instead of around back where Jack likes us to park. I go in the front door where the public is supposed to enter. He doesn't like us to do that either.

There are no windows in the small, rectangular room. There's a bench on each side of the doors, two surveillance cameras mounted to the low ceiling, and a large concrete keystone mounted to a boulder in the middle of the floor with the words ENFORCEMENT OF LAWS, and PRESERVATION OF DOMESTIC ORDER encircling it in gold.

Frank's working the desk today. He and Chuck trade off dispatcher and desk duties. He's on the phone behind Plexiglas, frowning, and gives me a nod of recognition as I pass through the door leading to Operations.

The rest of the building is made up of two holding cells in back, a booking room, an evidence room, an equipment room, a general-purpose room, and Jack's office.

There are four other deputies besides me. Two of them are named Chad.

Pierced Chad has four earrings he's not allowed to wear on duty, a pierced nipple, and a pierced tongue that Jack has never noticed. He's always spit-shined and ironed, his tie perfectly knotted, his pant legs creased. He lives with his mom.

Pregnant Chad always looks like he's spent the night hiding in a closet. He's owl-eyed and is usually bent over a scalding cup of coffee like he's trying to steam lines out of his face. He lives with his expectant wife and their three children between the ages of one and five.

Tripp Doverspike is a big, loud guy who raises ducks and has a pretty girlfriend.

Our other deputy is Todd Stiffy, whose name alone propelled him into an armed occupation.

Not one of them joined the sheriff's department because he wanted to fight crime or make the world a better, safer place. On the other hand, they also didn't do it because they like to bully people or because they get off being an authority figure with a badge and a gun. We're all well aware that doesn't mean much around here. The general populace is better armed than us, and most of them are better shots, too.

They're all decent guys, but they became deputies simply because they needed a job, and it's a good job with good benefits and a good retirement plan. Not to mention a free car or truck with a V-8 engine and a siren.

I became one because my reason for coming home was to confront a violent ex-con, then leave again. After Jack made the passing job offer to me in the State Store last summer, it occurred to me a few days later that being a law-enforcement officer might not be a bad thing for me to be when I eventually meet up with Reese. Unfortunately, I didn't stop to consider that becoming a deputy would mean I'd have to do a deputy's job. On the upside, I really like my truck.

Pierced Chad is on the phone at his desk. He nods a good-morning in my direction. Pregnant Chad and Doverspike are on transport this week. I don't know where Stiffy is.

Our desks are the only places where individuality is allowed to be expressed in the building, and even then it has to be done sparingly.

They float in the middle of the sterile sameness, little islands of distinction, the objects scattered on them and the pictures taped to them revealing the complexities of the man behind the deputy.

Stiffy's into sports. Pierced Chad loves cars. Pregnant Chad has kids. Doverspike likes ducks and has a pretty girlfriend. My desk is clean except for a calendar.

Jack's in his office, a remarkably empty, impersonal place considering how many years he's occupied it. He was first elected when I was a child, not long after Gertie blew, when the populace wasn't paying much attention to anything but survival.

His competition was a law-and-order career cop, a former Centresburg police chief, whose campaign focused on traditional crime-fighting issues in an area with little crime but a lot of death. Jack Townsend was a self-made businessman who liberally spread his money around and held lots of rallies with beer kegs and vats of ham barbecue where people could have a good time and get away from the ghosts.

His opponents pointed out that he didn't know anything about law enforcement, but his supporters pointed out that running a small sheriff's department with limited duties couldn't be more difficult than building a successful car dealership from the ground up.

Centresburg has its own police department, and the state police have a barracks in this township and flex the majority of the investigative and enforcement muscle around here. Our job consists mainly of transporting prisoners, assisting the coroner's office, and mopping up the unincorporated countryside.

And while a sheriff's deputy must complete specific training, meet certain qualifications, and maintain local certification, a sheriff doesn't have to meet any standards. He's elected.

Jack's done well. No one's held the office this long in this county. No one can touch him in an election. He's run uncontested for the past decade. He's considered gruff but not callous, tough but fair-minded, a decent hard-ass who will tell you he's going to beat the crap out of you before he does it. He often takes the moral high road, but, as with so many men who do, I've never been able to figure out if it's because he's a moral man.

He's reading the *Parade* section of the Sunday newspaper and doesn't look up when I enter, but I know he's seen me because he asks, "Where are your pants?"

I look down at my muddy jeans.

"In a closet at my sister's house," I answer him.

"How is your sister?"

"She's fine."

"How's your mother?"

"Closer to your age."

He rattles his paper.

"Next time I see you, I want your ass in those pants where it belongs."

"I really fail to see how they help me do my job."

"Your ass inside them," he says again.

I take a seat on a slippery, diner-booth-quality chair and stretch out my legs. My knee hurts. I need a drink or another pill or both.

"Were you working yesterday?" Jack asks me.

"Not to my knowledge."

"You want to tell me why you responded to a call, then?"

"I was in the neighborhood?"

He glances up. His hair is a metallic gray, perfectly oiled and combed, and his eyes are a dark, unreadable brown. He's kept a trim figure all these years, which is nothing short of amazing considering the diet of roast beef, mashed potatoes, and gravy his deceased wife used to feed him and the fact that he spends the majority of his time sitting behind a desk. He always dresses in full uniform, including a keystone-shaped belt buckle and matching tie clip. He never leaves the station without his hat on.

He glances down again, turning the page, and asks me the same question he's already asked me a dozen times since I've been back.

"When do you think Paterno's going to retire?"

"I think he's waiting for God to retire first."

He turns another page. The room is overheated and smells faintly of the smoked cheddar cheese spread he likes to eat on crackers.

"So you did respond to the call?"

"I dropped by."

"I'm going to assume you have a good excuse for not writing up a report yesterday and you plan on doing it today. I'm also going to assume that you didn't confiscate any guns, since the last time you pulled that shit, I suspended you for a week without pay, and next time it will be a month."

He finally puts the paper down, pushes it aside, and gives me his full attention. Jack's office doesn't have windows. Sitting here in front of his unavoidable scrutiny is like being a toad in a shoe box with a kid's big eye straining omnipotently through a hole in the lid.

"I don't care what the hell happens in a man's house," he goes on. "No statements, no complaints, no reports, no arrests mean no crime. Do you know what it's called when you go ahead and take a man's firearm from his home under those circumstances?"

"Thinking ahead?"

"Stealing."

I shift in my seat. I went back in the house while Jess was still out cold and took his other guns, including a handgun I found on a shelf in the bedroom closet.

"I don't want this department involved in some major-pain-in-the-ass lawsuit."

He tugs out another section of the newspaper and flips it open.

"God," he sighs, "I miss the good old days when men just used to beat the crap out of each other and women gossiped like crazy behind each other's backs when they had disagreements instead of hiring lawyers. It's so damn cowardly."

He eyes me briefly.

"I want a report today," he tells me.

Thirty years he's had this office. He could at least put a plant in it, or a picture of his grandkids. He has citations and plaques hanging on the walls, but not a single photo of him accepting any of them. There's no sign anywhere of his love for fly-fishing, Penn State football, or his deceased wife. It's as if he can only do this job if he steps away from himself.

"Fine," I reply.

"One more thing," he says. "You know Reese Raynor is getting released tomorrow."

Tomorrow: the immediacy of the word should fill me with anticipation or dread, but it does neither.

I wonder what's going through Reese's mind on his last day of captivity. Probably the same thing that was going through it on his first day. The same thing that goes through a dog's mind from the moment he's chained to his doghouse to the moment he finally drops dead: When am I going to be fed?

"I've told everyone to keep their eyes and ears open. But I want you at your desk for the rest of the week unless I personally give the word for you to do something else."

"What? Why? Because I answered that call yesterday when I wasn't on duty?"

He pushes his chair back slightly from his desk and laces his fingers over his gut. I see the glint of his belt buckle between his knuckles.

"Do you remember Reese's trial? You were there every day. It wasn't too long after you got out of the hospital after your first surgery. You were in a bad way. On crutches. Wearing a knee brace. Anyone could tell to look at you, you were in a lot of pain. But you were there every day. You never did tell me why."

His fingers begin to tap on each other.

"You want to tell me now?"

Jess was there every day, too. He was the only one from their family who ever showed up. I wonder if Jack ever wondered why Jess was there.

"No," I answer him.

He slides his chair back up against his desk and tugs out another section of newspaper.

"So what are you saying? I'm tied to my desk for the week because eighteen years ago I went to the trial of a guy who's being released from prison tomorrow?"

"You've been a little off lately. I can't quite put my finger on it. Distracted, maybe. And making too many judgment calls when you're out on the job. Thinking too much for yourself."

"Sorry about that. I'll try and think less."

"Leave the thinking to me. I've got something for you to do before you get to your paperwork. Do you know Ronny Hewitt?"

"Yeah. We played football together."

"Do you remember where he used to live? Out near the Run?"

"Yeah."

"He still lives there. He and his wife built a house next door to his folks. I want you to go out there. Apparently Andy Lineweaver's picnic table was washed down the creek during that last flood we had. He thought it was gone for good, and then he spotted it last week in Ronny's yard. Ronny says it's his now. Andy waited until Ronny left for work this morning, and then he showed up with his truck to take it back. Turns out Ronny forgot his wallet and came back to the house, too. They're in the process of beating the shit out of each other. It's getting bad enough that Ronny's wife just called us. Apparently it's a helluva nice picnic table. Andy just bought it last year."

I stare back at him. "Are you kidding me?"

"I don't want to send Chad or Stiffy. Breaking up a fight is messy."

He opens his new section of newspaper, shakes it out, lays it flat on the desk, and begins reading.

"They might get their pants dirty."

# SEVEN

THE ROADS TO COAL RUN ARE HILLY, TWISTING, RUINED ONES with broken shoulders and potholes made a generation ago by coal trucks too heavy to travel them and left unmended by a generation who doesn't come out here anymore. Clumps of houses, lone trailers, gap-faced barns, a beer distributor, and a one-pump gas station fly past my window before I plunge into a corridor of trees, several miles long, where the day's weak light filtered through the bare branches onto the blacktop makes the air look watery and gray.

I resurface suddenly to an isolated place where the hills roll away from the road on all sides in purplish-gray waves. Surrounded by the emptiness, I feel suspended, floating, like I'm bobbing in the middle of an ocean of earth. Then the landmarks of Coal Run begin to appear: an abandoned ball field scarred with gopher holes, my boarded-up elementary school, a drive-in theater where rows of rusted speaker posts stand at attention in the weeds like a suicide cult waiting for instructions from the great peeling white screen.

I avoid the road that goes past my old neighborhood and head straight to the Hewitts' house.

It's a pretty little ranch painted barn red with white trim. A little farther down the road sits the other Hewitt home like a proud parent wearing the same colors, but it's about twice the size and beginning to show its age.

I come to a rolling stop about twenty feet away from Ronny's well-tended front yard, where a guy, who I assume is Andy Lineweaver, has him pinned to the ground and is beating him with pistonlike arm movements.

Ronny's wife is standing by screaming, crying, and holding a mobile phone. I slam the door loudly when I get out. She looks my way, intense relief showing on her face.

"Thank God you're here!" she cries, and comes stumbling toward me.

I look past her to the men. Ronny doesn't seem to be moving much. "Hey!" I call out. "Hey!"

I jog over to them. I glimpse the picnic table in back of the house, at a slant, half in and half out of the bed of a pickup truck. It *is* a nice one.

"I said, Hey."

I grab Lineweaver by the back of his shirt collar and pull him off. His arm is still pumping. He jabs me in the ribs with his elbow enough times that I start to get annoyed. I wrench his arms behind him and push him to his knees. He tries to bite my ankle. I lodge my good knee into the small of his back, hold his wrists with one hand, and lean onto the back of his neck with my other forearm until he finally stops thrashing around.

"Son of a bitch!" he bellows.

"It's a picnic table," I explain to him through clenched teeth.

Ronny's wife runs over to where he's sprawled out on the ground. His chest is rising, and I hear moaning.

"It's my picnic table!" Lineweaver shouts. "He stole it!"

The wife looks up from Ronny.

"He didn't steal it!" she screams. "It washed up in our backyard!"

"He's stealing it now! Son of a bitch!"

Lineweaver tries to break free. I put more weight on him.

Ronny struggles to a sitting position. His wife uses her shirt to wipe the blood off his face. He holds himself around his gut, moaning. He starts to cough. I watch him to see if he spits up blood.

Lineweaver jerks beneath me. I give his arms a sharp yank.

"Are you going to behave, or do I have to cuff you?"

"Fuck you!" he says.

I pull his arms back until his chest is lifted off the ground.

"I didn't hear your answer."

"I said yes!" he cries out.

"Yes what?"

"Yes to whatever you said."

"It was an either/or question. Pay attention."

"Let go of my fucking arms!" he screams.

I drop him. He lies in the grass, cursing.

I get up very slowly, listening to the internal scream coming from what's left of my knee joint. Sweat stings my eyes, not from exertion but from pain.

"Are you all right?" I ask Ronny.

He blinks at me from a face that looks made of purple putty. He starts to speak. It's hard to hear him at first as he mumbles through his swollen lips, slick with blood and spit.

"When a man owns a piece of land and it's registered legally with the courts and everything," he begins, "then everything on it is his until he dies or gives it to his kids for all perpetuity, and it don't matter how it gets there."

Lineweaver brings his arms around in front of him and slowly raises himself off the ground.

"What the hell is he talking about?" he asks me.

"I think he's quoting the Magna Carta," I reply.

"So you're saying even if you steal something, it's yours," he says to Ronny.

"The police can come and take it from you if they know you stole it, but once you get away with stealing it, it's yours and no one can take it back."

Lineweaver takes a step toward Ronny.

"You're so full of shit," he says.

"Besides, I didn't steal that table. It landed here." Ronny turns to me. "Ain't that an act of God, Ivan?"

"If it isn't, I don't know what is."

"So it's mine," he says boldly to Lineweaver.

I find myself smiling at him. Ronny wasn't exactly the brightest guy I ever knew. I admire his attempt at logic for the same reason I always admired the truly ugly girls in Jolene's pageants. There were always a surprising amount of them, girls who didn't have a chance in hell but were out there anyway with their Vaseline-coated teeth and duct-taped cleavage giving it their all. They didn't know it, but they were there to pad out the roster, to finance the pageant and the queen's reign with their six-hundred-dollar entrance fees that they had to beg, borrow, and sacrifice for. Pageant officials called them "plugs." The girls called them worse things. Jolene called them "worker ants."

"Right," I say.

"Are you a fucking retard or something?" Lineweaver snarls at me. "It's my table. Everybody knows it's my table. He even knows it. I'm taking it back."

"Is the table his?" I ask Ronny and his wife.

"But . . ." Ronny starts to say.

"Is the table his?" I repeat.

"He can't prove it," the wife jumps in.

"Everybody knows it's mine," Lineweaver snaps.

"Unless you have some kind of legal documentation proving this table is yours," I tell him, "I have no choice but to rely on my knowledge of property statutes and the nuances of state and local zoning ordinances to arrive at a fair judgment."

They all watch me with last-lottery-ball intensity.

"What is it?" Lineweaver barks.

"Finders keepers, losers weepers."

Ronny smiles, and his wife hoots. I don't notice what Lineweaver's doing, so I don't see the fist coming.

It catches me square in the eye. There was a time in my life when my spontaneous reaction would have been to strike back. Now I simply content myself with the knowledge that the blow had to have hurt his hand as much as it hurt my face while I watch a million pinpricks of light explode in front of my eyes before I stumble backward and fall on my ass.

Ronny's wife hurries over to me.

"Aren't you gonna arrest him?" she asks.

I think about the paperwork. Assaulting a peace officer on top of everything else. I don't want to deal with it. At least Jack will be happy to hear they solved their problem like in the good old days, instead of hiring lawyers.

"I don't think so," I reply.

The truck peels out. The table falls off the bed and crashes to the ground, where it rolls onto its side.

She helps me up. Ronny has managed to get to a standing position, too. He's holding his sides, but he's smiling as I walk over to him.

"This is Ivan," he says to his wife. "Ivan Z. You know him."

"Well, I never actually met him." She turns to me. "I went to Punxsy same year as you two, so I got to see both of you whup our butts a bunch of times."

"Hell, Punxsy." Ronny spits some blood in the yard. "We could've just sent Ivan and Jess Raynor and nobody else, and they would've beat you guys."

"Be nice," she says to her husband. Then to me, "I'm just curious. Why'd you let us keep the table? It's really his, you know."

"I don't like him."

"Do you know Andy?"

"I just met him."

"Do you want to go to the hospital?" I ask Ronny.

"Nah, I'm okay," he says.

He looks at my face.

"Do *you* want to go?"

The area around my eye is throbbing, but for the moment it helps to keep my mind off my hangover headache, which helps to keep my mind off my leg. I lean my head back, close my eyes, and begin to mentally isolate each injury to my body the way I used to after a game, then jump from one to the other like I'm striking keys on a keyboard, trying to create a tolerable harmony from the individual tones of pain. Knee. Head. Eye. Do-re-mi. Eye-knee-knee. Knee-eye-head. Fa-so-la-ti. Head-eye-knee-knee.

Ronny and I are thinking the same thing: Deets would have told us to get up, shut up, and get back in the game.

"I'm okay, too," I tell him.

"Do you want to come in?" his wife asks me. "Can we get anything for you? Coffee? Breakfast? Ice? Some aspirin?"

"No, I'm fine. I should get going."

I start walking to my truck. I notice another pickup pulled over to one side and idling on the road. It's not Lineweaver's. This one is an old Chevy made back when the cab's roof was a different shade than the body. The roof is white; the rest of the truck is a sky blue with a couple rust patches.

The guy driving it has one arm hanging out the window. A trail of gray smoke rises from between his fingertips. It's Val.

I pick up my pace until I'm almost jogging. My knee is killing me, but I don't care.

"This is what you do for a living," he says when I reach him.

"On a good day," I tell him.

I peek into his truck. He's got a six-pack of Red Dog, a carton of cigarettes, a blue plastic Wal-Mart bag filled with Chef Boyardee products, and a bunch of loose red lollipops sitting on the seat next to him.

"This isn't what I was planning on doing," I say all of a sudden. "Being a deputy, I mean. I was a football player. Well, you know that. I was more than just a player. I was good. Great, actually. I was an All-American. Leading rusher at Penn State three years in a row. We won a national title my freshman year. Won the Sugar Bowl my sophomore year. I was drafted by the Bears. The Chicago Bears. Back when Ditka coached. Jim McMahon, Walter Payton, Mike Singletary. All those guys. I never got to play with any of them because I got injured. I never even got to meet any of them except Ditka. He sent me a letter when I was in the hospital. Joe Paterno came and visited me a couple times. Brought me some ice cream. Peachy Paterno. That's his flavor at the Creamery. It's great stuff. I used to have a flavor. Ivan Z's Tacklebreaker Brickle. They don't make it anymore. . . ." My voice trails off.

He finishes his cigarette and flicks the butt onto the ground.

"You're gonna have to shorten that if you want it on your tombstone," he advises me.

He pulls out, and once again I let him get away before I ask him where he's staying. I just stand there like an idiot and watch his brass Gertie tag swing from his rearview mirror as he drives away. He got to keep his tag, too, that day, even though he wasn't killed.

I decide to pursue him this time. I drive the main road back to Centresburg for a while, and when I don't find him, I head for our old neighborhood. If this really is his first time back here in thirty-three years, I'm sure he felt the need to check out the place. Hopefully, he knew ahead of time about the mine fires and wasn't expecting to find a town anymore.

The houses are all gone now. Cracked foundations and piles of chimney rubble are left in their places. The sidewalks that used to lead to front doors are broken and buckled. Rusted mailboxes ragged with bullet holes hang from splintered wooden posts. Grass doesn't grow, and the weeds that do are an inexplicable shade of snot.

A lot of women used to plant flower gardens in dump-truck tires laid flat and painted white. A few of the tires remain, along with other little pieces of each family's identity: swing-set skeletons, rolls of chicken wire, doghouses, flat-tired bikes, a rotting picnic bench.

Keeping watch over all of it is a small, randomly stationed army of forsaken lawn ornaments, their colors chipped and faded. From a distance their cracked faces look real to me. Frozen deer and rabbits. Dogs and Madonnas and elves. Their bodies bleed mud and grass like victims of some perverse crime of nature.

My favorite is a St. Joseph lawn ornament housed in an upturned, sawed-off half of an old claw-foot bathtub. It's survived better than any of the others. The tub has been an effective shield against rain and wind and pickup-truck snipers. White porcelain shrapnel litters the yard, but the saint has never been hit. The white dove that used to sit perched on his finger wasn't so lucky. It's gone, but his finger is still raised as if he's saying, "Hey, wait for me."

I slow my truck to a stop in front of what used to be our house and where Val's garage was never built for the truck he never completely fixed. The silent, empty black mouths of the coke ovens are strung across the distant hillside like a sutured wound.

Our backyard was the first place where the problem was detected. It was late May at the end of my senior year in high school. I was grabbing some breakfast. Mom was upstairs getting dressed for work, and Jolene had run outside to feed her pet white rabbit.

When she came back inside, she had a strange look on her face. It wasn't pure worry or fear, but a little of both mixed with confusion. The pen was gone, she told me. The ground was torn up in a straight line like someone had taken a backhoe and overturned the earth, leaving broken roots and rocks the size of her head in its wake. But strangest of all was the intense heat around the spot and how it seemed to be coming from the ground.

I reluctantly followed her outside. Jolene wasn't a liar, but she had a knack for missing the obvious. If she said the pen wasn't there, I believed her, but I also knew there had to be a reasonable explanation. Probably one of the more ambitious members of her legion of simpleminded, greasy-overalled admirers had dragged the thing off with his dad's tractor, planning to replace it with a new one, painted pink, that he'd spent an entire school year building in shop class.

I could see right away that the pen was gone and the ground was ripped up. I was confident of my tractor theory until the heat hit me like an oven door had been thrown open in my face.

I should have hesitated, or I should have gone to get help, but I was entranced by the horrible possibility of what I suspected must be true.

By then, almost fifteen years after Gertie blew, everyone in town knew we were sitting on top of a mine fire. It was a predictable final outcome after an explosion of that magnitude. Isolated sections of the coal bed had kept burning long after the initial fireball raged through the tunnels, and eventually the heat and gases reached the topsoil.

Scattered patches of plants and trees had begun to wither and die. There was always a strange burned smell in the air no one could identify. People were constantly ill with headaches and nausea, but no one suspected that these symptoms could be related to anything other than a recurring flu bug.

Even with all these developments, people weren't too concerned. Mine fires were common in coal country, and everyone knew they were next to impossible to put out.

A great, soft, simmering cloud of steam was spread across the ground where the rabbit pen had been. I noticed something strange jutting out of the torn clods of grass and dropped to my knees to check it out. I began moving the dirt away and realized it was the corner of the pen.

I called out to Jolene and started digging more vigorously when suddenly the ground split apart and I found myself tumbling headlong into a chasm where gusts of heat billowed up at me and a hot wind howled around my ears. I grabbed onto the yard above me, but I could feel the dirt crumbling in my hands. Beneath me flames flickered in a black so infinite I couldn't tell if they were near or far, small or raging. I started slipping.

When I opened my mouth to yell for help, a scorching rush of air tore through my throat and lungs and burned the breath out of me. Jolene grabbed my hands and was able to help pull me out.

Only a split second had passed, but my eyebrows had been singed off and the bottoms of my gym shoes had melted onto the soles of my feet. The physical pain was nothing compared to the fear I felt. I was sure I had seen all the way to the center of the earth. Maybe all the way to hell.

By the end of that day, a motorcycle, a prized rhododendron bush, a clothesline post, and a birdbath had all disappeared in other yards. No one was sure what to do. People were still more confused than scared, but that changed in the middle of the night when everyone on our road was awakened by a loud boom. We all came outside in our pajamas and watched in dumb amazement as a neighbor's Harley was consumed in flags of brilliant orange flames while it was slowly sucked into the earth. The gas tank had exploded. No one could say why.

The wife went back inside and called Sheriff Jack.

For the next few days, the town crawled with scientists and engineers sent by the Department of Environmental Resources, Penn State's mining-engineering department, UMW, and the state Bureau of Deep Mine Safety. Some reporters and a few spokespeople from various concerned interests showed up, too. The guy from the federal Mine Safety and Health Administration had the shiniest black shoes I'd ever seen. No one from J&P put in an appearance.

The hole in our yard turned out to be four hundred feet deep and 370 degrees hot. Toxic levels of carbon monoxide and sulfur dioxide were found in the air and drinking water.

The final verdict was announced at a public meeting in the elementary school's multipurpose room by a guy from the state secretary of Environmental Protection's office: All the ground beneath Coal Run was on fire.

Barbed wire and a warning sign went up at the junkyard. The government paid people for their homes and gave them six months to relocate before the town was bulldozed under. Most people were satisfied with the money.

Mom found a house in Centresburg. Jolene and I tried to convince her that it was probably for the best. Now she'd be a lot closer to where she worked, and she'd have all the amenities that come along with living in a big town.

She did her best to act like she didn't care too much. At times I almost believed her.

Val's obviously not here. I try the junkyard next.

I'm hopeful at first when I notice a pickup truck parked there, but it doesn't turn out to be the truck Val was driving. It's a Dodge Ram, the same year and color as Jess and Bobbie's. I pull in front of it and see the smashed-in headlight and the scratched grille.

From where I stop, I can see down over the hill. Jess is standing with Danny next to the rusted remains of a Kenmore dishwasher. He's surrounded by rotting recliners and couches, washing machines, piles of tires and hubcaps, heaps of scrap metal, hundreds of beer bottles, and rusted refrigerator doors. All of the junk is riddled with bullet holes, including the menacing red-and-yellow DANGER KEEP OUT sign. The local boys shoot at anything, and if it doesn't run away, they often hit it.

I get out of my truck this time. The smell of sulfur hits me, a smell like a hundred struck matches mixed with a dozen rotten eggs. I blink and cover my nose with my hand and slam my door. The sound carries far in the absolute silence, but neither of them looks my way. I can hear Jess's voice floating over the hiss of the simmering earth, but I can't make out any of his words.

He's doing all the talking, waving one hand in the air while the other one grips a big stick that he has planted in the ground and holds at arm's length like he's just laid claim to a foreign land.

What's he doing here alone with Danny? is the first thing I wonder. What kind of mother leaves her kid alone with a man who hit him yesterday, even if that man is his father? For the moment I'm angrier at her than I am at Jess.

"Hey, Jess. What are you doing out there?" I call to him.

He turns and squints at me from beneath the bill of his J&P cap, then turns his back to me. He's also wearing his old company windbreaker with RAYNOR stenciled across the back in big yellow letters, a pair of jeans, and a pair of black Wolverine work boots with bright yellow laces.

Wisps of white haze crawl in and out of the tops of his boots and snake up his legs. On wet days like this one, the cool water makes the hot ground steam.

He points out something to his son on the dishwasher and proudly pats its side with the unintended affection blue-collar men feel for major household appliances that outlive their warranties.

"You shouldn't be out there," I try again. "It's dangerous."

"It's only dangerous over there." He points farther down the hill.

I start taking slow, tentative steps across the mud-slick hillside, maneuvering between tires, beer bottles, and gutted bags of garbage. I slide the final few feet, keeping my balance with my arms pinwheeling at my sides.

"You see that?" he asks when I join him.

He points off in the distance. I look down the length of his arm, but I don't see anything except the dead forest surrounding the junk. The trees lost their rough outer covering of bark long ago, and their interiors have been weathered and smoothed by years of exposure to the elements until they've taken on a muted silver glow. Some of them have broken free of the weakened soil and toppled over; their charred root systems look like snarls of barbed wire.

"What am I looking at?"

"There was a yellow Maytag dryer sitting there yesterday. Today it's gone. Sunk into the ground. It might be hundreds of feet below us by now."

"And you really think it's safe for Danny to be out there?"

"Shit," he breathes out. "Wasn't he just standing next to me two seconds ago? I swear he's part mountain goat."

"Come on away from there, Danny!" he yells.

The little boy is crawling on top of an overturned refrigerator. The bottom half is sunk partially into the ground. It's hard to believe he's the same kid I saw passed out and bleeding in his mother's kitchen yesterday.

Jess leans the stick against the dishwasher and reaches in his jacket pocket for a packet of Skoal. He offers me some. I pass. He puts a plug in his lower lip.

"You can find the damnedest shit here. People throw away entire doors and windows. Parts of roofs. Siding. Insulation. I've found some really good lumber before. That's why I'm here," he volunteers.

"Bobbie had a little accident at the house the other day, and the garage door got busted up. You saw it."

"Bobbie did that?"

His gaze and his voice falter.

"Yeah, well. It was my fault. The brakes on the truck are really bad. I've been meaning to fix them. Now she wants me to fix the garage door. Reese is coming to see us when he gets out, and even though Bobbie hates his guts, she wants the house to look nice. Does that make any sense to you?"

Danny arrives breathless in front of us. He's carrying a beat-up orange plastic jack-o-lantern bucket kids use for trick-or-treating.

His nose is badly bruised and swollen to twice its normal size, making his eyes look small. They have slashes of dark shadow beneath them.

He doesn't seem to be in any pain, though, and he certainly has a lot of energy. He doesn't seem afraid of his dad, and he doesn't seem upset with him either.

I watch Jess watching his son and try to figure out what he's feeling. I'm looking for guilt on his face, but I don't see any. I see a kind of rough affection and some concern over the boy's injury, but nothing that would make me think he's the one who inflicted it.

I want to ask him outright if he did it and, if he did, how could he? Danny holds the bucket out to his dad.

"Can I keep it?" he asks.

"What are you going to do with it?"

"Put stuff in it."

Jess takes it from him and turns it around in his hands.

"Okay."

He hands it back to him.

"Did you say hi to Deputy Zoschenko?"

The boy looks at me suspiciously, then casts a quick glance at his dad, who nods his assent.

"Hi," he says, and scoots away.

"Well, he seems to be feeling okay today," I comment.

"Yeah." Jess reaches behind his head and touches the place where I hit him with the board. "I think he feels better than I do."

"I'm sorry about that."

"No you're not."

"Yes I am."

"No you're not."

"Well, what was I supposed to do? Let you shoot someone?"

"I wasn't gonna shoot anybody. I was shooting at the tires so Bobbie couldn't leave."

"Yeah, your brother-in-law tried the same thing with your mother yesterday and almost shot her head off. Did you hear about it?"

He nods.

"What is with your family? Can't you just let people leave and then call them when they get where they're going and continue the conversation that way?"

"I didn't know what was happening. I thought Bobbie was leaving."

"Leaving?"

"Yeah, leaving."

"You mean, really leaving?"

"Yeah, leaving."

"You guys having problems?"

"I'd say that's none of your business."

He looks away from me across the valley at what's left of Gertie. The complex is miles away but easily visible from where we're standing. The coal silo, the locomotive shed, the rail sidings, the operational buildings and repair shops, the massive corrugated iron walls of the loading tipple, and the exterior structure of the shaft with its huge wheels and rusted cables attached to the cage that dropped men like rocks over five hundred feet into the black tunnels below—it all sits eternally still and silent like a bombed-out village.

"What about Danny?" I ask him. "You knew he was hurt and had to go to the hospital. You saw Dr. Ed there. Why didn't you think that's what it was all about?"

He looks down at his feet. Feathers of white mist land gently on his heavy black boots before vanishing.

"You did know Danny was hurt?" I press him.

"I was already gone when it happened," he replies.

"When what happened?"

"When he hit the wall," he says slowly, watching me carefully.

"You're sure you weren't there."

He turns his head and spits behind him. "I think I'd know if I was there or not."

"You were pretty drunk."

"I wasn't there."

"Bobbie said you were there," I lie.

"She did not," he shoots back, but he doesn't look completely convinced.

"What are you trying to pull?" he asks me, anger rising in his voice. "You got something you want to say to me, say it."

We both look at Danny. He's sitting at the top of a small mountain of ragged tires.

"I'd just like to help if I can. That's all."

"Help?" He spits again, this time near my boot. "Who says I need help?"

"I know what it's like. That's all I'm saying."

"Know what what's like?"

"To have your life turn out"—I search for the least offensive way to put it—"not as great as you thought it would."

He gives me a questioning look with something like a smile on his lips, and for a second I think he's going to bust out laughing. He doesn't go that far, but his resentment is temporarily lifted. His attention drifts back to Gertie.

"It's been fourteen months since I got laid off at Lorelei," he volunteers. "I was one of the first guys to go. Even though I'd worked there a lot of years, there were a lot of guys there a lot older than me.

"I was working graveyard the day I found out. I didn't know why at the time but I decided not to shower after my shift, and I drove straight home wearing all my gear. Everything. Even my belt and my helmet. Even my knee pads. My arms were stiff, and my back was aching, and the dust that always got inside the collar of my shirt felt like ground-up glass eating into my skin. I was still shivering from the cold and sweating from the work.

"So I showed up at home still in my work clothes, and I just took a seat in the backyard in a lawn chair right when the sun was coming up over the hills. I heard the screen door open, and I looked over and saw Danny peeking out at me. Bobbie was leaning outside with him, handing him a cup of coffee to bring me. She took one finger and pressed it to her lips to warn him not to bug me and when I saw her do this . . . I don't know, I can't explain it. It was this kind of joy I felt that I had this woman who respected me and she was teaching my son to respect me, too. And all of a sudden I realized why I kept everything on and didn't shower at work. 'Cause I was afraid I was never going to get to feel this way again. And being tired and dirty and aching and shivering and sweating at the same time was how I knew I was alive.

"Reese missed out on all that. He never wanted to go into the mines. He was like you."

"What?" I say automatically.

I wasn't prepared for Reese to enter into that particular description or for me to be compared to him.

"He and my dad used to go at it. Fighting over the mines. I didn't understand Reese, but I didn't hate him for feeling the way he did. Not like my dad. My dad took it as a personal insult. He hated him. He even told him that."

"I'm not anything like Reese," I insist.

"In a lot of ways you're not, but in that one way you are."

"He beat his wife into a coma," I remind him.

"Yeah, I know that. And in that way you're not the same. But of course you ain't never had a wife, have you? So we can't really be sure."

He stops talking long enough to yell at Danny again. I see the bright orange pumpkin bucket bobbing amid the junk.

"I never thought Reese would ever get married. I don't think he did either. But if you're screwing around, there's always the possibility you're gonna get a girl pregnant, and that's what happened, so he did the right thing and married her."

I remain silent.

"What I don't understand is why she would've been screwing around with him in the first place. They weren't exactly compatible, and Reese wasn't exactly oozing charm when it came to girls. I know that's not a nice thing to say about your own brother, but hell, I know him best. We're twins. I shared a womb with that guy."

He stops talking. A blanket of quiet immediately falls over everything.

Birdsongs, insect clicks and buzzes, rodent rustlings, the far-off rumble of machinery, a car engine approaching in the distance, a dog's bark: sounds so common I once considered them part of silence don't exist here anymore, and in their absence I've discovered that true silence is anything but peaceful.

"Point is, you got no right coming back here after all these years and telling me my life didn't turn out all that good when you don't even know what a good life is," he tells me while he scans the junk for

Danny. "You're just pissed 'cause your own life didn't turn out the way you wanted it. That's your fault."

"I broke my leg."

"Fuck your leg. I'm not talking about football. I'm talking about you. You could've done whatever you wanted. You ran away."

He calls for Danny.

"You're the worst kind of coward," he says as he picks up his stick and begins moving away from me. "You're a guy who's afraid of himself."

He starts up the hillside with a coordination and speed I could never manage now. I watch him go and watch his son follow.

I take a final look at Gertie before I leave. It's the place where my father died and my career died. I should hate the sight of it, but I can't.

Despite my mother and father's hope that I would go to college and not work in the mines, and despite my own claustrophobic childhood fears of the miles of dark tunnels, I expected to live and die tied to Gertie. My commitment to her was like a marriage vow a man gives to a woman he doesn't really love but one he knows will make a good wife.

The night my leg was crushed, I was drunk out of my mind. I walked around the gutted complex with my bottle of whiskey, staring at the ragged gaps in the equipment walls, the maze of stilled conveyor belts, the rust-streaked iron hull of the massive loading tipple. I was overwhelmed by the power still echoing in the silent, forgotten machinery. I felt insignificant, like an unchewed morsel of flesh waiting to be digested inside the bowels of a wounded metal beast.

That's the way I wanted to feel. I had done something unforgivable, something I could never fix, and what was even worse than what I had done was the fact that I was so callous and self-absorbed I never even realized I had done anything wrong until two lives were destroyed.

I took a seat on the ground inside one of the buildings and drank until I passed out. When I woke up, it was dark. A shaft of moonlight fell through a hole in the ceiling into the center of the room like an empty spotlight.

The first thought I had was of my dad. Not my dead dad. Not the dad I knew briefly before he died. But the dad I never got to know. The dad I would have known now.

I was sad when my dad died because I loved him. He brought security and stability to my life, and he made my mom happy. But I was a very young child. I had only known him for a few years and then only known him through a child's eyes with a child's perception.

As the years passed, I missed him much more than I did those first days, weeks, even years after his death. I constantly found myself in need of his guidance. I always had to wonder if he had lived and I had been able to know him as I grew older, would I have been a different person? A better person? Would I have made different choices? Better choices? Would a young mother not be lying comatose in a hospital bed? Would her son not be an orphan?

I'm pretty sure I went to Gertie that night looking for my dad and the other miners. I wasn't expecting ghosts to appear and give me advice or warnings. I was looking for an explanation of them that could somehow lead to an explanation of myself.

Long before Gertie became the site of so much death, it had been a source of life for all of us. For me it was the closest thing I had to God.

The skittering of an animal made me look up, and a shower of rust flakes and soot rained down on my face. I caught sight of a tiny twitching nose and beady black eyes peering down at me for a second; then they were gone, and I was left staring at the teeth of a gear wheel lying half off the ledge, teetering above me.

A lot of people have told me I was lucky. It could have crashed down on my skull or my chest instead of my leg. It could have crushed my femoral artery, and I would have bled to death long before I was able to crawl to the road and get help.

A lot of other people have told me I'm the unluckiest bastard on the face of the earth to have that kind of freak accident happen and have it ruin a promising career and the fame and wealth that would have come with it.

I always believed the latter, even though I never cared much about the fame-and-wealth part of it. Football was what I did best. It was what I was supposed to do, and when I couldn't do it any longer, I was lost.

I didn't run away from home. I don't know if I can ever make Jess or Jolene or anyone else understand this. I was thrown into the dark, and I never gave up looking for a way back.

# EIGHT

JOLENE'S FRONT DOOR BURSTS OPEN, AND EB COMES TEARING
out of it wearing his pirate costume from last Halloween, complete
with a plastic-hook hand, eye patch, and Jolly Roger hat. He's also
wearing a red necktie striped with gold and green.

Harrison trails behind him, his hands plunged deeply into the
pockets of his baggy, oversize jeans.

Eb yanks open the passenger-side door and hops in. He makes himself comfortable on the seat of my truck after he messes with some
knobs on my radio and checks out the TuffNet computer screen
where I've shown him how to run license plates. He removes his Jolly
Roger hat, sets it in his lap, and grins at the LICK M——E— bumper
sticker. His gold hair is dark with sweat, and the skin beneath the sprin-
kling of freckles on his cheeks and nose is pink with exertion.

He scrunches up his entire face like the top of a drawstring bag and
asks, "How's Grandma Zo?"

"Well, she's fine. As fine as she can be."

"You mean she's dead."

"Well, yes. You and your mom talked about that, right? You know
that's not going to change."

"You checked at the funeral?"

"I did. But you know what? Grandma Zo looked very peaceful. I
know she's up in heaven now. She's where she wants to be."

"With Liberace."

"Right."

He falls silent and sticks a finger in his mouth to wiggle a loose tooth.

"Okay," he says.

"So did you have fun yesterday?" I try to change the subject. "Josh baby-sat, right?"

His sadness passes, and he brightens up as he begins one of his breathless narratives.

"Josh made Harrison cry. He said we're all bass turds 'cause Mom wouldn't marry our dads. He said being a bass turd is bad and people don't like you 'cause of it and make fun of you. Then he made Harrison cry 'cause he said at least we know who our dads are but Harrison doesn't. So he's like the biggest bass turd. A huge one."

He notices Harrison standing outside the truck and clamps his mouth shut and gives me a look that tells me we're supposed to keep our conversation a secret.

Harrison leans in the open window.

"Hey," he says to me.

"Hey," I say back.

"I told Uncle Ivan we're bass turds," Eb bursts out, having kept the secret for as long as he could.

Harrison stares at him with older-sibling disbelief burning in his dark eyes.

"I don't get why you got so sad," Eb adds. "You know who your dad was. He was Passing Through."

"That's what he was doing, you idiot. Not who he was."

"Come on. Get in," I tell him. "We'll go for a quick spin, and I'll let you turn on the lights and siren."

"That's not a thrill for me, Uncle Ivan," he sighs.

"It's a thrill for me," I tell him.

"Me, too," says Eb.

He stares at my face for a moment, and then he and Eb exchange knowing looks.

"How was your day?" he asks me.

Eb suppresses a giggle.

Jolene already discussed my black eye with them. Jolene's only objection to it was that her boys might think it was cool that I was in a fight, so I agreed to let her tell them that a woman did it.

"It was good," I reply. "I saved a picnic table. I bought a bunch of footballs at Wal-Mart and signed them to donate to the hospital auction tonight. And I spent the rest of the day at my desk doing paperwork. How was your day?"

"We're doing a cool project in school," Eb begins before Harrison can even draw a breath. "I need a can. It can't be a big can like a coffee can, and it can't be flat like a tuna-fish can. It has to be a soup can or a can that looks the same as a soup can, and it has to be cleaned out, and the label has to be tooken off, and the lids, too.

"If we have extras, I can bring them in, too. Some kids might not have any cans. You never know. Miss Finch says it's okay. We can bring in lots. Do we have those kinds of cans?"

"I'm sure your mom has those kinds of cans," I answer.

"But not empty ones. We have to have empty ones. We had potato-chip chicken last night, and it didn't use any cans. You missed it. Why didn't you eat dinner with us last night? Why didn't you sleep on the couch last night? You said we were going to play Mario Kart before I went to school when Mom wasn't looking."

I clear my throat. Harrison looks away from me down the street. He knows I don't have any excuses Eb would understand or ones that he would understand or even ones I understand.

The same thing is true when it comes to trying to justify all the years of their lives that I missed.

Eb had dressed up for the occasion of my return home in navy blue pants, a white shirt with a collar, and a clip-on tie with cartoon dinosaurs on it.

He marched up to me and extended his small hand with the gumption of a tiny businessman about to try to sell me futures in his company.

"Hello, Uncle Ivan. I'm your nephew, Everett Craig. We met once when I was very young. We have pictures."

I took his little hand in mine and felt a kind of calm I hadn't felt in years, the calm of not being judged. Everett Craig didn't care what I was now or who I was then. He had never seen me play ball. He had never seen me run down a field darting in and out of defensive backs with the grace and abandon of a deer fleeing through a grove of trees. He had never seen me recently on bad days take fifteen minutes, with tears of pain streaming down my face, to lower myself onto a toilet to take a crap. He had never seen me drink tequila shooters in a Tampa Bay Hooters until I passed out with a disgusted waitress caught in my drunken grip promising to fuck me real good later if I'd just let her go now.

He was happy to know me just because we shared Jolene.

She comes out of the house. She stops in the middle of the sidewalk to check her purse for something.

"Did you get boxes?" she shouts at me.

"They're in the back of the truck."

"Okay, boys," she calls as she walks to her car. "Get back inside with your brother. Harrison, you've got homework. And Ebbie, you are not going to the auction with Hannah and her mom wearing a pirate costume. Go change."

"You're going to the auction?" I ask him.

"Yeah," he says, his small, bright face turning thoughtful. "I like to attend events."

From outside the truck window, Harrison snorts a laugh and shakes his head.

"I'll be home later tonight," I assure Eb. "And I'll whup your butt at whatever game you choose."

He gives me a lopsided prizefighter's smile with one of his top front teeth missing, and a bottom one, too. He holds up his eye patch so I can see both eyes.

"You wish," he says.

He gets out of the truck and starts to race away, then stops suddenly and comes racing back. He reaches inside his plastic hook and takes out a small white envelope covered in stickers. "Uncle Ivan" is written on the outside in red marker.

He hands it to me through the window.

"This is for you," he says, as he slips his fist back into the hook. "You can read it later."

---

Zo's house is square, made of old, powdery, dark-red bricks, trimmed in white, full of windows, with a wide front porch supported by four white pillars.

It's in pretty good shape for a hundred-year-old house. Some of the floorboards on the porch are starting to rot. The downstairs window trim could use a fresh coat of paint. The hedges need to be cut back. The roof leaks in one of the upstairs bedrooms. One of the hinges on the outside cellar doors has rusted through. The showerhead in the bathroom needs replacing. These were all jobs I was hoping to get to before she died.

Between Safe Haven and her other charitable pursuits, I know Zo just about depleted her inheritance before she passed away. Randy and Marcy are about to hear the news formally, sitting in a lawyer's office: All that's left is the house.

I'm assuming Randy will sell it and the two hundred acres of untouched wooded hills. He has no interest in moving back here, plus he won't be able to pass up the money. J&P has been after his family to sell for three generations. It's prime land for strip mining.

I walk through her back door and drop a load of empty boxes I picked up at Bi-Lo. There's a small room before the kitchen where she kept an extra freezer, her washer and dryer, her husband's gun rack empty now except for one rifle she used to shoot raccoons that got in her garbage cans, and an old gray filing cabinet containing what she ominously referred to as "her papers."

Jolene's standing in the middle of the kitchen with her hands on her hips doing a silent inventory. Her hair is pulled to the top of her head in a gilt ponytail.

"This is insane, Jolene," I call out. "There's no way we can pack up this whole house by ourselves."

"You're right," she says. "Let's quit already."

I pull out one of the drawers in the filing cabinet and quickly close it again. I don't even want to think about going through that mess. Me and my stupid promises.

On the wall next to the cabinet is a wooden plaque with GREETINGS FROM MIAMI spelled across it in tiny silver seashells. I take it down and turn it over. On the back is a piece of masking tape with her mailman's name written on it.

After her latest heart attack, Zo had become obsessed with preparing for her inevitable demise. She knew she had a son and a daughter-in-law who had no interest in any of her personal possessions and wouldn't think twice about getting rid of any of them. Fueled by nightmares of her mother's hope chest being auctioned off to a stranger or her favorite gravy boat being sold at the Goodwill store for a quarter, she labeled every object in her house with a piece of masking tape and a name.

I reach for one of the three J&P ball caps hanging on a set of hooks near the back door.

"Christ," I say.

"What?" Jolene calls out.

"She's even labeled the hats."

She joins me. I hand the plaque to her. She turns it over, looks at the name, and sighs.

"I'm only going through the personal stuff," she tells me. "Her dishes and pots and pans are going to the church. Her clothes are going to Goodwill. Randy's hired someone to take care of the furniture. I think he's going to have an auction. Is it wrong for me to take the canned goods?"

I walk into the kitchen and take a beer out of the refrigerator. Zo always kept a few around for visitors.

"So this is what it all comes down to," I observe between gulps of beer. "You accumulate stuff your whole life. You die. And it all gets thrown away."

"It's not getting thrown away. It's being given to other people."

"For them to throw away."

"Don't say that. People will treasure this stuff. It's being recycled."

She gives my face a frank stare.

"You just can't relate to any of this because you don't keep anything," she says. "You're a grown man with only one box."

I follow her into the kitchen. The box she refers to is sitting in a closet in her house behind a kaleidoscopic curtain of all the evening gowns she ever wore in a pageant, beginning with the emerald green taffeta that won her Laurel County Fair's Pine Princess and ending with the slinky gunmetal blue sequined number she was wearing when she was temporarily crowned Miss Pennsylvania.

I donated most of my football memorabilia to the high school, but I kept a few things, not for myself but with the sole intention of giving them to my son someday: a Penn State jersey signed by my teammates the year we won the national title, one of the game balls from our Sugar Bowl win, a signed framed photo of Bob Hope shaking my hand, and the letter Mike Ditka wrote me after I broke my leg.

It was a nice gesture from a man I had met only twice and who didn't owe me squat. It was brief and not what I would've expected. He didn't say anything about my leg. He didn't make any references to our similar blue-collar Pennsylvania backgrounds or our blue-collar Ukrainian fathers. He didn't even mention football. He wrote about heart and how people who have it will succeed at whatever they commit to, and how people without it can still succeed but will never be invited to his house for dinner.

Jolene starts picking up things off Zo's kitchen counter and flashing pieces of tape at me before packing them into an empty box: a ceramic spoon rest shaped like a rooster for the pastor's wife, a Steeler cookie jar for a family down the road with three little boys, a marble rolling pin for a girl at her church who just got married, an electric can opener for her cardiologist.

"I wonder what Zo left for me?" she asks herself loudly.

Fortunately Jolene recognizes all the names. Zo knew she would, and this is probably why she asked her to deliver the things. She made me promise I'd help her, but the process is still going to take months. She should just put an ad in the newspaper and one on Zo's church bulletin board alerting everybody that ever knew her in any capacity to stop by her house and pick up their reward.

I walk over to one of Zo's china cabinets filled with everything but china. She has even more knickknacks than my mom does. They're all gifts from people who knew her through Safe Haven, or miners' wives, or the generations of kids she's taught in Sunday school.

The kids got into the habit of buying or making her angels for Christmas every year, and she must have hundreds of them, representing every craft material known to man: ceramics, wood, plastic, Play-Doh, gold plate, resin, marble, papier-mâché, wax, Styrofoam, pewter, elbow macaroni. Some are too big to fit in the cabinet. Others are as small as Hershey Kisses. Some are actually made from Hershey Kisses. Some are obviously expensive. Others were made with fifty cents' worth of pipe cleaners and glitter. They fly and kneel and twirl on top of music boxes. They hold harps and gifts and hymnals and candles.

I open the door and pick up an angel with a swirling red gown and enormous wings, blowing on a trumpet.

I don't even bother turning her over to see if there's a piece of tape. Dispensing the angels alone is going to take Jolene months.

I put the angel back and reach for another one. She's porcelain with a perfect painted face and soft brown curls. She's dressed in layers of stiff golden fabric and holds a baby fawn.

I do turn her over, and I'm so excited by what I see I look toward heaven and mouth a silent thank-you to Zo.

I set the angel aside where Jolene won't notice her.

On a different shelf is Zo's framed photograph of a small crowd of miners sitting and standing on the front steps of the old J&P company store circa 1915. If I had to pick her most prized possession, it would be this photo.

The men are filthy, on their way to the bathhouse after a shift, dressed in work clothes, wearing their hard hats with lamps attached to the front. Some are carrying metal dinner buckets. One has a Napa lamp hanging from his belt, a new innovation at the time for testing the air for methane, much to the relief of canaries everywhere.

The miners called the company stores "pluck me" stores because their prices were about 25 percent higher than stores' in surrounding towns, but if a miner bought his supplies somewhere else, he was fired and blacklisted. His pay was a pittance to begin with, and, along with feeding and clothing his family, he also had to buy his own tools, dynamite, and carbide. The pluck-me stores gave credit, and miners ended up so far in debt to the company they could never leave the coalfields. The debts didn't die with them either. They were passed on to their sons and to their sons' sons.

The store in Zo's photo is a nondescript box without any signs. During the era it was built, most miners couldn't read. The companies didn't provide schools, but they were quick to provide jobs for the children sorting coal or digging it in the deep shafts where the tunnels were so narrow only a child's small body could fit inside them.

A little boy, no more than ten years old, sits at the feet of the men, as filthy as they are, wearing a familiar grin. It's Eb's grin. The boy is his great-grandfather, Zo's dad.

He was a breaker boy for five years before he went into the tunnels. His job was to sort and clean the coal. He would sit against a wooden chute, where raw coal streamed past in a black river, and pick from dawn to twilight, removing debris and breaking large chunks of coal into smaller ones. In the picture his hands look like the claws of a crow.

It was dangerous work. Hands were mangled, legs crushed. There were stories of very young children at other mines who had been sitting astride the chutes and fell in and were smothered by the coal.

Zo's dad never lost a finger. This was a great source of pride for him, Zo always said. That and the fact that he never sold his two hundred acres to J&P.

I pick up the photo. I don't need to check. Zo's most treasured family heirloom will go to her only son, but as I take it down from the shelf, I glimpse a piece of masking tape on the back. I turn it over and read the name: Val Claypool.

# NINE

MARCELLA'S HAS BEEN AROUND FOR ABOUT A YEAR, AND, LIKE the few other upscale restaurants in the area, it serves Italian food and steaks. The tablecloths are made of cloth. The lighting is dim. The menus are bound with gold tassels. The bartender knows how to make a manhattan. Most of the wait staff can pronounce "gnocchi."

I look in the direction of the cigar and gift shop adjoining the lobby of the restaurant. From this table I can see a corner of the shelves where figurines and music boxes are displayed. The blown-glass rooster sits near the window. He's a fiery glint of color.

Chastity takes the angel and holds it up to the candlelight like a jeweler examining a gem.

She checks out the small snip of masking tape I left underneath her skirt with the name Chastity Morrison written on it in Zo's frail script.

"She's beautiful," she says, and sets her down next to her veal marsala. "It was nice of Zo to think of me."

She picks up her wine and takes a long, slow sip. I watch her lips grip the rim of the glass. She's wearing her hair up. The style shows off her long, slim neck and the shape of her shoulders beneath her cream-colored sweater.

I ache for her. I don't mind. It helps take my mind off my knee and my eye. I try to compose one of my pain harmonies. Knee-eye-eye. Knee-balls-knee. La-di-da. Do-re-mi. Balls-balls-knee.

"And very nice of you to take time out from your evening to deliver it to me," she says, smiling knowingly at me.

She's seen right through me. I tracked her down through the hospital. She was on call tonight and ended up missing most of the auction because she had to perform an emergency appendectomy. She's having a late dinner now.

Once I found out where she was, I was so caught up in the fact that I had a legitimate excuse to see her again that I didn't stop to think that delivering a remembrance from a dead old lady might not be considered an urgent enough reason to show up at a restaurant.

"Do you want to join me? I was supposed to meet someone, but it doesn't look like he's going to make it," she says.

What could possibly be more important than sitting across a table from this woman and watching her put things in her mouth? I wonder as I take a seat.

"So what happened to your face?" she asks me.

"It happened in the line of duty."

The words are out before I can stop them.

She's kind enough not to make a smart-ass comment. She lives in this town. She knows what kinds of duties I perform.

"It was a picnic-table-related incident," I add.

She smiles and nods.

"I've heard those can turn really ugly."

She's not wearing a ring, and her boyfriend is standing her up. There's no way she's engaged.

"It turns out we have a lot of mutual acquaintances," she comments. "It's strange we haven't met before now."

"Yes," is the only response I can come up with.

"There was Zo. There's Dr. Ed. Your mother and your sister."

"You know Jolene?"

"Only casually. I met her and her sons a couple years ago when Josh was in that fender bender and was brought to the ER. I was on call. All three of her sons look very different from one another."

"They have different dads."

"Really? I thought Randy Craig was their father. I thought they were all Zo's grandchildren."

"No, just Eb. Josh never knew his dad."

"Oh, I'm sorry. Is he dead?"

"No, a marine."

The waitress shows up, and I order a Jack Daniel's.

Chastity takes a bite of her veal, then puts her fork down.

"Actually we have met before."

Her fingers reach for the strand of gold around her neck. She plays with it, then smoothes it against the soft fabric of her sweater.

Knee-balls-balls. Balls-eye-balls. Balls-balls-balls.

"We have?"

She nods slowly.

"You don't remember me, do you?"

The word "Clearfield" flashes through my brain. I start to panic. Clearfield. We played Clearfield every year. I did some partying in Clearfield. Clearfield girls did some partying down here. Did I make out with her? Did I have sex with her? Did I promise her I'd take her out sometime and then blow her off?

She picks up her wineglass again and leans back in her chair, watching and waiting.

"I have a bad memory," I try to excuse myself.

"I'll help you out," she offers. "September 1980. Clearfield High School."

Shit, I say to myself. Is it possible I made out with her? Is it possible I had sex with her, and I don't remember her?

I clear my throat. It's possible.

"Last game of the season," she goes on. "You guys killed Clearfield, forty-five to six. You scored three touchdowns."

"Right," I say. "And after the game . . ." I leave the words hanging, waiting for her to finish the sentence for me.

She's not going to help me out at all. She cocks her head to one side and smiles sweetly at me.

"Yes?" she says. "After the game . . . ?"

I remember the game. I was on fire. No one could touch me. We were district champs that year. We had a huge blowout of a party that night, but it was back in Centresburg.

"After the game"—she grins at me—"when your team bus pulled in to the McDonald's, a bunch of cars and pickups pulled in behind you, and when you got out of the bus, a bunch of kids egged you."

"That's right," I tell her. "I remember it now. Someone got me in the side of the head."

"Yes," she says excitedly. "That was me."

I find myself grinning back at her.

"Really? You had great aim."

"Thanks," she says. "When I was a kid, I used to crawl out my brother's bedroom window onto the roof and spend hours throwing rocks at my neighbor's lawn jockey, trying to smash the lantern he was holding."

"Well, it paid off," I congratulate her.

"Thanks," she says again.

"So why did you pretend not to know me or anything about football when we met?"

"I was just having fun."

"At my expense. Again."

"Yeah."

"Is there anything else you like to do for fun besides abuse me?"

"I like to embroider. Cross-stitch, mostly."

"Rock throwing and embroidery," I ponder.

"And I'm a surgeon," she adds. "What do they all have in common?"

"You need good aim."

She gives me a gorgeous smile, full of all the delight of a little girl getting what she wants for Christmas and all the sudden sensuous attention of an intelligent grown woman encountering a man who says something she finds smart and funny.

"And a nimble wrist," I add.

The smile continues glowing, and the dark brown centers of her eyes expand until there's nothing but a rim of copper around them, like twin solar eclipses.

She leans forward over the table and purses her lips like she's about to kiss me or spit on me.

Balls-balls-balls. La-la-la. Balls-balls-balls.

"That's right," she says, and leans back again.

"You sure you don't want something to eat?" she asks and pushes her side dish of linguini and clams in my direction. "I'll never be able to eat all this."

I pick up the fork in front of me, meant for the missing mystery date.

"Do you mind if I ask how a girl goes from growing up in Clearfield to becoming a surgeon in Pittsburgh and then ends up in Centresburg?" I ask before I dig in.

"Do you want the real, corny truth, or do you want a cynical, sensible answer, like real estate is much cheaper here?"

"I'll take the corny truth."

"Okay." She pauses to eat another bite of veal, then launches into her story.

"All I ever wanted to do was escape. The minute I turned eighteen, I was gone. Off to college in the big city. I went to CMU. Did my residency at Presby. Started on the staff there. Worked my butt off. I rarely had time for a social life, but when I did, I had plenty of offers.

"Well, even with everything I had going for me, I was unhappy, but I couldn't figure out why. It wasn't as simple as saying I was exhausted and stressed out from my job. I was truly unhappy.

"One night I was on a date. I was listening to this guy go on and on about some mutual fund or something financial. For a minute I couldn't even remember his name. All the men I had known since leaving my hometown just blurred together. They were all the same.

Always whining and complaining. All they ever talk about is money and their careers and how everything in their lives is so difficult, when nothing in their lives is difficult.

"I suddenly realized how much I missed the guys from back home, which was a real shock for me, because at the time I left, one of my worst nightmares was that I would end up married to one of them, living in a trailer with five kids."

Her fingers begin pulling apart a chunk of garlic bread, leaving the pieces uneaten in a pile on the edge of her plate. Her voice drops to a husky whisper, and her words pour out rapidly.

"I started tearing into my date. I said, 'Can you do anything? You have this job that pays you a lot of money to make more money for a big company that makes more money for a lot of other men just like you, but what can you do besides that? Can you do anything real? Can you fix a carburetor? Paint a house? Pitch a tent? Plant a tree? Tap a keg? Sing a song? Catch a fish? Install a dishwasher? Carve a turkey? Build a table? Build a fire? Can you even fix my toilet?'"

I quickly go through her list in my head. I'm falling short.

"This is the corny part. I had this moment of homesickness that hit me like a truck. I missed everything. Even all the stuff I used to hate. The peace and quiet. The absolute lack of anything to do on a Friday night. People I used to think were dumber than me and less sophisticated. People I used to get so frustrated and disgusted with because I'd think to myself, How can you be content with this? But I realized that was the key. They were content. Everyone I knew in my current life had everything and was miserable.

"I started keeping my eyes and ears open for a staff position at a hospital in a smaller town. When this one opened up, I took it."

The moons pass by, and the eclipse is over in her eyes. They're a glowing golden brown again.

"I know what you mean about the being-content thing," I tell her. "I used to think the same way about my dad. Even though he died when I was only five, I still knew him long enough to get this strong sense of how content he was with a life I didn't want to have. It wasn't that he loved mining. But he was devoted to it.

"Yet at the same time, he didn't want me to have it either. He wanted me to go to college and work with my mind, not my hands and body like he did. He wouldn't have wanted me to be a football player, because in his eyes professional athletes—even though they made a lot of money—were no different than factory workers or miners or farmers. We were all *sovok* to him."

"*Sovok?*" she asks.

"Men who did physical labor," I explain. "It's a Russian word. To be called *sovok* literally means 'you are a shovel.' He never looked down on this way of making a living or men, like him, who did it. He had great respect for them, but he didn't revere them the way he did artists, and inventors, and teachers. According to him, a strong back or fast feet could always be replaced, but original thoughts could only come from the individual who thinks them."

"Is that the way you think of yourself?" she asks. "Just another strong back and a pair of fast feet?"

I try to casually throw away the thought, even though it's always plagued me.

"I'm sure as hell not a pair of fast feet anymore," I say.

She stares back at me. She looks like she might want to argue the point with me but decides to go in a different direction.

"My dad was the same way," she says. "He worked for Brockway Glass until it closed down, and I never got the feeling he wanted to do anything else, but I had two older brothers, and he always kept after them to go to college and have some kind of white-collar career. It turned out I was the only one who did."

"So he was the one who encouraged you to be a doctor?"

"No, not really. No one encouraged me in an intentional way. My brothers had more to do with it than my dad. I was always trying to keep up with them and prove I could do anything they could do. When they'd hunt and clean their deer, I'd make myself watch, and I really became fascinated with the insides of creatures. I also used to help them build and fix things."

"In other words," I volunteer, "it was a natural progression from liking guts and fixing toasters to wanting to be a surgeon."

"Right. Plus, I wanted to help people, but I didn't want to have to deal with people. I could never be a general M.D. and listen to people whine all the time about their problems."

She wrinkles up her nose when she says this. I'm studying and memorizing every move she makes, every thought she voices, every shadow she casts and glimmer of light she captures, every scent that comes off her body, from the slight antiseptic smell of the hospital soap on her hands and the floral scent of her shampoo to the hint of wine on her breath when she said hello to me to the rich female odor that's more of a premonition than a smell, attracting me and pulling me forward with hope, the same way morning always does no matter where I wake up and how hungover I am.

"You just want to knock them unconscious and cut them open," I say.

"Exactly."

Her cell phone goes off. She takes it out of her purse and answers it.

"Can you excuse me?" she asks. "I'm going to go to the lobby to take this. I can't stand people who talk on cell phones in restaurants."

I watch her walk away from the table. Another short skirt today. Balls-balls-balls-balls-balls-balls.

My eyes wander to the dark red glass of wine sitting next to her plate. An imprint of her lips clings to the rim, a soft, smoky smudge compared to the smear of carnival colors Jolene leaves behind.

I reach for the glass and bring it to my own lips. I want to taste her. I don't drink the wine.

While she's gone, I make short work of my own drink. I'm eyeing the remaining heel of garlic bread she didn't destroy when I hear an exaggerated laugh coming from the bar area of the restaurant. It's Mike Muchmore in a salmon sweater, a corduroy L. L. Bean ball cap, and tan slacks with a little white leather golf glove hanging out of his back pocket. He's got one hand resting on some guy's shoulder and another clutching a Dewar's and water.

He sees me and acts like I'm the last person in the world he expects to find here, and I probably am. He lowers his head to the men at the bar. They laugh. He laughs. He slaps some bills on the bar and starts walking toward me, already extending his hand, straight-armed, like he means to get a good running start and impale me with it.

"Ivan, good to see you again."

I stand up and give him my hand. He takes it loosely and releases it again without a pump. Val used to call this a "suit shake."

"Mike," I respond.

He looks me over, starting with my black eye, my grass-stained deputy's shirt, pausing at my badge, and ending at my jeans and boots. He ends by studying my eye.

"That's quite a shiner you've got there. Did you start the fight or was it the other guy?"

"It happened in the line of duty."

"In the line of duty? That's interesting. What exactly constitutes 'in the line of duty' for you? No matter what time of night or day I run into you, you're always in uniform. Well, partially in uniform. But I rarely see you armed. Does that mean you're on duty, off duty, or somewhere in between?"

"I don't like to carry a gun."

"Why not?" he laughs.

"I'm afraid I'll kill someone."

He laughs harder. I sit back down and wipe my hand on the leg of my jeans.

"This must be the time of year you get the itch," he says.

"Excuse me?"

"You know. The itch." He clenches his hands into fists and shakes them. "The itch to play football."

"Oh, that itch. Why would I get it now?"

He sits down in Chastity's chair, which really bothers me.

"Training camp," he says slowly.

"It's only March."

"You must miss it," he commiserates. "What do you miss most? The fans? The fame? The parties? The women?"

"The availability of painkillers."

He laughs again. I look around desperately for my waitress. I catch her eye across the room as she's bringing out a tray of food. I make a drinking motion at my mouth. She smiles.

"Where's Chastity?" he asks, pushing her chair away from the table, settling back in it, and cradling his scotch in his crotch.

"You know Chastity?"

"Know her? I'm going to marry her."

At first this information doesn't register. The fact behind the words is too inconceivable for my brain to grasp.

I think of all the truly terrible things I can: my father's death, my town's destruction, Crystal's fate, Stalin's gulags, Vietnamese villages being torched by guys like Val. Nothing seems quite as horrifically unjust as the thought of Muchmore having this woman.

"We love this place. We come here a lot. I get my cigars at the gift shop and just bill them to my table."

He leans forward and stabs the tabletop with an index finger. I've seen him make the same gesture in court.

"This is my table, by the way," he informs me.

The waitress comes by with another whiskey. I drink half of it and tell her I'm going to need another one.

"Actually, I'm glad I ran into you," he says.

His lips stretch into a slack smile. He has washed-out blue eyes and a lazy mouth that seems to move a beat behind the words coming out of it. All his facial expressions form predictably and unavoidably, like the slow spread of a stain.

"I've had a family approach me about taking legal action against

Dr. Ed. I was hoping you might talk to him and convince him to talk to them. Reasonably talk to them. I think litigation can be avoided if he'd just apologize."

I don't respond. I feel like I'm coming out of a coma.

"Apologize for what?" I finally ask.

"He went to their house and gave their child a DTP immunization."

"Holy shit!" I cry.

Muchmore jumps, and a little bit of his drink sloshes onto his pants. A few customers and waitresses look our way.

"I hate that," I exclaim. "The next thing you know, he'll be prescribing antibiotics for ear infections."

"You know the situation, Ivan," he says in a placating tone. "You accompany him sometimes on these little outings of his. His methods are illegal."

"You're right. I do know the situation, and he's not doing anything wrong. The children he's vaccinating are all going to eventually be required by law to have these immunizations in order to start school. He's just making sure they're getting the shots when they're supposed to. Some of these parents don't bring their kids in because they don't have health insurance. Some of them are just lazy and ignorant."

"His mere presence on their doorstep is an act of coercion."

"Haven't you ever heard of house calls?"

"Unsolicited?"

"Any idiot can go to your door and try to sell you magazines or tell you about Jesus Christ. Why can't Dr. Ed try to get you to vaccinate your kid? He doesn't charge for it."

"There's no one policing him."

"He's a doctor. He knows how to give a shot."

"His skills aren't being questioned."

"He's protecting children."

"He's violating adults."

"Who's the family?"

"I can't tell you."

"What exactly did he do that they're upset about?"

He hesitates.

"The father wouldn't allow him in the house, so he pretended to leave, parked down the road, walked through the wooded area behind the house, and let himself in the back door. Once he was in, he managed to distract the father long enough to give the baby the shot."

"How'd he do that?"

He hesitates again.

"He brought a case of beer and a bucket of fried chicken with him."

I smile.

"It's not funny."

"You're right. It's not. Can Dr. Ed countersue? Oh, wait. I forgot. There's no crime against being a fucking moron."

"No, but entering someone's house against his will and injecting his child with a chemical substance without his permission is a crime."

"Only in the legal sense."

He swirls his ice cubes. I close my eyes and listen to them clink.

He's seen her naked! my brain screams at me.

"I'm on Dr. Ed's side," he says.

"Fuck, you are."

"He's his own worst enemy. He's crude and pushy. He has no tact or social skills. I suppose it's not his fault. Considering."

He's touched her naked.

"Considering what?"

"Look, I'm the last person who would hold a person's roots against them, but let's face it, half the county's welfare goes to someone he's related to."

He's fallen asleep with the warm, soft weight of her pressed up against him. He's kissed the back of her neck while she sleeps. He's listened to her breathe. He gets to see her eyes do that solar-eclipse thing every day. He's reached for her, and she's come to him. He's been inside her. He's felt what she's like inside.

I stand up.

"Come on, Ivan. Take it easy."

He laughs nervously and glances around him looking for potential witnesses if I make the mistake of touching him.

"All I'm saying is, you can take the boy out of the trailer park, but you can't take the trailer park out of the boy."

"Ed grew up on a farm."

"You know what I mean."

Chastity comes back. I silently beg her not to kiss him. I beg God, too, even though I don't believe in him, and if there was the slightest chance in hell I might start again, he completely blew it tonight.

She doesn't kiss him. He kisses her. But she did not kiss him. This is an important fact. Their lips have touched. I saw it before my very eyes. I can't deny that it happened. But he was the one who made the first move.

"What's going on here?" she asks, smiling, looking back and forth between the two of us.

I'm too stunned to answer. I can't believe the same woman I was just talking to could have anything to do with Muchmore.

"Nothing," I say.

"Nothing," he says.

"Do you two know each other?"

"Sure," Muchmore booms, slipping his hand around Chastity's waist. "Everybody knows Ivan. He put Centresburg and Coal Run on the map. He made this place famous. To this day he's considered one of the all-time-greatest college players. He should've won the Heisman. He was robbed," he tells Chastity confidentially.

"You were robbed," he says to me.

"I know who he is," she says, frowning at him. "I grew up around here, remember? I meant are you friends?"

Neither of us answers.

The waitress returns with my Jack Daniel's. I take it from her and drink it in two swallows.

I look down at the empty glass in my hand. I put it on the table.

"Congratulations on your engagement," I tell Chastity.

"Oh," she says, looking a little surprised. "Thank you."

"I've got to get going."

I stop at the gift shop on my way out. The girl behind the cigar counter greets me. I nod at her and head straight to the rooster.

The lighting in the store makes him sparkle fiercely. I pick him up and run my thumb over the smooth glass plumes of his rainbow tail. He's forty-five dollars. An Italian name is scripted in tiny looping gold on the underside of his feet.

I hold him up to catch the light again, and through the window I see Chastity talking to Mike. She looks concerned for an instant. I wonder what he's telling her. Her expression calms. She smiles. She leans into him, and she kisses him this time.

I walk over to the cash register. I pick out a few boxes of prime Dominican Republic cigars. It's the best I can do in America. I think about my old boss, Mr. Perez. He always said the things he missed most about leaving Cuba were the cigars and the Cubans.

I hand the rooster to the girl. I tell her to gift-wrap it and charge everything to Mike Muchmore's table.

# TEN

SHE'S GOING TO MARRY MUCHMORE? I CAN'T BELIEVE IT. I won't believe it. There's no way she could want to spend even fifteen minutes with that guy, let alone her whole life. What could she possibly see in him? What could they talk about? What could they do? What opinions could they share?

There's only one answer. Money. Money and power and social status. She's a doctor. Of course she's going to marry a fucking lawyer. Who else would she marry? A mechanic who can fix her carburetor?

What was all that bullshit about guys who can't do anything and missing guys from back home? Muchmore is a perfect example of a guy who can't do a single goddamned useful thing. It's all bullshit. Every word that comes out of a woman's mouth when she talks about what she wants in a man is bullshit. Oh, I want a man with a good sense of humor. Oh, I want a man who can plant a tree.

You never see a beautiful woman with a poor man. It's a fact. Okay. Bobbie Raynor. Okay, every once in a while they pick a guy who doesn't make a fortune. Okay. My mom was married to a coal miner, too. Okay, another example but it's rare. Money and the things it can buy. That's all they want.

She's totally screwed up. She has no idea what she wants. She doesn't know. He can't make her happy. She doesn't even know what happy is.

She doesn't even need his money. She's a doctor, for Christ's sake, living in a cheap little shithole town where you can buy a draft beer for

$1.50 on $1.50 night at Brownie's. She's got to be packing the money away. She doesn't need Muchmore and his BMW. I hate fucking BMWs. I hate Germany for making them. I hate that whole fucking country.

What can I do to get her to like me? Shit. I don't have any money. I don't have any way to make money. Do you know what a deputy makes? Muchmore's mechanic probably makes five times what I make. Shit! Even if she wasn't lying. Even if she does want a man who can do all the shit she was talking about . . . hell, I can't even fix a toilet.

"Ivan."

"Yeah?"

I look up at Art standing behind the bar.

"You're talking out loud," he tells me.

I try to bring his form into focus. He stays hazy around the edges.

"I'm sure nobody minds," he adds. "I just wasn't sure you knew."

"Thanks."

I look up and down the line of drinkers. They don't care. They're all thinking modified versions of the same thing.

I can't imagine how great it must be to find the right woman and have her feel the same way about you. The concept sounds simple, but it's the most complicated process on earth.

I'm not talking about settling. I'm not talking about people who find someone they think they can care about. They're fairly compatible. Around the same age. They date for a while. What the hell? Let's get married. Let's have kids. That's what we're supposed to do. I'll be the husband, and you can be the wife. We'll probably split up in about ten years, because we're going to get really sick and tired of each other, because deep down we don't have a bond. We're not together because we can't live without each other. We're doing this because we've got nothing better to do and because we're scared of being alone.

I look up from my drink again. Art's down at the other end of the bar. No one's looking at me. I'm pretty sure I was quiet this time.

I want what my parents had before it was ruthlessly ripped from them. They were destined to be. No one could have conceived of or planned the way their separate lives would eventually entwine. Not even God. It was something in their individual souls calling out to each other across an ocean, then across a nation, and finally across a dinner table.

Before my mother met Rado Zoschenko, she had heard of him. He worked in Gertie with her father. He was a foreigner originally, but he'd lived in America for ten years mining coal in Illinois. He spoke pretty good English, her dad had told them, and he had the damnedest tattoo.

My grandfather brought him home for dinner one night. Rado was a single fellow who had just moved here and didn't have any family. Grandpa thought he could use a home-cooked meal. All Rado ever brought in his lunch pail was a hunk of bread with a tough brown crust and a cold boiled potato. He was meticulous about removing every shred of peel from the potato before eating it, and once Grandpa asked him why, and my dad replied, "For four years all I ever get to eat in camp was peels."

Grandpa was dying to ask him more about this camp and what kind of parents would send their child to it, but prying into a man's background wasn't something he did. Instead he invited Rado home so his wife could do it.

I can only imagine what my relatively sheltered, teenage mother, who had never traveled farther than the twenty miles it took to get to the Crooked Creek campground where J&P had its company picnic every year, thought the first time she met this mysterious, jet-haired stranger from another land who took her hand in his and announced with Old World ceremony, "Meeting you is pleasure."

Grandma had been prepped beforehand and knew to steer the dinner conversation to this camp Rado had talked about. It couldn't have been that bad, she had scolded her husband earlier.

"Didn't you have wienie roasts or sing-alongs?" she asked my dad.

He gave serious thought to her question, finding nothing offensive or amusing about it.

"No, we didn't have these things," he said after he finished swallowing, placed his fork on the table, dabbed at his mouth with his napkin, and folded his hands in his lap.

"I suppose worst thing was fleas. They were so bad we would wake up in the morning and our arms would be bleeding from where we scratched so hard in the night."

Everyone at the table stopped chewing.

"Or maybe not," my father corrected himself. "The worst would be the radiation poison, of course. It's what killed most of us. It was a slow way to die. It started with throwing up and headache. Then your hair falls out and your toenails fall off.

"A lot of the Russians would kill themselves once they knew what was happening. They don't have problem with this. Suicide is a way of life for them. They treat as a romantic thing. Not for Ukrainians, though. Nothing would ever cause a Ukrainian to take his life. This is only for God to do. Or Stalin, I suppose."

Grandma clapped a hand over her mouth, and Grandpa fumbled with his fork before it clattered onto his plate.

"Did you call this place a camp?" he asked my dad, squinting at him over the meat loaf.

"Sure. Yes, a camp. A work camp." My dad struggled to find the right word. "Gulag."

"You mean like one of Hitler's concentration camps?" my mother's younger brother, Kenny, asked.

"Yes . . . well, in a way." My dad continued to struggle with words. "We were workers, not prisoners."

"Then you could leave?" my grandmother asked.

"No, we couldn't. It's hard to explain. I was prisoner, yes, but I was also *sovok*. I was worker. It was important that we thought of ourselves as workers. I was a miner. I mined uranium."

A dumb, awkward silence fell over the room. My mother was the one who broke it, speaking to my father for the very first time in her life.

"And now that you're free . . . you're still a miner?" she asked him.

My dad looked at her. She stared back at him and saw in his gaze a man who had endured more suffering than she could ever imagine, yet he hadn't been made weak or bitter or numb because of it.

He smiled at her and reached for his third helping of mashed potatoes, soft and fluffy white without a trace of peel, and shrugged.

"It is something I know."

She was eighteen. He was thirty-three. Four years would pass before he would approach her with any romantic intentions. She went to college in Slippery Rock and got her degree in home ec. She wanted to be a dietitian on a cruise ship and travel the world, then maybe open up her own restaurant someday, or a catering business.

The summer she graduated, my father presented himself at her family's home with flowers for her mother, vodka for her father, and for her an album of Tchaikovsky's Symphony no. 6 in B Minor, "Pathétique," performed by the Leningrad Philharmonic Orchestra.

In his own way, he would show my mother the world without ever taking her anywhere.

I look up again and try to find Art. I need another drink.

I can't find him. I look down the bar. I think I see him, but his head has taken on a bizarre elongated shape and his skin has turned brown.

I eventually realize I'm staring at the mounted deer head near the door. At closing time some drunk always pulls up a chair and stands on it to stroke the velvety nose and touch the amber glass eyes.

I look to the other side of me.

"Hey," Jess Raynor says to me.

"Hey," I say back, maybe a little too loudly.

I didn't hear him come in, or for all I know he's been here all night.

"Why aren't you home with the little lady?" I ask him. "Trouble in paradise?"

Art comes by and hands Jess a beer. I push my glass forward, and he pretends not to see it.

"Least I get some paradise now and then," Jess answers in his low rasp.

"I can get paradise anytime I want it."

"Yeah," he snorts.

He looks all around him, up and down the bar at the entirely male clientele except for two women with big hair and screeching laughs sitting at a dark corner table that no one is drunk enough yet to approach.

"I can see that," he laughs.

I get off my stool and position myself in a way I'm pretty sure is almost a little intimidating.

"You know what?" I say. "You're a fucking bass turd."

"Yeah?" he says back.

"Yeah."

"I got the feeling you've got something you want to say to me. Something you really want to say to me."

"Yeah, I do."

"Yeah? Well, I've got something I want to say to you, too."

"Yeah?"

"Yeah. You want to say it here, or you want to say it outside?"

"Let's go outside. I'll say it outside."

"Hey, guys," Art says.

"Don't try and stop us," I warn him.

"I'm not. I want paid."

I throw some odd bills on the bar. They're crumpled and greasy-looking. Jess takes a couple clean, crisp ones out of a nice leather wallet and lays them flat on the bar. The wallet's probably a gift from Bobbie, or maybe Danny. When he's not busy picking his teeth up off the floor, he's out working a paper route to earn money so he can buy dear old Dad a wallet for Christmas.

What the hell is that? I have three nephews. I never hit one of them, and not one of them ever bought me a wallet.

We step outside. The streets are deserted. Nighttime commerce and entertainment belong to the mall now. Downtown is used only for drinking.

"Your kids get you that wallet?" I ask him immediately.

He plants himself a few feet away from me. Behind him white plaster flakes litter the sidewalk in front of Woolworth's like the building has dandruff.

"What?"

"Your wallet. Your kids get it for you?"

"No. Bobbie did. What's it to you?"

"I fucked her once, you know that?"

The words are out before I can stop them. I wouldn't have stopped them anyway, even if I had been given the chance. The best and worst thing about being shitfaced drunk is that it allows you to say all the things you've always wanted to say but didn't out of respect for yourself and others.

I brace myself for his attack. Nothing comes. He tilts his head a little like he's studying a blueprint. He smiles at me.

"Yeah, I know. Bobbie told me. We were having a big fight when that happened. She saw me giving Kelly Kowalski a ride one day after school, and Kelly was wearing that pink miniskirt of hers. You remember Kelly's pink miniskirt?"

"Who doesn't?"

"Bobbie got mad at me and accused me of some shit, and we kind of broke up. She only did it with you to get back at me. When I asked her how it was she said . . ." He pauses, and a big grin plays across his face. "She said, 'The rumors are greatly exaggerated.' And we laughed so hard I almost threw up. And then everything was okay between us again. In a way you were responsible for getting us back together."

I throw the first punch. He steps aside, and I miss him. The momentum from my swing turns me around, and I'm left facing the door of the bar, and for a split second I can't remember where I am, why I'm here, and who I'm with, but I do remember I'm pissed about something. I can't remember what exactly, but I know I'm willing to fight to the death in order to defend my right to be allowed to be able to continue to be pissed about it.

I feel a hand on my shoulder. Jess yanks me around to face him again. He gives me a shove in the chest, and I stumble backward. It occurs to me he's not as drunk as I am. It occurs to me he's not drunk at all.

I'm not afraid, though. Jess doesn't fight. I remember a time Reese beat him up in school. Reese with the bill of a grimy ball cap yanked low over his flat stare, wearing a black T-shirt with a cracked Judas Priest decal on the front, standing in the hall next to Jess at his locker, and then there was a sudden eruption that ended in Jess's being beaten to a bloody, snotty pulp and Reese's being ushered off to the principal's office kneading his bruised knuckles.

Jess didn't even try to shield himself. He just took it. The next day the two of them were sitting together at the end of the cafeteria table, eating their brown-bag lunches in their traditional stiff silence. Jess had to stay after practice for a week and run laps as punishment for letting himself get beat up when we had a big game that Saturday.

The memory gives me added optimism. I regain my footing and take another swing. This time he blocks the blow with his arm.

"What the hell are you doing?" he asks me.

"You're a fucking loser, Jess. Look what you did with your life. Nothing. You did nothing. You're nothing. You're less than nothing. You're nothing."

"Shut up. You don't know shit about my life."

I say the one thing I know will humiliate him the most.

"You beat up your little boy."

He rushes at me. He picks me up by my deputy's jacket and smashes me against the wall.

"That's a lie!" he shouts. "Take it back!"

I take another swing. This time I connect with his stomach. It

knocks the air out of him, and he lets go of me. I follow it up with a
punch to his jaw, but he still has more coordination than I do. He
grabs me by the hand when I try to throw another one and wrenches
my arm behind my back.

"I want my guns," he says into my ear.

"What?"

"I want my guns back," he says again, his grip tightening.

I feel all the bones in my hand grinding together. Even at my most
fit, I never had the kind of raw brute strength he still possesses now.
When I was playing in a game, I might have had it, or if I had to rescue someone from a burning building, I might have it, but it would require an adrenaline rush to rouse it.

"I don't have your guns."

He pushes me up against the wall, and I feel my face scrape against
concrete. He gives me a punch in the kidneys that brings tears to my
eyes.

"I want my guns," he tells me again, this time with a sense of ur-
gency in his voice.

"I'll get them to you," I wheeze.

"I want them now."

I turn my head to try to look at him. His face is right next to mine.
I can see a small cut on his chin where he must have nicked himself
shaving, and a few faint Barbie choker scars still circling his neck. Jess
always had a hard time keeping his head up.

"I don't have them."

"I want them by tomorrow," he says, "or I'm coming to get them.
They're mine. You got no right to them."

"I'll bring them by your house," I promise.

He lets go of my hand. I bring it around in front of me and look
down at it expecting to see it bent and crumpled like a cartoon paw
that's been crushed under an anvil.

I slide to the ground and sit there. I won't give him the satisfaction
of curling into a fetal position until he's gone.

"Jess," I call out.

He stops and turns around. I look up at him. His bottom lip is split, and there's a small trickle of blood on his chin.

Seeing the injury I inflicted gives me a momentary thrill of triumph, but then I feel bad. It brings back all the conflicting emotions that always surrounded my relationship with Jess.

When he made a great play, I was happy for him, but I also secretly wished he'd screw up next time, making me look better in comparison. When he failed, my gut reaction was to feel bad for him, but I also felt glad for myself.

I remember once when I was ready to quit the team after a bad sandpapering for pussyfooting, Jess joined me in the locker room and explained to me that Deets knew what he was doing. How he was a man who thought inflicting a punishment you could survive was the highest form of praise and sending you home happy with yourself was an insult. How he wasn't preparing us to play college ball or pro ball the way I thought he should be, how he was preparing us to live the kinds of lives our fathers did in case we couldn't play ball. The playing-ball part was easy. How Jess was right, and I thought he was smart for figuring that out, but I couldn't admit to him that I thought he was smart. How he was going home to his dad because his dad was alive, and how he was supposed to be happy about that, but how he must have had days where he wished he was going home to a ghost instead.

We were great football players, Jess and I, because football, like our lives, was about love and rage and feeling both at the same time for the same reason.

I reach into my jacket pocket and toss a key ring to him. He catches it in midair.

"Zo left you her tractor mower," I tell him.

I watch his mud-caked boots and the frayed cuffs of his jeans walk away while I stay seated on the ground.

I feel something else tucked inside my jacket, and I take it out, too. It's the envelope Eb gave me earlier in my truck.

I open it and read it in the light cast by the buzzing Miller Lite sign.

It's a birthday-party invitation with all kinds of balls on the front: baseball, soccer, football, basketball, golf, and tennis. Across the top in big block letters is the promise WE'RE GOING TO HAVE A BALL!

Inside are the details to Eb's seventh birthday party, including the time we're all supposed to meet at the Chuck E. Cheese restaurant. The date is six months away.

He's written a note to me on the back. I can hear Harrison's sighs of frustration as Eb asked him to spell every word.

*Dear Uncle Ivan,*

*I wanted to tell you about my party early in case you have other plans you need to change.*

*From, Everett Craig Your Nephew*

I put the little card back in its envelope and back inside my jacket pocket.

I don't get up for a while.

# TUESDAY

# ELEVEN

THE FIRST TIME I SAW HER, SHE WAS A SPECK OF A PERSON sitting on a guardrail. She could've been a boy or a girl, an adult or a child.

I realized she was a kid before I figured out her sex. She had short, dark hair and was wearing jeans, tennis shoes, and a blue western-style shirt. As I approached her, I saw that the shirt had colorful stones, cloudy with age, set all over it in a confused zigzag pattern that made me think of Volodymyr's crown. Some of the stones were missing, and only the empty settings remained.

I was out doing my Saturday run. I was going to say hi, but I wasn't going to stop. Then I noticed she was holding one of her shoes in her hand and she had been crying. Both shoes and the cuffs of her jeans were soaked in black, tarry muck.

I pulled up to a stop.

"What's wrong?" I asked her, breathing heavily and wiping sweat off my face with the bottom of my sweatshirt.

She looked at me for a moment, then dropped her eyes and wouldn't look at me again as she spoke.

"I stepped in some kind of sticky mud," she began. "I didn't see it. These are new shoes. I'm gonna get in trouble."

I took the shoe from her and examined it. I smelled it to see if it was oil or asphalt or paint. I wished Val was with me. He knew everything that came out of the ground around here. It didn't smell like anything except dirt.

"I think it's just mud. I wouldn't worry about it," I told her, and handed the shoe back to her. "It should clean off. Are you going to be all right?"

She shrugged her thin shoulders and still wouldn't make eye contact with me.

I looked at her. I decided she wasn't a child after all. She was probably around Jolene's age but nowhere near Jolene's developmental plane. She didn't have much up top, but the bottom half looked good. She wasn't ugly.

She wore a tiny tarnished gold cage on a chain around her neck with colored glass chips inside it.

"That's a pretty necklace," I said.

It was a piece of crap, but when I said it, I meant it.

"Thanks," she replied.

"Well, I've got to get going," I told her, and jogged off.

I never gave her another thought until the next Saturday when I went running again.

She was sitting on the same guardrail. It wasn't an accident. I was certain she had come here at the same time hoping I ran the same route every Saturday morning.

She was wearing the same tennis shoes and jeans. They were both shadowed in gray where the stain hadn't completely come out. She had on the cage necklace and a pink shirt that clung to the lumpy bra covering her little breasts. On both wrists she wore charm bracelets dangling with more colorful fake jewels.

"You waiting for a bus?" I asked her.

She smiled. If she hadn't smiled, I might have kept on going.

I slowed down and smiled back at her.

"You live around here?" I asked.

She nodded.

"I don't recognize you from school. What grade are you in?"

"Sophomore."

"You're in the same grade as my sister, Jolene. Do you know her?"

"Everyone knows Jolene," she said.

"Yeah, I guess so. Do you know who I am?"

"Everyone knows who you are, too," she said.

I wanted to fuck her. It was an instantaneous impulse. I wasn't sure where it came from. I wasn't wildly physically attracted to her. I wasn't hard up for female companionship. I could run back home, take a shower, make a phone call, and be screwing a girl who was better-looking.

It was her innocence that got to me. Not her virginity. I had been with virgins who were about as pure as acid rain. She was untouched. She wanted, but without knowing she wanted. She had breasts and hips, but she was still a child. She didn't know anything about dicks and pussies and tongues and cum. She wanted me to hold her hand. To make her feel as pretty and as important as Teen Queen Jolene. Maybe she wanted me to kiss her. It would be the way she had seen it in movies. Something with a soundtrack and a happy ending.

It didn't make much sense, but my next thought was of Val and the only time he let me shoot his gun. I remembered the feel of his callused hands on mine and his whispered tobacco breath near my ear instructing me to look my prey in the eyes. I remembered the thrill and fear that came with the power. And I remembered his advice afterward: It would be pretty stupid to try to kill something I didn't want to kill.

I brushed the memory away. I didn't care what Val thought. Val was gone. Val was worse than gone. Val had decided to stay away.

I looked around me at the calm, green hillsides that I loved, and I hated them for having something hidden inside them that could lead to their destruction. I looked at the girl.

I let my soul be corrupted that day, although it would be years later before I accepted what I had done. I forgot who I was and what I should do and only thought about what I wanted and what I could do.

I stepped toward her. It was a bold move, even for me.

She didn't move away from me. I bent my head down and kissed her. She kissed me back, then suddenly pulled away and blurted out, "I have to go," and took off down the road.

"I'll be running past here next week," I called after her. "Maybe I'll see you again."

She was waiting for me the next week. I didn't waste any time. I got her to take a walk with me. I took off my sweatshirt and laid it down on the ground so she'd have a place to sit while we talked. We didn't talk.

She let me take her clothes off, but not the necklace. I told her it might get broken. She asked how, and the look she gave me made me realize she didn't have any idea what we were about to do, but she didn't stop me. She trusted me. She thought she loved me. She couldn't imagine I didn't have her best interest at heart.

When I pushed inside her, her eyes grew huge and she asked me to stop. I told her it would be okay. She didn't ask me again. She didn't say anything.

I watched her face the whole time. I tried to imagine the images going through her mind. I was convinced she was picturing the life we were going to lead. The dating. The hand-holding. The love I was going to give her. Maybe love she desperately needed. I didn't know anything about her. About her home life. She seemed to be poor, but we were all poor. I knew she had a little girl's love of cheap, sparkly jewels, but I didn't know a girl around here who didn't. How far did it go? Did she see our wedding, our happy home, our baby?

Then it was over in a pleasurable, physical spasm. I had taken what I wanted. I was done. She had been penetrated, destroyed, and now would be left in ruins like any other source of precious ore.

I left her on the side of the road. I never even bothered asking her name. I wouldn't learn it until a couple months later when she got up the nerve to talk to me in school, and I went home afterward and looked her up in the yearbook. She was wearing the necklace in her picture.

Her name was Crystal. I didn't even offer to walk her home that day. I wasn't planning on ever seeing her again.

Tapping wakes me up, and I'm grateful that the memory slips away from me.

The tapping grows louder. I wonder if I could have managed to crawl inside a very big tree last night and now there's a woodpecker outside looking for his breakfast.

I open one eye and see daylight outside a windshield badly in need of a washing. I try to move. Every part of my body hurts, some more than others. My face. My head. My arm. My back. My knee.

I turn my head and smash my nose against a steering wheel.

The tapping becomes banging.

"Stop," I groan.

"Hey, Uncle Ivan," I hear.

The voice is muffled, like the speaker has a jar over his mouth.

I crane my neck back and see an upside-down Eb waving madly at me from outside the driver's-side window.

He cups his hands around his mouth and puts them right up against the glass.

"Rise and shine!" he calls.

"Stop," I say again.

I look around to get my bearings. I'm curled up on my side on the seat of my truck. The sharp bones of Val's lucky rabbit foot are digging into my hip. At my feet is a big box filled with some of Zo's belongings I told Jolene I'll help her dispense. I can't remember getting here. I don't remember anything after my encounter with Jess.

Eb bends down, then pops back up again with a coffee mug in his hands.

"Open up," he says.

I open the door. He hands me the coffee.

"Mom says to give you this. She says you're going to need it."

He's ready for school. He's wearing a yellow rain slicker and his backpack and is exuding more energy and excitement over the act of handing me coffee than I will probably ever feel about anything ever again for the rest of my life. I take the cup from him. Steam rises slowly from it. The heat feels good in my cold hands.

"You said you were going to play a game with me last night," he reminds me.

"Something came up."

"Why'd you sleep out here in your truck?"

"I was tired."

"Too tired to come inside and sleep on the couch?"

"Yeah."

"Harrison says you were passed out drunk."

I take a sip of the coffee.

"Harrison's a bass turd."

"Me, too," he says, smiling. "You know what else I am?"

"What?"

"My name is a verb. I learned it in school yesterday. Miss Finch taught us about oceans. Ebb is what the tide does. It means to move away from something."

He backs away from the truck, holding his hands out like he's on a tightrope.

"See, I'm ebbing."

"I see."

"Did I get to see the ocean when we came to visit you in Florida when I was little?"

"Yes."

"Did I like it?"

"You ate a lot of sand."

The front door of Jolene's house opens and bangs shut. Harrison steps outside and starts to stroll down the sidewalk with his trademark slouch.

"Come on, midget!" Harrison shouts to Eb. "You're going to miss your bus. Mom wants to talk to you, Uncle Ivan."

Upon hearing this information, Eb gives me an even bigger smile before racing away from the truck to catch up with his brother. He gets in front of him and starts walking backward.

"I'm ebbing to school," he proclaims.

"No, you're not," Harrison says disgustedly. "You're going toward school. You're ebbing from home."

"Yeah, that's it," Eb corrects himself. "I'm ebbing from home."

I wait until they're gone before I try to get out of my truck. I don't want them to see how I move.

I walk around to the back door. Through the window I see Jolene standing at the sink in her Valley Dairy uniform holding a soapy tiara in one hand and scrubbing at it with a toothbrush.

She doesn't turn and look at me when I come inside.

Josh is sitting at the table finishing a bowl of cereal and reading a magazine.

He has a mop of dark blond hair he keeps shaved around the bottom. A few years ago, he had his initials shaved into it. Jolene sent me a picture of it. Then he had the word "dawg." Now he's matured into a very tasteful lightning bolt. I'm going to suggest "bass turd" before he leaves for college this fall.

"Hey, it's Hobocop," he says when he sees me.

"Funny," I tell him.

I can still remember the day he was born like it happened yesterday. I drove over the mountain from State College in the middle of a blizzard to represent the male gender at his birth, since his father had run off to basic training. When I got there, Josh had already been born and was sleeping soundly and pinkly in my mom's arms, and Jolene was reading out loud to her from a fashion magazine about the dos and don'ts of wearing leg warmers, giggling wildly at the don'ts.

"It's a boy," she announced when she noticed me standing in the doorway. "Like you."

I take a seat across from him before he can stand up and carry his bowl to the sink. He's as tall as me now. Some days I don't like to be reminded of this.

I have my back to Volodymyr, and that's the way I like it. I'm in no mood to meet his all-knowing stare.

Mom gave the portrait to Jolene when she moved here with Josh. It never felt right having him hang in the house we moved into after our Coal Run home was bulldozed under. His presence in the new house seemed more like a betrayal to Dad's memory than a tribute.

Josh gives Jolene a peck on the cheek on his way out, the same thing I used to do every morning with my mom. A sudden pang of guilt stabs at me as I think of all those lost years I avoided her, and not because of anything she had done. I'm still avoiding her. I'm back home, but I still don't see her enough. She's never complained.

I look around me and bury my face in my hands. Jolene's kitchen is one of the worst places for a hangover. The walls are papered in hundreds of little bright red apples with a border of little red and blue houses and the greeting WELCOME FRIENDS WELCOME FRIENDS WELCOME FRIENDS covering the entire perimeter of the room.

I've had a couple late nights sitting in this kitchen with a bottle wondering if there's a border out there somewhere that says: GET THE FUCK OUT GET THE FUCK OUT GET THE FUCK OUT.

"So you're pissed at me," I break the ice.

"No, why would I be pissed at you?"

"Because I didn't come home last night like I promised Eb," I sigh.

She tosses the toothbrush inside her sink, where it clangs loudly, and turns on the water with more force than she needs. The stream bounces off the small crown in a spray of dish soap bubbles that spatters the front of her uniform. She finishes rinsing it and gives it a few shakes before setting it to dry in a rack with some breakfast dishes and rinsed-out cans with the lids taken off.

"No, why would I care how many promises you break to Eb? Or why would I care what kind of example you set for him? Why would I care if my six-year-old son finds you passed-out drunk in your truck?"

"He wouldn't have known I was drunk if Harrison hadn't told him."

She grabs a dish towel from a hook near the stove and begins to dry her hands furiously.

"Is that supposed to be funny?" she asks.

"Why do I have to set any kind of example for anybody? I'm not their father."

"You are the most selfish person I've ever known."

"What are you talking about? He's only six. I'm not having a bad influence on him. I'm not having any influence on him."

"You were the same age Eb is now when Val was drafted. Are you going to tell me you were too young for him to have had an impact on you? Were you too young to remember Dad?"

I don't say anything.

"I was, you know," she says quietly. "Too young to remember Dad."

She hangs the towel back on its hook, pausing to adjust it so the colorful scene of smiling fruits and vegetables is properly displayed. The crown, leaning against a cereal bowl, sparkles noticeably in the midst of the dishes and cans. She gives it a deep, thoughtful glance, as if she might consider wearing it today.

Her crown collection resides in a small white curio cabinet in the upstairs hallway. She cleans them one at a time in no apparent order, usually with a soft blue cloth made from a square patch of Josh's first security blanket. She likes to do it at night after the boys are in bed when she's watching TV, in much the same way Zo used to take out her knitting or my mother used to take out her pair of scissors and newspaper flyers filled with coupons. Most of the crowns are from pageants; a few are gifts from childhood; some she bought for herself.

When Jolene first started competing in beauty pageants, I couldn't figure out why. She's one of the least competitive people I've ever known. She's always been aware that she's pretty; she's never needed a panel of judges to tell her so. She didn't need the titles as a professional springboard. She never had any interest in the kinds of careers beauty pageants usually lead to. She didn't want to be an actress, a TV newscaster, or a gyrating girl in a rock video.

My mom was puzzled, too, but she was never the kind of mother to pry too deeply or lecture. As long as we promised to never do drugs, drive with someone who'd been drinking, drop out of school, spend money foolishly, or vote Republican, we were fairly free to pursue whatever interests we wanted, even those she didn't completely understand or wholeheartedly approve of.

I never heard her voice an opinion, good or bad, about beauty pageants or give Jolene any kind of advice. The only time I ever heard her say anything to Jolene before a pageant was before her very first one, standing in the hallway outside the junior-high auditorium.

Mom took her by the hands and said, "You know what really impresses me? A good lemon meringue pie. Where the filling is just right—not too tart, not too sweet. And the meringue is perfect—not too stiff, the peaks not too browned."

Jolene said, "Me, too, Mom."

And Mom looked immensely relieved.

It only took until her third pageant before Jolene won one. She was fourteen when she was crowned Laurel County Fair's Pine Princess, and at the precise moment when that crown began its journey from its satin pillow to the top of her golden head, the answer to why she wanted to be in pageants became blindingly obvious.

I was there. I had reluctantly left the fairway with a group of my buddies and our girlfriends, loaded down with stuffed-animal trophies and big clouds of pink cotton candy, to join my mom and Zo in the grandstand to watch the event.

Jolene stood absolutely calm and poised in a green strapless dress with her hands clasped prettily in the folds of her skirt while all around her the shoulder pads and sequined appliqués and torn hemlines of the other girls' attempts at cutting-edge eighties fashion jostled and squirmed and vied for attention.

The chairman of the Laurel County Fair's Events Committee, acting as emcee in one of the organization's official red blazers stained with black patches of mud from awarding the tractor-pull ribbons earlier, made the announcement. Then he took a little silver tiara off a dusty yellow satin cushion held by the year's previous princess, who was smiling bravely and scanning the audience for her mother and the funnel cake she had promised to have waiting for her once she had conceded her throne.

Jolene's fixed gaze followed the crown's journey. She watched the arc it made from the pillow through the fairground air, thick with the sound of cheering and the smells of livestock, cooking grease, and diesel fuel, until her eyes rolled back in her head like she was having a seizure as she tried to see it actually descend upon the top of her own head.

Mom paused in her whooping, grinned at Zo, and looked relieved once again.

"She wanted the crown," they said in unison.

"Which pageant is that one from?" I ask her.

She glances back at it again.

"Miss Mid-Atlantic Seaboard," she says. "Do you remember my talent?"

"Modern prance?"

"Modern dance," she corrects me. "Do you remember the girl who went right after me? She did a lame gymnastics routine, but she had a great body and she wore a knockout glittery multicolored bodysuit that made her look like a rainbow trout."

"Yeah, I remember. It completely changed the way I looked at fish."

"She has a porn Web site now."

The word "porn" makes me think of Chastity. The words "glittery," "bodysuit," "Web site," "gymnastics," "girl," and "trout" all make me think of Chastity.

"I e-mailed her."

"You e-mailed her porn Web site? What did you say?"

"I asked her if she remembered me. Congratulated her on her Web site. Asked her what else is going on in her life. That kind of stuff."

"You congratulated her on a porn Web site?"

"Sure. I admire that kind of confidence. I really do. I could never let a stranger see me naked, unless, of course, I was having sex with him."

She walks out of the room and comes back wearing a denim jacket with suede fringe over her uniform and carrying her purse.

"So what do you have planned for today?" she asks. "Are you going to work?"

"Of course I am."

"You'd better shower and change your clothes first."

"Yeah."

She turns to leave, then stops.

"Tell me something, Ivan. Why did you come back here? Definitely not for me or for the boys or for Mom. Why? I want to know."

I don't say anything.

"I never blamed you for needing to leave," she goes on. "Mom and I were prepared for that. You went away to college, and then we were ready for you to go on with your career and move to Chicago. That was fine. That was great because we knew it was best for you.

"But I do blame you for what you did instead. Cutting us all out of your life the way you did. I never understood it, and I still don't. You never said you were sorry."

"I never realized I did anything wrong."

"You have a responsibility to people who love you. And I don't mean you have to do things for them. I mean you have to let them do things for you."

"I couldn't." My head begins to pound. "You don't understand."

"Okay. I don't understand," she says, trying to calm me. "Then explain it to me. What happened, Ivan? What could possibly be that bad? What did you do? I can't believe this is all about your leg. You're not that shallow. You're not a quitter either."

My need for a drink is automatic. There's no desire involved anymore. I know it won't bring me pleasure or even relief. It's become instinct. A learned instinct.

"Look at you. You've been here for almost a year, and you still don't even have a place to live. You're drunk every night. You're getting into fights. I have to nag at you to bathe and put on clean clothes. You're worse than all three of my boys put together. What's going on with you?"

"I don't know," I tell her.

The pain in my head is getting worse. I stand up suddenly, knocking my chair over. We both look at it lying on the floor.

Jolene waits for me to set it up.

Despite the indignity of wearing a uniform the same color as a traffic cone and a name tag promising the customer "Service with a side order of sunshine," there is nothing subservient about her. She is in control here. This is her domain.

She faces me with her back against the kitchen counter, her hands gripping it on either side of herself, like a protester defending a condemned landmark from the wrecker's ball.

For the first time since I showed up unannounced on her doorstep eight months ago, after I got the newspaper clipping telling me Reese would be getting out of prison within the year, I get a glimpse of the possibility that I could become unwelcome. I don't believe she would ever completely shut me out of her heart, but she might be able to lock her front door.

"Okay," she says, slipping into her jacket. "You do what you want. You're a grown man. But you're not going to do it here anymore. I don't want to see it, and I don't want my boys to see it. I'm not going to let you make me pity my big brother."

She leaves through the back door.

"Was that an ultimatum?" I call after her.

She doesn't respond.

As soon as I hear her car drive away, I head for the cabinet where she keeps her booze. There's nothing in it but a bottle of grenadine, a half-empty bottle of Old Granddad, and two bottles of Tequila Rose. I grab the bourbon and take a seat at the table again.

A Welch's jelly-jar glass with a Pokémon character on it sits in front of me. It has a little orange juice in it. I pour it half full of whiskey.

I take a drink. It tastes like shit.

I look up and find Volodymyr staring at me.

I have no way of knowing how old the czar was supposed to have been in this portrait. His long hair and drooping mustache are youthfully dark, without a touch of gray, and his pose with one leg bent, his foot on an altar stair, holding a scepter topped with a jeweled cross out and away from him as if ready to take a swipe at a pesky fly or bash in a Mongol's head is the casually aggressive stance of a young, confident king wanting to show forward movement and religious endorsement, but his eyes belong to an old man. Not a defeated or bitter old man who curses his age, but an enlightened one who knows that his years are a gift and only with the passage of time can a man gain an understanding of life that makes him fit to guide others.

They are alert but calm, full of ancient composure and wisdom but also hope and curiosity. He's a grown-up wearing a child's simple, awkward crown made of iron, not gold, set with stones chosen for the variety of their colors, not for their value.

As a child I was convinced this was what God must look like before I stopped believing in him.

Dad loved that portrait. He was so proud of it. He showed it to everyone who came to visit us.

He would explain exactly where it used to hang in his family's small, spare farmhouse in Ukraine. He would tell the story of how he eventually traveled back there after his release from Magadan to find all the members of his family dead and the house destroyed but the portrait somehow miraculously whole, lying in the ashes, ripped from the frame, singed, scratched, bent, but salvageable. He would tell of his mother's respect for the artist who painted it, her love for the rich colors, her devotion to the subject: the man who brought peace and Christianity to her people. He would insist it was the last thing she saw before she closed her eyes permanently against the starvation that had already taken her two young daughters. When describing the women in his family, Dad never mentioned the war. He called them casualties of faith.

I get up and walk over to the sink. I pour out my drink. I turn the bottle upside down, close my eyes, and listen to the sound of the whiskey disappearing down the drain. It's a very small victory.

# TWELVE

I DRAG MY BODY UPSTAIRS. IT'S NOT EASY. MY KNEE IS KILLING ME.

I strip in the hallway and check out the damage to myself in the mirror on the back of Jolene's bedroom door. My knee is the size and consistency of a small, rotten grapefruit. I have a fresh purple bruise on my lower back from Jess. I have a black eye. My knuckles hurt. My joints ache. My head is pounding.

The image in the mirror doesn't bother me. It's almost comforting. It reminds me of my ball-playing days. It reminds me of my dad and the other miners when I saw them without their shirts on or in a pair of shorts in summer. Almost all of them were scarred in some way, but somehow none of their injuries made them want to stop working. They only seemed to further ignite their desire to go back inside. The more battered a man was, the more alive he became.

I'm not sure where I stand with Jolene right now, if I've been kicked out altogether or if I can redeem myself and stick around a little while longer.

Last night, after we found the photo for Val at Zo's house, I mentioned that I had seen him in his pickup earlier. I also mentioned the lollipops sitting on his front seat and how I knew they came from Dr. Ed. Like the man himself, Dr. Ed's lollipops have remained unchanged during the forty-five years he's been giving them out. They are no-frills suckers, simple, solid-colored candy disks wrapped in clear cellophane with white sticks bent into loops to make it easier for young children to hold.

Val went to see Dr. Ed, which means Dr. Ed might know where he is. Jolene insisted that I talk to Dr. Ed today and find out what he knows about Val's whereabouts. She also insisted that I let her deliver the photo. I said no. We compromised, and I agreed to let her do it if I went with her.

She accused me of being overprotective of her. I told her I was protecting Val.

I decide to go see Dr. Ed before going to work. I'm avoiding Jack. He was out yesterday afternoon and didn't see my black eye. He won't be pleased about it. It was okay for Ronny Hewitt and Andy Line-weaver to resolve their difficulties the old-fashioned way, using fists instead of lawyers, but it's never okay for one of his men to get sucker-punched.

This house has only one bathroom. Jolene gave up any claims of ownership to it a long time ago without much of a fight. She understood that she was simply outnumbered by the filthy-footed tribe of towel-dropping, urine-spattering, toothpaste-spitting men she had created, and quietly removed all her cosmetics to a vanity table in her bedroom and all her female necessities to a shelf in her closet, including her own tube of toothpaste, toothbrush, shampoo, soap, and a set of plush clean towels. She doesn't use her own bathroom; she visits it like a guest spending the night or a girl going to the communal showers in a dorm, bringing along the items she needs to get clean, then taking them away with her again.

I step over the damp towels heaped on the floor and the puddles of water, pull back the shower curtain hanging by half its rings, and step into the bottom of the tub stained a permanent gray from dirty feet. A cake of green soap with black fingerprints on it sits in a slimy soap dish. I use the Spider-Man shampoo.

The sink bowl is caked with formations of dried toothpaste like tiny pale blue stalagmites. A tall plastic cup with a smiling cow on it and Valley Dairy's promise for free soft-drink refills holds four toothbrushes with crushed, shaggy, petrified bristles. I find the one that belongs to me and brush my teeth.

The rest of the area around the sink is scattered with small plastic dinosaurs and pirates Eb takes in the tub with him, a couple crumpled Dixie cups, Josh's deodorant, a comb with half the teeth missing, and my razor. I can't find any shaving cream, so I use Mr. Bubble.

Next I head to Eb and Harrison's room for a clean shirt, underwear, socks, and jeans. I've been granted temporary usage of a dresser drawer and part of a closet in their room.

Harrison's side is picked up and orderly. Eb's side of the room is covered in junk. At first glance it appears he's just a run-of-the-mill slob, but upon closer inspection the random mess takes on meaning in the form of distinct piles of very specific objects: tabs from pop cans, receipts from stores, popsicle sticks, drinking straws, fortunes from fortune cookies, plastic spoons, colored toothpicks, regular toothpicks, hardened pieces of gum, beads, crayon tips, nails, screws, kernels from Indian corn, rocks, painted rocks, sticks, rubber bands, hundreds of little scraps of paper with writing on them, marbles.

The individual collections are either pushed into round piles or laid out in straight, measured lines.

I look down at the stuff and notice a couple photographs sitting in the middle of it. At first I'm not sure they're my dad's Magadan photos. The idea that one of the few precious remaining pieces of my dad's history could be carelessly left on the floor of a six-year-old boy's bedroom, where they could be trampled, fingered, wrinkled, or ripped, makes so little sense to me that I'm certain I must be mistaken.

I walk over and pick them up.

There are four of them. My dad received them in the mail before I was born from a fellow survivor who had gone back to see the Siberian work camp.

The first time I saw the photos, I couldn't figure out what they had to do with war. They weren't anything like the pictures in magazines and history books my dad had shown me about World War II. They didn't show soldiers or flags or clean, hopeful girls with shiny hair and red lipstick waiting in America for their husbands and boyfriends to come home.

One was an aerial shot of Magadan as it was then, almost fifteen years after the war, a grimy gray grid of a city set firmly into the gray rock that makes up the northern shoreline of the great gray Sea of Okhotsk.

The other three were taken at the site of the work camp. The first was a distant shot of the jail. A small, square building with iron bars on its single window. It was the only structure that had survived the passage of time and the brutality of the elements, and it jutted from the bare rock like a last remaining tooth stub in a dead man's gums.

The second photo was of a mountain of curled and cracked shoes and belts. When the workers died from starvation or radiation poisoning, the precious leather was saved to be used for other purposes while the bodies were buried behind the pile in endless rows marked by sticks with can lids nailed to them with the worker's number engraved on them.

The final photo was of this. Most of the markers were gone, but here and there were a few sticks, and one had a lid that had somehow managed to catch the weak daylight and reflected it back in a flash of startling silver.

I don't understand what the pictures are doing here. I feel momentarily betrayed by my mom. She's supposed to be the caretaker of Dad's artifacts. What is she doing giving them to Eb?

But my misgivings quickly pass. Why not? What good are they doing sitting in a drawer where no one will ever see them? I can't know what impact they're having on Eb—if the effect will be great or trivial, if he will learn something from them or learn to deny something in them—but whatever the lesson is, he's entitled to experience it as much as I was at his age.

I put them gently back on the floor next to a pile of unopened sugar packets from Eat'nPark, and I get dressed.

Dr. Ed still has his practice in the same small brown brick professional building he started out in. Very little has changed in his waiting room since I used to sit in it as a kid. He has the same pictures of clowns and frisking puppies on the walls and the same poster of a grinning cow explaining the benefits of milk, but now he also has a poster of a pierced, tattooed, green-headed Dennis Rodman explaining the benefits of HIV education.

The toys are different: padded, rounded, plastic, safe. Gone is the wooden pounding bench I used to beat the hell out of and the talking pull-string Raggedy Ann doll Jolene used to love, that I wanted to beat the hell out of by the time she finished playing with it.

One little boy pushes beads up and down twisted tracks of bright-colored wire, and two little girls are clustered around a big pink plastic dollhouse, but for the most part, kids sit and silently play their GameBoys or watch the big TV mounted in the corner. The room resonates with muted electronic beeps, occasional coughs, and the symphonic swells of a Disney soundtrack.

I present myself to Dr. Ed's thick-necked, flush-faced sister, who's been his receptionist for as long as I've been a patient.

She's holding a phone receiver between her cheek and shoulder while taking a clipboard from a mother. She hangs up the phone and tells the mother her HMO has a copayment of twenty dollars, then eyes the box of cigars I'm holding and the clock set inside the belly of a grinning red Buddha.

"Is he busy?" I ask her.

"No," she says before answering another call. "These kids are here for show. He doesn't really see any of them."

"I need to talk to him for a minute. I'll let myself in."

She wags a finger at me while she takes care of the caller, then gets up from her seat with the murderous, sluggish resentment of an elephant being poked and prodded into performing a headstand. She opens a door marked STAFF ONLY and beckons for me to walk through it. She always insists on opening the door herself. I think it's a form of territoriality.

"Room Four," she tells me, and points down a hallway wallpapered in the alphabet.

"Thanks," I say.

The cold, silver-topped exam table of my youth has gone the same way as the pounding bench. It's been replaced by a padded mint green table. I put the cigars and the clock on the floor beside it, lie down on it, stretch out my legs until my boots dangle off one edge, put my hands behind my head, and study the colorful map of Nursery Rhyme Land on the wall opposite me.

As a kid I used to want to live there, but as an adult I've noticed it's a miserable place filled with nothing but crime, poverty, and domestic violence.

There's Peter Peter trying to stuff his unwilling wife into a giant pumpkin shell, and Jack and Jill taking a vicious tumble down a hill. Bo Peep is sobbing in a field next to a clothesline where the royal maid is having her nose ripped off her face by a gigantic black crow. Old Mother Hubbard gazes piteously at her skeletal dog, while Tom Tom the Piper's Son has been reduced to stealing pigs. Little Miss Muffet fends off a gruesome spider, and three mice in dark glasses scurry away from a knife-wielding farmer's wife. Humpty-Dumpty is sunny side up.

In the middle of the map stands a tattered boot exploding with filthy, screaming children. A haggard old woman holding a wooden spoon chases a few of them.

The door opens, and Dr. Ed appears in his blue exam coat with a stethoscope draped around his neck and a couple strips of stickers peeking out of his breast pocket.

"I used to imagine that's how Reese and Jess Raynor lived," I say to him, staring directly at the shoe.

He glances at it on his way to the sink to wash his hands.

"The shoe is better insulated," he tells me.

He walks over holding a tongue depressor.

"How was the hospital auction?" I ask him.

"A big success," he replies. "Your balls were a big hit. Say ah."

I open my mouth and stick out my tongue. I try to ask him, "So what do you think about Reese coming back?" but all I hear come out of my mouth is, "Ah-ah-ahahahah-ah-ah-ah–ahahahaha-ah-ah."

He has no problem understanding me.

"I'm not exactly jumping up and down over it. I know he's going to stay with Jess and Bobbie for a while. I know that's only going to make a bad situation worse."

"Ah-ah-ah-ahahahaha-ah-ahahahaha-ah-ah?"

"I've been their pediatrician since the day Gary was born, and I never noticed any signs of abuse on any of them until Danny yesterday."

He removes the tongue depressor and walks over to the garbage can to throw it away.

"So you're sure it's abuse?"

"Let's just say I know he didn't do that running into a wall."

"Why would Bobbie protect Jess? I know I don't know them very well, but Bobbie doesn't strike me as the kind of woman who'd tolerate someone doing that to her kid."

He returns holding an otoscope. He gives my right ear an authoritative tug.

"A lot of women try to deny it and live with it," he says, peering inside my head. "They choose to defend the man."

"Out of love?"

"Hell, no. That's not love. That's cowardice. Those women don't have any damn courage."

"That's what I mean," I say. "That's not Bobbie. She's not a coward. Her family went through a lot when her dad was killed. She's a survivor. And she was always fun. Never down on anything. At least not in front of other people."

He moves on to my other ear.

"Jess lost his job. His unemployment ran out. He hasn't been able to find anything else steady. He's got four kids and a wife to feed. He's under a lot of stress. Financial and otherwise. Just because a guy loses his temper once isn't reason to write him off as a monster. Maybe that's what Bobbie's thinking. But regardless, I don't want to see it happening again."

I think about Jess last night and the way he reacted when I accused him of hitting Danny. I think about the two of them at the junkyard and how comfortable they seemed with each other. I'm not convinced that Dr. Ed is right, but at the same time I feel like we haven't been told the truth.

He steps around in front of me and puts his stethoscope in his ears.

"Unbutton your shirt," he tells me.

He puts the stethoscope against my chest.

"Take deep breaths," he tells me.

He leans forward, listening intently.

"Did Val Claypool come here yesterday?" I ask him.

He nods.

"What can you tell me about him?"

"He had his tonsils out when he was five, and he's allergic to cats."

He straightens up and slips the stethoscope out of his ears and back around his neck. He brings out a blood-pressure cuff from one of his pockets and straps it on my arm.

"Why did he come see you?"

"He had a tummyache."

"I'm serious."

"So am I."

"Any other reason?"

"He wanted to talk."

"He wouldn't talk to me. Did he tell you he saw me?"

"I think he mentioned that."

"What did he say?"

"He said he saw you."

"That's it?"

He gives the rubber ball a few squeezes and studies the gauge.

"What did you expect him to say? 'I saw Ivan Zoschenko. He's a fine-looking man. Do you think he'd sign a football for me?'"

"I just meant did you talk about me at all?"

"No."

"Not at all?"

"No."

"Did you talk about why he never came back?"

He rips the cuff off and walks over to the sink to wash his hands.

"How's your knee?" he asks me.

"Pretty bad," I reply.

"Val's staying in that abandoned house across the road from Bert Falls's place for a couple days. It's still in pretty good condition. It has a good roof. Why don't you go talk to him yourself?"

He comes walking back toward me, and his eyes light on the box of cigars and the Buddha sitting on the floor.

"Those are for you," I tell him. "The clock is from Zo. The cigars are from me."

He stoops to pick them up. When he does, I notice some brown age spots on the top of his scalp beneath his white crew cut. The idea that age could ever triumph over Dr. Ed has never occurred to me.

He must be close to seventy by now—maybe over seventy—but the years have not dulled him or slowed him down.

The sight of white hair and a few wrinkles never bothered me, but discovering age spots is like noticing the first rust scabs around the door handle of a reliable, beloved vehicle. They don't command respect or confidence. They can be covered up or ignored, but what they signify is inescapable. He's starting to corrode.

I don't want Dr. Ed to die. I want us to be able to hang out a lot longer.

He holds up the clock, turning it this way and that, then reads the quote from Confucius inscribed on the back.

"'The way of the superior man is threefold. Virtuous, he is free from anxieties; wise, he is free from perplexities; bold, he is free from fear.'"

He sets the clock down on the exam table along with the cigars. He opens the box.

"Don Sebastian," he murmurs as he takes one of the gold-wrapped cigars and runs it under his nose. "Bless you."

He pulls his prescription pad from another pocket. I'm glad to see it. I could use some more pills.

"One more thing," I remember to tell him, reluctantly. "I ran into Mike Muchmore last night. He wanted me to talk to you about apologizing to some family that wants to sue you because you gave one of their kids a DTP shot in their home. You had to bribe the dad with beer and chicken."

A slight smile crosses his lips, and he chuckles under his breath.

"Do you know who he's talking about?" I ask.

"Yeah. I'll take care of it."

"It might not be that easy. Muchmore is their lawyer."

"Good."

"What do you mean, good?"

"Didn't you say he asked you to ask me to apologize?"

"Yeah."

"So he wants to avoid litigation, right?"

"Right," I say warily.

"Do you know how much money he'd make in legal fees if they actually sued me? Or even began the process of suing me? He's trying to help me, not hurt me."

"I don't think he has any interest in helping you. You should've heard the things he said about you."

"I know what he thinks about me. He's told me to my face. He thinks I'm loud, vulgar white trash, but he knows I'm a good doctor. I think he's a self-righteous, conceited, obnoxious ass, but he's a good lawyer, and it's good to know a good lawyer.

"There are certain situations in life where you have to have one whether you want to or not to help make shit go away. They're like enemas."

He puts down his pen and rips the page off the pad with a veteran doctor's flourish, then folds it and hands it to me.

"Your blood pressure's high. Your color's bad. You have wax in your left ear, and somebody punched you in the face," he reports.

He gives me a pat on the shoulder.

"Now, if you'll excuse me," he says as he heads for the door, "I have much cuter patients to see."

I walk back through the office, grabbing a lollipop out of the basket on his sister's desk on my way past before she can slap my hand.

Back at my truck, I unfold the piece of paper and look down at Dr. Ed's scribbled prescription. It reads "Sober, he is free from making an ass of himself."

# THIRTEEN

THE RAYNOR BEAGLES ANNOUNCE MY ARRIVAL WITH A PITCH-perfect blending of their solemn voices. As one tapers off, the other begins its climb to a drawn-out tenor so solid with longing I imagine I could stick my hand into the air above their freckled muzzles and feel the notes twine around my fingers.

I park my truck on the road. Wet brown-and-green fields rough with winter stubble fall away in waves of hills. A few splotches of red-and-white cow lurch slowly across the top of a rise where one massive, sprawling, gnarled oak has been spared out of respect for its usefulness as a shade tree and its ornery appearance.

A long, leafless bank of level trees runs behind the house, the mesh of crooked black branches reminding me of the border of mourning lace on the handkerchief Zo gave my mother the day of the miners' funeral. She held it throughout the entire service but never used it. I knew she wouldn't. She considered it too pretty.

The yard has been picked up since I was here on Sunday. The pieces of wood are gone, but the tire tracks remain and the garage door still has a ragged, gaping hole in the middle of it. A clear plastic tarp is tacked over it. One side has already come loose, and the rest of the tarp expands and collapses in the cold breeze with a definite rhythm, like the house is breathing with the help of an oxygen tent.

I pause before the front door holding Jess's guns and listen. I don't hear any sounds coming from inside. Not even a TV. If Bobbie's home, I know she's standing on the other side of the door waiting for me to knock. Between the barking dogs and the sound of my truck, she has to know I'm here. She's trying to decide if *she's* here.

I was sincere when I told Jess at the junkyard that I wanted to help, but after last night at Brownie's, I've begun to doubt that I can help by talking to him. I've decided to try talking to Bobbie, which may be even worse than talking to Jess. The other day she wanted to rip my head off.

But I've got a half hour before I'm meeting Jolene at Bert Falls's place in hopes of finding Val. Jess and Bobbie's place is on the way. I don't need more of an excuse.

I knock.

Bobbie opens the door immediately and stands there in a tight black T-shirt and a pair of faded jeans cinched around the waist with a rolled-up bandanna, leaning in the doorway, her bare arms folded across her chest and one bare foot with bright blue toenails scratching the top of the other one.

She stares at me with the calmly vacant yet wholly alert gaze of a cat.

"What's that old saying?" she asks me. "'Beware of geeks bearing arms'?"

"I think it was originally 'Beware of Greeks bearing gifts,' but yours makes even more sense."

She takes the rifles from me, one in each hand, and props them up in the nearest corner. I don't return the handgun. She doesn't ask for it. Chances are she doesn't know it's missing.

"Why'd you take them in the first place?"

"Things were a little volatile out here."

"Volatile?" she says with a slow smile. "Did they teach you that word in deputy school?"

"No, I already knew it."

She pokes her fingers into her coppery hair and gives it a mussed look, like a little boy who just woke up.

"So what if it was volatile? You think we're the kind of people who go around shooting each other?"

"Jess was about to shoot someone."

"No he wasn't. He was going to shoot out our tires so I couldn't leave."

"Oh, right. I keep forgetting about Raynor hospitality: If you're not leaving with a smile on your face, you're not leaving."

She narrows her green gaze at me and fixes me again with feline scrutiny.

"Is this some kind of official visit? Because I've got nothing to say about what happened the other day. Everything's fine. Danny's fine. Jess is fine."

"Where is Danny?"

"With Jess. They're running an errand."

"How can you trust Jess alone with him?" I try to trip her up and get her to admit what really happened, but either she's too smart for it or she's been telling the truth all along.

"He's fine with Jess. Why wouldn't he be?"

She turns on one bare heel and starts to walk out of the room.

"If you're here as a blast from the past, you can come have a cup of coffee with me. If you're here as one of Jack Townsend's goons, you can close the door on your way out."

I think about the guys I work with: the two Chads, both of them young and relatively idealistic; one a clean-cut, good-looking, recruiting poster of a guy, still living at home with his mom; the other a perpetually baffled-looking, premature family man who reminds me of a dog who's just spent an hour chasing Frisbees each time he comes tromping into the station and flops into the chair behind his desk.

Stiffy is a solid, compact vault of composure and inner strength that's enabled him to endure a lifetime of abuse over his name to get to the point he's at now, where he's so proud of it he only goes by the one name. All day long, his phone is answered, "Stiffy here." And Doverspike—though large and loudmouthed—wins a ribbon at the fair almost every year with one of his prize white ducks. "Goons" is one of the last terms I'd apply to them as a group, but I'm not about to waste my breath arguing with Bobbie about this.

I follow her into the kitchen. It's a pleasure. She has a great butt.

As I watch her hips moving and her fingers start to play with her hair again, I feel jealous of Jess.

I'm jealous of his pretty wife, his devoted kids, his wallet, even his shitbox house. At least it's got a nice view of the valley.

Jess's words at the junkyard surface in my head, and the reality of how my life turned out clashes hard with the old assumption about how I thought my life would turn out, but I remind myself that even when I still had a wide-open future, I never wanted any of this. I don't want it now either, although I'm the first to admit I don't know what I *do* want.

How can I envy something I don't want? How can I admire a situation I pity?

The contrast of conflicting emotions is familiar. It reminds me of how I felt as a kid about the way people went on with their lives after the explosion.

Most people, men and women, just kept going. On the surface, at least, they appeared to treat the deaths of all those men as just one more big pothole in their road of life. They didn't stop and protest or get angry about it. They didn't try to get it filled in or put a warning sign near it for others. They walked around it and kept going forward.

I thought they were wrong to feel and act that way. I saw their lack of rage and their failure to cast blame and seek some kind of revenge against some kind of enemy, real or imaginary, as weakness and apathy, yet at the same time I knew that their steadiness and refusal to feel sorry for anybody—least of all themselves—made them braver and more virtuous than I could ever hope to be.

Bobbie was one of them. Her family really struggled financially. She worked in the kitchen at the high-school cafeteria, and she did it without shame or resentment. She always had an after-school job, and the money she earned was used to buy groceries and winter coats for her little brothers, not records or lip glosses for herself, or nights out at the movies.

I can't know what went on inside her, but outside she seemed unaffected. She was never sad or angry. She did well at school. She worked without complaining, and she pursued fun and pleasure without guilt.

Her kitchen is spotless. A small wooden table, immaculately painted in a glossy white, sits in the precise middle of glowing dark green floor tiles. The backs of the chairs match the floor. The countertops match the floor, too, and the cabinets are white with polished-gold door handles.

I marvel now as I did on Sunday at how clean and picked up she manages to keep a house with four kids and Jess in it.

She probably cleans constantly. I'm sure her mother set the example. I'm sure she was like my mother and Zo and most of the other women I knew growing up. They always worked too hard and were always tired, but they never questioned this way of living, because they never knew of any other way to live. Everybody worked all the time, because there was always more work to do.

Bobbie has this ingrained in her. Jess does, too. Unfortunately, there's not enough work for either of them to do around here anymore, and they weren't raised to understand the concepts of wasting time or leisure time.

"Did Jess do that to your face?" she asks me as she reaches inside a cupboard for a coffee mug.

"Why do you ask?"

"He came home with a fat lip last night. He wouldn't tell me what happened."

"Then I guess I won't either."

She brings me a mug of coffee and a sugar bowl. Then she comes back a second time with her own mug and a bottle of whiskey. She holds it over my cup. Her hazel eyes have lost their cat-green intensity. They're a soft gray in the unlit kitchen, except for a glint of mild malice in them.

"You want me to Irish that up for you?"

The words are in the form of a question, but it's delivered as a challenge.

"My dad never drank straight coffee," she explains.

I watch the bottle wavering over my cup. I see the first brown drops gathering at the mouth. My own mouth grows dry, and my throat tightens. My pulse quickens.

My hand springs forward without my conscious knowledge or permission and flattens itself over the top of my cup. A splash of whiskey hits the back of my hand. Bobbie pulls back the bottle, apologizing, while I wipe off the booze on my jeans, all the while fighting an intense urge to lick it off instead.

"No, thank you," I say shakily.

She knows I wanted to say, "Yes, please." She puts the lid on the bottle but doesn't put the bottle away. She leaves it sitting on the table as a sign that we are not completely friendly.

"So Reese gets released today," I say to her.

She takes a seat across from me and sips at her coffee. "He called Jess this morning at the crack of dawn. Woke us up. He told Jess he'll be getting here later today."

"Today?"

"Yeah, I was surprised, too. I assumed he'd have some urgent things to take care of before he headed down this way, like getting drunk and getting laid. I figured he'd try and get laid somewhere where he's anonymous. I'd like to think it would be impossible for him to do it around here, but I suppose we have our skanks just like everywhere else."

She fixes me briefly with a gaze of sincere remorse.

"I don't mean that disrespectfully to Crystal. I admit I never understood what she saw in Reese and what could have possessed her to want to marry him and have his child, but he wasn't a complete monster back then. He had some good points. He was still salvageable, and maybe that's what she saw in him. Nobody knew what was coming. Nobody knew he was capable of that. Now we all know, and any woman who'd screw him now, knowing what we know, would have to be as disgusting as he is."

"So I take it you're looking forward to his visit."

She smiles at me. "Jess can't turn him away. Blood is thicker than water, you know."

"And stronger than common sense."

"That, too. Plus, they're twins. They've got that weird intrauterine bond between them. Who knows what went on in there? Did you know identical twins come from the same egg? Two sperms. One egg. If you stop and think about it, it's really kind of creepy. They really are one person split in half."

"Or maybe not. Two sperm, two people."

"No." She shakes her head. "Two eggs, two people. Two sperm in one egg is like one of those horse costumes with one guy being the head and the other guy being the rear end."

"Which one is Jess? The head or the ass?"

She smiles again. "You sure are asking a lot of questions about Reese. Jess said you asked him a bunch, and his sister Bethany said you asked her, too. Any particular reason?"

I don't answer her right away, and then something catches her interest out of the corner of her eye before I come up with an excuse. She gets up from her chair suddenly and darts toward the back door, where she picks up an old football covered in dried mud and scowls at it.

"What's this doing inside?" she angrily asks the absent offender.

She looks over at me, and the earlier spark of ill intent I saw in her eyes becomes a blaze.

"Think fast," she calls out and throws a pass at me.

I catch it but fumble it afterward. It hits the table and jars the cups. Some coffee spills out.

The soles of my feet burn, and my head instantly fills with the muted roar of the crowd, like the surf outside a seaside cave, as the name of our team is announced while we stand in the alleyway beneath the bleachers outside the locker room door. Deets's bald head gives off an eerie phosphorescence in the dark, like the poisoned mushrooms that grew in the woods behind my house.

"What's with you?" Bobbie laughs. "So much for the great Ivan Z."

"I never play anymore," I say, trying to defend myself. "I haven't touched a football since I broke my leg except to sign them."

"Never? Not once? You've never even tossed a couple passes to Jolene's boys?"

I shake my head.

"Why not?"

"I don't know."

She walks over and takes the ball from me.

"I don't get it. How could you just shut it off like that? Jess plays with all the kids. Our oldest girl's actually the best in the lot. You should see her catch a football. Her form reminds me a lot of Jess in high school. 'Sticky Fingers,' he calls her."

She walks to the back door, opens it, and tosses the ball outside, then bends over to rearrange some muddy rain boots lined up on a mat outside the door. I feel the beginnings of a hard-on while I stare at her ass in the tight jeans.

I briefly entertain the idea of walking over there and making a play for her. I even allow myself to carry it to the point where I imagine her responding the way she did more than twenty years ago in the backseat of her grandmother's Buick.

What if she did? I ask myself. Do I really want her because I want her, or is it because I want her to want me, or because I want to try to redeem myself after the "rumors are greatly exaggerated" comment, or because I want what Jess has, or because I can't have what I really want—which is Chastity—or just because I have a cold, lonely penis attached to my lower body?

My hard-on dies before it has a chance to live. The heat of desire becomes a chill of doubt that sprays through me, congeals in my crotch, and solidifies there like a protective cup.

She stands back up again, closes the door, and walks back to the table.

"All the time and energy you used to put into football," she says as she sits down again, "where have you been putting it all these years? Into drinking, I guess."

"What's that supposed to mean?"

"Everyone knows you're a drunk."

Her comment is unexpectedly harsh. At this point my dick has curled up and is set in solidified self-pity like a bug trapped in amber.

"So's Jess," I tell her.

"He's not a drunk. He drinks. There's a difference."

"You're an expert on this?"

"My dad was one of five Irish brothers. I have three of my own. What do you think?"

"And they're all drunks."

"I have two uncles who are drunks, and one brother. The rest are hard drinkers. That's what my dad was, too."

"And the difference is . . . ?"

"A hard drinker is a man who drinks to help him cope. A drunk is a man who drinks because he can't cope."

"What is it I can't cope with?"

She gives me the same sly smile she did before, the one where we're sharing a sinister secret that I don't want to share.

"I love Jess," she tells me. "He's my one and only. But we're different. You and me, we're the same. Our dads were far from the blast. That means they were crushed to death or they suffocated. Do you ever think about that? How they died?"

I take a quick swallow of coffee.

"No," I reply.

"Do you ever blame your dad for dying?"

"No. Do you?"

"Sometimes."

She stops smiling, but she continues watching me intently and suspiciously, like she's afraid I'm going to blurt out something I'm not supposed to.

"You know Jess could've gone to college and played ball just like you did. He could've got a degree and had a career somewhere instead of just a job. But he had his priorities straight. He stayed here where he belonged. He was a real man."

"That's your definition of a real man?" I ask her. "Someone who lives and dies within two miles of the place he was born, even if it means being unemployed and having to suffer and struggle every day of his life just to survive?"

"Pretty much."

She puts her elbows on either side of her cup and makes a bridge with her hands, where she rests her chin while she studies me with pretty eyes full of an ugly intent to harm.

"You did what you wanted to do, not what you should have done. You know your dad would've never let you do something like that. He would've been real disappointed in you."

A chill much stronger than the one in my crotch spreads throughout my entire body. She can't know about Crystal.

"Do something like what?" I whisper.

She smiles magnificently. She knows she got to me. I don't know where her hostility toward me is coming from. It may be as simple as seeing me as a threat to her family. I could expose their dirty secret.

Two can play at this game. I can get to her, too.

"We all know Danny didn't smash into a wall," I tell her. "Jess told me what happened. At the bar last night. He was drunk. Drunks tell things they're not supposed to. That's why we got in the fight."

Panic and suspicion flash across her face.

"What did he tell you?"

"The truth."

She thinks about it, and her calm returns. She shakes her head confidently.

"He didn't tell you anything."

"Why are you protecting him?"

"Protecting him?" she asks. "What do you mean? What did he tell you?"

"He told me he hit Danny."

It takes a moment for my words to sink in. Her face becomes an absolute blank. She grows pale before my eyes.

She stares straight ahead so intensely I think she might be in a trance. Then, all at once, she falls apart. Tears begin rolling down her cheeks, and her shoulders shake with sobs. She covers her face with her hands.

"That's the kind of guy he is," she says from behind her closed fingers.

At first I think I didn't hear her right.

"What kind of guy?" I ask her. "The kind who beats his kids?"

She drops her hands and shakes her head.

"No. You don't understand. He's so good to me, and I've been awful to him."

"You're right. I don't understand. I don't understand anything you're saying."

"Some days I feel like I can't take it anymore. I just can't take it. And now Reese is coming."

She stops talking suddenly. I can tell by the look on her face that she thinks she's said too much.

"Of course you can't take it," I try to console her. "You've got four kids, and your husband's out of work. Things are really hard, but that doesn't give Jess an excuse to do this. Nobody wants to get him into trouble. He isn't a bad guy."

"You don't know anything about Jess!" she screams at me, the same rage returning that she showed on Sunday when Dr. Ed accused Jess. "Don't you talk about Jess!"

"Did he hit Danny?"

She thinks about it. I can see the terrible struggle going on in her thoughts and her heart. It shows on her face. Anger, fear, sorrow— even love fights for a place.

She stands up and takes her coffee cup to the sink.

"If he says he hit Danny"—she chokes on a sob, with her back toward me—"then I guess that's what happened."

When she turns around again, she's regained her composure admirably.

"It's still none of your business," she tells me. "I hope you understand that. I really mean it. Now I want you to go, and I don't want you to come back."

She walks out of the room. I leave by the back door. A calm, delicate rain has begun to fall. It feels like stepping into a cool, wet breath. From here I can see points of bright green on the bare branches that looked dead and black from the road.

Next to the row of dirty boots are two dirty Ball jars with jagged holes poked in the lids with a screwdriver.

I pick them up to see if their prisoners are still in residence. They're empty. I put them back where I found them.

Steve and I used to spend hours of our summer vacation standing in the cold, murky water in the creek behind my house, overturning rocks, searching for crayfish and filling jars with them. They were especially exciting and meaningful prey, because they had claws and could hurt you if you weren't smart and careful.

Some days we let them go. Other days we forgot and left them in the sun and accidentally boiled them. Still other days we set them loose on the packed dirt around the doghouse in Steve's backyard and watched his Lab mutt strain at the end of his chain while the crayfish skittered witlessly from snapping jaws to our prodding sticks until they succumbed to dust and exhaustion.

We were always really impressed with the size of the mud-brown piles of claws and antennae we were able to capture. We used to love to give the jars a couple violent shakes and watch, grinning, as the crayfish responded to our cruelty by trying to rip each other apart.

# FOURTEEN

NINETY-SEVEN MEN DIED IN GERTIE. THE REMAINS OF SIXTY-four were recovered and laid out in rows on the floor of the Coal Run Elementary School multipurpose room on plain white bed sheets donated by the housewares department of Woolworth's. The others are still buried deep inside the collapsed tunnels along with my dad.

The rescue crews worked for two weeks before giving up. It was a painstaking, time-consuming process. The miners had been swallowed by the mountain when it collapsed in on itself, and the only way to free them was to manually mine them out with picks and shovels the same way their forefathers used to mine the coal.

The workers weren't looking for survivors by the end of their search. They were looking for something to be dug from the earth to be given to a loved one to put in a box and bury again: a hand with an engraved wedding ring, a foot still in its steel-toed safety shoe, a piece of torn shirt with a piece of torn skin permanently fused to it by a glue of baked black blood, an unharmed hard hat with its lamp still glowing and tufts of hair in grayish pink spatters of flesh stuck to the inside of it.

I never saw any of these things. I only heard about them, but I knew that the stories were true. It was why there were so many small coffins at the funeral, a size usually reserved for babies, Val reluctantly explained to me when I asked.

Val helped dig for the entire two weeks. He was one of the first men in and one of the last to give up. He probably would've continued to dig in that same spot forever like a determined dog with a misplaced bone if J&P hadn't called off the search. He also needed to get back to work. He had already lost two weeks' pay.

I was never allowed back to the site after the day of the explosion. I only saw Val one more time that day, hours after we'd first seen him. I found him sitting on the ground gulping oxygen from a mask attached to one of the tanks donated by the Centresburg hospital and staring at a dozen dogs that had strangely gathered in a group far away from the people and silently lay in the dirt, watching, with their muzzles on their paws.

I ran over to him and told him about how my mom had dislocated my shoulder but we found Dr. Ed and he fixed it and gave me a shot of something that made it kind of numb and a bunch of lollipops. I offered him one. He took the red one and put it in his pocket.

Then I asked him if he knew anything I didn't, and he asked me what I knew. I told him I knew an explosion had caused the mine to cave in. I knew a lot of the dads were dead. I knew my dad was one of the men on the list posted on the office door who was working Left 12, but until my mom said so, he wasn't dead. I knew his number was 342. I knew that the official name of Gertie was J&P Coal Company Mine No. 9. I knew Stan Jack named all his mines after women. I knew that Gertrude was his mother.

He said I was a smart kid. He said he didn't know more than that.

After that first day, he was gone every morning by the time I woke up. He came home every night at dusk, the black mine dirt covering him like shoe polish, too tired and filthy to do anything but fall into a heap in the middle of his backyard, where he'd lie so still I was always certain he was dead.

I'd walk over to him and call his name. I'd nudge his leg with my toe. I'd offer to get him a beer.

Maxine would come out and beg him to get up, beg him to take a shower, beg him to eat dinner, beg him to go to bed. She'd promise him things she couldn't deliver. She'd make threats that didn't scare him. She'd start to cry. Then she'd finish by shaking him awake and screaming at him that he was going to catch his death of a cold if he kept lying on the ground.

Then he would push her away, growling something about dying from a cold's being a fine fucking way to die, and fall back asleep.

The only person who could rouse him was my mom.

Once Maxine had gone back in her house sniffling about the futility of a mother's love, my mom would cross our backyards pulling her old nubby biscuit-colored sweater closed around her and hugging herself against the cold night air.

She'd kneel down next to him and lightly touch his arm, and his eyelids would fly open.

"Why don't you go inside, Val?" she'd ask in her quietly assertive voice. "Get cleaned up. Have a hot meal. Get some sleep."

He'd elbow his way up to a sitting position. The eyes behind the grimy black mask would look at her like she was a creature he'd never seen before—something mythical like a unicorn or a wood nymph—and he wasn't sure if he should be terrified or enchanted.

She'd watch him with her new haunted, blasted stare that was impossible to turn away from but equally impossible to hold.

When I found myself trapped by her new gaze, I felt a strange, sweet pain, like when I finally scratched a maddening bug bite until it bled, reveling in the relief it gave me but knowing I was going to be tormented by a burn afterward. I needed her more than ever now, but it killed me to look at her.

Her eyes were the only things about her that had changed. Her voice was the same. She still kept up her physical appearance. She still did her work. She did more than her usual work. She helped the women who couldn't cope. Our house was filled with kids.

A stranger wouldn't be able to tell there was anything wrong with her, except for her eyes. They were her *nakolki*. They made me feel the same way I did when I used to trace the outline of Dad's Stalin tattoo: a respect and admiration for what he had survived, but also the sadness of isolation, knowing he had been through something I could never understand that made him somehow better and stronger than I was.

"Okay," Val would say to her. "I'll do that."

From the day of the explosion to the day he left for Vietnam, I only remember one time when he spoke about my mother without his feelings' being in the form of a question about a chore he could do for her.

It was the day before the miners' funeral. He had come home earlier than usual. There were still a couple hours of daylight left.

I was sitting on the bottom step of our back stoop looking at my *Wonders of Nature* book. The stoop was made of concrete, and my mom was always warning me this time of year not to sit on it or I'd catch the same death of a cold that Maxine was always warning Val about.

I could never quite figure out why the cold you caught from sitting on something cold could kill you but a regular cold could be easily vanquished with St. Joseph Chewable Aspirin for children and Vicks VapoRub. Whatever the reason, it was a fear all mothers seemed to harbor, and I usually respected it, but that day Mom had forgotten to warn me.

Val saw me sitting there and motioned me over. I was surprised and happy to see him home early and not sprawled out on the ground asleep. I put my book down and ran over to him. Being around Val made me feel like I was part of the men. Before the explosion I didn't mind being part of the women and children, but now it felt like a betrayal.

He started stripping off his filthy work clothes. During his regular shifts, he always cleaned up at the bathhouse, but these past couple days working on the rescue crew, he came home dirty.

He didn't stop until he was wearing only his underwear. Sitting on the edge of his back porch was a scrub brush and a hard blue-gray chunk that looked and felt like granite but was actually soap. He grabbed both and turned on the water spout on the side of his house where the hose was attached in summer and stuck his head beneath the freezing-cold water.

He made a noise like a dog that's been kicked, then set about vigorously scrubbing his head, face, hands, and arms with the rock-hard soap and wire brush.

When he finished and he was glowing a raw red, he shook his head hard and walked to the back door, dripping and covered in goose bumps. I could see a towel hanging inside on a coat hook. He grabbed it and went inside, returning a few minutes later dressed in jeans, a clean flannel shirt, a Penzoil ball cap, and his dress pair of boots, usually reserved for social occasions, a soft yellow suede with bright red laces.

"You want to go for a ride?" he asked me.

"Sure," I replied instantly.

"Go ask your mom."

He was already sitting in his truck when I came running back. We drove in silence. I didn't mind it, except for one point where I had a sudden intense longing to hear him belch the alphabet, but I let it pass without mentioning it to him.

We parked on the side of a road with nothing around us, for apparently no good reason. He got out and started scaling the hill, and I followed him into the woods. We walked along for a while, until we came to a spot with a good view of my school.

Today was the day they were removing the bodies to get them ready for tomorrow's funeral.

The remains of sixty-four men meant sixty-four coffins. Sixty-four coffins meant sixty-four burial plots, sixty-four headstones, sixty-four hearses, sixty-four preachers delivering sixty-four eulogies.

Coal Run didn't have a funeral home. The nearest one was in Centresburg. We didn't have a big empty cemetery waiting to be filled all at once. People buried their dead sporadically in church graveyards. We didn't have a morgue where we could store the bodies while we figured out how to bury them. The school needed the multipurpose room back for gym class and lunch period.

The widows couldn't afford expensive coffins and plots in pricey private cemeteries, although a few did drain their savings accounts or used a chunk of precious insurance money to buy a fancy casket.

Taking into consideration all these factors, everyone agreed that the miners should be laid to rest all at once. It only made sense that these men who worked and played and lived and drank together should be buried at the same time, in the shadow of the same hillside, with the same words said over them.

A local lumber company donated enough wood for sixty-four coffins. Every man with carpentry skills donated his time. Mike Muchmore's dad donated ten acres of land he owned between Coal Run and Centresburg to be used as a cemetery for the miners and eventually their families. Packard Mining Equipment donated their flatbed trucks to transport the coffins.

J&P wouldn't provide any of their own trucks. It had something to do with insurance reasons. They posted a memo on the Gertie office door explaining their decision. It hung between the memo telling the families of the dead miners that they could keep their numbered work tags and the one reminding everyone that J&P was no longer obligated to provide money for burial costs, since the union had voted against the mandatory burial fund.

Val and I stared down at the coffins stretched out in a seemingly endless line running the length of the school parking lot and far enough down the road that we lost sight of them. Each man's last name was painted on top. Fathers and sons were given first initials, too. I tried to find my grandfather and Uncle Kenny, but I couldn't. They had both been identified. Uncle Kenny was in one of the baby coffins.

I looked up at Val. I couldn't read his expression. He was staring in the fierce, vacant way a man stares at something he can't believe he's seeing.

"You ever been to Ocean City?" he asked me out of the blue.

I shook my head. "My dad always said he was going to take us to the ocean someday. He said everybody should see it. He came across it on a boat once."

"They have this thing called a boardwalk," he went on. "It's for people to walk on along the beach. It's up high on stilts so you got a good view of the ocean on one side, and the other side has restaurants and games and souvenir shops and all the hotels behind it lit up at night."

He pointed at the line of wooden boxes stretched out below us. A dog was sniffing around them.

"It looks like that."

He quickly found a rock and let loose with a rocket throw. He had a great arm and perfect aim. He hit the dog square in its side. It twisted its body around and gave a high-pitched yelp before loping off.

From above me I heard him say, "I'm glad we didn't find your dad. I'm glad she didn't have to see him."

I looked up and saw his eyes gleaming. I had never seen Val cry. It didn't even occur to me that his eyes could be wet with tears. It seemed more like they had been varnished with something that could seal in his sorrow.

"Is my mom always going to be sad?" I asked him.

He picked up another rock.

"She'll stop being sad someday. But I don't think she'll ever be able to be happy again."

This time he threw the rock purely for distance. I watched it disappear across the road, behind the school, and beyond the boardwalk of coffins. I wondered if there was some bug over there, minding his own business, who had just been crushed beneath it.

The hills bordering Union Road have been strip-mined for as long as I've been alive. There's a section farther north where they're still mining and a section farther south where the replacement saplings have finally begun sprouting sporadically on the bare hillsides like a crew cut.

Here they stopped working about three years ago. The land hasn't been backfilled yet. In some spots the terrain is as barren and lifeless as photos sent home from the Mars probe, but without the red haze.

No one inhabits this stretch of road except for Bert Falls and his lawn-mower graveyard.

His half acre of land is blanketed with mowers of all colors in various stages of rust and mobility. Push, tractor, self-propelled. They are parked in packed lines and from a distance provide a festive splash of color against the bleak landscape. Up close they're alive with snakes and rats.

Bert's not licensed to run a repair shop. To my knowledge no one has ever seen him work on a mower. But whenever someone wants to get rid of one, they bring it here, knowing it will get a good home. If he's around and awake and feeling ambitious, he'll come outside of his small, mint green shoe box of a house to greet the donor and gesture with a glowing cigarette where to park it.

Across the road from Bert's place is an abandoned house that used to belong to one of the Gertie miners and his family. I don't know his widow's specific story, but I imagine she was one who couldn't find a job or a new husband and couldn't make ends meet on her own, so she took her kids and left. It happened to a lot of people. I could never understand why the bank didn't just let them keep the houses. No one new was going to move here and buy them. They were just going to sit here empty as reminders to those who got to stay that some were forced to leave, and that's what happened.

I can tell that this house was no prize to begin with, or maybe it was until the death of the husband and then it went from being a happy home to a constant reminder of grief and a source of fear.

An elm tree, stricken in its youth, leans against the front of the house, dead but not down. Its bark has fallen away in patches, and the wood underneath is the greasy black color of the mummified faces I saw in the ancient-Egyptian exhibit at Chicago's Field Museum when I went there on a tour the day after signing my contract with the Bears.

Except for the tree sagging into the sagging roof, the yard is empty. No shrubs. No weeds. No wild carpet of briars and underbrush. Grass barely grows. For some reason nature has decided not to reclaim this place.

Val's truck is parked next to the house on a section of yard that used to be a driveway. I park on the road behind Jolene's car.

She's sitting inside it with her head bobbing in time to some music she's playing on the radio.

After our talk at her house this morning, I'm not sure how she's going to treat me. She was civil to me on the phone when I called to tell her I'd found Val, but civil from Jolene is a bad sign. It's like getting a piece of cake without frosting.

She gets out of the car.

"For Christ's sake," I say.

"What's wrong?"

"Could you be any more transparent?"

"You have a problem with this dress?"

She's wearing one of her most attractive dresses: a short, low-cut, fuzzy, pale pink sweater dress. Eb calls it her cotton-candy dress. Harrison calls it her man-candy dress.

"Where's your uniform? You told me on the phone you weren't able to get much of a break. How were you able to go home and change?"

"I drove home with my uniform unzipped. I had it off before I reached the staircase. I pulled this dress over my head as I was running back downstairs. Then I had to run back up and grab my shoes out of the closet, but that only took a second, since I keep these ones up front. I don't wear them too often, since they're pink and they don't go with much, but I love them, so I keep them up front where I can look at them when I want to."

She looks down at her shoes, turning her feet this way and that.

"How long have you been sitting here?"

"Five minutes."

"He hasn't come out?"

"He's probably sleeping."

"Or maybe he's spying on you with a compact."

Our eyes meet, and I search hers to see if she's still mad at me. I'm not assuming she didn't mean what she said in her kitchen—I just want to know that there are no hard feelings between us.

"Very funny," she says, and starts toward the house.

She doesn't hate me.

As we walk across the yard, I realize it's not bare at all. My boots crunch over scraps of wood, rusted tool parts, bits of trash, and beer cans crushed flat that have become fossilized into the dirt. Val's not the first person to have bunked down here for a night or two.

The front-porch steps are newer than the rest of the house but not as well made. Someone has built them recently. They're poorly constructed of wood that was probably already rotting when it was nailed together. The bottom step is split down the middle. The second is stained on one side with a red crust of animal guts.

Despite the outward appearance, there's a calm lingering here. Unlike well-tended, valued homes that reject decay, this place has slipped easily and gratefully into collapse, like the very old greet the realization of painless death in their sleep.

Before we can knock, the front door opens with a yank and a musty groan. Val's suddenly there, not six inches from me, behind a brittle black screen, in a pair of torn jeans and no shirt. He's not wearing the hat. He has his hair pulled back in a ponytail. He looks better in the hat; it muffles his stare.

He's in his bare feet. I take a second look and realize he's in his bare foot. The other jean leg is tied in a knot above where his knee should have been. He's holding a rifle in one hand, with the stock on the floor, using it as a crutch.

He looks Jolene up and down, then looks at the brown paper bag she's holding that has the photo from Zo in it and one of the boxes of cigars I took from Marcella's.

"I don't get Meals on Wheels anymore," he says.

"We're not with Meals on Wheels," Jolene tells him.

"Then maybe this is a new way to help the homebound? Feels on Wheels?"

"If that's a reference to my appearance," she says, smiling, "I'll take it as a compliment."

"You take it as a compliment that a guy would want to cop a feel from you?"

"Why not?"

His eyes rest briefly on her face, then flick past her at the shifting shadows of lawn-mower vermin across the road.

"Do I get an extra feel since I'm a decorated war hero?" he asks, scratching his chest.

Jolene watches his fingers rake back and forth beneath the dark hair.

"What were you decorated for?" she asks.

"Christmas. The guys put tinsel in my hair and used me for a tree."

"I suppose it was hard to find an evergreen in Vietnam," I jump in, trying to become part of the conversation.

I regret the comment instantly, even though I'm not sure what was wrong with it. He's still physically standing in front of me, but the person I was talking to vanishes. He doesn't turn hostile. He doesn't even seem outwardly upset. He just disappears behind the same untouchable, dark calm I witnessed at the funeral home.

"You want to know about 'Nam, go rent *Platoon*. I don't have time for that shit."

"I wasn't asking about 'Nam. I don't care about 'Nam."

I regret this comment instantly, too. I do care about 'Nam. I care a great deal about 'Nam, for purely selfish reasons. The war there took him away from me, and it's always been easier for me to blame the war than to blame him for the fact that even after it was over, he never came back. He never wrote either. He promised he would write, but he didn't.

He wrote to his mom. I saw those letters. They were always brief, and the words didn't seem to come from him. I imagined the army handing out form letters for each soldier to copy in his own hand and sign his name to. He talked about how the war was coming right along, as if it were a worthwhile project requiring a lot of time and a lot of men, like the building of a bridge. He talked about the weather being hot, the food being terrible, the guys in his platoon being okay, the rain coming suddenly in thick sticky downpours like a gush of gray milk, the Vietnamese people being nice, the terrain being jungles and rice paddies and slick red mud, all of it hard to maneuver in. He never wrote about the fighting. He never wrote about death. He never wrote about an enemy.

He always ended by saying he missed everybody, but he never specified anyone in particular. He never asked about me.

"I don't mean I don't care about it. I don't mean it's not important. I just mean you don't have to talk about it." I fumble miserably with my words, all of them seeming to be the wrong ones. "That's not why we're here."

"This is for you," Jolene interrupts, trying to save me.

She holds up the bag.

"Well, well," he says.

He pushes open the screen door with his free hand and grips his gun more firmly.

"This must be pretty damn special to warrant a police escort and one of Centresburg's finest and most beloved waitresses taking time away from her coffeepot to get all dressed up and drive the whole way out here to deliver it to me."

He looks directly at Jolene.

"Course we both know the real reason you did that."

She moves a step closer to him.

"Why is that?"

"Because I'm the first man you've ever had more than a three-word conversation with who didn't try and get into your lacy pink panties."

"That has nothing to do with it."

"It has everything to do with it. You didn't come out here to be nice to me. It isn't in your fuzzy pink biogenetic makeup to give a rat's ass about some one-legged freak show. It's all about those lacy pink panties. Proving to yourself how goddamned precious they are."

"Stop saying that. You don't know anything about my panties."

"I know they're pink and lacy."

"How do you know that?"

I realize at some point I'm supposed to jump in and defend my sister's honor, but she's always done a much better job of it than I have.

Val has something close to a smirk on his face. For the first time since I've seen him again, there seems to be an emotion forming in his eyes. I'm not sure what the emotion is, but the blankness is breaking up.

"I am not a stereotype," she states.

"You're a stereotype of a stereotype. You're a surroundsoundtype."

"I've had enough of this. Here I was, trying to be nice."

"No, your brother here is trying to be nice. You're trying to get me interested in your lacy pink panties."

"Stop it. Okay. I've had enough of the panties."

"Lacy and pink."

"They are not."

"Prove it."

"That's it. Here, Ivan."

She hands me the bag.

"I don't have time for this. I've got to get back to work."

She starts to leave, then turns back.

"I almost forgot. Would you like to have dinner at my house Thursday night?" she asks Val. "Our mom is coming, too."

"Sure," he says.

She turns again and makes it the whole way down the steps this time before deciding she's not done yet. She comes charging back up and gets so close to Val I think she's going to lick him.

"If you had any class at all or knew anything about women, you'd know it was a compliment to you that I put on this dress. A compliment. Not an insult. Not a way to make fun of you. And definitely not some stupid game, some stupid competition over who can get who to want the other person first. Everything with men is a competition. It's so boring."

"Lacy and pink," he responds.

This time I see authentic frustration on Jolene's face. I even see her fists begin to clench.

She turns around suddenly, and I'm certain she's not coming back, but she stops halfway across the yard and starts hopping around as she takes off one shoe, then the other. Next she yanks off her pantyhose like she's pulling brown taffy off the ends of her feet. She balls them up, turns around, and throws them in the direction of the road, then reaches up under her dress and pulls off her panties.

She marches across the yard, back up the steps, and throws them at Val. They hit him in the face and fall to his feet. He doesn't flinch. They're lacy and pink, of course.

He waits until she storms off again, then holds on to the doorjamb and uses his rifle to spear the panties. He flips the gun upright, like the color guard in a parade, and the panties slide down the barrel until they're resting against his hand holding the trigger.

"I have some shit to do," he says to me while watching Jolene stomp across the yard in her bare feet, with her pink shoes swinging at her side. "If you want to come in while I'm doing it, you're welcome to."

He swings around with a hop and disappears into the shadows. I wait until Jolene pulls out, and I follow him.

He has a fire going in a hole in the wall that used to be a small fireplace. It's a nice blaze, and I head straight for it.

The room has a card table and one chair in it, and a couch taped in several spots with duct tape. A red-and-white cooler and a blue Wal-Mart bag full of empty baked beans and Chef Boyardee cans sits against one wall. A small pyramid of empty beer cans is stacked neatly in one corner. Old newspapers, crumpled cigarette packs, dirty rags, bits of straw, sticks, string, feathers, and other nesting materials have been swept against the other wall, leaving the main section of floor clean.

He puts Jolene's panties and the paper bag on the card table.

I feel like I should say something about Jolene but decide I can't possibly explain her better than she's just explained herself. I know Val isn't going to explain anything about either one of them.

I must be smiling, because he asks, "You find this kind of lifestyle amusing?"

"It reminds me of my old place in Florida."

"Florida?" he says. "When'd you live in Florida?"

"I just came back here eight months ago. I lived there for almost sixteen years."

He hops over to the cooler using his rifle for balance.

"Why?" he asks, pulling open the lid and reaching inside.

"I don't know. It's warm there."

"It's a fucking sauna there. You like that kind of heat?"

"Not really."

He tosses a beer my way. It's still morning, and for all he knows I'm on duty, but I don't ask what would make him think I'd want a beer right now. I pop open the can.

"At the time I wanted to get far away from here and go somewhere completely different and someplace that would be easy to live in," I explain further. "No weather problems. Easy access to alcohol. No more state stores and beer distributors that close at nine. Lots of good-looking girls in bikinis."

"You bag a lot of good-looking girls in bikinis?"

"Some."

"Did it make up for the fact that you were living in fucking Florida?"

I laugh. "I guess you don't like Florida."

"Never been there."

I take a seat on the edge of the couch. He sits at the card table where there's a pack of cigarettes and a lighter. I try not to look at his missing leg.

He opens a beer for himself and drinks, staring out the screen door at the mowers and the place where Jolene's car was.

"You never came back before now?" he asks as he taps out a cigarette and sticks it in his mouth.

"No. How about you?"

"I came back once," he says, lighting up. "For an afternoon. It didn't work out, so I left."

"You were here?"

"Yeah. Once. About a year after I got back to the States."

"You were here?" I repeat, feeling strangely panicked. "You saw your mom? You went to your house?"

And you didn't see me? I say to myself, silently.

"I didn't make it that far."

"I don't understand."

He finishes his beer, crushes the can, and tosses it at the pile of cans in the corner. It hits near the top and balances there.

He starts to get up to get another one out of the cooler. I hurry to get it for him. He gives me a glance of disappointment and annoyance. I stop midway from crossing the room, realizing he thinks I'm getting it for him because I think he can't do it on account of his leg. I think about sitting down again. I think about getting it for him anyway. I stand rooted to the middle of the sagging floorboards.

"Just get the fucking beer," he growls at me.

I give him one and sit down. He falls silent again, and I watch him drink and smoke.

He's not old. He'd be in his fifties now, and some men are definitely old in their fifties, but he has the ageless quality about him that most miners used to have: guys who never seemed young when they were young or old when they were old, their appearance and general deterioration seeming to have nothing to do with the passage of time and their place on the time line.

I start to fidget on the couch. I want to know about the day he came back. I want to know what he meant when he said he didn't make it that far. I want to know why he didn't come and see us. But I'm afraid to ask. I don't want to antagonize him. I feel he might kick me out at any minute.

"I tried to come back," he says, staring out the door again and taking a final drag off his first cigarette, then tossing the butt into an empty Chef Boyardee ravioli can he's using as an ashtray, "but I didn't feel right being here anymore."

"What do you mean?"

"When I left, I was a stupid kid who had never been farther than Centresburg. When I came back, I was only twenty-two, but I was an old man already. I'd been on the other side of the world and lived in a jungle. I left a part of my body in that jungle. I killed people in that jungle. People. Not squirrels. People."

He takes a long swallow of beer, lights another cigarette, and clears his throat.

"I came back to the same place and the same people. Nothing had changed here, but I had changed a shitload. It was worse than being a stranger."

"But you're here now."

"Yeah, I'm here now because of some asinine promise I made an old lady over thirty years ago," he answers me irately. "I saw Zo the day I came back. I had to drive by her place on the way out of town, and she was down at the road getting the mail out of her mailbox. She invited me up on the porch for a beer. I told her I was leaving for good, and she made me promise I'd come back for her funeral if I didn't make it back sooner. She even made me promise to subscribe to that fucking excuse for a newspaper for the rest of my life so I'd be able to see her obituary when it ran. It's pretty damn weird when you think about it. That was over thirty years ago. She was only in her forties and already talking to me about her death like it might happen any day, and if it did, it was no big deal.

"Yeah, I'm here now," he finishes, "but only for a few days. That's all."

"You're not staying?"

"Did you hear what I said? I don't belong here anymore."

"Yes you do," I blurt out.

He pauses in his drinking, smoking, and staring out the door to fix me with the kind of look he used to give me when my chattering presence in his backyard began to wear on him.

"This is where you're from," I keep going. "You always belong where you're from. It's the one thing that can't be taken away from you.

"You can lose a job. You can lose a woman. You can lose a bet. You can lose a war. You can lose a leg. You can lose your sanity. You can lose your memory." I come to the end of my list, almost short of breath.

"But you can't lose the place you're from," I finish. "It's always there. The land and the sky. It's always yours. No one can turn you away as long as you can say, 'This is where I'm from.'"

"You talking to me or you?" he asks.

I fall silent. Val's the next one to speak. I think the topic's been dropped, but he returns to it.

"I've seen people turned away from the place they're from. I've seen them slaughtered for the simple reason that they wanted to stay in the place they're from."

"Sure. I know," I tell him. "Look at my dad. He didn't want to leave his home, but it was destroyed and there was nothing left there for him anymore. So he left, but he took a piece of it with him. Every time he told a story about it, every time I saw him look at his portrait of the czar, he was back there in his mind. I know he was.

"The people you're talking about who were killed were killed because of outside influences. They didn't kill each other. If anything it proves exactly what I'm saying: Some people would rather die than leave their home."

He nods, still staring out the door.

"Your dad told me once Americans don't live through wars; they send men off to fight in them. It was an important difference to him. I told him I understood what he meant, but I didn't until I was in 'Nam. Then it was clear what he was saying. He meant, no matter what we like to tell ourselves over here, we can't understand what other cultures feel who have wars fought in their own backyards. War is a rape, and we've never been raped. We've been spit at a couple times. Nothing more. We pick and choose when we're going to fight. Sometimes we try and stop a rape. Other times we're part of one. But we always have the luxury of choice."

He takes a swallow of beer.

"And that's one big fucking luxury."

I nod my agreement.

"Your dad didn't talk much, but when he did, he always had something to say."

I nod my agreement again.

"So what'd you and Zo talk about the day you came back?"

"She did most of the talking."

"Did you talk about me?"

"I asked her if the Zoschenko kid was still a pain in the ass, and she said you were."

A trace of a smile plays across his lips. It's there so briefly it could almost be mistaken for a slight grimace of pain or a nervous tic.

"I sat there with her for about an hour, and she never once asked me about Vietnam or my leg. Then, right before I'm about to go, she says to me, 'Did you hear about the new bonus plan the Pentagon has for the military brass?' And I said, 'No, I never heard anything about it.' She said they get to choose two points on their bodies they want to be measured from, and then they get one thousand dollars for every inch."

The smile returns, and this time he lets it take over his whole face.

"Now, I'm beginning to think this sounds a little strange, but it's Zo. I can't really suspect much. She's sitting there drinking from a yellow coffee mug that says 'Good things come in small packages' with baby ducks and rabbits on it, and she's wearing a pink sweatshirt with an angel on it with big silver wings. It looked really homemade, like one of her Bible-school kids made it for her. And she's wearing those tan canvas tennis shoes she always wore, with the little socks with white lace around the tops."

I smile at the memory of her feet.

"She says first they take an air force colonel. He's a real tall guy. He says he wants to be measured from the top of his head to the bottom of his feet. It turns out he's six foot five. That's seventy-seven inches. Seventy-seven thousand dollars. The next guy is a navy admiral. He holds his arm straight out from his side and says he wants to be measured from his fingertips to the bottom of his feet. Turns out to be eight feet. Ninety-six inches. That's ninety-six thousand dollars. Next is an army general. He tells the guy doing the measuring that he wants to be measured from the tip of his dick to his balls."

"Zo is telling you this?" I marvel.

"I swear it's true," he assures me. "Now, when the general says this, the guy doing the measuring looks embarrassed and makes some comment about how he's sure the general is a well-endowed man, but, 'We *are* talking about a thousand dollars an inch, sir. Are you sure that's what you want measured?' The general says yes. So the guy tells him to drop his pants, and he bends down to start measuring. Then he stands back up, looking amazed. 'General,' he says, 'Where are your testicles?' And the general says, 'In Vietnam.'"

We both bust out laughing.

"Zo told you that?" I ask again.

"Yeah."

"I've been meaning to ask you, how did you know Zo in the first place?"

"She was my Sunday-school teacher," he tells me, and we crack up all over again.

"I have a hard time imagining you in Sunday school."

"I could belch the twenty-third Psalm."

Once our laughter subsides, the little house becomes awkwardly silent. I realize, after it's over, how rarely I ever heard Val laugh in the past. The same was true for myself.

"If you don't mind, I've got some shit to do," he tells me.

"That's what you said. You mind if I ask what?"

He takes the cigarette out of his mouth and raises the beer can in my direction.

"This is it," he says.

I rise to go.

He puts his palms on the table and pushes himself out of the chair. I stop myself from telling him he doesn't need to get up.

"Is Miss Slag Heap a good cook?" he asks me.

"Yeah, she's a good cook. She does a lot of it. She has three sons."

"What about a husband?"

"She doesn't have one."

"Divorced? Widowed?"

"Picky."

"But she had three kids with the guy?"

"She had three kids with three guys," I correct him. "And she didn't really have the kids with them. It was more like she had the kids despite them."

"The American way," he says, reaching for the brown paper bag sitting on the edge of the table. "We hurt the people we love and fuck people we should hate."

He opens it and pulls the framed photo of the J&P company store out of it.

"It's a picture of—" I begin to explain.

"I know what it is." He cuts me off.

His eyes gloss over it for a moment before he slides it back into the bag and leaves it on the table.

He puts all his weight on one hand and grabs the rifle he'd left leaning against the wall. With the help of the gun, he reaches the door in three hops. He pushes the screen open and stands in the doorway, a one-legged silhouette against the gray light.

I hold out my hand to him, and he grips it firmly with a dry, callused palm and scarred, battered fingers. It's the kind of shake that has an incorruptible promise behind it. We shook the day he left to go to war, my small, smooth hand in his big, rough one, both of them marred with scratches and scabs and traces of dirt in the lines of the knuckles and under the nails.

That day he told me he would be back, but in all fairness to the man, he never told me when.

I take a slight detour on the way back to Centresburg and drive past the junkyard. I come around the final curve and see the hill in front of me. The steam is thick today, and active in the wind. It snakes out onto the road like snapping lengths of frayed white ribbons.

There's a boy on a bike halfway up the hill. He's lost all the momentum he might have had at the beginning of his climb. He's standing upright over his seat, his legs pumping in slow motion, the bike leaning low to one side before flipping to the other side after the straining downward push of the sneakered foot on the opposing pedal.

I come up behind him slowly and roll down my window. The burned-sulfur smell from the junkyard fills my truck. I can hear his labored breathing and the sound of his BB gun, slung across his back, hitting the fabric of his raincoat with dry rattles. His face is red and frowning with exertion. The hair at the back of his neck is damp with sweat.

"Shouldn't you be in school?" I call out to him.

He glances my way, then quickly goes back to staring straight ahead. I get the feeling this is a necessary form of concentration for him in order to keep the bike moving forward.

"I missed my bus."

"You planning on riding your bike the whole way to Centresburg?"

"I'm riding to my grandma's," he answers me in huffs. "She's going to give me a ride. There's nobody home at my house. My mom works."

"You want a ride there?"

"No thank you."

"What's the gun for?"

He looks from side to side at the trees that will be hectic with birds and squirrels and the roadside grasses where groundhogs will be hiding once he gets past this lifeless stretch of poisoned, simmering road. He fixes his eyes straight ahead again, almost losing his balance on the zigzagging, barely moving bike.

"You never know what you're gonna find," he replies.

"Okay," I tell him. "You be careful and stay on your side of the road. And tell your grandma to have a nice day."

I pull away from him, watching his progress from my rearview mirror.

My thoughts return to Zo, and I find myself smiling. It was just like her to ask Val to make a promise to come back when she died. More than thirty years before it happened, she was already making sure that even her death would serve a purpose. She knew that her obituary would bring him back again the same way a mother's cry at dusk brings her child home for bed.

The junkyard is covered in a blanket of mist as thick as fuzz. I come to a rolling stop at the top of the hill and wait for the boy to reach it so I can watch him fly down the other side.

# FIFTEEN

MY TALK WITH VAL SHOULD HAVE MADE ME FEEL GOOD, BUT AS I drive back to town, all I'm feeling is jealousy and the familiar ache of loss: Val knew my father better than I did.

I give up looking for excuses to avoid work and go to the station. I don't know why I've had such a hard time doing my job lately. I don't have any real complaints about it.

Certain aspects of it can be tedious and sometimes just plain boring. A lot of it is grunt work. When I first started here, Stiffy told me most of the work I'd be doing would be "secretarial, janitorial, and transportational," and he was right.

There's a lot of frustration: moments when I find myself wanting to shake some sense into the victim I'm supposed to be helping as much as I want to do it to the criminal I'm supposed to be subduing, times when I feel the law I'm enforcing is more dangerous than the so-called violation it's correcting. But there are also times when I feel like I've helped someone. Not necessarily because I've resolved a problem. Not because I've restored property to a rightful owner, or assuaged a fear, or assisted someone in dealing with the aftermath of an accident or tragedy. It's the fact that I showed up at all. A call was sent out, and that call was answered. I represent dependability.

Not much is going on when I get to the station. I park around back and go in through the personnel entrance, which takes me past the holding cells. One has an occupant who's giving off the worst stench I've ever smelled in my life.

He's sitting on the cot in his underwear and tube socks full of holes, with one of the department's stiff pea green blankets held loosely around his shoulders, providing him with all the warmth of a paper towel and all the comfort of a shower curtain. His face is distorted into a severe wince that might be caused by regret or anxiety or the inability to escape his own smell.

We don't have a shower, so he was probably told to clean up in the sink, but small, occasional patches of some kind of black filth still cling to him in unlikely places: behind an ear, on the tip of his elbow, the back of a hand, a big toe poking through the end of his sock.

He gives me a pleading look when I walk in. His eyes are weepy and bloodshot, and they're not that way from crying.

"How about a drink?" he says to me.

"I'm fresh out," I tell him, and I feel a slight wave of disgust at myself that I had a beer already this morning, even though I've had more than my share of mornings when I took my first drink before my first piss.

I pass on through the room as quickly as my knee will let me.

Pierced Chad is at his desk, sitting straight and tall, talking on the phone. He has the receiver in one hand and is twirling his black-mirrored sunglasses with the other. He's the only one of us who wears sunglasses. He says he does it so people can't see his true feelings in his eyes when he's interrogating them. I've noticed he also wears them when he's talking to women in bars and paying for his gas and shrink-wrapped sticky bun at the Kwik-Fill.

Stiffy is pouring himself a cup of coffee. He's not wearing any shoes.

As I get closer to him, I get a slight whiff of the smell from the guy in the cell.

"Holy shit," I say.

"Not exactly holy," Stiffy replies. "Chicken."

"Chicken what?"

"Chicken shit," he says. He jerks his head toward the back of the station. "Our guest back there. He got into a disagreement with his boss at Wertz's Chicken Farm, and they ended up in deep shit, so to speak.

"Chad's over at the Wash N Go right now trying to do something about the stink in the car. I smell this way just from riding in the same vehicle with him. I left my shoes outside. His clothes are out in the Dumpster. We were going to burn them, until Jack pointed out the only thing worse than chicken shit is burning chicken shit."

"I guess he's right about that," I reply, and reach for the pot to pour my own cup of coffee. "Is Jack in?"

Stiffy smiles. "Yes, he is. And he made some mention of wanting to see you when you came in this morning."

"I'm sure he did. I guess I should go get it over with. I have it coming. I've been kind of slacking off the past week or so."

"Happens to everybody now and then," he tells me with a shrug. "It's not the slacking off that bothers him so much; it's the not knowing why you're slacking off. Jack needs to know everything."

"I've noticed that."

"You got a message, too. A Dr. Morrison called you. She wants you to call her back. I left the number on your desk. She sounded nice."

Being reminded of Chastity fills me with momentary glee and lust, until I remember how we left things at Marcella's. She's marrying Muchmore. I still can't believe it.

"That's too bad," Stiffy says.

I guess I'm talking out loud again without realizing it.

"Yeah," I say as I dump spoonful after spoonful of sugar into my coffee.

I walk over to my desk.

Chad nods at me. His phone conversation is peppered with phrases like "not at liberty to say," "ramifications of his actions," and "alleged offenses." I think he's working, but it turns out he's renting a band for a friend's wedding.

I sit down and pick up the piece of paper with Chastity's number on it. She gave two numbers: her office and her cell. I try not to let myself read anything good into it. The fact that she gave me her cell-phone number, which is an invitation to call her anytime, is probably only because she wants to use me in a professional manner again. She probably wants to talk to me about another charity event. Maybe she's organizing a fund-raiser to help struggling young lawyers buy their first BMWs before age thirty. Or maybe she wants to finance a series of seminars teaching corporate executives how to dig holes and change spark plugs.

I'm good and mad by the time I pick up my phone and dial her office number first. It's a Tuesday morning. She's probably at her office. Unless she's in surgery or at the hospital or Safe Haven visiting patients.

I look at the message Stiffy took. It doesn't say where she called from. It doesn't say when she called. It doesn't say why. It doesn't even hint at her mood or what she was wearing. If it's another short skirt, or maybe a longer one today. Or maybe a pantsuit with high heels. She'd look great in a pantsuit: one of those tailored ones where the jacket matches the pants and women don't wear anything underneath the jacket except a lacy piece of some kind of lingerie.

I've seen them worn that way in magazines and on TV, although I've never seen a real woman wear one. Jolene assures me women in New York wear them, and she also assures me that most of them don't look good in them because you actually have to have a better body to pull off a pantsuit than you do to wear a dress.

I hang up before her secretary can answer. Of course she's not in her office. It's probably the last place she'll be, and if she is there, she's seeing a patient. That means she'll have to get back to me between patients. She'll be rushed.

I take a drink of coffee. It's way too sweet.

The cell phone is better. She'll only answer if she's really free. And if she doesn't answer, I'll get to leave a message with my own voice. It won't be her secretary's interpretation, who might get it all wrong. I can't put this in the hands of a stranger who's never met me, or, worse yet, maybe she has met me. Maybe I went to school with her. Maybe I dated her. Maybe she's from Clearfield, too. I don't know who the hell her secretary is.

I hang up before her cell phone answers. Shit, a message. I need a message. I start rehearsing them in my head when my phone rings.

"Laurel County Sheriff's Department. Zoschenko speaking."

"Hello, Zoschenko. This is Morrison," she says in a playful voice. "What are you up to?"

She's calling me back. She wanted to talk to me so badly that she didn't even wait for me to return her call. This could be good.

"Not much," I tell her.

"I'm calling to thank you."

She's calling to thank me. That's better than calling to ask a favor, but not as good as calling because she's crazy about me. Unless the reason she's calling me again so soon is because I'm a chore she wants completed as quickly as possible. I'm probably on a list of a hundred people she's calling to thank for donating their time to the fund-raiser.

"Hello?" she says. "Ivan, are you there?"

"Yes." I clear my throat without much success. "I'm here."

"I wanted to thank you again for donating those autographed footballs. They were snapped up right away. And so was the dinner with you."

"It was?"

"Yes, and it looks like I owe you an apology. You were right. You weren't bought by a man."

"I knew it."

I feel happily vindicated, until I remember that all that's been proven is that she was wrong in thinking that no woman could be interested in me. It doesn't change the fact that she had the thought in the first place.

"So is my owner attractive?"

"Very attractive. I know this is short notice, but can you make it for dinner tomorrow night at six at Eat'nPark?"

"Are you kidding me? Eat'nPark?"

"They donated the dinners as part of your package. Zo always told me they make a mean baked scrod. And you'll get a free smiley-face cookie. Or, if you'd prefer to pay for dinner for the two of you somewhere else . . ."

"No, that's okay. Eat'nPark at six."

I happen to glance in Chad's direction. He's giving me a thumbs-up.

There's a few seconds of silence that I'm certain are going to be followed with a polite farewell, but then I hear a soft intake of breath that makes me think of her testing her bathwater with the tips of her toes and finding it too hot.

"I wanted to apologize for what happened last night at Marcella's," she says. "I'm not sure exactly what it was, but there was some definite tension there between you and Mike."

"There's always definite tension between me and Mike. It has nothing to do with you, and it's not something you need to apologize for," I reply.

I should just leave it at that. We've had a nice conversation, and she thinks I'm an okay guy; maybe not a guy she wants to go out with or sleep with or marry, but at least a guy she likes, but I've got to ruin that, too.

"The world is full of incredible women who throw themselves away on assholes. I should just get used to seeing it and not let it upset me," I decide to add.

"Oh, I see. That's what you were upset about? I'm an incredible woman, and Mike is an asshole."

"If you say so."

"What about all the great men who throw themselves away on bimbos?"

"Here's a thought: Why don't you find a bimbo for your asshole and I'll find a great guy for you?"

"What exactly is your definition of a great guy?"

I think about Bobbie. To her a great guy is one who never leaves town.

I don't have an answer for her. I don't want to talk about it anymore. I just want her to tell me it's not true; she's not going to marry Muchmore.

"I don't understand it. What is it? The biological-clock thing? Do you need to settle down and make many more Muchmores?"

"I'm not in any hurry to have kids," she replies calmly. "Can I ask you why you hate him so much, aside from the fact that he's a lawyer?"

"Isn't that enough?"

"Does it have anything to do with something that happened when you were kids? I know you went to school together."

"I never knew him in school. He was a couple years older than me and already a condescending pain in the ass. And it wasn't because his family had money. His dad wasn't a bad guy. He could put on an old Woolrich coat and a pair of shitkickers and down a few at Brownie's with the miners, and nobody thought anything of it. His dad gave us the land for the J&P cemetery. We wouldn't have been able to keep them together otherwise. They would've been split up. Nobody wanted that. Even the guys like my dad that were never found. They were still given a spot. If you go there, you'll see a stone with his name on it. It's not to show you where he is but to show you where he was."

My voice dies in my throat. I look up and realize both Chad and Stiffy have left. I'm all alone.

"I'm sorry about your dad, Ivan."

"Yeah, everyone's sorry. I doubt I'm ever going to run into someone who's going to say I'm really glad your dad was killed when you were a kid. I didn't mean to get off the subject. Let's just end this by saying I don't like the guy and nothing could ever change my opinion of him."

"Nothing?" she wonders. "Do you know that woman who was beaten into a coma by her husband twenty years ago? Crystal Raynor? Mike defended her husband. It was one of his very first cases as a public defender right out of law school."

"Yeah, I know all about it."

"Mike's the one who's paid to keep her in Safe Haven all these years. I think that's fairly decent of him."

I'm not able to say anything more. I hear her make her apologies and say she has to get back to work.

I hang up the phone and stare at the calendar on my desk. Today has a red circle around it. I can't remember if I'm the one who put it there.

Jack's slow, even, hard-soled tread, like a principal crossing a gym floor in his street shoes, intrudes on the brief silence. I don't look up. The footsteps stop, and I hear a faint creak that could have come from the adjustment of his belt and holster or the shifting and settling of various joints and bones as he arranges himself in what he considers to be a stance of infinitely unrushed importance. I sense he's standing near the doorway to the reception area.

I look up in that direction. He's wearing his jacket and his dark brown sheriff's Stetson with its polished silver shield, which means he's on his way out. He crooks his finger at me.

"Meet me outside," he says.

I join him. He's standing with his thumbs hooked in his pants pockets, elbows out at his sides, lips pursed, already nodding for me in anticipation of the agreement I'm going to have for everything he says to me.

He always begins by looking at a man's feet, then sweeps his gaze up the body, ending at the face, where he finally meets the eyes and then extends his hand for a handshake. It has the disconcerting effect of making you think he's noticed something about you that you didn't know yourself, and you're never quite sure if it's a good or bad quality.

With me this time, his eyes don't rise past my jeans.

"Pants," he says to me.

"Shirt," I say back.

His eyes flick to mine.

"I thought we were doing word association," I explain.

"All right, then," he says. "Sky."

"Blue."

"Gun."

"Shot."

"Raynor."

"Chimp."

"Reese Raynor."

"Fucker."

"Father."

"Mother."

"Sheriff."

"Jack."

"Chicken."

"Shit."

He lifts his hand in greeting to someone driving down the street bordering one end of our parking lot.

"You want to tell me about your shiner?" he asks me.

"Not particularly."

"I know where you got it."

I wait for him to go on. Jack dribbles information. It's one of the ways he gets people to say things they didn't have to say. They want to finish his accounts for him and prove they know more than he thinks he knows.

"I want you to stay away from that situation," he says after it becomes clear I'm not going to say anything.

"Okay."

"Obviously, I'm concerned. There are children in that household. But it's none of our business. If Jess wants Reese staying there, there's nothing we can do about it."

I'm confused for a moment. Then I realize he only thinks he knows how I got the black eye. He heard about the bar fight. He thinks it came from Jess.

"You know I'm not a hard-ass about your conduct off the job," he continues. "I don't feel you disgraced the Laurel County Sheriff's Department by your behavior last night, but I do believe you disgraced yourself and your mother and your sister."

"Since when are you opposed to brawling?" I ask him. "The other day you were waxing nostalgic about the good old days when men used to beat each other up instead of calling lawyers."

"I still stand by that. I'd rather see two men have a fistfight than take some pissant problem to court and spend their life savings on a lawyer instead of the camper they always wanted. Are you telling me you and Jess were resolving a legal issue last night? A property dispute, maybe?"

"I don't even remember what we were fighting about."

"You want to tell me what's going on with you?"

"No."

"Jolene and the boys doing okay?"

"They're fine."

"Your mother?"

"She's fine, too."

"How about if I insist you tell me what's going on with you?"

"How about if I admit that there is something going on with me but I'm not sure exactly what it is?"

"That's a start."

"You have any advice on how to figure out what's bothering me that doesn't include seeing a shrink or talking to God?"

He cups an elbow in one hand and scratches his chin with the other.

"Fly-fishing."

"I don't fish."

He nods, his hand still resting on his chin, sort of caressing it now. I can't see the slightest shadow of stubble on his face, not a single dark pinprick of a hair beginning to surface. I've never believed he shaves; I think he uses a kind of facial herbicide.

"That's too bad," he says.

He drops his hand and hooks both thumbs back in his pants pockets. His eyes sweep the parking lot. He notices another passing car he feels compelled to acknowledge with a brief raising of his flattened hand, like an Indian chief in an old western greeting the white man.

"I don't want you going out on any calls for the next couple days unless there's absolutely no one else available," he tells me, "and I don't foresee that happening. Friday we'll all be at Gertie. I'm assuming you'll be going, too."

"I've heard about it. What is it exactly?"

"Just a little memorial service at the mine we have every year."

"What time?"

"Nine thirty-three. Same time it blew."

He looks at his watch.

"I've got to get over to the dealership. The new Broncos came in today. I want to check them out."

He gives my legs a final disapproving glance, adjusts his hat, and starts across the lot to his car. I wait until he's out of sight, then I get in my truck and drive to Safe Haven.

My mom and Zo both insisted they didn't know who paid for Crystal's care and that as long as her expenses were being met, they abided by her benefactor's wishes and didn't attempt to find out who he was.

I have to know for sure. I have to know if Chastity's information is true and Muchmore has a conscience. Not only a conscience but integrity. He's kept his generosity hidden all these years when he could have made it public and received the respect and affection of a community that otherwise doesn't think too highly of him.

Not just integrity but compassion. He could have lessened his guilt in a lot of ways: done pro bono work for battered wives, given a hefty donation to a women's shelter, left the public defender's office or maybe even left criminal law altogether. Instead he chose to pay a very large sum of money out of his own pocket to keep Crystal in a clean, respectable place where she'd be well taken care of and exposed to nice people, even though it probably doesn't matter, since she's incapable of knowing where she is. She lost everything else. He made sure she got to keep her dignity.

His kindness eats at me, because it wasn't my kindness.

I want to believe I would have cared about her and her orphaned son even if I hadn't broken my leg that night at Gertie. I want to believe that their fates would have plagued me the same way they have for the past sixteen years even if I had gone on to have a successful career and a good life. I want to believe that my conscience didn't kick in just because my own life had been ruined and I found that blaming myself for what happened to Crystal and the boy added welcome fuel to the blaze of self-pity that was already consuming me.

But I'm afraid the truth is that after I recovered from the initial horror of the crime itself and the guilt I felt over my own personal involvement in her life, I would've gone on with my life uninterrupted and never given them a second thought. The same way I did from the very beginning. I never thought about them before they were harmed.

The drizzle has stopped. The sky is still lead-colored, but a bright crescent of white sun has begun to appear from behind a sooty gray cloud. The corridor of light it casts is harsh, since there's no blue sky to absorb it, only metal clouds to reflect it. It falls across Safe Haven making the wet blacktop of the parking lot glimmer and the white walls of the building look freshly scrubbed.

The reception area is empty except for a young mother sitting on one of the overstuffed couches, straightening her little girl's overall straps while instructing her not to run or touch anything.

The receptionist is on the phone. I nod at her as I pass by and begin following the Christ night-lights lining the baseboards. Even during the day, they have an opalescent glow to them.

The place is quiet. Breakfast is over. Midmorning naps and cable reruns of *Murder, She Wrote* and *Matlock* have begun. It's a weekday, so there aren't many visitors.

The first-floor hallway is empty except for food trays carrying the beginnings, ends, and middles of meals. I raise the battered tan plastic covers on a few plates. Strips of brittle red bacon. Scoop-shaped yellow mounds of scrambled eggs. A bright green lettuce leaf with a shiny-slick slice of bright orange canned peach. Untouched pieces of tan toast with hard, unspread squares of pale butter lying on top of them.

I look up when I hear a strange sound.

It's Jess and Danny coming at me from farther down the hall. Danny's carrying the orange pumpkin bucket he found at the junk-yard the other day. He's swinging it at his side. The noise is coming from whatever he has inside it.

They stop a few feet away from me. Jess has changed his shirt since last night, trading in one checked flannel for another, and he's wear-ing a different ball cap—a black one with the call letters of a Pitts-burgh hard-rock radio station emblazoned across it in red—but he still has on the exact same face. He hasn't slept or showered or eaten. The hollows beneath his eyes are smudged with purple shadows. His lower lip is swollen, and he has a red tear at one corner of his mouth, but nei-ther of these injuries is painful enough to prevent him from chewing. He takes a tin of Skoal out of his back pocket and holds it in his palm in preparation for going outside.

"What are you doing here?" I ask him.

"Visiting my sister-in-law."

"Since when do you visit Crystal?"

"I do it from time to time. I didn't realize I had to clear it with you first."

We stare at each other. I have nothing to say.

My method in getting Bobbie to tell me what really happened to Danny may not have been honest, but I don't feel bad for telling the lie that got her to admit the truth.

I wonder if she's seen him since this morning. Probably not. It wouldn't have made any sense for him to drive into Centresburg this morning to run errands, then go home, then come right back again.

When she does see him again, she's going to tell him about our conversation. I'm confident of that. She's going to tell him I know, and that will be the end of any possible friendship Jess Raynor and I might have left.

In my zeal to find out the truth, I never stopped to ask myself if I really wanted to know it. Now that I know, I'm sure I don't want to know. What good is going to come out of it? Am I going to save Danny Raynor? Am I going to save Jess or Bobbie? And exactly what would I be saving them from? Each other? Their own lives?

Suddenly the shitbox apartment I left in Tampa doesn't seem so bad. Not having a single meaningful social relationship outside my friendship with my boss and his son sounds great. I fondly recall my job killing bugs, and it seems almost enjoyable. I'm able to convince myself that I actually miss the fumes, that I miss putting my ear up against a stucco wall and hearing the skittering of a nest of three thousand cockroaches, that I miss doing battle with palmetto bugs the size of sparrows, that I miss the inability to ever adjust my body temperature between the sticky white heat of the great outdoors and the refrigerated blasts from people's homes and apartments. It would be so easy to go back.

Val's words ring in my ears: We get to pick when we fight. We have the luxury of choice. And it's one big fucking luxury.

My silence seems to enhance my ability to hear other sounds. I hear water being poured from a pitcher. I hear the phone ring at the front desk. I hear Danny shift his bucket from one hand to the other.

When Jess speaks again, I feel like he's shouting in my ear, but he hasn't stepped any closer and he's using his usual quiet tone of voice.

"Maybe a better question is to ask what you're doing here? Why you visit her all the time now that you're back? And bring her presents? Maybe even ask you after all these years why you were so interested in Reese's trial? And why you're so interested in him being released now?"

I hear the creak of a body shift on a mattress. I hear Angela Lansbury reveal the murder weapon and the murmurs of approval from patients watching the show.

Jess looks down at his son.

"Did you say hello to Deputy Zoschenko?" he asks him.

"Hi," Danny says, staring into his bucket.

"Hi, what?"

He looks up for a moment at his dad, but not at me.

"Hi, Deputy Zoschenko."

"How are you, Danny?"

"Good."

His nose and the skin around it are an iridescent collage of gray and green and yellow.

"What have you got in there?"

He holds out the bucket. It's half full with rocks and some hard candy he took from the basket at the reception desk.

Jess puts one hand lightly on Danny's shoulder. Danny moves closer to his leg and slips a hand around his dad's thigh. I know I'm not mistaking what I'm seeing. There's no fear between this boy and his father.

They start to move past me.

"If I were you," Jess says to me, "I'd go see her right now."

I wait until they're gone before I go to her room.

She's awake, staring straight ahead at constant blankness. Viewed from the doorway, her body makes an inhuman hump, like several scrawny cats curled up beneath the sheet.

I walk over to her and set the gift-wrapped box from Marcella's on her bedside table.

The damp, unclean smell of the bedridden is overly strong around her today. No amount of floral-scented soaps and mountain-fresh laundry detergent can cover it up completely. It comes from within. The unhurried internal rotting of organs and muscle. The spoilage of blood.

I pick up her hand full of dissolved tendons and pebbly pieces of bone. It feels like a small glove filled with marbles.

An aide has dressed her in my least favorite nightgown. It's a pink, gauzy, clearance-rack negligee that exposes the knobs of her shoulders and the ridged boniness of her chest.

I stare at her and think about the small handfuls of breasts she had and how they would have grown larger when she carried her child. Did she nurse him? I wonder. Did she teach him "The Itsy Bitsy Spider"? Did she ever think about what he might be when he grew up?

I know nothing about her years as a wife and mother, nothing about her years as a girl and daughter, nothing about the time before and after me. I'll never know anything about her except for the three afternoons we met on the road and the one day she got up the nerve to approach me in school.

My worst fear is that she's whole and well inside. That the walking, talking, smiling, moving, thinking, watching, wanting, waiting, willing girl I knew briefly is buried alive inside a body that can't move, see, speak, or feel. What if her memories are intact, the good and bad, and this is all she has to keep her company forever in her frozen darkness?

I sit down in my chair and pick up the gift. I show her the box before I unwrap it. I tell her how surprised she's going to be. I take my time and tell her about the weather and the guy who rolled around in the chicken shit. When I pull the rooster out of the box and hold it up to the light, I can almost convince myself that she's fine and she understands.

A nurse has combed and parted her dark hair and fastened it back on either side with small silver barrettes. Her eyes, though sightless, are still a clear brown. Her limbs, though useless, aren't petrified into unnatural poses. She can hear out of one ear. What she hears, no one knows but her. Can she interpret sounds, or are they nothing more than stuttering, skittering signals trapped and doomed among the broken connectors and crushed circuits of her brain?

I get up and walk over to the shelf where the rest of her animals and figurines are displayed. That's when I see the boy. I'm so startled by his presence I almost drop the rooster on the floor.

"I'm sorry," he says.

Young man is a more accurate description than boy. I'm sure he'd be offended by the term "boy." He's standing in a corner, half hidden by the other bed. I don't get the feeling that he was hiding on purpose, but that he had moved there before I even arrived to get as far away from Crystal as he could without leaving the room.

He stares at us raptly, without horror and pity for her but also without any desire to try to understand what he's seeing, adapting to her condition but not accepting it. His eyes are glassy and bloodshot from crying.

I don't move or make a sound. His face shows embarrassment, but it's quickly defeated by the more powerful grief, then replaced for a moment by the mechanics of good manners.

He takes a step toward me. He has on a long-sleeved shirt with a collar, a pair of dark gray pants, and black loafers. He dressed up for this visit.

I stare at him boldly, helplessly, searchingly. I try to understand as much as I possibly can about him in that split second before he opens his mouth to speak.

I decide that he has a good home and a good family. He gets good grades. He has a steady girlfriend he likes to buy presents for. He's not filled with rage or confusion or an unbearable emptiness. He believes in God and hard work and that every vote counts. No one and nothing has dug a hole in him until today.

He walks toward me and puts out his hand. I'm not sure I want to shake it. I'm not sure what it will do to me.

"I should have said something the minute you walked in. You must be Deputy Zoschenko. I'm John Harris."

He catches himself and looks over at Crystal.

"I mean, John Raynor."

I can't take my eyes off him. His presence has the paralyzing power of a great stag stepping out of a line of trees into a wide-open field. Even the most hardened hunter has to take a moment and marvel at his majesty before he pulls the trigger.

"Sorry," he says again, and drops the hand.

I'm not even conscious of my rudeness.

"I wasn't eavesdropping or anything like that."

"No, it's okay," I say, finally finding my voice.

He makes a nervous, apologetic laugh.

"This must be a shock for you. Finding me here like this."

"It's a shock."

"The nurse told me how you come and visit her all the time. She said you've been really nice to my mom."

His voice breaks off. He looks at Crystal. He's forcing himself to do it. In his eyes is the hope that it will get easier the more he does it. I don't have the heart to tell him it won't.

"I never knew about her. I never knew about any of it until about a month ago. My parents—" He stops again. "My adoptive parents," he goes on after a deep, shaky breath, "decided to wait until I turned twenty-one to tell me. They felt I had a right to know, but they didn't think I could handle it until I was an adult.

"I wanted to see her if we could find her. They didn't try and talk me out of it. They helped me find her."

"It sounds like you have great parents."

"Yeah, I guess I do."

He looks bewildered for a moment, and then his eyes travel all over the room, making a wide arc over Crystal this time. They end at the shelves of blown-glass animals. I hand him the rooster. He sets it down gently, then starts picking up the others one at a time.

"She was a good mother to you before this happened to her," I tell him.

He makes himself look at Crystal again. He stares at her face, at the blind empty eyes, at the chin caked with drool, at the caved-in cheeks.

He breaks into gulping sobs.

"I don't remember her at all."

"That's okay," I tell him from a distance.

I'm still afraid to touch him. He probably doesn't want to be touched. He turns his back to me, and I watch his shoulders shake. He's holding the ruby red prancing horse.

"How could someone do that to a person?"

"I don't know."

"He's still in jail, right?" he asks, turning around to me suddenly.

An iron wave of protectiveness rises up inside me. My eyes dart to the clock on the wall. Reese has been a free man for several hours.

"You don't ever have to worry about him," I promise him.

"My parents said the adoption documents were sealed by the court so he wouldn't be able to track me down if he ever got out."

"That's right."

"Did you know him, too?"

"Yes, I did."

He begins to calm down. I walk over to the nightstand next to Crystal and pick up the box of Kleenex. While I'm over there, I give her a kiss on the top of her head.

He watches me with guilt and a mild sort of horror. I reach out the box to him, and he plucks out a tissue. He blows his nose, still holding the little red horse.

"What you're doing for her is amazing to me. I guess you must have been really good friends. Either that or you're the nicest person on the face of the earth."

"No," I tell him. "Believe me, I'm not."

I put the box back and take out my wallet.

"Here," I say, and hand him a picture of Crystal I cut out of our high-school yearbook. "You should have this. She was sixteen in that picture."

He takes it from me.

"Are you sure you don't mind if I keep it?"

"I don't mind."

He stares at it for a moment. He can't help glancing up at what she is now. He quickly returns his eyes to the picture, then darts them to the glass horse.

"She was pretty," he says.

"Yes, she was."

"I don't look like her, though. Do I?"

"No."

"I guess I look like my dad, then."

"Yes, you do."

He walks back to the shelves and carefully returns the horse.

"I better get going."

"Do you mind if I ask where you're going to?"

"Back to school, I guess. I go to Ohio State."

"How's your football team this year?"

"Not bad," he says with something close to a smile.

"You play?"

"No." He shakes his head. "I did in high school, but I wasn't good enough for college ball. I run track, though. Middle distance."

I'm back to being unable to talk or move. He seems to be having the same problem. We stand awkwardly until he speaks again.

"I feel like I need to get out of here. I'm going to come back and visit her again, but right now . . . do you know what I mean?"

"I understand completely. So you're not even staying overnight?"

The protectiveness rushes through me again. I know Reese could be back in town today.

He shakes his head.

"I always thought I knew who I was, and now I don't know anymore. Like, I always thought I was born in Cleveland. Now I find out I'm really from . . . what's the name of that town again?"

"Coal Run."

"I might even have other family around here. Aunts and uncles. Cousins. Grandparents. Do you know if I do?"

"You have some."

"None of them cared what happened to me? They just let me disappear out of their lives?"

"It was beyond their control."

He looks back at Crystal. The struggle going on inside him shows clearly on his face. I think of the stag again, stepping into the field, this time realizing the hunter has him in his sights. He must decide to run or stand his ground, knowing either way he can't escape his fate.

He walks over to her, bends, and quickly kisses her on the cheek.

We don't say anything more to each other. He walks out the door and down the hall, and I walk along with him, each of us accepting the other's presence in silence, without explanation, as if it were the most natural thing for me to accompany him and him to want my company.

Outside, the sun has won its battle and the storm clouds have departed, leaving behind ragged wisps of black and gray hanging in the blue sky like chimney smoke.

Danny Raynor is squatting next to the border of shrubs lining the walk leading to Safe Haven's front door, intently picking through the whitewashed gravel and pieces of rose-colored quartz spread at their bases. I glance around for Jess and find him behind me, standing off to one side, his hands in his pockets, rocking slowly back and forth on the heavy soles of his work boots. He doesn't look my way.

John stops, and we finally shake hands. It's a hand like any other. It doesn't burn or crush or turn me into stone. There's nothing painful about its touch, except that I'm feeling it for the very first time.

I watch him walk across the parking lot to his car. It's a blue Nissan. A couple years old. A nice car, but not too nice. I'm glad to see he's not spoiled, and he's also not suffering.

I don't know I'm crying until I feel a tear crawling down my neck.

Jess comes up beside me.

"That was your son," he says.

I nod.

Out of the corner of my eye, I see a brown stream of tobacco hit the cement walk.

"You better fix that," he says.

# SIXTEEN

I TOLD HER TO HAVE AN ABORTION. AFTER I GOT PAST THE annoyance of being approached by her in the hall in front of my friends, and past the initial panic at realizing she was serious, and past the anger that my own life could be compromised in any way, my mind searched and found the answer. Abortion. What a beautifully clear-cut, foolproof word. To terminate before completion.

She gave me a look of absolute disbelief. She wasn't upset that I said it. She wasn't about to cry or hit me. I don't even think it was the word itself that startled her. It was that I could say it to her so quickly and so carelessly.

"I don't want to have an abortion," she said, dropping her gaze to the same mud-stained tennis shoes she was wearing the day I met her.

"Are you out of your mind? You're sixteen," I whispered harshly. "Why would you want to do something stupid like that? Do you think having a baby is a joke?"

"No."

She didn't matter enough for me to hate her. She was too innocent and easily manipulated for me to fear her. All I felt looking at her standing in front of me with her downcast eyes and cheap chips of color inside the tarnished gold cage she wore around her neck was the same petty irritation I might feel for a knot in the laces of my cleats.

I wanted rid of her.

"If you think having this baby is going to get me to marry you or even pay any attention to you, you're wrong. I'll deny it's mine. To tell the truth, how can I be sure it's mine? Maybe you screw guys on the side of the road all the time."

I thought I saw her flinch. I was afraid she was going to start crying and make a scene. I wasn't home free yet. I still had to be careful how I played her. If I did it correctly, she'd have an abortion or she'd have a baby she'd be too intimidated to claim was mine.

"I don't like you," she said softly to the floor.

I was shocked by her nerve in standing up to me. Didn't she know who I was? Didn't she know her place?

"You think I care?"

"I won't tell anybody it's your baby," she added quickly, almost in a mumble. "I don't want anybody to know."

She turned and walked off down the hall. I felt great. I had won, and I had also dodged a bullet. It was amazing I hadn't got a girl pregnant already. I didn't always use protection. Luck had cut me a break by making my one and only victim too selfless and naive to pursue me. She was going to take care of it alone.

I saw her and John only one more time before that night in a State College bar when I watched her bloody body being wheeled out of her home on a stretcher and him being carried out with his gutted stare and one small hand like a starfish clinging to the back of a deputy's neck on the eleven o'clock news. She was walking down the main street in Centresburg with him. He was about two years old. I looked right at him, but he didn't exist for me. All I saw was Crystal. I didn't want any trouble. I wasn't even willing to put up with a couple minutes of awkwardness.

I hid from them.

I was not myself, I've tried arguing with myself. That mean, cowardly, self-absorbed boy wasn't me. He was someone I sent out to do my dirty work, because sometimes we have to make tough decisions and do unpleasant things to people who don't deserve them.

I had my own stresses. On the surface it may have seemed I had a charmed life, but I was about to leave for Penn State, where I was expected to be the Golden Boy again, where I was expected to perform at a level I had never approached before, where I was going to be under the tutelage of a coach who instructed and guided instead of terrorized and manipulated. Common sense may have said that I should prefer his methods, but I had never encountered them before. I was comfortable with fear and the blind pursuit of duty. It was something I knew just as my father knew mining.

I'm driving too fast. I'm not even sure where I am. I'm still in Centresburg. I'm in a neighborhood I've probably known since I was a child, but I can't recognize anything. The street is noiseless. Kids are in school. Adults are at work or quietly going about the activities they pursue alone in their homes every day. The houses look blurred and browned around the edges, like they're made of singed paper, until they disintegrate altogether into puddles of dirty gray.

I pull my truck off to the side of the street and dig through the junk on my seat and floor hoping there might miraculously be a single unopened beer I forgot to drink or a bottle with an inch or two of whiskey left, but I haven't had a beer in the truck since Jolene cleaned it out on Sunday, and I threw away the empty bottle of whiskey I drank that night.

I lean my forehead against the steering wheel and watch tears drip off my face and leave dark wet spots on my faded jeans.

It is something I know: Those were my dad's words to my mother explaining why he chose to work in a mine when he was free after years of being forced to labor in one as a prisoner.

I think of him meeting her for the first time, sitting at that long-ago dinner table with my grandfather and uncle, living ghosts of able men who would meet their ends too soon for no reason other than that they were doing their jobs.

They went every day. They did what they were supposed to do. And I thought I was doing what I was supposed to do. Be a ballplayer. I was good. I brought my town glory. I made people proud, not just of me but of us. That's what I was supposed to do. Not have a wife and baby dangling around my neck when I was only eighteen.

*Roby sho kajut.* Do what they say. That's what my father's mother screamed at him when a pair of starving, half-crazed Russian soldiers with patches of black frostbite on their hands and holes worn through their boots told him he was going to go labor in a death camp to help make bombs to win the war, after they gunned down his father for saying no.

*Roby sho kajut.* Do what they say. Work this job. Fight this war. Take this ball and run down that field. *Roby sho kajut.* Do what they say, and you may have a chance at life later.

I shouldn't be crying. I always told myself if I ever got to meet him, I wouldn't cry.

I was certain that since I had lived for so long with the knowledge of his existence and with the ugliness of what I had done, eventually coming face-to-face with him wouldn't have any impact on me. I thought I was prepared for it.

But no amount of drunken obsessing could prepare me for his flesh-and-blood hand in mine. For his living, breathing presence in a room with me. For the flash of my father I saw in his features when he smiled.

I took my son from his mother; I took my son's mother from her son. Jess was wrong in his assumption. Some things can't be fixed. How can I fix that? By telling him the truth now: that his real father was a spineless, self-absorbed son of a bitch who callously abandoned a pregnant sixteen-year-old girl who then felt her only alternative was to find someone else to screw as quickly as possible and hope that this time when she told him she was pregnant he'd have the decency to marry her? And that person turned out to be Reese Raynor, a man who would beat her routinely until one day he put her into a coma? Does he really need to know this truth after just finding out the truth about the existence of Crystal?

We'll sit and have a beer, maybe? Pick up where we left off? Hope to have some kind of future grow out of the death of our father-son relationship? Could we build a new relationship over the murdered fact of the one we should have had?

His past is dead to me, and his knowing me as his father is dead to him. No amount of bargaining, negotiating, apologizing, promising, pleading, or a bribe of cold, hard cash will get back his life for me. What I threw away can't ever be retrieved, replaced, or imitated.

I try to picture him at every age: crawling over junk and collecting rocks like Danny Raynor, full of gap-toothed enthusiasm and unconditional love like Eb, going through the trying transition of boy to man that Harrison is experiencing, where he begins to look at a hole in the ground as a place to bury his mistakes and his treasures, not just a place to explore.

I gave up my son's life. I'm incredulous at the thought of these words and the fact that for the last twenty-one years I didn't understand their meaning.

I make it back to the station, although I have no conscious memory of doing so. I have no problem staying at my desk for the rest of the day. I take calls and catch up on paperwork and help several people who show up at the station with various complaints. I'm an automaton, and I think that maybe this is what I should be: a man behind a desk who never leaves the desk, who has nothing outside the desk. No woman, no family, no community, no life. Just a desk. A square, solid piece of furniture that I can't hurt or help.

After work I stop at the Kwik-Fill with the sole intent of getting gas. It never crosses my mind that the mother of Reese and Jess Raynor works here, or even that a human being works here.

The fluorescent glare, the customers standing mutely between regimented shelves staring hypnotically at the brightly colored, plastic-wrapped items, the polished silver and glass of the refrigerated section, the complete absence of smells, the constant unidentifiable insect whine makes me think of an alien spaceship and a race of zombie space clones.

Edna Raynor could easily be part of the intergalactic flight crew in her Kwik-Fill uniform and name tag, with her teased hair like a helmet and her complexion an unnatural shade of fleshy orange in the blue-white glare from an overhead set of lightly buzzing tubes.

I can tell by the carefully arranged stiffness and the highlighted silver-gray glint of her hair that her hairdresser squeezed her in after all. I can picture her on the phone Sunday, later in the day, after getting over the shock of being shot at, pouring out her domestic woes to the woman on the other end in exchange for an appointment. Rick's worst nightmare—the reason he tried to disable her vehicle in the first place—was her getting to a phone, and she probably ended up using his as he was passed out in the mud next to his wife's lawn goose and his own puddle of piss.

She gives me a nod of acknowledgment when I walk in, and then her eyes dart to a display of Middleswarth potato chips where a man is standing with his back to us, one hairy, muscular, pale arm hooked around one of the cardboard barrels. The lid is lying on the floor. He digs his hand into the container and pulls out a couple yellow chips that he shoves into his mouth. He wipes his greasy fingers on the leg of his jeans.

I get the feeling that I know him. I glance back at Edna, who's glancing back and forth between him and me. She's trying to communicate something without speaking. It's not fear, exactly, even though there's wariness in her eyes.

I think back to the times Val let me tag along with him when he went hunting. He'd shoot me a similar look when he sensed that a deer was nearby. Don't scare him away, he'd say with his eyes. That's what she's saying, too.

I take a step toward him. He's going bald. His scalp shows between the oily stripes of his hair. He turns around with another handful of chips poised in front of his open mouth.

Our eyes meet for a moment. Our stares lock. On first sight he only sees a deputy and I only see an asshole. Then recognition begins to dawn for both of us. He gives me a dog's smile that's nothing more than the physical act of drawing his lips back from his teeth.

He pops the chips into his mouth and crunches them loudly.

"Well, well, well," he says. "If it ain't the great Ivan Z."

I feel the skin on the back of my neck tighten. I'm not bothered by his presence as much as I'm bothered by his use of the exact same words of greeting that his twin used a couple days ago. I don't like to be reminded that they're two parts of the same whole.

He extends his hand. I think of him holding the baseball bat in it.

When I don't take it, he draws it back and wipes the grease on his jeans again and holds it out for another attempt.

I don't want to take it, but I can't afford to arouse any suspicions in him or in anyone watching us.

He has a bully's grip. He wants praise and a show of fear and thinks they're the same thing. He expects me to try to wrest my hand out of his, then give it a disbelieving flex and compliment him on the pain he inflicted.

I don't. I beat him by distraction. I ask him a question.

"How long has it been, Reese?"

My ploy works. The exertion of concentration forces him to abandon the handshake. He sincerely tries to do the math and come up with a sum of years—and fails.

"Since high school, I guess," he says, and shoves some more chips in his mouth. "Shit, I missed these chips in Rockview. Most of the guys did. Some liked Wise, and there were a few shitheads who said Snyder's is the best, but they usually only said it once. If you know what I mean."

"You should contact the Middleswarth people," I tell him. "I think you may have just stumbled on a great new ad campaign for them."

He gives me another dog grin.

"I remember when you broke your leg. It was before my trial. I heard about it in jail. Man, it was all anybody talked about for days.

Guys were really torn up. It was like they took it personally. You know what I'm saying? 'Cause you weren't just some great ballplayer nobody could imagine knowing. You were one of us."

"Except for the part where I didn't kill or maim anyone."

He tilts his head a little, like he's trying to hear better. His chewing slows. His stare hardens, and I'm reminded of the fact that he beat a man to death, a man the same age and size as himself with a similar history of violence who had spent years behind bars, which is an entirely different crime with an entirely different reason behind it than attacking a defenseless woman. Beating Crystal into a coma was an act of cowardice; beating that inmate to death was an act of insane rage.

I had a moment in the Safe Haven parking lot this morning where I almost went after John and asked him to stay. I wasn't sure if I was going to be able to tell him the truth or just try to convince him that Centresburg was a happening place where a guy like him could have a good time hanging out with a guy like me between visits to see his mother, the vegetable, and nightmares about the monster who put her in that condition, whose blood he believes runs through his own veins.

I thought better of it, and now, standing here face-to-face with Reese, I'm glad the boy isn't anywhere near here. He should be back to school by now, safe and sound in his dorm room or apartment, maybe hanging out with some friends, maybe studying. I didn't ask him if he has a girlfriend. He probably has a girlfriend. He probably has a bunch. He's a good-looking kid. No, he could have a bunch, but I got the impression he's a little on the shy side. He's probably trying to get up the nerve to ask out a girl he's crazy about, but every time he's around her, he makes an idiot of himself.

"Jess told me you just moved back here last year," Reese says to me while he bends down and picks up the lid off the floor and puts it back on top of the barrel of chips. "That makes you kind of fucked up, don't you think? Far as I know, people leave here and people stay here, but they never do both."

Does he know? I wonder. Did he marry Crystal thinking John was his son, or did he always know he was someone else's?

Jess knew, or had he only previously suspected? I didn't ask him. By the time I finished watching John walk to his car and finished watching the car pull safely out of the parking lot onto the road and drive away in the direction it should have been going, Jess and Danny were gone, too.

If Jess always knew, did he send the clipping?

One thing I'm sure of: If Reese does know he wasn't John's real father, he doesn't suspect that I am. That's the kind of history between two men that he would feel compelled to address.

"So you've seen Jess today?"

"Yeah, I'm supposed to be staying there." He snorts something close to a laugh. "But I'm reconsidering. Things were calmer in prison. More quiet and less violent."

He snorts again. I get a sick feeling in my stomach. I can't believe it. I can't believe Jess is at it again.

"He's your brother," I say coldly.

"Yeah, I know he's my brother. What do you want me to do about it? He's crazy about her. She's got a nice ass and nice rusty brown hair but, shit, so do his beagles. He can't see how fucked up she is."

"What do you mean?"

"What the hell have we been talking about? The way she smacked her kid. The little guy. You know him? I think she broke his little nose. It's all swollen up, and his whole fucking face is one big bruise."

The sick feeling remains, but the reason behind it changes.

"What makes you think Bobbie did it?"

"I heard them talking about it. Her and Jess. Something about him telling someone he hit the kid so people wouldn't think she did it and her thinking he was a great guy for doing that, but she didn't want people to think something bad about him. It started out nice, then she was crying, then they got in a whup-ass fight, and the little guy went and hid in the truck."

He begins stacking as many barrels of chips as possible on the one he already has.

"I don't suppose you'd help me carry some of these out to my car?"

"No," I answer him.

"Hey, Mom," he calls out to Edna. "Come help me take some of these out to my car."

She blinks at the absurdity of his request.

"In case you didn't notice," she says back to him, shooting a stern look over the long line of heading-home-after-work customers waiting to pay for their gas, snack cakes, and cigarettes, "I'm working."

The fact that he beat his wife into a coma, murdered a man, spent most of his adult life in jail, and is about to walk out of a store with a bunch of stolen foodstuffs that she'll end up paying for out of her meager paycheck are things she apparently just accepts in her son, but his disrespect for an honest job is something she won't.

"All right, then," he says to her. "Good seeing ya again, Mom. Shame you're not a widow yet, but don't give up hope. It'll happen someday."

He turns his back to me and starts heading toward the door, the stack of chip barrels leaning against his chest and reaching to the top of his head. He's having a hard time seeing around them, so he's moving at a shuffle. A little kid breaks ranks with his mother and sister waiting in line and runs over to open the door for him. It's hard to be afraid of him right now.

"He never forgave Chimp for not going to work that day," Edna says to me when I finally arrive in front of her cash register.

It takes me a moment to understand what inspired her comment, until I remember what Reese said on his way out.

"Chimp hated him for thinking that way, even though he knew he was right. Things were never the same between them after that. They were always at each other."

She rings up my charge at the pump outside and my can of root beer.

"I've often thought if Chimp had died with his shift like he was supposed to, both my boys would've turned out fine. That's twenty-three fifty-four."

I think I understand what she means: A dead father you respect can be better than a living one you don't.

I pull out my wallet and hand her three tens.

"I didn't get a chance to thank you for what you did for Rick and Bethany the other day," she says as she pops open her cash drawer.

"I didn't really do anything, unless you mean I didn't arrest him. He was having a bad day. That's all. No reason to ruin the rest of his life because he had a moment of poor judgment."

"I meant signing the football. He built it a little stand and they put it on top of their TV. They're real proud of it."

She gives me my change, pats my hand, and slips me a couple free Slim Jims.

# SEVENTEEN

I DON'T LIKE TO PLAN GETTING DRUNK. PLANNING TO PARTY IS perfectly fine. Planning on meeting someone for a drink is great. Looking forward to a nip after a hard day's work or a beer after a good hard mow is okay, too. But scheduling and setting aside a time to simply put as much alcohol into your system as you possibly can, with the sole intent of forgetting everything about yourself and your life so you can eventually arrive at a point where you pass out so completely you won't even dream, is not a good thing.

Even those of us who do it understand that we shouldn't do it. We don't want to do it. We know how we're going to feel the next day. We know how we're going to piss off, sadden, hurt, and worry people we care about. We know that the drinking won't solve any of the problems that have led us to drink in the first place; it will only make us more incapable of solving them.

I think back to Bobbie's definition of hard drinkers and drunks. I'm not either. I don't drink to help myself cope, and I don't drink because I can't cope. I drink because I need an addiction to replace the loss of my old one. It would have been nice if my new addiction could have been fly-fishing or stamp collecting, but the easiest, most familiar thing to reach for at the time was a bottle.

My old addiction still plagues me. It's been eighteen years, and I still wake up every morning with the smell of a wet practice field in my nose and the echo of a coach's instructions in my ears. I still feel the initial anticipation of knowing I will get to play ball today. It's what used to get me out of bed.

People can't seem to understand that the habit of playing football isn't any easier to break than the habit of gambling on it. Addictions are not always to bad things.

For the most part, people are sympathetic when they're around someone who's trying to kick an addiction. They will go out of their way not to smoke in front of someone who's trying to quit smoking. To drink in front of an ex-alcoholic would be cruel. If someone is dieting, most people would never dream of sitting down in front of him and eating a hot fudge sundae. But no one thinks twice about constantly reminding an ex–football player about football.

One of the main reasons I went to Florida and stayed there is because there was nothing there that reminded me of football. My kind of football. The only kind of football. Pennsylvania football.

The thrill of a crisp, clear Saturday afternoon. Stepping out onto the bright green field underneath a pure blue sky with the sun glinting off the silver bleacher seats before they begin to fill up with fans. The hills beyond, surrounding and keeping us, wearing their riot of fall colors, like they've dressed up in party clothes for the occasion. Just enough chill in the air to make you want to run. The feel of your cleats gripping the packed black earth. The rich smell of the dirt and the fragrance of the grass.

Fans cheering, pennants whipping, brassy battle calls from the marching band, coaches bellowing, the thuds and grunts of bodies slamming. The salty taste of blood in your mouth, the gritty taste of dirt when you go down too hard. The adrenaline rush when the ball is yours. The pounding of your heart when you see the opening. The feeling in your legs that you can run forever. That you will be young forever. That no one and nothing can touch you. That you are yours and yours alone, yet you belong to all these others. The satisfaction of being good at something. The pride of having a purpose. The joy of breaking free.

My intent is to get drunk tonight. Stinking drunk. I go straight to the State Store after the Kwik-Fill and buy two bottles of whiskey and one of rum.

I'm on my way out the door and heading back to my truck when I hear a woman shouting. I can tell she's not in any danger even though she's calling for help.

I spot her easily. She's standing outside the entrance to the Dollar General store gesturing wildly with her arms, two full plastic bags of dollar items hanging from two fat clenched fists. She's short and pear-shaped, with long, stringy, margarine-colored hair.

I begin to make out what she's squawking about. Someone stole her car.

Ironically, I'd be more tempted to help her if I weren't a deputy. I look back and forth between my bottles in their brown bags and the distraught woman, knowing if I walk over there wearing my uniform, I could end up spending most of the rest of the evening dealing with her and a stolen auto report, or maybe even dealing with the person who stole the car.

I'm contemplating escape when I notice she has two kids with her. Probably around eight and five years old.

I walk over.

"Good evening, ma'am," I say. "What seems to be the problem?"

The words barely leave my mouth before she comes rushing at me. She stops right in front of me, and I take a step back. She smells the way I'm planning on smelling a couple hours from now. She starts to shout at me, and my eyes tear up from the fumes coming out of her.

"He stole my car! That son of a bitch! Thinks he knows goddamned everything. He stole my car. I want him arrested."

"Who stole your car?"

"He did."

She points to the nearest row of parked cars. Dr. Ed is leaning against his Impala talking on his cell phone. He acknowledges me with a wave.

"Dr. Ed stole your car?" I ask her.

"Yeah. And it was premeditated, too. He should go to jail longer for that, right?"

"No one's going to jail."

"I want him to go to jail!" she shouts.

"Don't make Dr. Ed go to jail," her little girl says from behind her.

"Yeah," her little brother echoes.

The mother turns around and snaps, "Shut up!" at them.

Dr. Ed comes walking over.

The sight of him coming our way makes the woman livid.

"There he is! Arrest him!" she starts shrieking. "He stole my car!"

"I didn't steal it," Dr. Ed replies calmly as he joins us. "I moved it."

"Same thing if I don't know where you moved it to. That's what stealing is. Taking something of someone else's and moving it somewhere where they can't find it."

"Did you move her car and now you won't tell her where it is?" I ask him.

"Yes."

"Will you please tell her where it is?"

"No."

"See, he's a car thief." She sticks a finger in his face and shakes it at him. "And what's more, he planned it. I mean, really planned it. He probably followed me into Lowe's just to do it."

"I was already there when you came in," he tells her.

"I was in Lowe's buying some paint," she starts to explain to me.

"She was in Lowe's staggering down the paint aisle, screaming at her kids," Dr. Ed interrupts.

I look down at them. The girl is staring at her feet, but the little boy is nodding.

"He sees me and comes over and starts talking to me nice as can be," the woman starts up again. "Asking me about the kids and all. Then he asks me if he can help me check out and take the stuff to the car for me, since it's so heavy, and then I could go ahead and take the kids and start my other shopping, and he said he'd bring the car keys back to me at the dollar store. Well, I said sure. I thought he was being nice. Never would've occurred to me to think my own kids' doctor was a car thief.

"So I give him my keys and the stuff, and then we come over here to the dollar store. He finds me and gives me my keys back. Then, when I go to get in my car, it's gone. Just plain gone, but all the stuff we bought is sitting in the parking space."

"Is that what happened?" I ask Dr. Ed.

"Are you entertaining tonight?" he asks me, glancing at my bottles.

"Don't try and change the subject. Is that what happened?"

He scratches at his white crew cut.

"Sounds like a fair description."

"Where's her car?"

"I'm not letting her drive with her kids in the car. She can barely stand up."

"It's none of your goddamned business!" the woman screams at him.

I motion him away from her, and we talk in private for a moment.

"Why don't you just bring her car back. Then, when she starts to drive, I'll arrest her for DUI."

"I don't want her arrested in front of her children."

"What the hell? Either you think this woman should be held responsible for her behavior or not."

"She should be held responsible, but my way is better."

"You being arrested instead of her is better?"

"I called her sister. She's a great gal. Very reliable. She's coming to get her. What are the bottles for?" he asks me.

I don't answer him. I walk back to the woman.

"Ma'am, I've been told that your sister is on her way here to pick up you and your children. Why don't you just go home and have a good evening, and I'm sure Dr. Ed will return your car to you tomorrow—"

"Tomorrow?" she cries. "I want him arrested now!"

Dr. Ed comes up beside me.

"You better arrest me."

"No," I bark at him. "I'm not going to arrest you. I'm off duty. I have things to do."

"I think you have to arrest me, even if you are off duty."

The woman puts her hands on her hips and fixes me with a glassy, drunken stare.

"He stole my car, and I want him arrested. And if you don't do it, I'm gonna call the sheriff."

Dr. Ed shrugs.

"You better arrest me."

He insists on getting his doctor's tackle box out of his car and taking it with us. We drive away together in my truck for appearance's sake. Then I drive him to his home first and then his office and beg him to go away. He won't budge. He talks about how that kind of woman is exactly the kind of woman who is going to show up at the station tomorrow to make sure I did what I promised I was going to do, and if it turns out that I didn't, then she's going to try to get me fired.

I tell him I don't care about being fired, but he says he won't have it on his conscience, and that's the end of any further arguing.

I'm so pissed at him that I decide not to tell him what I found out about Jess and Bobbie. I don't tell him I saw Reese either. Or that I tracked down Val. I'm punishing him for making me postpone drinking until I'm sick by not sharing interesting information with him that he doesn't know I have. It makes sense to me at the time.

Pregnant Chad is the only one working when we arrive at the station. He isn't on duty either; he's just looking for a way to avoid his wife, who has just entered her second week of being overdue with her fourth baby.

He doesn't seem at all surprised or upset by the facts I lay out for him. He puts on a fresh pot of coffee, finds Dr. Ed a clean blanket, and starts pumping him for free medical advice regarding his kids' latest coughs and earaches. I try to make my escape, but Dr. Ed insists I stay and have a cup of coffee with them before I go. Chad agrees with him. He says it's the least I can do after arresting my own pediatrician for grand theft auto.

"You better watch it, or you're going to get into big trouble one of these days," I warn Dr. Ed while he's standing with his broad back to me, pouring coffee and digging around for some aspirin in his tackle box.

"What kind of trouble?" he asks.

"I don't know. Somebody's finally going to sue you or kill you or leave a bag of flaming dog shit on your front porch."

He brings me a mug of coffee.

"Drink this," he says.

I take it from him. It's really shitty coffee.

"I need to go," I tell him.

"Sit," he commands, "and drink your coffee while we reminisce."

"Reminisce?" I groan.

"You never got to see Ivan play, did you, Chad?"

I start to get up.

"Sit down," Dr. Ed says, more forcefully this time.

"Actually, I did get to see him play once," Chad admits, almost shyly. "It was his senior year of high school. I had a cousin who was two years behind him. He took me to a game against Purchase Line. I was six years old."

He takes a seat and pulls his chair up not too far from where Dr. Ed is reclining on a cot in a cell. I drink some of my coffee.

"I'll never forget it," he says to Dr. Ed. "It was the most exciting thing I'd ever done in my life. Going to a football game at night. All the lights and the people cheering and the band playing.

"He scored three touchdowns that night. The first two I missed, but the third one I was watching when it happened, and I'll never forget it as long as I live. The ball was snapped, and he came running up behind the quarterback, and every single player on the field came together in one huge lump of bodies. There were arms and legs everywhere, and all this grunting and shouting. Then all of a sudden he came bursting out from the middle of it like a rocket exploding off its launch pad. No one could believe it. Everyone in the stands jumped up and started screaming. My cousin grabbed me and held me up over everybody's heads so I could see. The other players on the field didn't even realize what had happened. They were all still in a lump. He never looked back to see if anyone was coming. He never looked over at any of the fans cheering for him. He just ran. Looking straight ahead like he saw something special in the distance, and it made everybody else look down there, too. He ran all by himself the whole way down the field, across the big red Centresburg flame at the fifty-yard line, and when he got to the end zone, everybody was going crazy in the stands. People were just going out of their minds. And the players had figured out what happened by then, and his teammates were jumping up and down, and the other team was standing there shaking their heads. He didn't spike the ball or do a fancy dance or jump around. He didn't even look up in the stands. He just slowed to a jog and stopped for a moment, and then he turned and started jogging toward the sidelines like nothing had happened."

"He did his job," Dr. Ed says.

I start to nod off to sleep.

The last thing I remember hearing is Chad saying, "Yeah."

# WEDNESDAY

# EIGHTEEN

I WAKE UP IN ONE OF THE HOLDING CELLS WITH PIERCED CHAD standing over me.

One of Dr. Ed's prescription slips is pinned to my shirt. It reads "I slipped you a mickey."

The man himself is nowhere to be seen.

Chad doesn't comment on the situation at all, except to ask me what I think of the cots. Are they comfortable? He says he was thinking of bringing his girlfriend here once. He was never able to get up the nerve to ask her, but someday he's planning on asking her or some other girl. He's pretty sure somewhere out there is a girl who'd be turned on by the idea of sex in a jail cell.

I get to my desk before Jack or anyone else arrives. I spend my whole day there, not quite knowing how to deal with the fact that I feel physically well. I had planned on being violently hungover all day long.

I don't even leave the station to get lunch.

Stiffy reminds me at the end of the day as he's on his way out and heading for home that I have a dinner date at Eat'nPark. Otherwise I would have forgotten about it. Pregnant Chad gives me a wink and wishes me good luck. It's never too late to meet the right woman and start a family, he tells me.

An elderly hostess in a yellow cardboard HAPPY BIRTHDAY crown holding a water pitcher aloft in one hand and clutching a stack of

large plastic menus to one side stands serenely in the doorway separating the milling would-be Eat'nPark customers from the vista of
happy seated customers like a Statue of Dining Liberty beckoning to
our teeming, hungry masses.

I wait my turn standing in front of the glass display case full of
brightly painted, plate-size cookies and rows of pies topped with glis-
tening meringues and shiny glazes and sparkling sugar crystals. I
glance around secretively, looking for my very attractive owner; that
was the way Chastity described her.

Considering that she thinks of me as nothing more than a has-been
dumb jock, she probably thinks the only kind of woman I can find attractive is a dim-witted, twenty-something blonde with large breasts
and a boundless capacity for enduring endless, exaggerated tales of my
past exploits and physical prowess. I can only hope.

I finally arrive in front of the hostess. I begin to explain who I am,
but she interrupts me with a shake of her head. In a creaky voice both
ominous and pleased as punch, she tells me she knows why I'm here.

I follow her through the dining room, fighting back the temptation
to ask her if my date's pretty or does she at least look easy or desperate.
Little old ladies are usually a good judge of these particular personal-
ity traits.

The last time I had sex was right before I left Florida, with a woman
who had just moved into the apartment two doors down from mine.
The night was memorable to me only because I've hit the outskirts of
middle age and the fear of fading appeal, where I believe that every
time I have sex may be the last. It doesn't make the sex act itself any
better than previous times. It only makes me more determined to enjoy
it more than previous times, which usually has the opposite effect.

It's no different than all the times I've tried to quit drinking and I've
sat with my final whiskey forcing myself to savor it when all I want to
do is gulp the whole thing down at once in order to get any kind of a
buzz, no matter how small or fleeting or ultimately unsatisfying.

If I gulp, I feel like I missed out on something; if I savor, I feel frustrated; but either way I always remember that last drink, until I have the next one a couple days later.

I scan the booths and tables for an unattached female. I don't see any.

We make our way toward a small, round blond head barely visible above the back of a booth. The hostess stops next to his table and automatically fills the water glass sitting across from the boy. He hops out of the booth and extends his hand to me.

"You must be the great Ivan Z," he says, grinning so broadly I think the smile might sever the top of his head from the bottom, like an ax stroke to a tree. "I'm Everett Craig. It's great to finally meet you."

I take his hand. He's wearing a pair of tan corduroy pants without grass stains on the knees that are a little small on him, a blue shirt, a navy blue blazer that's a little big on him, and a yellow adult-length necktie patterned with tiny blue airplanes that hangs below his belt.

"Mr. Craig," I respond. "It's a pleasure."

"Have a seat," he says, and hops back onto his.

The hostess hands me my menu and totters away.

"You bought me?" I ask.

He nods.

"Don't tell me you actually used your own money for this. Your allowance money or your birthday money?"

He has a mug of hot chocolate sitting in front of him. He leans into the little white tufts of whipped cream on top and slurps loudly. When he pulls back, he's wearing half the drink on his nose and chin.

"Dr. Ed was there, and he gave me a loan. He said I could pay it back by not being sick for a year."

"Was it his idea for you to bid on me?"

"No, it was mine. I thought this would be a good way for us to get to know each other."

The guilt I've been trying to keep at bay for the past two minutes triumphs momentarily. My shoulders sag under its weight. I've been living, or at least half living, in the same house with him for the past eight months, but he has to buy an hour of my time in order to get to know me. I'm ready to start being seriously depressed when I stop and take another good look at Eb.

He's thrilled about this meeting. He's thrilled that he came up with the idea, and he's thrilled to be spending time with me. I should be equally thrilled.

He's not holding a grudge over times I've let him down in the past. He's not feeling bad, and he's the one who has reason to, not me.

I've always believed that feeling guilty showed a person was basically decent: Even though he did something wrong, he at least realized he did something wrong and felt bad about it. But right now it seems painfully obvious to me that guilt is nothing more than a device to make yourself feel better over something you did that hurt someone else while cutting the person you hurt out of the equation.

"I agree," I tell him. "I only wish I'd thought of it myself. For us to go out together just the two of us and do something."

"Don't worry about it." He takes another slurp of hot chocolate. "Now you can do it with Harrison or Josh and be the first to think of it."

"So did your mom drop you off?"

"She went out. Dr. Morrison did."

"Dr. Morrison?"

The birthday-party table erupts into applause when the hostess, followed by a knot of waitresses, comes into view carrying some kind of pink-cream-topped pie ablaze with candles. I assumed that the party was for a child, but it turns out to be for a large, flannel-shirted man with touches of gray in his hair, wearing a crown similar to the one the hostess wears but with BIRTHDAY BOY written across it.

They begin to sing "Happy Birthday," and soon the entire restaurant joins in.

I hunch down and lean across the table so Eb can hear me through the din.

"Did she say anything about me?" I ask him.

He hunches down, too.

"You mean, did she say if she likes you?"

"Yeah, something like that."

He shakes his head.

"The only thing she said about you was she asked if you could fix a toilet."

"What'd you tell her?"

"I told her I didn't think you could. I told her I'd never really seen you fix anything, except the one time you stepped on the remote when it was lying on the floor and you cracked the back off it and you kind of put it back together and put a rubber band around it to hold the batteries in."

The singing ends. The restaurant grows silent as the man blows out his candles. Cheering ensues.

"But I told her *I* know how to fix a toilet," he adds.

"How do you know how to fix a toilet?"

"Mom taught me."

"Your mom knows how to fix a toilet?"

"Sure. Grandma taught her. Some guy named Val taught Grandma. Mom said Grandpa never bothered teaching Grandma because he thought he was always going to be around to do it for her. That's why Mom says you always have to learn to do everything for yourself. You can never count on anyone always being around."

We both sit up again now that we can hear each other without shouting.

"Don't be sad, though," he tells me with a furrowing of his smooth forehead and a concerned pout that's hard to take seriously with a ring of chocolate and whipped cream around it. "She said to give you a message. She said after you take me home after dinner, if you want you can pick her up at the hospital and you could go have a drink or something. If you want."

"She really said that?"

"Yeah. Do you like her?"

"She's all right, I guess," I reply with admirable detachment. "What about you and this Hannah girl you went to the auction with? I've heard you mention her from time to time."

"We're just friends."

I nod my understanding of their situation.

"Can I ask you a personal question, Mr. Craig?"

"Sure, Mr. Z."

"I have to confess I've seen you around town, and I've always been impressed by the amount of neckties you have. Is there any particular reason you collect them?"

"Nope. Not really."

He takes another drink from his hot chocolate. This time I can't help reaching across the table and swiping the whipped cream off the tip of his nose with my finger.

He takes the hint and wipes off his mouth with his napkin.

"My dad wears a tie now," he tells me, staring at the chocolate staining the paper. "That's why he moved away. 'Cause he got a good job with a tie."

He looks up at me, and I have a powerful moment of déjà vu from when his mother, my baby sister, used to look at me with those exact same eyes filled with the exact same bewildered hurt. I think it was only this morning.

"It makes you feel different when you wear one. Did you ever wear one?" he asks.

"I have on occasion."

"Didn't you feel more important?"

"To be honest, I feel more important right now than I ever felt when I was wearing a tie."

"You look pretty bad," he says, his grin returning. "Maybe you should borrow my tie before you go see Dr. Morrison."

"Maybe I should."

"Hi, how are you fellas doing tonight?" our waitress asks us.

"Great," Eb pipes up.

"Do you know what you want, or do you need some more time?"

He doesn't pause for a breath.

"I'm going to have chili, and a grilled cheese sandwich, and spaghetti, and cottage cheese, and chocolate pudding with sprinkles, and can you keep them from touching each other?"

"I sure can, honey."

She turns her smile in my direction. I slide my unopened menu across the table to her.

"I'll have the same."

I've been inside the Centresburg Hospital about a dozen times since I've been back. Each trip here has been work-related, escorting someone after a car accident or a bar fight or a home-repair mishap.

Prior to this rash of visits, I hadn't been back here since I broke my leg. I was only here a few hours that night, long enough to get me stabilized after the blood loss and shock, before moving me to a hospital in Pittsburgh and a team of specialists Joe Paterno already had waiting for me.

My mom was with me the entire time. I sensed her more than saw her. I drifted in and out of consciousness, rarely remembering anything that passed before my eyes, but I felt her sitting next to me, and I heard her voice inside my head.

During my years of drinking, I've given a lot of thought to what she must have been thinking that night, even though we've never discussed it. She had lost her husband, father, and brother to Gertie, and now, in some cruel twist of fate, she was going to lose her son to it, too, years after that threat had supposedly passed.

One thing my mother had been spared along with the other young widows of Gertie was that they weren't going to run the risk of losing their sons to the mines. It was a state of affairs they actively worked toward, even before the mines closed on their own for economic reasons and the mine fire gutted our town.

After Gertie blew and these women no longer depended on J&P to put food in their children's bellies and roofs over their heads, they adopted a different attitude toward the mines. Many of the opinions they began to voice to each other were opinions they had always held but kept from exploring even within their own minds, the way a child will consciously deny that an abusive parent is doing anything wrong by striking him, telling himself instead that he deserves it.

After the explosion it was more important than ever that the profession of coal mining be respected. None of us left behind could allow ourselves to believe that any of those taken had died pointless deaths.

We could never hate the industry for the same reason the families in our midst whose sons were going to die in Vietnam would never allow themselves to hate the country they had fought for, but it was perfectly acceptable to hate the men who owned the companies or the men who wanted the war.

It was no different than my dad's being able to continue being a miner in America after he had been a miner in a Magadan gulag. The fact that he had been taken away from his family at gunpoint, starved, beaten, and forced to live and work under deplorable conditions against his will never seemed to affect his respect for the actual job. He could hate the man tattooed on his arm who made him be there against his will, but he couldn't hate the work, because to hate the work was to hate himself.

Once the enemy had been identified and given human qualities like ourselves, even if their faces had never been seen, a fair fight could ensue. The gloves could come off. Excuses no longer had to be made. Patriotism no longer had to be confused with the pursuit of power. Morality no longer needed to be attached to something based on greed, and gratitude was no longer given to something based on exploitation.

For my mother and the other miners's wives, it was a battle fought in the quiet, subtle form of guidance. They were going to make sure when the time came that their sons would have opportunities outside the mines and the armed forces. They urged them on to college or vo-tech school, pushed them to learn job skills, or just simply tried to instill in them the desire to look beyond the end of their own road as the only possible place for work.

The mines ended up closing on their own for reasons other than lack of a workforce, and Stan Jack pocketed his fortune and moved on to do whatever it is men like him do next.

It had to come as a relief to our mothers, because they knew deep down that as long as the jobs existed, some of us would fill them.

No one had said the forbidden names at the time, but they had sat on the tongues of every man and woman present when Gertie blew: Monongah, Centralia, West Frankfort, Darr Coal. A hundred men dead. Two hundred men dead. Burned, dismembered, crushed corpses spread out on high-school-gymnasium floors waiting to be identified. Others buried too deep to be recovered. Local lumberyards unable to provide enough pine for the coffins. A hundred men dead. Three hundred men dead. Three hundred new men ready to fill their jobs the next day.

The causes behind these explosions were never known for sure. Reasons were given, but there was no way to effectively conduct an investigation at a scene buried under tons of earth and rock.

The companies blamed it on miner incompetence; the miners blamed it on the company's disregard for miner safety, but this particular battle had become one of unspoken demands and silent arguments kept inside their hard hats by the time of my dad's generation of miners. All the legislative battles that were going to be fought had been fought; all the improvements that were going to be made had been made.

The miners themselves knew that working in a mine could never be safe, just as a seasoned soldier never believed in a commander in chief's promise of a quick and easy war.

These promises were made for the well-intentioned but ignorant public by the well-informed but equally ignorant powers that be about subjects neither understood or wanted to think about.

Those who did understand, like my father and my mother, shook their heads and wondered at the games these luxuriously removed people played to ease their uninvolved consciences. Then they went ahead and did their jobs and lived their lives, knowing full well there is no such thing as a safe mine or an easy war.

There's a used-book sale going on in the hospital lobby. About a dozen folding tables have been set up, all of them crammed full of rows of books arranged in no particular order. A teenage girl plugged in to a portable CD player and engrossed in a magazine sits at a card table with a red cash box and a hand-painted sign telling everyone that all proceeds will go toward the building of the new children's ward.

The sale is proving to be popular, if only because it offers an alternative to sitting in waiting rooms or lying in hospital beds. People walk from table to table—some in patients' gowns, others in regular clothing—picking up books, opening them to the first page, and putting them back again.

I leave word at the front desk to have Chastity paged, and then I do some browsing for my mom. She has a couple favorite authors who have published enough paperbacks between them to assure there's always a few copies floating around any book sale.

I move on to a different table. Sitting cross-legged on the floor in front of it with a big book open in his lap is a boy who looks familiar. It takes me a second to place him as the same one I passed this morning riding his bicycle.

He's engrossed in the book. I stand next to him, and he never looks up. I try to get a look at what he's reading.

The page he's on has pictures of big jungle cats: a leopard sleeping in a tree, a pouncing black panther, a roaring lion, a crouching tiger. They catch my eye because they're not photographs or the traditional style of illustration for a book like this. Each picture is a miniature work of art, a painting, not an ink drawing, almost impressionistic in the way the colors are softly blended and light and shadow play against each other.

A thrill of recognition races through me, and I have to stop myself from reaching out and yanking the book away from him.

He looks up at me.

"Hi," I say.

"Hi," he replies suspiciously.

"Did you get to school okay?"

His expression relaxes as he remembers me.

"Yeah. My grandma took me."

"Could I see that book for a second?"

He pulls it closer to himself.

"I didn't do nothing wrong."

"I know you didn't. I want to show you something."

He looks from me to the book, then back again. He decides he can trust me and reluctantly holds the book up to me.

I take it and hold it in my hands like it might break into a million pieces at the slightest pressure. I close it and run my hand over the old hard cover bordered in orange with a collage of plants and animals pictured on it and the title in capital letters: THE WONDERS OF NATURE.

Inside the cover my name is written in faded lead by a sprawling five-year-old hand. Two other names come after it. This isn't the first time it's been passed along. My mother must have given it away for the first time years ago.

I skim through it, recalling every section as clearly as if I had read it yesterday. The African rain forest. The Australian outback. The American woodlands. The desert. The ocean. The Arctic. The prairie.

I find the page I'm looking for and hand the book back to the boy. He stands up to take it.

"That's a prairie-dog town," I tell him. "Have you ever seen one of those?"

He shakes his head no as he studies the picture.

I wait for him to finish. I hope he puts it back on the table. I want the book. If he doesn't give it up willingly, I'll be forced to try to convince him I should have it. I can show him my name on the first page. What if he argues: finders keepers, losers weepers? The same rationale I used to solve Ronny Hewitt's picnic-table crisis?

Maybe I could beg and make him feel sorry for me. Maybe I could offer him cash. Of course, there's always the fact that I'm bigger than he is.

He looks up from the page.

"Cool," he says simply.

He gives me a quick version of the same grin he wore coasting down the hill this morning on his bike.

"Thanks"—he looks me up and down and decides to call me—"Officer."

He tucks the book under one arm and walks over to the girl with the cash box, his other arm swinging at his side.

I feel Chastity come up next to me. I don't have to turn to know she's there. Her presence charges the air like the arrival of a game day.

I turn and look at her. She's changed out of her work clothes. No sexy pantsuit or a short skirt with her long legs showing. Instead her long legs are inside a pair of slim jeans tucked into stack-heeled, brown suede cowboy boots. Her hair is down and loose, except for a thin brown leather headband. She's got on a pale pink T-shirt with a well-worn denim shirt over it tied in a knot. I can tell by the shape of her breasts beneath the fabric that she's not wearing a bra.

"Ready?" she asks me.

# NINETEEN

CHASTITY NEVER HAD TIME TO GRAB DINNER, SO I TAKE HER to the Valley Dairy. She said she had a craving for a chocolate milkshake and fries.

It's not very crowded. It does most of its business during breakfast and lunch. Jolene likes to say this is because she doesn't work nights. She could be right. The pep level for the three waitresses working tonight is running low.

The customers are subdued, too. People eat in silence for the most part, occasionally speaking to each other in low tones. It's the exact opposite of the Eat'nPark chaos.

We've already done our word jumbles and crossword puzzles on our menus, and Chastity even drew a picture of a barn with cows and chickens around it, using the broken crayons sitting on the table in a juice glass.

During the drive over, she said she felt bad about our phone conversation and wanted to make it up to me. She said she didn't want us to get off on the wrong foot.

I'm trying to figure out why she'd want to get off on any foot with me and exactly what we'd do once we started off on the foot. I know she's engaged. She seems to like me but not be interested in me, yet I sometimes see flashes of something sensual in her eyes. Maybe she's a flirt. Maybe this is some warped kind of vengeance for all the times we beat Clearfield. Maybe she's preparing to hit me in the head with the ultimate egg: leading me on to think I might get to sleep with her, then blowing me off? Or maybe she will sleep with me once and then dump me? I can only hope.

"So tell me about Florida," she says, dunking a fry into the ketchup on her plate. "I've only been there once, and the whole time I was there all I could think was, why would anybody want to live here? No hills. No trees. Too hot outside, too cold inside. Everybody and every-thing feels so temporary. I don't know how anybody could ever do any-thing serious there."

"I don't think anybody ever does. I think that's the whole point."

I watch her raise the fry to her lips and take a bite. I must be doing it with a longing look on my face, because she pushes the plate across the table to me and nods that I should take one. It's not the fry I want, but I take one.

"It is a strange place if you actually try to live there, and you're not retired," I tell her, "because no one is from there. Everyone has come from some other place because they failed at something or they couldn't cope with something. Everybody you talk to has a similar story, and almost all of them start with, 'Yeah, I just couldn't deal with . . .' and then you fill in the blank: couldn't deal with an ex-wife, couldn't deal with so-and-so looking for me because I owe him money, couldn't deal with snow, couldn't deal with a certain job, couldn't deal with having any job."

"Then why were you living there?"

"If America were a yard sale, Florida would be the table in back with all the discarded crap and all the broken, unidentifiable pieces that went to other things. I fit right in."

"Well, I know your mother and your sister, and I know this town, so I know you weren't discarded," she says, reaching for her shake. "And you're easily identifiable. So you must have thought you fit in because you were broken. Are you referring to your knee?"

"I guess."

"You ran away because you broke your leg."

"I did not run away," I practically shout at her.

"What do you call it? A smart career move? You always secretly harbored a burning desire to kill bugs for a living? I admit Florida's the place to be if that's your calling in life."

"I didn't care where I went. I just knew I couldn't stay here."

"Why not?"

"I couldn't play ball anymore. That's all I was to people around here. A great ballplayer. I didn't want to have to be reminded every single minute of every single day what I'd done."

"What do you mean, what you did?"

"What?"

"You said you didn't want to be reminded about what you had done."

"I did?"

She slips her straw between her lips and takes a sip.

I look at my own drink: a Coke. I'm surprised not to have an urge to put rum in it, but I'd love to have a beer. I asked one of the waitresses if they make beer shakes yet. She just smiled and said I'd be amazed how many times she gets asked that question.

"I must have meant what had been done to me," I explain. "You know, what happened."

"I still don't see why having to stop being a great ballplayer should make you feel like you had to leave."

"I let everyone down."

The words are out before I can stop them. I realize it's the first time I've ever said them out loud to anyone.

She seems to grasp the seriousness of what I've just said, even though the words themselves are simple, almost juvenile.

She knits her brow.

"How?" she asks.

"I told you. I'm not a great ballplayer anymore."

"I highly doubt that anyone expected you to be one forever."

I shrug a reply.

"I can tell you one thing," she says, still looking concerned. "There wasn't a single person at that auction looking at your balls that had even the slightest bad feeling about you."

I look over at her. She's waiting for me to smile at her comment. The best I can do is roll my eyes at her.

"You were a source of happiness and pride for them. Someone would start talking to someone else about you. They'd say you should've seen Ivan against Notre Dame. You should've seen him against Ohio. That time on the fifty, he took the snap and disappeared into this wall of linemen and everybody thought he was buried; then he popped out on the other side and ran for a touchdown. Or that time everybody thought he was out of bounds, but somehow he managed to run seventeen yards down the sidelines for a touchdown like he was walking on a tightrope."

I reach for another fry off her plate while she keeps talking.

"The next thing you'd know, there'd be a bunch of people all huddled around, smiling and nodding and talking about you, and then that led to talking about other things. You make them feel good about their town because you're from it, and then they feel good about themselves."

"That's sort of what I mean," I tell her. "Everybody talking about me. I can never escape it. Even now."

"Why do you want to escape it?"

She takes another slurp of her shake.

"I just do."

"If it's so bad, then why did you come back?"

"I came back to do a favor for a friend."

"But you have a job here."

"It's temporary."

She looks up at me with the straw still between her lips.

"You're not staying?"

"I don't know."

"Do you like the job?"

"I'm not sure about that either. Some days I do. Some days I don't."

"I think that's true for any job."

She goes back to eating fries. She holds each one between her thumb and forefinger and picks it up delicately like she's playing a game of pick-up sticks. After she eats a few, she licks the salt off her fingers before she puts them around her milkshake glass again.

"I haven't seen you in action," she says, "and I don't know you very well, but I've been around people talking about you, and it seems to me that you're one of those people that other people automatically look to for guidance."

"That's scary."

"I think given the opportunity to talk to a lawyer about a legal problem or an accountant about a tax problem or a teacher about a math problem, they'd rather talk to you. And not because you were famous once. They just seem to trust your judgment."

"Well, that's kind of weird, considering how badly I've screwed up my own life."

"Maybe that's because you've never really listened to yourself."

She stares into her glass and stirs what's left of her shake with her straw.

"You might laugh at this," she says, then looks up at me almost shyly, "but I think you'd make a good sheriff."

I do laugh at it.

"No chance of that for a while. Jack's going to be sheriff until the day he dies. He'll be rolling around in a tricked-out wheelchair with a siren and a regulation shotgun strapped to the back of it. He'll have keystone-shaped bifocals."

We both laugh at the image. Then I suddenly don't find it funny. I find it all too real.

"What's wrong?" she asks.

"Jack's getting up there. Dr. Ed, too. I was thinking about Zo. You ever been out to her place?"

She shakes her head.

"The house is great, but it's the property that really sets it apart. Two hundred acres of untouched hills and forest."

She makes a big slurping noise as she drains the rest of her shake.

"Sounds great," she says.

"You want to go?" I blurt out before I realize how stupid the suggestion is.

"Go where? To Zo's house?"

"Yeah . . . well, I have a key. Jolene and I are sort of in charge of packing up her personal belongings."

"So you're asking me if I want to go to a dead old lady's house in the middle of the night and go through her dead old lady things?"

"Something like that."

"Are you springing for the beer?"

We end up at Zo's house with a couple six-packs. The house is cold. The heat's not working. I start a fire in the living-room fireplace, but it only makes the living room warm. We start packing boxes in the other rooms but are gradually drawn there by the heat.

The work, the nearness of Chastity, the comfort of being in a place that has always been safe helps distract me from my troubled thoughts of John, and Jess and Bobbie, and my dark wish for Reese.

Surprisingly, after the day I've had, I don't feel the need to get shitfaced, but I do need some alcohol in my system like a diabetic needs his insulin. A few beers provide enough. I concentrate all the rest of my desire on Chastity. Having her in the same room with me and being able to watch her simple loveliness as she engages in common household tasks like packing a box and dusting a shelf is just as arousing to me as seeing her in her high heels and miniskirts.

She picks up a vase off an end table, checks the bottom for masking tape, cleans it off with a rag, and puts it in one of the dozen boxes of objects to be dispensed by Jolene. Unmarked objects go in a different box. So far it contains an air-freshener night-light and a broken windup alarm clock.

I pop open a new can of beer for her. She takes it from me while she picks up a framed photo off the same end table with her other. She shows it to me: two small children, sitting Buddha style on their big padded diaper bottoms, graze on a plate of Ritz crackers and cheese cubes in the middle of a room enclosed by a perimeter of sturdy plastic fencing.

"Those are Randy's legitimate kids a couple years back," I explain.

"They're cute," she says.

"Like pandas," I add, "only less endangered."

She laughs and takes a gulp of beer.

She has a small birthmark where her jaw meets her throat. The first time I noticed it, I thought it was a tattoo of a lavender rose. I watch it pulse as she swallows.

She flips the picture over. Finding no masking tape on it, she puts it in the We-Assume-This-Goes-to-Randy box.

I ease myself back down on the couch. It's made from a nappy, crumbly-looking upholstery, the same light brown color as the spice cake Zo used to serve here to her guests, with an ivory afghan over the back and two matching doilies on the armrests the same color as her sour cream frosting.

I reach for the drawer I removed from Zo's filing cabinet and brought with me into the warm living room and start browsing through its contents.

A lot of it is junk: old insurance statements, instruction manuals and warranties for everything from toasters to septic tanks, a bunch of old patterns in their original Butterick and McCall's envelopes, with ink sketches of willow-thin girls wearing short zippered jumpers and hot pants with matching vests.

Some of it's not junk, though. At least it wasn't to Zo. A brochure from the Liberace Museum in Las Vegas. Homemade birthday cards from her grandchildren. A newspaper clipping of a widow with a J&P executive in a suit handing her a gigantic fake cardboard check while her four kids stood around her in their best clothes and scrubbed faces. The caption reads "J&P reaches out helping hand." It didn't mention that the hand only contained three hundred dollars for each family.

I find an old math test of Randy's. He only missed three. The teacher wrote WOW! in red ink at the top. It's the only one of his school papers I find. There's also a safety-patrol patch from grade school, and a small clipping from the local paper listing the graduates of his high-school class. His name is underlined.

I guess that was one of the advantages of having a boy like Randy. You didn't have to devote too much storage space to his achievements.

"So what do you think Randy will do with the house?" Chastity asks as I toss his test into the Randy box. "Do you think there's any chance they'd move back here?"

"No. He has a good job in Maryland. He'll sell the house. The land, too. I'm just afraid he's going to sell it for strip mining."

"Do you think he'd do that?"

"I don't know. I'd like to think he wouldn't. Both his parents will spend the rest of eternity spinning in their graves if he does it. J&P's been after his family for generations for this land. Now they're going to see their opportunity to pounce. They're going to know he's the one who moved away and doesn't have any more loyalty to this place. And they'll know he has a wife and two kids to support. They'll offer him more money than he could make selling it as a home. This isn't exactly a hot real-estate market out here."

She suddenly turns and walks to the window. She pulls back one of Zo's celery green curtains and looks out at the shadows of the dark hills like giant sleeping bodies huddled under blankets for the night.

"Destroying this land would be awful," she says.

"Yeah. But we all need money."

"Too bad we don't seem to need anything else."

She lets the curtain fall. I watch her walk to the fireplace and crouch down in front of it.

She moves off the balls of her feet onto her knees like she's about to start praying, but she puts her palms out to the fire instead of clasping them, like she's caressing God instead of begging him for something.

The white light from the fire gives her face a porcelain perfection.

I think about an angel my mother used to set out at Christmas. She was dressed in layers of stiff golden fabric. Her face was flawless, but beneath her robes every inch of her slim white body was finely fissured with hairline cracks.

I find a sealed brown envelope in Zo's drawer. "For Ivan" is written on it in her delicate and careful handwriting.

Chastity turns her head in my direction and looks up at me. Her eyes are copper in this light. I can just make out the rose-shaped mark on her throat. It's where I would place my thumb if I were going to kiss her or strangle her.

She takes off the denim shirt. The shapes of her nipples push against the pink T-shirt.

I put the envelope down.

She starts to move toward me, crawling on her hands and knees.

The various points of faded pain on my body begin to spark and throb again as the heat she generates in me spreads and settles around them.

My fingers itch at my sides. If I don't touch a part of her soon, I will have to hurt yet another part of myself to distract my desire.

I stop breathing as she arrives between my legs and lowers her head.

"Look what I found," she says excitedly.

She pulls out a wooden box from underneath the couch. My breathing starts again, but it can't possibly keep up with the pounding of my heart. I finish my beer in one long gulp.

She opens the gold clasp. The box is lined in black velvet. A beauty of a hunting knife with a cut-bone and brass handle and a polished stainless-steel blade about four inches long lies inside it, along with an old, cracked, dusty black leather sheath with a boot clip.

"I'll be damned," I say.

I lower myself carefully from the couch to the floor in front of the fireplace to sit beside her.

"That's Bill's hunting knife. She gave it to him on their wedding night. See, it's engraved."

I put my hand over her hand holding the knife and tilt it so she can see the words.

"'Zo and Bill. Always and Forever,'" she reads.

"He wore it all the time in his boot. When they found what was left of his body, it was unidentifiable. Until they found a crushed lower leg with a boot and his knife in its sheath completely unharmed. It was still polished when she took it out."

She holds the knife directly in front of her chest between the two dime-size shadows of her nipples. The firelight plays over the blade hypnotically. I watch until it's hard to tell what is reflection and what is real, if it's a knife or a solitary flame of steel.

She's looking for the masking tape. When she doesn't find any, she picks up the box and searches it. She turns it upside down.

"Who's Judy?" she asks.

"My mom."

I reach for the back of her neck and put my thumb on the pretty birthmark at her jawline and tilt her head back to kiss her throat.

She doesn't move except for a slight shudder that takes me back to the last tremor of life I felt in the rabbit Val slaughtered in order to give me its lucky foot before he left for 'Nam. I apply a slow, steady pressure. Her breathing turns ragged. My own takes up the rhythm of her pulsing blood beneath my thumb.

I drag my lips and my fingers down her throat until I have her breast in my hand. Her nipple nudges against my palm.

She puts her arms behind her, and her back tenses into an arc. My eyes fix on the curve where her breast dips into the hollow near her armpit. I kiss her there through the fabric of her T-shirt.

She pulls away, and I think it might be over. She stands up, and panic races through me. She wants a man with a purpose, I remind myself. Not a man who can barely walk who sleeps on his sister's couch every night. A man who didn't even give her his free smiley-face cookie from Eat'nPark. I ate it in my truck on the way to the hospital.

She wants a man like Muchmore, who silently provides quality medical care at great personal expense for women who've been beaten into comas by their husbands.

Then I notice her smiling at me and her eyes eclipsing into disks of black and bronze. She pulls her shirt off over her head while gently swaying her hips and tosses it into one of the boxes packed with Zo's stuff.

She unzips her jeans and slides them down her legs, pulls them off her feet, and tosses them, too. They end up in a different box.

I stare at her standing in front of me, angelically naked, her skin pearlized by the firelight, and let my eyes absorb her curves and shadows.

I used to view women as a bunch of parts with obscene and silly names, but she is one slow, seamless stroke of flesh with only one name.

She reaches out her hand to me to help me off the floor. It's not easy, and there's no way for me to do it gracefully or to maintain any masculine dignity.

As she helps me, I watch her and think of a taut, sleek, tawny female jungle cat being approached by a scraggly, scarred, limping old male with one eye missing and his tail dragging on the ground. I hope she's not thinking the same thing.

She kisses me, and I close my eyes and consume her through touch like a blind man placing his hands all over a loved one's face, trying to remember.

I don't even realize I've undressed when she leads me to the couch and stretches out on it, waiting for me.

"I can't do it like that," I tell her. "My knee," I start to explain, but she stops me with a look.

She has me sit on the couch and crawls on top of me and takes me inside.

I watch her the entire time, unable to take my eyes off the vulnerable body of a woman, so delicate compared to a man's, yet moving so powerfully beneath my hands controlling me, my pleasure, and my fate.

She says my name only once. A sort of wild cry.

I close my eyes and hear my mother's young voice sounding the same as it rose above the other desperate voices at the smoldering remains of Gertie, calling out my father's name for the last time.

I try to make this first time last, and I fail. My surrender is quick and unconditional. I've never been afraid to let go before. I've always rushed toward the release without investing emotion. This time I fear the place I'm going to, yet I want to be there more than I've ever wanted to be anywhere.

# TWENTY

I CAN'T SLEEP. I WANT TO WATCH HER.

Chastity's asleep on the couch, naked and perfect as a sculpture, lying on her side with her hands tucked beneath her cheek like Zo's sleeping angel figurine on the fireplace mantel.

I notice the envelope with my name on it that I found earlier.

It was licked and sealed at one point, but the adhesive wore off years ago. When I undo the clasp, it breaks off in my fingers.

Inside are some sheets of paper covered front and back with small, deliberate handwriting in faded blue ink. The pages have been smoothed out flat, but the fold lines are still evident.

I pick up the top sheet and begin to read.

*December 8, 1968*

*Dear Zo,*

*How are you? I hope you're well and your son, too.*

*Sorry I haven't written for so long. Things have been tough. About a week after I wrote you my last letter, we were lead platoon out on patrol going through these low mountains that remind me a lot of the ones back home except the ground here is this slippery red clay crap and back home it's good old-fashioned dirt and bony. We were heading down into a valley, going along the ridgeline, when all of a sudden we spotted two NVA divisions coming into the valley like an army of ants. We radioed* back for assistance, but we knew we only had one company behind us. About 140 men.

There was a big hill in the middle of the valley and we went for it. We dug in, set up what weapons we had, and basically started dying.

They tried everything. Machine guns, rockets, rifles. They even set the hill on fire. We just dug holes and let it burn over us, then came back out and kept shooting. Nothing stopped them. Sometimes they'd come at us on a dead run screaming their shit. Other times it would be a very professional, well-controlled assault.

Water was our biggest problem. Ammo second. Choppers tried making passes on the top of the hill with resupply and taking what wounded they could, but it was crazy. A lot of guys died waiting to be taken out.

Everyone who managed to survive got wounded. I got shot in the arm. The bullet went in and out and hit the guy behind me—Webster Hicks, a guy from Detroit—in the chest. He took it in the right side, so it looked like he was going to be okay.

You only get one bandage, so the disadvantage of having the bullet pass through you is you have to make a choice if you're going to treat the exit or the entrance wound. We decided on the exit because it was more of a mess.

Hicks was saying about how I slowed down the bullet for him. He actually, seriously thanked me. I heard later he went into shock on the chopper and died.

Five days into it, the Fourth Marines came in and overran our position, and we got a little breathing room. By then we'd lost over half our platoon. The battle went on for over a month. There wasn't a single one of us who thought we were going to get out of there.

The whole time we're fighting, I kept thinking about back home and trudging off on those freezing cold mornings when it's still pitch black outside carrying my lunch pail with my extra sandwiches in it in case there's a cave-in. In case there's a cave-in? Jesus, did you ever stop to think about that? Of course not. We didn't because it was just part of our lives, but we were taking sandwiches with us in case we got buried alive and got hungry waiting for the rescue team.

So I kept thinking to myself I'm used to having a tough job, so I kept telling myself this is my job. It's my job. It's my job to defend America, and that's a good job. What job could be better than that? And that's what I kept thinking the whole time. This is my job. I blocked out everything else.

It helped me out on the hill, but now that we're out of there, the same thoughts are bugging the hell out of me, and I'll tell you why. I had a good reason for working in the mines. We all did. I was helping take care of my mom and working on my truck. There was this girl I wanted to ask out. I won't tell you who, 'cause you know her. I didn't want to do it until my truck was running perfect. I wanted to paint it, too.

It's not that different here than back home. It's a quiet place with lots of hills and quiet people who just want to farm and eat their rice and trade their chickens and be left alone. It reminds me a lot of back home, if home were in a fucking hellhole full of bugs.

My problem lately is trying to figure out the reason for doing the job I'm doing now.

I love my country. I'd give my life to protect someone like Mrs. Zoschenko and her kids. Mr. Z gave his life just to get a paycheck. But I'm not so sure exactly what I'm protecting them against by being here. Buddhist monks? Farmers? Little quiet villages surrounded by miles of nothing but rice paddies and jungle? Cute Vietnamese kids with their arms blown off but still smiling at you? Communism? What communism? Where is it?

It's hard to believe it. That's all I'm saying. You don't see any signs of anything bad here, except us and the VC. It's too bad when governments decide to go to war they can't just take their armies and put them in a contained space to fight like a football stadium and not have to fuck with innocent people.

*I don't know when you'll get this, but if you get it before Christmas, have a merry Christmas. I hope it's snowing there.*

> *Your friend,*
>> *Valentine Claypool*
>> *Rifleman*
>> *101st Airborne Division*

*March 11, 1969*

*Dear Zo,*

*It was good to hear from you. It sounds like you had a nice Christmas. Thank you for your prayers.*

*I just finished eating, and I've got some time to write before I go on patrol. We've been living on cold C-rations out of our helmets for a month. I can't even look at the ham and lima beans anymore. We call them snot and nipples. That gives you an idea what they're like.*

*Last time I wrote, I forgot to tell you Lucius took a bullet in the throat when we were on the hill. I saw it happen. He dropped his gun and clapped his hands around his neck and fell to his knees. He started looking around and saw me.*

*He tried to say something or, I don't know, maybe you just make this gargling sound when you get shot in the throat. It was in his eyes, though. He knew what it meant. It wasn't fair. He should've died instantly. That's what I kept thinking.*

*I crawled over to him, and he started shaking his head at me, but I kept going. Jesus. He just sat there on his knees holding his neck, all this blood coming through his fingers and coming out of his mouth, and he wouldn't die. He wasn't even weak enough that he had to lie down.*

*He bled to death. I sat down beside him and put my arms around him. Eventually he sort of slumped against me, but he still wouldn't die. He wouldn't let go of his throat either. It was almost like he didn't want me to see it. Like he was embarrassed or something.*

*Dying is one thing. Knowing you're dying is another. Maybe I'm a chickenshit, but I don't want to look death in the face. I want him to come up without me knowing and sit on me.*

*A lot of guys died, but he's bothering me the most. I can't stop thinking about how long it took him to die and how much time he had to think about what it was going to be like.*

*Mr. Zoschenko told me this story once about when he was a prisoner in that work camp in Siberia where he got that wild tattoo.*

*He had this Russian friend there named Dmitri who was a political prisoner. He had been caught with some friends at college running a printing press printing pamphlets against Stalin. They were also printing pamphlets against Hitler. I asked Mr. Z if that meant Dmitri was for the Americans, and he said they were against them, too. I asked him who they were for, and he said they didn't know yet. They only knew who they were against.*

*He and Dmitri used to talk a lot about what was the best way to die, since they were pretty sure they were going to die there. There was starving to death. Freezing to death. The radiation poisoning from the uranium. Blood poisoning from a bad tattoo. Committing suicide with a pickax. Throwing yourself off a cliff into the sea. Being beaten to death by a guard in a bad mood or a fellow prisoner in a bad mood. They could never decide which would be the best way to go.*

*Dmitri had a girlfriend back home named Alla who he got pregnant, but he wasn't able to marry her before he got arrested. This bugged him a lot, because he really wanted to give the baby his name. He was always talking about escaping, and one day he did.*

*About a month later, they brought him back. He was in real bad shape. He was almost starved to death and had lost the tips of two fingers to frostbite, and he'd been beaten up bad.*

*He told Mr. Z that he had been able to find out about Alla and the baby before he got caught. Alla died in childbirth, and the baby died, too. Mr. Z told him he was real sorry but they were both in a better place now.*

*Then Dmitri said, "Rado, I've been thinking about our conversations about what is best way to die. I think I know the answer now." And Mr. Z asked him, "What is it?" And he said, "First."*

So I've been thinking of that story a lot. I keep telling myself Lucius is the lucky one. I think about him being in heaven. Not a clean white heaven with clouds and angels and harp music and nothing to do, but a place where he could just be himself and do what he wanted. Shoot some pool with his dad. Have a couple beers. Paint some houses. He was a house painter before he got drafted. Most of the guys I know would still work a job even in heaven.

I think about Mr. Zoschenko a lot, too. He was kind of like a dad to me. Sure as hell more like a dad than my real dad, wherever the hell he might be. I think about that painting of that czar he had in the kitchen. It looked like something that should've been hanging in a museum, but he had it in his kitchen. Supreme sovereign of our stuff, Mrs. Zoschenko called him. I think about his boy, too. He used to come and hang out with me sometimes.

I told him I was going to write to him, but I can't write to a kid. I can't tell him about this shit, and I can't lie to him either the way I do to my mom.

If I don't make it back, do me a favor and tell him that story his dad told me. Wait until he's more grown up and can understand it. Thanks.

> Your friend,
> Valentine Claypool
> Rifleman
> 101st Airborne Division

P.S. Dr. Ed sent me a couple bags of lollipops like I asked him. I told the guys I got them to give to the kids whenever we run into them, but they've all started calling me Candy-ass anyway.

June 6, 1969

Dear Zo,

We're all getting medals for the last battle I told you about. They were just going to give one to the lieutenant, but he put up such a stink we're all getting them. None of us care too much one way or the other.

*You asked me once what my first impression of 'Nam was, and I don't remember if I ever answered. To be honest, it was probably the smell of shit. Somebody was burning shit from the latrines near the airstrip, which is how they get rid of it over here. Or maybe that was second. Probably the heat was first. It hits you when you walk off the plane like somebody's thrown open a furnace door. For a second I forgot to be afraid of the fighting, and instead I was afraid of the place. Holy fuck, I thought to myself. I'm in a jungle.*

*Then I thought about the Zoschenko kid next door and this book he was always dragging around. Natural Wonders or something like that. It was this big book the size of a phone book, and it had this section on the jungle. He loved that section. He was always showing it to me. And the prairie-dog town. The kid was obsessed with the prairie-dog town. I told him once he had a much better chance of seeing one of those than a jungle, and now here I was in a jungle.*

*But I'll tell you what, as many guys as come through here, you don't ever see any rich kids over here. I don't know what they're telling you back home, but there are no rich kids here. No movie stars either. It's not like World War II, when everybody from Clark Gable to Jimmy Stewart signed up.*

*There's even a class system within the army. It hit me the other day that our platoon is always sent out on ambush. We're always point platoon when it comes to combat or contact. And we have the most blacks, rednecks, and guys who have a history of problems with authority figures, like Lucius and Cunningham. We have a lieutenant with a girlfriend back home named Rosita. Is this a coincidence?*

*Sweeney says I'm getting fucking paranoid, but I'm sorry. When I see this shit. When I think about how many guys died just on that one fucking hill. When I see the body bags getting dumped off the choppers and some of them rip open and shit pours out you can't even identify as human. The piles of boots with guys' names on them and blood inside them. Do you know what has to happen to someone to get blood in the bottom of his boots?*

*I don't know what I think anymore. I guess all I'm saying is, there's an endless supply of rednecks, blacks, Hispanics, and fuck-ups between the ages of eighteen and twenty-two. That's all I'm saying. If we ever have to call up Stan Jack's son, we might want to reconsider this war.*

*The reason I'm telling you this is because I've decided I'm going to do another tour. Here's the way I look at it. I'm just getting good at knowing what to do here, and if I leave, I'm going to get replaced by a guy who's just as green as I was, and when he gets good at it, he's going to get replaced, too. What kind of fucking sense does that make?*

*I'm not noble or brave or any of that crap. I'm feeling good about my decision. I'm like one of those people who donates their dead kid's organs so another kid can live. I bet sometimes when it gets hard for them thinking about their dead kid, they think about the kid they helped who's still alive, out there smiling and happy and running around, and how happy his folks are that he's not dead. That's sort of the way I think at my lowest moments. I think about the guy back home I've never met and I'm never going to meet who's going to get to keep his life.*

*It's my one small stand against stupidity.*

*Take care of yourself.*

> *Your friend,*
> *Valentine Claypool*
> *Rifleman*
> *101st Airborne Division*

I finish reading and slide the letters back into their envelope. Chastity stirs slightly. I reach out and touch her.

# THURSDAY

# TWENTY-ONE

WE SPEND THE NIGHT IN ONE OF ZO'S GUEST ROOMS. CHASTITY'S absence next to me wakes me in the morning, and I find her standing in front of a window with her bare feet in a patch of sun-soaked throw rug on the honey-colored wood floor, wearing nothing but her pink T-shirt, tugging her fingers through her curls.

The smile she gives me lets me know that I didn't dream last night, and I didn't dream making her feel the way I'd been dreaming of making her feel.

"If it isn't the great Ivan Z," she says, her voice still throaty with sleep.

She turns her back to me so I can see her bare ass while she steps into her panties.

"You're doing that on purpose."

"Of course I am."

"Come here."

"I can't. I'm late. I have surgery this morning."

"Come here."

She walks over to me, smiling. I grab her and pull her back into bed with me.

She pushes me back and straddles my chest, clamping my sides with her bare legs, the triangle of her panties inches from my face. For the first time in my life, I'm beginning to see the bright side of being a man no longer able to perform in the missionary position.

"You're very cute," she tells me.

"Cute? Puppies are cute. You're supposed to tell me I'm strong and sexy and I've got a lot of stamina—"

"And that you have a big dick?"

"That's always good."

She hops off me before I can grab her again.

"I'm late," she says.

She picks her jeans up off the floor.

I get out of bed as quickly as I can, but she's fully dressed by the time I do.

"Do you want to have dinner tonight?" I ask her.

"Ivan, last night was great."

"I sense a 'but' coming."

She hands me my own jeans so I don't have to bend down.

"No, there's no 'but.' It's just that I am involved with someone else. Seriously involved."

"You stayed the night."

"I know. I wanted to."

She goes back to the window. I'm putting her on the spot and I don't want to do this, yet at the same time I want her and I'm not sure how to get her. I still don't understand what happened last night. I would have never thought of a dead old lady's house as a love nest.

"How about if I put it this way?" she says, turning back to face me. "I'm not a woman who usually sees more than one man at a time."

"So if you're seeing me, that means you're not seeing him?"

"That line of reasoning was practically algebraic," she says, smiling. "Pretty impressive for a dumb jock."

"I know what a hypotenuse is, too."

"That's geometry."

She hands me my shirt.

"Or are you trying to tell me if you're seeing him, you don't want to see me?"

"I'm in a hurry. Can we work on your math skills later?"

I stop her from leaving by grabbing her around the waist.

"Do I have a chance? That's all I want to know."

She smiles up at me, but her dark eyes are serious. "Maybe you don't realize it, but when I look at you, I have to ask myself the same question: Do I have a chance with this guy? You're not sure of anything in your life. You're not even sure you're going to be living here a couple months from now."

I have no honest reply to give her.

"I can't make any promises or even predictions about what will happen between us," she continues, "but I want to keep seeing you. That's the best answer I can give you."

She kisses me.

I feel pretty good. It's a better answer than I was hoping for.

I load my truck with a couple boxes of Zo's stuff to take to Jolene. I put the envelope with Val's letters in my glove compartment, under my gun and Vicodin.

Even though Chastity's late, I drive slowly. I'm trying to prolong the time we're together and avoid the moment when she'll get out of my truck and maybe walk out of my life.

"Have you ever been out to the Coal Run junkyard?" I ask her as we approach it.

She nods. "Of course I have. My family made a special trip once right after they declared it a disaster area but before they put up the barbed wire. We wanted to see the chasms with the fire burning inside them."

"You were part of the masses that actually walked out here and risked falling into four-hundred-foot-deep fiery sinkholes?"

"Sure. Who could resist that?"

I slow near the top of the hill so we can look around. Whether drawn by curiosity, disgust, or fear, it's impossible to speed past this place. It's nature's version of a haunted house.

There's a truck parked at the side of the road. I pull up behind it and stop.

"Do you mind?" I ask her.

"Mind what?"

"There's someone down there I need to talk to."

"Are you kidding? Down there? This was a cool place to come to as a kid, but now I'm a grown-up and I'm late. To perform surgery," she adds emphatically.

"Five minutes. I promise. That's all."

I get out before she can convince me not to, and I start down the hill.

Jess is standing near the bottom between a rust-speckled filing cabinet and a shattered microwave.

By the time I reach him, he's moved farther away and is toying with the knobs of a Hotpoint stove. He has his head bowed over a burner, and the brim of his cap conceals his face from me.

He straightens up and studies the clock. He bangs it a couple times with his fist.

"Nice stove," I comment.

He opens the oven door and peers inside. He crouches down and rests his hands on his thighs while studying the interior. Then he puts the entire upper half of his body inside.

"Reese get to your house okay?"

"Yeah," his voice echoes from inside.

"Is he there now?"

He pulls back out again and adjusts his cap.

"He closed down Sweetwater's last night. Then he closed down Brownie's. I expect he'll sleep most of the day, then do the same thing tonight."

"So Bobbie and Danny are alone with him right now, and you're messing around in a junkyard? You're okay with that?"

He turns his back on me and starts walking toward the spot where the dryer disappeared. I trail after him and catch up as he stops to examine a VCR by turning it over with his foot.

"I know about Bobbie," I tell him. "I know she hit Danny, not you."

His gray eyes narrow with suspicion, which makes him look a lot

like Reese except there's no malice in his expression, only the beginning paranoia of a man realizing he needs to protect his family but he's
not sure from what.

"What the hell do you want from me?"

"What do you mean?"

"You lied to Bobbie and said I told you I hit him. What the hell was
that all about?"

"I was trying to get her to tell me the truth."

"And you decided the truth was I punched my son in the face."

"It was an easier truth to accept than thinking Bobbie did it."

He starts pacing. His heavy, careless footsteps make me nervous. I
keep expecting the ground to split open and him to disappear inside it.

"She's not a bad mother," he blurts out, his eyes pleading with me
now. "She isn't. She's a really good mother."

"I'm sure she is."

"You don't understand. Things have been rough for us. It's not easy
having all those kids and me losing my job. She worries all the time.
And now Reese coming."

He stops pacing. A few wisps of steam crawl up his boots and disappear behind his jeans.

"That day we had a big fight about Reese. She told me if I let Reese
stay with us, she was leaving. Him or me, she said. And I picked him.
Course I was really mad at her and I didn't think she was serious, but
it still don't make it right. What I said. It was a rotten thing to say.
Maybe the worst thing I've ever said to her."

"That's why you thought she was leaving?" I ask him.

He nods.

"I went off with a bottle and a six-pack and my gun. She yelled after
me I'm no different than Reese: a good-for-nothing drunk who gets his
kicks killing things."

He takes his cap off and clutches it in both hands the way the sur-
viving men did for weeks after the Gertie explosion whenever they'd
see my mom or any of the widows.

"I guess after I left, Danny was crying, and she yelled at him to shut up, and he wouldn't, and when she asked him what was wrong, he said he didn't want her to say bad things about his dad like that, and she smacked him. She said it was a reflex. She said she didn't even feel herself doing it.

"It don't give her an excuse for what she did to Danny. She knows it. She feels worse about it than anybody else could ever make her feel. She hates herself now. And I don't want her to. Danny doesn't either."

I realize what he's been doing lately, why he always has Danny with him. He wants to believe in his wife, but he's afraid to leave her alone with his son now.

"That's all I'm going to say about it. It's our business, and we're going to be okay."

He puts his hat back on and starts walking away from me. I follow.

His hand suddenly reaches out to stop me from taking another step. We've arrived at a ragged depression in the earth. There's a drop-off about five feet deep, and then the land resumes again in steaming, crumbling peaks and valleys like a small, smoggy canyon.

He kneels down. I start to speak, and he hushes me with a finger to his lips. He waits until he hears a faint hiss like a tire leaking air before dropping the finger and pointing into the hole.

"There," he says.

I look down but don't see anything except broken dirt and torn roots. He gets up and wanders off, returning with a mop handle.

"How long have you known John was my son?"

"I didn't know until I saw him yesterday. He looks like you."

"Then you didn't send me a newspaper clipping about Reese getting out of prison when I was still in Florida?"

"I never even knew you were in Florida. Maybe Bobbie mentioned it at some point since she sees Jolene now and then, but I don't remember."

He kneels again and sticks the handle deep into the crevice and scrapes at the walls. Sparks glow inside the black dirt like tiny red jewels.

"But you knew he wasn't Reese's son?"

"Yeah, but I didn't know who the father was."

"Did Reese know?"

"That you're the father? Hell, no. He would've called the newspapers. 'I'm raising Ivan Z's son.' He thought you were hot shit."

He sets down the mop handle and feels around in the dirt with his hands.

"He knew Johnny wasn't his, but he didn't want anybody to know," he goes on. "He never told anybody, not even my mom. I only found out by accident, and then he made me swear I wouldn't tell, and when Reese makes you swear to something, you usually stand by your promise."

"How did you find out?"

"One time I tried to talk to him after he beat up Crystal pretty bad. He got all upset and said it was none of my business. Then it hit me all of a sudden that I never once saw a mark on Johnny. So I asked him about it, and he said he never touches the boy. And I asked him why not? And he said, ''Cause he ain't mine.'"

He pulls out his hands, claps them together to brush off the dirt, and looks up at me.

"He wasn't raised in a barn, you know. My mom managed to get some values into him. One was you don't mess with other people's stuff."

He moves a few feet away from his original digging spot, kneels down again, and leans his ear to the ground.

"John was your mom's grandson, or at least she thought he was. Why didn't she try and keep him? Or at least try and stay in touch with him?"

"I guess she thought he was little enough he could start over and never know about what happened. He had a chance for a brand-new life. If he had stayed here, he would've had to live in this town knowing his daddy was in jail for almost killing his mommy and knowing everybody around here knew about it. He could've never had a good life here. Too much pain and gossip. She would've been keeping him because *she* wanted him, not because it would've been best for him. My mom may have her failings, but being selfish ain't one of them."

I think about how selfish I was. I never thought about my mother in regard to John. She never got to know him either: a descendant of her union with the man she loved and lost, a living piece of my father's identity, not a photograph of a lid on a stick or a portrait of a czar. I kept her from knowing her first grandson.

"You think she was a bad person for thinking that way?" Jess asks me.

"No," I tell him.

He stands up and takes a small white box out of the pocket of his Woolrich coat.

"I was going to drop by the sheriff's department today on my way to work and give you this."

He hands me the box. I take it and open it. Inside, lying on a piece of cotton, is Crystal's necklace.

"Bobbie and I took her personal effects when it turned out her folks didn't want them," he explains. "I think it was too painful for them. I think they decided to try and pretend she never existed. Some people deal with a lost child that way."

I stare at the cage the size of my thumbnail and the chips of dull color captive inside it.

"You should give this to your son," he urges me. "It belongs to him now."

"I didn't tell him who I am," I reply, still staring into the box. "I think it's best. I'm not planning on seeing him again."

He picks up the mop handle and moves about two feet away from where he last knelt. This time he stretches out across the ground on his stomach, grips the pole two-handed, and starts plunging it into the gash in the earth.

"That's your business."

"You think I'm wrong?"

"Not my place to say."

"I wouldn't know how to find him."

"You're a cop. Can't you find people? Ain't that part of your job?"

He hits something solid with a clunk. I see a trace of a smile on his face.

"The dryer," he proclaims.

I close the box and slip it into my jacket pocket.

I don't particularly want him to see the shape I'm in, but my curiosity wins out over my pride. I slowly, painfully get down on my knees, but I can't see anything.

I stretch out on my stomach next to him. He gives me the pole and points at a spot. I lift and plunge and feel the impact travel up the wood.

"You're right," I marvel.

"Ivan," I hear Chastity call out, and she doesn't sound happy.

"Damn. I'm in trouble," I say to Jess, even though he can't have any idea what I'm talking about. "She was late to begin with. Now she's going to be really late."

I hear her heavy breathing and light footfalls approaching us.

I wait to hear scolding, but I hear laughter instead.

We both roll onto our sides and look up.

She has her hands on her hips. Her cheeks and lips are flushed with color from the cold. The wind tosses her hair around behind her in a wild, dark tangle.

"This is what was so damned important?" she asks. "You had to come down here and play in the mud with your little friend?"

"Chastity, this is Jess Raynor." I make the introductions. "Jess, this is Chastity."

"Nice to meet you," she says to him.

Jess touches the bill of his cap with his filthy hand.

"Likewise," he says back.

She crouches down between us while rubbing her hands together and blowing into them.

"You cold?" Jess asks.

She nods.

"Is it true what they say about the land around here?" she asks him.

In reply he sticks his hands into the gaping scar in the ground and brings them back brimming with dirt.

She cups her cold hands and holds them out to him, and he fills them with the warm, steaming earth.

---

Muchmore has his practice in a big blue Victorian house trimmed in white about a block away from downtown, where the business district starts to blend with a residential neighborhood.

The large front porch has two long wooden flower boxes bursting with bright red, yellow, and orange flowers. It's still too cold for them to survive the nights. I have an image of a couple of his high-heeled, tight-skirted paralegals out there at the end of every workday and first thing every morning, one at each end, lugging the heavy boxes in and out of the office to keep the flowers warm overnight. I make a mental note to find out if this is how they do it and, if so, to cruise by some morning and watch.

A pretty young receptionist smiles brightly at me when I walk in and approach her desk. The house still looks like a house, not an office. Her desk is off the foyer in a room that was probably a parlor and is still decorated like one, with a grandfather clock against one wall, lace curtains, and a mahogany curio cabinet filled with law books now instead of figurines.

Her smile falters for a moment when she notices how dirty I am. She stares forlornly at the glowing finish of the hardwood floor I'm standing on, then glances past me, trying to see if I left muddy footprints on the pristine rose-patterned carpet in the hallway. When she sees that I didn't, the smile returns.

"Can I help you?"

"I hope so. I need to see Muchmore."

"Mr. Muchmore is due in court. He's on his . . ."

Her voice trails off as we hear footsteps coming down the hallway.

"I should be back around noon," Muchmore says as he steps into the room, carrying a briefcase and wearing a long, cream-colored wool coat and the glossiest black shoes I've ever seen aside from the ones the politicians wore the day they announced in the school multi-purpose room that all the ground beneath Coal Run was on fire.

"Ivan," he announces.

He comes at me with his jousting pole of a handshake. I'm tempted to step aside at the last minute just to see if he'd keep going and end up putting his arm through the window, but I restrain myself. As usual, the actual clasp of his hand is quick and weak.

"This is a pleasant surprise," he says, then steps back, smiling, and raises his briefcase in front of his face as if he's defending himself against me. "Wait a minute. Are you here as friend or foe?"

"Neither."

He laughs.

"No hard feelings about the other night then?"

"No hard feelings."

She's mine, I want to shout. But she's not mine. She wasn't his either. She's hers.

"Good. Good," he says, nodding. "Are you here about Dr. Ed? About what I mentioned at dinner the other night?"

"No. I told him what you told me. I guess he'll be in touch if he feels he needs to be."

"Good. Good."

He glances at his watch.

"Hey, I'm due in court. Let's walk and talk."

"Hey, why not."

We step outside. It's a clear, sunny day, but cold. He pulls a pair of black leather gloves out of one pocket and slips them on. The court-house is a five-minute walk from here.

"I wanted to ask you something about Reese Raynor. You remember Reese Raynor?"

"Of course I do. That was a big case for someone to try their first year with the public defender's office."

"Were you happy with the outcome?" I ask him.

"As his lawyer, it wasn't really up to me to be happy or unhappy with the outcome. I felt I did a good job of defending him, so I guess you could say I was happy with my performance."

I give him a hard stare.

"But I guess it's safe to say that you weren't happy with the outcome," he adds.

"I'm an eye-for-an-eye kind of guy. I thought he should have been taken outside and beaten into a coma with a baseball bat."

"Well, that's not the way the system works." He gives me his slow, superior smile. "The district attorney's office accepted the reduced plea. The jury found him guilty. The judge gave him the sentence. They all had much more to do with the outcome than I did. I just defended him because that was my job at the time. But for the record, that case was the beginning of the end of my interest in criminal law."

"Why's that?"

We arrive at my truck. I lean against the hood. He's about to do the same, then notices how dirty my truck is and stands back.

"About a year after the trial, I was defending a man involved in a drunk-driving accident. I needed to interview his father, who was also involved and was dying in Cherry Tree State Hospital. While I was there, the name of the hospital seemed very familiar, but I couldn't remember why. Then it suddenly came to me. It was the hospital where Crystal Raynor had been committed.

"I decided to visit her. I can still remember feeling smug about it. Thinking I was such a great guy for visiting her. I was very impressed with myself and my so-called compassion. Then I saw her."

He looks past me down the street.

I wait for him to tell me this is when he decided to pay to put her in Safe Haven. He doesn't, and I feel a grudging respect for him. Maybe he did it to ease a guilty conscience, or maybe he did it because he truly wanted something better for her, but he definitely didn't do it in order to make other people think he's a great guy.

I understand why he told Chastity, though. She's the kind of woman who motivates men to concoct stories about saving children from burning buildings and delivering home-cooked meals to elderly shut-ins in order to impress her. I told her about Ivan Z's Tacklebreaker Brickle. She asked me why I didn't get to have something chocolate named after me.

"Have you ever been inside Cherry Tree Hospital?" he asks me.

"Yeah."

He shakes his head. "It's a terrible place."

"Yeah."

"So what did you want to ask me about Reese?"

"Did you know he's been released?"

He nods. "Yesterday, I believe. Last time I talked to Dr. Ed, about a month ago, he told me his release date."

"Isn't that a strange thing for you and Dr. Ed to be discussing?"

"Not really. Ed was involved with the case, and he's also maintained a correspondence with the people who adopted John Raynor."

"You're kidding."

I'm not sure what to make of this new bit of information.

"I thought the records were sealed and no one was allowed to know who adopted him."

"You know Ed," he laughs. "Sending John's medical records to his new pediatrician wasn't good enough for him. He wanted to talk to the new parents, and somehow he was able to convince the district attorney to let him. As we all know, Ed has a knack for convincing people to see things his way.

"I guess the parents were impressed with him and his concern for John's welfare, and they've kept in touch with him all these years. They send him a school picture every year. They sent him a high-school-graduation announcement and a clipping from the newspaper last year when he won some sort of track award. He's doing very well."

"So you're saying Dr. Ed's seen a recent picture of him?"

"Fairly recent."

After Chastity's revelation that Muchmore paid for Crystal's care at Safe Haven, I began to think he might be the one who sent me the clipping about Reese's release. If he's that committed to Crystal, I thought he might want to seek some kind of revenge for her, but in order for him to realize I'd be the perfect person to send after Reese, he'd have to believe I had a good reason for wanting him dead, too.

"You said Dr. Ed was involved in the trial. How?"

"He came to me with some information about John that he thought might be important."

"What kind of information?"

"I can't say."

"Was the information that Reese wasn't the boy's real father?"

"You know?"

"Yeah, I know."

I check his face for his reaction. He doesn't show any sign that he thinks I'm personally involved.

"Ed figured it out the first time he saw John as an infant," he continues. "Apparently there was no way the combination of Crystal's blood type and Reese's blood type could make John's blood type. When he asked Crystal about it, she admitted that the baby wasn't Reese's, but she would never tell him who the real father was. She did tell him that the real father knew about the baby, and he didn't want anything to do with either of them."

Hearing myself described that way is unpleasant but truthful. I try to ignore the sting of the remark.

Muchmore doesn't need any encouragement to continue telling his story. He seems to be enjoying giving me the details.

"I asked Reese about it during the trial. He admitted that he wasn't the boy's real father, but Crystal put his name on the birth certificate, so unless parentage is contested in court by the biological father, he is legally the father.

"It was a fleeting consideration of Ed's that if John had a real father out there, maybe we should attempt to find him. Then we decided that if in fact what Crystal told him about the real father was true, if he was living anywhere in the vicinity, possibly even the state, he would have heard about the case and would have had ample opportunity to step forward and claim his son. Otherwise he was long gone. In the end we decided not to tell the district attorney what we knew."

"Thanks." I stop him from going any further. "You answered my question about Reese."

Dr. Ed knows my blood type. He saw me attending Reese's trial. He's seen a recent photo of John.

"All right, then." Muchmore checks his watch again. "I really do need to get going."

"Wait a minute," I tell him. "I have something for you."

I reach into one of the boxes in the back of my truck and hand him a J&P ball cap.

"It's from Zo Craig," I explain.

I show him the piece of masking tape on the underside of the bill with his name on it.

"She's dispensing her possessions from the great beyond."

He takes it from me in one of his gloved hands, grinning broadly, and sets it gingerly on top of the meticulously arranged haystack of his hair, where it sits like an undersize derby on a clown's wig.

"How do I look?" he asks.

Pretty damn stupid, I think.

"You look good," I tell him. "And this is for you, too."

I hand him one of the boxes of cigars from Marcella's that I billed to his table.

"Ivan, this is very generous of you."

"Well, I came into some good fortune lately. I'm feeling generous."

He smiles at me.

"This is one of my favorite brands," he says.

"I had a feeling."

I watch him start down the street, waiting to see if he takes the hat off. He doesn't, but he doesn't pull it down tight on his head either. It's still miraculously balancing on top of his hair when he turns the corner.

I take the clipping out of my wallet and read the words written in the margin: "What are you going to do?" Of course it was Dr. Ed. Only Dr. Ed would ask me that question. I'm amazed I didn't figure it out before.

"The son of a bitch," I mutter under my breath.

He knew I needed a reason or at least an excuse. He knew it would bring me back.

# TWENTY-TWO

EB SUDDENLY PINGS INTO THE KITCHEN LIKE A COIN LET LOOSE inside a dryer. He manages to touch every surface within thirty seconds of his arrival, including his brother, who shoves him. He shoves back. They get into a small scuffle, which my mom has to break up.

"Behave," she tells them gently.

Her eyes fall appreciatively on the sparkling lemon meringue pie sitting on the counter that Jolene made for dessert. Then they fall on me.

"Aren't you going to change?"

"I already changed once today."

"I know. I saw your shirt lying on top of the laundry basket. What were you doing? Rolling around in the mud?"

"Not rolling. Just lying in it."

She gives me a suspicious frown.

"It's Val, Mom. He doesn't expect me to put on a suit. Besides, I have to work tonight."

"I thought you worked all day?"

"I had transport. I spent the whole day on the road, and I never got around to anything else. I have some paperwork to take care of tonight. That's all."

The frown deepens. She always knows when I'm lying. She rarely pursues trying to find out why I'm lying or trying to find out the truth, but we both know that she knows I'm hiding something.

"You look very nice tonight." I try to change the subject.

I'm not lying. She does look nice. She's wearing a dress. It's nothing fancy, but I've never seen my mother in a fancy dress since my father died. She used to wear pretty dresses to church on Easter and Christmas Eve and to the family dinner at her parents' house on Christmas Day.

Tonight she has on a long-sleeved, deep blue dress. The color compliments her eyes, and the fit shows off the fact that she still has a slim figure. She's wearing her hair down. It's straight and shoulder length.

Unlike most women her age, she has refused to cut it short and perm it and wear it in an old-lady bob. She can get away with it because her hair is still shiny and thick. Jolene is always telling her if she colored her hair, she could pass for forty-eight, and my mother is always telling her she doesn't have the energy to go undercover.

"You're trying to change the subject," she tells me. "But thank you anyway."

We each take an end of the kitchen table and pull it apart so we can insert the addition. Jolene had to borrow two folding chairs from a neighbor. I know I'm going to have to sit in one of them.

She breezes into the kitchen looking great in one of the dresses she bypassed for Zo's funeral. It's short black lace with fringe around the hem and the low-cut neckline.

Harrison takes one look at her and asks, "Who's the victim?"

"There's no victim. We're having a dinner guest, so I wanted to look nice."

"That's what I mean. Who's the victim?"

"He's an old friend of the family we haven't seen since Uncle Ivan was Eb's age."

They both stare at me, trying to imagine me at Eb's age, then trying to imagine Eb at my age.

"He used to live next door to us in Coal Run," she finishes.

She's carrying a tablecloth that she snaps into the air. It floats onto the tabletop, and she and Mom position it.

"Did you check the turkey?" Jolene asks Mom.

"It's perfect," Mom replies.

"I can't believe we're having Thanksgiving in March." Eb hops up and down. "Stuffing and gravy. This is so cool."

He's wearing his green Thanksgiving tie with a bug-eyed, terror-stricken turkey on it.

Jolene pauses in checking the contents of every pan on the stove and glances at me.

"Aren't you going to change?"

"That's it." I throw up my hands. "Who wants to play Nintendo?"

I grab my can of beer, and Eb and I race from the kitchen. Harrison always saunters, and he pays for it this time.

"Harrison, set the table," I hear his mom command.

The house was already filled with the smell of turkey when I arrived. By the time Val arrives an hour later, we've all begged Jolene a dozen times to let us start without him.

Mom answers the door when he knocks.

He's wearing a clean pair of jeans, the same army boot and big heavy shoe at the end of his prosthetic that he wore to Zo's funeral, a barn red corduroy work shirt, and the Castro cap. He's carrying a six-pack.

Mom's eyes gleam with tears when she sees him.

"Val," she says simply.

She reaches out, grasps him by the shoulders, and kisses him on the cheek. He stands stiffly, his eyes like cleats nailed to the floor. His free hand rises slightly, as if he means to put it on her back, but then it falls to his side again.

She pulls away, fixing him with a radiant smile that reduces the man to a boy. Its sincerity is overwhelming. She rarely smiles, and only when something truly enchants her or strikes her as funny. Her surface always reflects her depths.

"Hey, Mrs. Zoschenko," he mumbles.

"It's so good to see you again," she tells him.

"You look the same," he tells her.

"I do not."

"You do to me."

Tears start to roll down my mother's cheeks. I don't know what to do. Jolene stands by watching happily, as if she fully expected this reaction.

For the first time in my life, it occurs to me that maybe Val had a crush on my mom.

He extends the six-pack to her.

She wipes the tears away, smiles again, and takes it from him.

Jolene introduces her boys. Their desire to eat is stronger than their curiosity about this old neighbor of ours with the limp and the funny shoe who made Grandma cry.

It's not until we've spent a full ten minutes with everyone stuffing their faces in silence that Eb breaks the ice with a heaping spoonful of mashed potatoes and gravy halfway to his mouth.

"Isn't Val a girl's name?"

The eating frenzy is temporarily suspended. Josh swallows a laugh. Harrison turns very serious, glancing back and forth between Eb and Val. Jolene and Mom each sit back in their chairs and take a sip of their beers, poured in Jolene's good glasses.

"What kind of name is Eb?" Val asks in his rasp of a voice.

"It's a verb," he replies eagerly.

He jumps up from his chair and starts walking backward away from the table.

"I'm ebbing from dinner."

Harrison rolls his eyes. "It's a nickname for Everett," he explains to Val.

"Val's a nickname for Valentine."

Eb returns to his chair.

"You're named after a card?" he asks.

"I'm named after a saint."

"You mean like Volodymyr?"

We all automatically look over at the portrait hanging behind my mom.

"He's not a saint," Harrison corrects his brother. "He's a czar."

"What's the difference?"

"A czar is a king. A saint is a religious guy."

"He was religious, too. He's got a cross on his stick."

"It's a staff."

"He was a religious king," Josh speaks up.

I look over at him. He pulls one of Jolene's rolls apart and pops half into his mouth and washes it down with a gulp of milk.

When Val was his age, he was already working in the mines.

I remember when he made the decision not to go back to school his senior year. He told my dad one summer night when the two of them sat drinking at our kitchen table: Val with a beer he was too young to drink legally in this country, which my father considered ridiculous, and my dad with his warm tumbler of one of his vodkas that came in bottles with pictures of czars or snowy landscapes on the labels.

I had been sent outside to catch fireflies, but I lingered near the screen door instead, holding my jar and straining to hear their conversation over the whir of the fan Mom kept running in the open kitchen window. I heard Val's gruff confession and my dad's soft, precise broken English advising him to finish high school first.

The next day Val let me tag along with him to the junkyard to dump some old tires for a neighbor.

I went off to play in the junk. When I returned, he was sitting on the arm of an old couch with the back torn out and stuffing spread everywhere like snow.

He was staring at an old claw-foot bathtub with a big crack down the middle.

I asked him if he was going to finish high school like my dad said he should. He never answered me.

He just stared at the tub for a while, smoking a cigarette, occasionally picking up an old beer bottle and whipping it out into the junk abyss, where it would either clunk or break with a loud, clean crack or shatter like wind-chime music, depending on what it hit.

Eventually he got up, walked over to the tub, and gave it a kick. He cocked his head to one side and listened intently to the sound with a small, grave smile on his lips, as if it could tell him something mystical about life from the echo inside it. Then he glanced at me and said, "I got a job for this."

He lugged it home for a different neighbor and turned it into the shelter for her St. Joseph lawn ornament.

I keep watching Josh. Val was a year or two older when he wrote those letters Zo saved for me all these years. The idea of Josh's being in the mines or fighting in a war is inconceivable to me.

I look at him, and I think he's a child. When Val left for war, I thought he was a man. When I was eighteen, I was certain I was a man, but I behaved like a child. Am I right now? Or was I right then?

I'm absorbed in my own thoughts. I don't even realize the conversation has moved on until I hear Eb ask, "What happened to your leg?"

I'm impressed by his nerve. At his age I would have never been able to ask Val that kind of question. I wouldn't even be able to ask it now, but Eb doesn't seem put off by the disturbing green eyes with their troubled brown calm or by Val's intimidating silence.

Val puts his fork down and leans forward over his plate.

Jolene and Mom look a little apprehensive, concerned as much with Val's being offended as with Eb's being verbally attacked.

"What happened to your tooth?" Val asks him.

"It got loose, and I wiggled it with my tongue a lot until it came out one day."

Val seems satisfied with the answer and sits back in his chair. "I was fighting in a war," he explains, "and my leg got shot a bunch of times. I couldn't get to a doctor for a long time. By the time I did, my leg was dead and they had to cut it off."

"Did it hurt?"

"Yeah."

"Did you get a medal?"

"Yeah."

"Was it the same war Grandpa was in when he had to go to the place with the lids?"

"No, it was a different one."

Eb falls silent for a moment, and then a grin splits his face.

"Hold on a minute," he says eagerly. "I was saving this, but I'm gonna do it now."

He leaves the room and returns holding a bunch of lids, their edges ragged from being removed with a can opener.

"I had to have cans for an art project at school. We were allowed to bring in extra cans, for the kids who didn't have cans and I brought in a lot. Anyway, we just needed cans, not lids. Mom was going to throw them away, but then I remembered Grandpa's picture, so I saved them."

He dispenses lids and their explanations as he walks around the table.

"The biggest one is for Grandma. The shiniest one is for Mom. The dented one is for Uncle Ivan."

He stops next to Val.

"I didn't know you were going to be here. Is it okay if you get a regular one like me and my brothers?"

Val nods.

We all sit there looking at our lids. Eb watches us expectantly, beaming.

"They're for our graves in case we don't have anything else."

We continue nodding.

"I didn't want to waste them," he says. "They're good lids."

I make it through dinner and dessert before I get too antsy thinking about what lies ahead of me tonight. I wait until the boys leave the table in a thundering herd and Mom takes a cup of coffee into the living room, casting backward glances at Val, who's offering to help Jolene load the dishwasher.

I felt a little awkward around Val all night after reading his letters. I feel like a Peeping Tom forced to come face-to-face with the person he's been spying on, only what I've done seems even more intrusive. Watching someone through a window without his knowing is an invasion of his privacy; reading someone's innermost thoughts without his knowing is an invasion of his self.

But those letters belonged to Zo. She believed I needed to know his thoughts, no matter how many years had passed between us, and she was right. I needed to be shown that it's never too late to be told you weren't forgotten.

I make my apologies to them and duck out the back door with Jolene's protests ringing in my ears.

I know I'm leaving too early. I'll have to sit uptown half the night, but it's better than being around other people. I don't want anything to distract me or change my mind.

On the way to my truck, I grab Harrison's baseball bat off the back porch.

I drive out to the State Store and get a bottle of Jack Daniel's to keep me company, but I drink surprisingly little. Since seeing my son in the flesh, I haven't felt the need to drink as much. I'm not comforted by this. I don't believe for a single second that our meeting cured, reformed, or shocked me into being a nondrinker. I'm afraid of the opposite. I think I'm experiencing a dry lull before a very wet storm.

I got a look at Reese's car in the Kwik-Fill parking lot. Tracking him down is easy. He's parked uptown not far from the Golden Pheasant. I park my truck far enough away that he won't be able to notice it's a sheriff's vehicle.

I'm across the street from Woolworth's. I take slow sips off my bottle and think about the women who worked there, kindly old lifers who spent decades changing hamster litter and pulling out the tray of birthstone rings for little girls who would never be allowed to buy one because they didn't need one. I wonder what happened to them when their jobs disappeared.

I try to keep my mind focused, but it's not easy. I don't let myself think about John and what I have lost, or Chastity and what I may have gained. I don't think about Jess and Bobbie and what may or may not be going on in their house tonight. I don't think about Zo dying peacefully on her couch or Val's friend Lucius getting shot in the throat or Crystal the vegetable who will probably outlive us all. I don't think about my dad walking off for that final shift, waving up at me standing in my bedroom window as he crossed our moonlit front yard.

I don't even let myself think about Reese, because the rage that boils up in me is reckless, and I have to stay levelheaded to make this work.

It's a weeknight and near closing, so not much is going on. The couples have long since cleared out: those who came together and those who found each other. The women have left, too: the unsuccessful loners and the groups of giggling stumblers. The men who are left at this hour leave individually and sporadically. Each one bursts from the door and stops suddenly, squinting first at the streetlamp, then at the sidewalk in front of him, like it's covered in dog shit or daisies or something else he doesn't want to step in.

Reese is one of the last guys out. The relatively harmless-looking, greasy-haired deadbeat standing in the middle of a brightly lit convenience store trying to balance barrels of potato chips under the critical watch of his mother is gone. This Reese reminds me of the one I knew in high school. He has the same skulk. The same flat gaze. The same instinctive angry tensing of his arms and shoulders when he walks out into the open.

He waits outside the door and lights a cigarette before crossing the street to his car.

I try not to think of him as human. I think of him as I would any unpleasant but unavoidable chore.

I don't tail him out of town. There's no traffic at this hour, and I don't want him to realize a deputy is following him. I take an alternate route and pick him up about ten miles from Jess's house.

I could stop him at any time, but I don't want to take a chance of being interrupted, no matter how slim the chance might be on an isolated rural road in the middle of the night. I wait until we're about a mile from a coal road that used to cross a creek and lead to a loading tipple next to the railroad tracks. It's the same creek that eventually twists its way to Coal Run, where Steve and I used to catch our crayfish. The bridge disintegrated and washed away years ago. The road is overgrown with weeds and leads to nowhere now. I've never seen anyone use it except during deer season when hunters park their trucks there.

I know Reese won't stop immediately. His gut reaction will be to run. Then he'll remember he's on parole, and a drunk-driving charge isn't as bad as DUI plus reckless driving plus unlawful flight. He'll still consider running, but then he'll think about what that would mean. Staying with Jess and Bobbie and going out drinking every night is probably preferable to being on the lam or going back to prison. Then he'll think about running again, because he has just enough ego combined with stupidity to think he could actually get away with it. In the end, if he doesn't pull over for me, he'll pull over because he needs to take a leak. Arriving at either of these conclusions will take him about a mile of drive time.

I put my lights on and don't bother with my siren. My prediction proves accurate. He speeds up initially. Slows down. Speeds up again. Then he slows down, pulls over, and comes to a stop about twenty feet from the coal road. I roll down my window, stick my arm out, and motion at him to pull in. He does.

I get out, close my door behind me, and listen to it echo in the quiet night. I listen to my boots crunch across the bony and notice how some of the pieces glimmer in the moonlight like chips of ebony. I remember Jolene running around collecting jars of the stuff after I showed her the page in my *Wonders of Nature* book that showed coal being turned into diamonds.

He automatically holds a hand up to shield his eyes from the flashlight he's expecting me to shine in his face. I wait for him to figure out I'm not going to do it.

"Step out of the car," I tell him.

"For Christ's sake."

"Step out of the car."

"What the hell?"

He gets out and leans against the rusted-out fender. He seemed steadier in front of the bar. I realize now how drunk he is, and I wonder if I should wait and do this sometime when he's more sober so he can truly appreciate what's being done to him.

"If it ain't the great Ivan Z," he slurs at me.

"That particular greeting is beginning to get on my nerves, Reese. You think you could come up with something else?"

"I've never seen a deputy driving around these roads out here in the middle of the night," he slurs at me. "What were you doing? Waiting for me to leave the bar? Don't tell me you guys are gonna make my life a living hell now that I'm out. Is that it? You're just gonna harass me and fuck with me all the time? Why don't you just fucking plant some weed on me and send me back to jail already, huh? Why don't you just get it over with?"

"I considered that option."

My reply confuses him. He stops talking and peers into my face. He notices the baseball bat I'm carrying.

"What's that for?"

"You used to be pretty good with one of these," I say, gripping the bat near its end and slapping it loudly against my palm. "Football was always my game. I'm just a novice with one of these. I probably couldn't even crack your spine in two, let alone crush your skull."

A sluggish understanding begins to show in his eyes.

"What the hell is this all about? What do you want?"

"I want to know why you married her."

"Huh?"

I take a step toward him, and he flattens himself against the car.

"The child wasn't yours. She was pregnant when you married her. You married her and agreed to raise someone else's kid. Why?"

"I loved her."

"You loved her?"

"Yeah, I fucking loved her!" he shouts at me. "You got a fucking problem with that?"

I swing the bat without thinking and catch him across the knee-caps. He crashes to the ground on his side, screaming, and grips his shattered knees to his chest. I hit him in the kidneys, and he screams again.

I expect to feel good, but I feel sick. I realize too late I don't want to do this, but I have to do it.

My calm returns, even though my hands have begun to shake.

I take a deep breath.

"You loved her, and you beat her. You tried to beat her to death, and you're going to tell me you loved her?"

"I'm not saying I did a good job of it."

I lift the bat over him. He raises his hands over his head and cringes beneath them.

"Okay. Maybe I didn't love her. I thought I did. I guess I felt sorry for her. The guy who got her pregnant walked out on her. He dumped her. He told her she could never prove it was his. He told her to kill it. I felt bad for her, okay?"

I think of Val's letters. I think of him writing to Zo that the only bad things in Vietnam were the American soldiers and the North Vietnamese soldiers. The two enemies become one enemy to the people they were trying to save.

For one terrible instant, I feel we've been manipulated and pitted against each other, against our wills, for reasons we don't understand, by forces beyond our control. I see how we could have been and should have been on the same side. Reese and I come from the same dark place; we've just spent different amounts of time in the light.

The feeling isn't strong enough to make me forgive him or make me forgive myself.

I leave him moaning on the ground and walk back to my truck to get Jess's revolver. I return and show it to him. He cranes his head up, and his eyes flicker with terror.

"This is your brother's gun that you took out of his house today and put in your car. When I pulled you over for drunk driving, you shot at me."

I turn and shoot at a tree about fifteen feet away from us. Reese yells, "Holy shit!" when the gun explodes and pulls himself into a tighter ball on the ground.

"Fortunately you missed," I go on with my scenario, "and the bullet lodged in a tree. I was able to respond by shooting at you, and I didn't miss."

"That means . . ."

His face goes slack and pale.

"You're fucking nuts," he says shakily. "That's the most premeditated shit I've ever heard."

"It's not any worse than what you did to Crystal."

"I never thought about that shit before I did it. She'd just say something that pissed me off, and I'd hit her."

"You went out and bought the fucking bat."

"It was for Johnny."

"Don't call him that!" I scream at him.

"That was his name!" he screams back.

I grab him by the hair.

"Get in the car."

"Jesus!" he cries out.

"Get in the fucking car."

He starts to cry. I grab him under the arms and drag him over.

A pair of headlights appears in the distance. I keep dragging Reese, hoping whoever it is will keep going. We're far enough off the road they shouldn't be able to see anything.

The car slows as it gets closer, then turns purposefully down the coal road as if this were its intended destination. I stop, still holding Reese under the arms, and watch the headlights flick off and the car come to a rolling stop. The engine dies, and a door opens and slams shut.

Jack, in full uniform with a regulation shotgun tucked under one arm, comes walking slowly toward us.

"Let him go," he tells me.

I drop Reese. He skitters to his car and presses himself against it while Jack shines a flashlight in his face. He holds the beam steady for a couple seconds, then clicks it off.

"Hello, Reese," he says with a tightening of his lips that almost resembles a smile.

Reese half raises a hand but doesn't say anything.

"Deputy Zoschenko has been a little out of sorts recently," Jack explains.

"He's fucking nuts!" Reese shouts.

"Watch your mouth."

He turns to me.

"What's going on out here? Did he commit a crime of some sort?"

"He was driving under the influence."

"Ah." He rubs his chin. "I see."

He flashes the light at Reese, who covers his eyes with his forearm.

"Didn't you just get out of prison, Reese?"

"You know I did."

"Wouldn't a DUI be considered a parole violation?"

"Fuck you."

He turns the light off again, and we stand in silent darkness.

"I'll tell you what, Reese," he says. "I'll forget about the DUI, and you will forget about Deputy Zoschenko."

"How the fuck am I supposed to forget about him?" he cries.

"He won't bother you anymore unless I tell him he can. Now, get in your car and drive home and sleep it off."

"How the hell am I supposed to sleep this off? I need a drink."

"Go home," he orders him.

Jack takes a step toward him. Reese tries to stand and can't do it. We both help him up and put him in his car while he whimpers about his knees.

My own knee is killing me.

I take a seat on the rear bumper of my truck. Now that the adrenaline rush is over, I can barely move. I want to stretch out on the coal and die.

I hear one engine start and a car drive away. Then I hear a slow pair of shoes approach me.

"How'd you find me?" I ask him before he comes into view.

"You're not the only person who can stake out a bar."

"How'd you know what I was planning to do?"

He comes up next to me and puts a foot on the end of my bumper. "Do you know what this job is all about?"

"The pants?"

"Reading people."

My hands won't stop shaking. Aside from two target practices for the job and Val's letting me shoot his rifle, I've never fired a gun before.

"I got an interesting phone call from Bobbie Raynor today. You know Bobbie. She's married to Jess. Reese's brother."

I look up at him. I can't see his eyes. His entire face is hidden in the shadow cast by his hat brim.

"Yeah, I know Bobbie."

"She seemed to be under the impression that you might have a reason to want to harm Reese. That it might drive you to do something stupid. I believe those were her exact words: 'Jess and me don't want him to do something stupid.'"

"Did she tell you why she thought I might want to hurt him?"

"No. I couldn't get it out of her, and frankly, it doesn't matter at the moment."

"So what are you saying? I'm not in trouble for doing this?"

"If I thought for one minute you were actually capable of killing him, you'd be in trouble."

"You're not going to make me tell you the whole story?"

"Not tonight."

"I don't get it, Jack. You offered me a good job out of the blue that I wasn't qualified for. You've helped me keep that job when a different man would have fired me. You've cut me a lot of breaks. Now, after what I did tonight, you're still keeping me around. You're doing all this for me just because you love Penn State football?"

He takes his foot off the bumper.

"Maybe I'm not doing anything for you. Maybe I'm doing this for your sister."

He bends down and picks up Jess's revolver from the ground where I dropped it.

"I'm going to run by Jess and Bobbie's place," he tells me. "Make sure everyone gets settled in okay."

He starts to leave, then pauses.

"What was your plan? Make it look like self-defense?"

I nod at him.

He turns around and starts walking back to his truck. I hear a strange noise coming from him I've never heard before. At first I think he might be coughing or crying. It takes me a moment to realize it's the sound of Jack chuckling.

There are no clouds tonight. The sky glints a pure onyx black, and the cold seems to ricochet off its hard surface back to earth, where it shatters and pierces like needles.

I park my truck behind Val's and sit there with the windows open, staring at the bumper stickers on my dashboard and watching my breath leave my mouth in puffs. It's 3:22 A.M. I can't find a single star, but the moon is huge and bright. The strip mining beyond the house is so flooded with light it's taken on the shadowless appearance of a lethal, dusty, white planet.

Across the road the rows of lawn mowers look new and polished, their dents and scratches and scabs of rust repaired by the glare of the moon. The snakes move in and out and through them, steadily and almost invisibly, like looping currents of brown light. The rats are bolder and scurry out into the open. I don't see them until their eyes catch the moonlight and flash green for a second.

I get out and cross the yard. The scraps of junk and the sparse patches of grass have a dull gray glimmer to them, like they've been misted with iron. I drag my boot over the ground and leave a path. It's frost.

The house is dark and silent, but there's a wisp of smoke coming from the chimney. A flagpole has been erected since my visit yesterday. It's flying the Stars and Stripes and my sister's panties.

Val's sitting on the front porch steps smoking one of the cigars I gave him.

He doesn't seem surprised to see me.

I walk over to him without saying a word and sit down next to him on the steps.

"You gave me some hunting advice once. I don't know if you'll remember it. You told me it's pretty stupid to try and kill something I don't want to kill."

He takes a couple puffs off the cigar and blows some smoke in the air.

"That sounds like something I'd say."

"I thought I wanted to kill someone tonight. I tried to do it."

"But you didn't do it?"

"No."

"Then you must not have wanted to kill him."

"I have a son." The words catch in my throat.

I was planning on saying more, but I can't.

He hands me a cigar. I haven't smoked one since I worked for Mr. Perez.

"I wasn't drafted," he says simply. "I enlisted. After what happened in Gertie, I thought 'Nam would be better than working in the mines."

He flips open his lighter and holds out the flame to me.

I watch him in amazement. I don't know what to say.

"I was wrong," he explains. "We all make mistakes."

I look over at the mummified tree. In the moonlight it has the silver-gray sheen of a bone that's been sucked on. I wonder what killed it. We're too far away for it to be a victim of the mine fires. A disease or an insect, probably. It wasn't very old when it died. Its brittle limbs are smooth and have kept the thin, graceful swoop of youth.

Soft padding paws sound behind me, and I turn my head expecting to see a raccoon or a cat.

It's Jolene in bare feet and bare legs, wrapped in a blanket.

"He said my bedroom was too ruffly," she offers as an explanation.

I glance over at Val. His expression remains expressionless. I shake my head, smiling, and go back to watching the lawn mowers.

"That was quick," I tell her.

"Life's short," she replies.

She puts a hand on Val's shoulder and shakes something at me in the dark.

"You want to stay for Jiffy Pop?"

# FRIDAY

# TWENTY-THREE

THE NIGHTS I SLEEP ON JOLENE'S COUCH, I'M USUALLY AWAKENED by the boys getting ready for school. It's one of the reasons why I don't like sleeping on her couch and one of the reasons why she does like me sleeping here. She says I deserve it.

This morning I wake up on my own, with the sun in my eyes. The curtains on her front window are open, and the sun streams through, falling across my face and onto the coffee table, where signs of Val in the form of two beer cans and a full ashtray sit.

I raise up on one elbow expecting a hangover out of habit, but my head feels relatively clear. I'm still in my clothes, but my boots are off, which is a good sign. I feel better than I expected to feel.

I reach for the phone on Jolene's end table and dial Chastity's office.

She's on another line. Her secretary asks me to hold.

"Hi."

Her voice is a more effective wake-up than a dozen cups of coffee.

"Hi," I say back. "What are you up to?"

She laughs.

"I'm seeing patients. What are you up to?"

"Not much, so far. I thought I'd see if you were going to be free later tonight. Maybe have dinner?"

"Mm. I can't tonight."

"I'm sorry. I forgot. We're going to take it slow. I'm asking too soon."

"No, you're not. I'm just busy tonight, that's all."

"How about September fifteenth?"

"What's on September fifteenth?"

"I've been invited to a birthday party at Chuck E. Cheese's."

"Do they have one of those big ball pits?"

"I think so."

"You're planning on being around then?"

"Yeah."

"Okay, it's a date. In the meantime how about dinner Saturday night?"

"Sounds good."

"Are you going to Gertie today?" she asks me.

"I guess so. Have you been to this memorial service before? I hear they have it every year."

"Yes, I've been to it before. I think you should go."

"I haven't been back there since I broke my leg."

"You should go," she tells me again.

"Okay. Will I see you there?"

"If you don't find me first, I'll throw a rock at your head."

"Great."

After I hang up, I hear voices in the kitchen. I check the clock on Jolene's VCR. The boys should have left for school already, and Jolene should've left for work. I should've left for work, too, but that's never stopped me from being late before.

I walk into the kitchen and find Jolene and Randy having coffee at the table. She's in her waitress uniform. He's in a suit. He's taken off the jacket and has it hanging over the back of a chair. The tail of a necktie hangs out of one pocket. He looks tired.

"Hi, Ivan."

He practically jumps out of his chair to shake my hand. Randy has always been a little afraid of me since he got Jolene pregnant and they didn't get married. I don't know why. Eb was number three. I told him I was used to it.

"Hey, Randy. What are you doing here?"

"I was just about to find out," Jolene answers.

She gets up and brings back a coffee mug for me.

"Man, I must have been tired," I tell them. "The boys didn't wake me this morning."

"They're still sleeping," Jolene says. "They're going to the Gertie service, and then they'll go to school afterward."

"You let them miss school for this thing?"

She pours me a cup of coffee.

"You'll see," she says.

She sits down again and smiles at Randy.

"So what's this big news?" she asks. "You haven't even told me why you're in town."

"I came down yesterday to meet with Mom's lawyer about her will."

"I'd imagine that was pretty cut and dried," I comment.

"We've started going through her things," Jolene explains. "She has everything labeled with a piece of masking tape. I'd imagine the only thing left to account for in her will would be money."

"Well, there was something else she wasn't able to put a piece of tape on: the house and the land. She left it to you, Jolene."

"What?" Jolene gasps.

"See?" He hits the table with the flat of his hand. "I knew you didn't know anything about it. Marcy thinks you harassed Mom into leaving it to you."

Jolene is so stunned she doesn't bother to insult Marcy.

"Marcy's the one who made me come talk to the lawyer in person and see what we could do about it. She says we'll contest the will in court if that's what it takes."

"On what grounds?" I ask.

He puts his head in his hands and talks into them.

"I don't know. If the talk with the lawyer didn't go well, Marcy wanted me to talk to Jolene and see if I could convince her to give us the house."

"Marcy said this. Marcy wants that." Jolene finds her voice. "What about you? Do you have any say in this?"

He pulls his hands away and looks from her to me and back to her again.

"I have to admit when I first heard about it, I was upset. We were counting on the money we'd get from selling the house. We were already making plans for some of it. When I left the lawyer's office yesterday, I was ready to do whatever I had to do to get the house."

He gives us a strange, sad smile.

"I was ready to do whatever I had to do to get the house so I could get rid of it," he elaborates. "I drove out there all pissed off at Mom. Then when I got there and walked around a bit, I understood what she'd done.

"She knew I wasn't going to come back here and live. If she left the house to me, I'd sell it. And she knew who I'd probably end up selling it to," he adds guiltily.

"Have they contacted you?" I ask.

"The day her obituary ran."

"Sons of bitches," I say flatly.

"But it's more than that," he adds quickly. "It's more than her wanting to keep the land away from J&P and wanting to keep the house in the family. She knew with her and the house gone, I'd probably never come back here to visit anymore."

He drops his eyes and stares into his coffee as he talks.

"When she was alive, my mom never got on my case for the way I treated Eb. I knew she was disappointed in me, and I knew she wanted me to spend more time with him, but between the job and Marcy and our own kids and living all the way in Maryland . . . well, it was easier to just stay away. She never got mad at me or lectured me. Now that she's gone, she's making sure I won't forget I have a son here and I won't forget where I'm from."

We sit in silence. He keeps staring into his coffee. Jolene stares at him. I stare at Volodymyr and the history in his eyes.

Randy takes a deep breath and looks up.

"I want you to have the house, Jolene. You and Eb and the rest of your boys."

He slides a business card across the table.

"This is Mom's lawyer. I told him you'd give him a call. There's some papers for you to sign. Transfer of deed. That sort of stuff. Do it quick, will you?"

She stares at the little buff-colored rectangle and nods numbly.

He gets up from his chair, slips back into his suit jacket, and plunges his hands in his pants pockets.

"I've decided as long as I'm down here and there's still so much to take care of out at the house, I'm just going to spend the weekend. If it's okay with you, I'd like to spend some time with Eb."

"Sure, that's fine. What's Marcy going to say about all this?"

"That's my problem."

"Randy . . ." she starts to say.

"Don't thank me," he stops her. "I'm not doing anything great here except abiding by my mother's last wishes."

I stand, too.

"You're a good son, Randy," I tell him.

He jingles something in his pockets and rocks on his shoes.

"I don't know about that. I think I'm more of a coward. I don't want her haunting me."

The phone rings, and Jolene gets up to answer it.

"For you, Ivan. Work. It's Chuck."

She holds out the receiver to me.

"Hey, Chuck. What's going on?"

"We need you out at Jess Raynor's place. There's been a shooting." He pauses. "A fatality."

# TWENTY-FOUR

I DON'T WAIT TO HEAR ANYTHING ELSE. I TELL HIM I'LL BE THERE and hang up before he can give me any more information. I don't want to hear a name.

Ignorance is bliss, the saying goes. I try to embrace that philosophy during the drive to Jess's house.

It's a beautiful day with a cloudless blue sky. It was a day like this when we buried the miners.

I remember when I woke up that day being stunned at the callousness of nature, that force I revered and lugged around with me inside a book my dad had left for me one Christmas morning while masquerading as Santa Claus. The sun shone, birds sang, grass looked greener than it had in weeks, yet the men were gone. They were never coming back. We were all in mourning, numbed by our grief and disbelief. I thought nature should mourn, too. Not just for the men but for herself. Nature had suffered, too. We had gouged holes in her and ripped gashes in her. We had stripped her and stolen from her. But she didn't care. She didn't hold a grudge.

Zo saw that same day as a gift. She told me if it had been rainy, we would have got our shoes muddy.

I couldn't deal with a name, but I can deal with the word "fatality." Someone is dead, but I don't know who. I can think of the children and Jess and Bobbie, one by one, then tell myself that each one of them is still alive. It's a game of mental musical chairs. Death is the only remaining chair, and Jess and his family are still circling, not knowing that the person who wins will die. Until I get there, the music is still playing for me. My father's words in Val's handwriting keep reappearing in my head: The best way to die is first.

It's not until I've parked my truck down the road from the house and taken the first few steps toward the flashing blue and red lights of the ambulance and two sheriff's cars that I regret not knowing.

The beagles are silent but sit at attention on the roofs of their doghouses. Watching them, I'm filled with the same sick dread that turned my blood icy when I heard the first wail of Gertie's siren.

Their oldest boy, Gary, is standing outside with one of his sisters. I make mental check marks on my list of survivors. That leaves the other little girl. And Danny. And Jess. And Bobbie.

I swallow hard and make my feet move in the direction of the house.

I try not to dwell on the fact that I didn't kill him last night. That I had a chance to do what I should have done and I didn't, and now someone else is dead. I look away from Danny's orange pumpkin bucket, lying empty on its side in the middle of the yard.

Pregnant Chad comes out of the house holding the other little girl's hand. Jack is right behind him carrying one of Jess's rifles. He's followed by the paramedics wheeling out the body.

I run a clammy hand over my face. I don't want to see the size of the body.

I begin to pray to a god I don't believe in. I pray that it's not Jess, knowing that means he's lost his wife or his son. I pray that it's not Danny, knowing that means he's lost his mom or his dad. I pray that it's not Bobbie, knowing that means she's lost her husband or her little boy.

She called Jack last night to try to prevent this from happening to me.

I force myself to look. A pair of large, muddy boots stick out from the sheet at one end.

"Daddy!" I hear Danny cry.

Stiffy comes out of the house next, carrying Danny, who's clutching his blanket.

I watch the stretcher being wheeled carelessly over the ruts in the yard. The boots jostle against each other like they're keeping time to a frantic song.

"Daddy!" Danny cries again.

I feel the cup of coffee I just drank start to come up. I'm going to be sick.

I make myself look back at Danny. He's dropped his blanket. Stiffy doesn't notice and steps on it, grinding it into the mud.

Something doesn't fit. I'm not sure what it is, and then I realize Danny's looking back over Stiffy's shoulder when he's calling out to his dad. He's not crying over the covered body on the stretcher.

Shouting comes from inside the house.

Jack's eyes meet mine. I can't read anything in them before his gaze flicks away.

Doverspike escorts Bobbie outside. She has her hands cuffed behind her.

"She didn't mean to do it. It was an accident."

Jess comes after her. He almost stumbles down the front steps. One of his eyes is swollen shut, and bright red blood trickles from one ear, down his neck, and stains the shoulder of his T-shirt.

My heart starts pounding loudly in my chest. The body is Reese.

"I knew something like this was gonna happen!" Gary shouts when he sees his mom.

His young face turns red, and his lips start trembling.

"I just knew it!" he shouts again, and kicks at the ground before sitting down in the grass with his arms wrapped around his knees and his head hidden between them. His shoulders start to shake.

The girls stand beside each other.

"Mom!" the one cries. "Mommy!"

"It's okay, honey. I'm gonna be back. It's gonna be fine."

Jess misses the bottom step and falls on his face.

I jog over to help him.

"What happened?" I ask him as he gets unsteadily to his feet.

He wipes at the tears and spit on his face with a dirty hand that leaves his face streaked with mud.

"I don't know. I don't know. We got in a fight. Me and Reese. About going to Gertie. Next thing I know there's a gunshot. He's laying there dead. Bobbie's holding my gun."

He realizes Doverspike's putting Bobbie in the car. He takes off and runs over to them.

"She didn't mean to do it. It was an accident."

"He can't hurt you anymore, Jess," she calls out before Doverspike slams the car door shut on her. "I'm not sorry I did it."

He grabs at Doverspike's arm.

"She doesn't know what she's saying. She's upset."

Doverspike gently but firmly grabs Jess around the wrist and removes his hand from his arm.

"Sir, you're going to have to step away from the car," he tells him. "Sir," he says more forcefully when Jess doesn't respond.

A strange light dawns in his murky stares.

"You're going to have to step away from the car," Doverspike finishes.

"Sure," Jess mutters, all the fight seeming to have left him.

He sits down hard in the middle of the yard, just like his boy Gary did, not far from the spot where I left him unconscious a couple days ago.

I walk over to him.

"You all right, Jess?"

We watch the sheriff's car drive away with Bobbie and the ambulance drive away with Reese.

Stiffy puts Danny down. He runs over to us but stops a couple feet short of his dad.

Gary gets up off the ground, and he and his two sisters stand staring at us.

Jess doesn't seem to notice them.

"I'm going with Bobbie," he tells me.

"Can you drive yourself?"

"I'm fine. Do you mind taking the kids?"

"No, of course not. I'll look after them until you're ready to take them back or your mom can help."

"No, I mean take them to Gertie. Right now." He gives me a pleading look. "We always take them."

Jack joins us after putting the gun in his car.

"Don't worry, Jess. We'll take care of everything. You go on inside and get the keys to your truck."

"Did you know this was going to happen?" I ask Jack in a low voice after Jess is out of earshot.

"How could I possibly know? I'm a sheriff, not a psychic. Although I do know sometimes it's better to let families work out their own problems."

"That's what you call this? Do you feel this problem has been worked out?"

He kneels down and picks Danny's dirty blanket up off the ground and hands it to him.

"It's getting there."

I don't wait to see Jess again. The four kids cram into the front of my truck with me. Danny sits next to me, still holding his blanket. None of them move a muscle or make a sound while I drive.

We have to pass by the junkyard to get to Gertie. I notice more cars and trucks on the road than usual, but I don't think much of it.

The last few miles before the junkyard, snakes of steam begin to slither across the road in front of my truck and dart beneath the dead, wiry, black undergrowth dotting the banks like snarls of steel wool.

I round the final curve and see Jolene's car parked on the side of the road. I pull up behind it and cut the engine.

Four pairs of wide eyes turn in my direction and fix intently on my face.

"I want to check something out in the junkyard," I tell them.

Their stares don't waver. Their expressions reveal nothing.

"You want to come with me or wait in the truck?"

Gary, who's sitting next to the door, opens it, and they all bounce out, their feet moving before they hit the ground. They've all disappeared down over the hill before I even get out of the truck.

Small tumbleweeds of contamination bounce and blow in all directions.

I start down the hill and lose my footing for an instant. I slide on the slick, packed mud and grab onto the gutted shell of an old Zenith TV. The knob for changing channels has been ripped out like a limb from a socket, leaving behind a tangle of red and blue wires, reminding me of the way arteries and lengths of nerves are pictured in anatomy books.

Jolene is standing halfway down and turns in my direction as the TV goes somersaulting down the hill and I almost go with it.

The girls and Danny are off running around with Eb. Harrison is with Gary.

"What are you doing here?" Jolene asks me. "And why do you have Bobbie's kids?"

"Let's just say I'm helping them out. I'll explain it all later. What are you doing here?" I ask her.

"I always come here first. I like the view."

I follow her eyes across the valley to the remains of Gertie. Cars and trucks are parked all around it, in the same haphazard fashion they were left in the day of the explosion. I can even make out a few fire trucks and some police cars.

"What's going on?" I ask.

"Look," she says.

I begin to see the people. From this distance they're the size of ants, but it's a clear day, and I can see the colors of their clothing. They converge, split, converge, spread about, like speckles of paint in a water droplet.

In my mind I know who they are. I see husbands and wives getting out of their cars and holding hands. Guys running into other guys, buddies, coworkers, school chums, shaking hands. Daughters helping their elderly mothers, holding them at their elbows where their big white spring pocketbooks hang. They bring their purses everywhere, even to Gertie. Kids running off with their friends. A group of teenage girls casting glances at a group of teenage boys.

I know how they came to be here. I see Dr. Ed wash his hands in Exam Room 2, hang his blue coat on a hook, pick up his tackle box full of medical supplies, and flick the light switch on his way out. I see Muchmore outside a courtroom, checking his gold watch, ending a conversation with another lawyer, and offering his limp handshake before heading for his BMW. I see Chastity draw the blinds in her office, where she slips out of her skirt and heels and pulls on a pair of jeans and cowboy boots. I see Miss Finch glance around her empty classroom filled with art made from cans. I see Edna thank a coworker for filling in for her as she leaves her post behind the Kwik-Fill cash register. I see Chimp crawl out of bed, shaking off a hangover, and reach for his boots by the back door. I see Josh pick up some buddies in his truck. I see the tire shredders walk out despite a day's loss of pay. I see Randy standing on Zo's front porch looking at the hills. I see Val's old Chevy truck idling outside Safe Haven as he makes his painstaking, one-legged approach into the building to pick up my mom, who meets him with my dad's brass tag worn around her neck today and tucked secretly beneath her blouse. I see Jack taking off his hat to polish the shield before he drives up in his sheriff's car. I see Crystal forever in her bed.

Behind us, on the road above us, traffic has picked up. Cars and trucks roar past, a few at first, then a constant rumbling stream.

"I wonder what Zo left for you?" Jolene says.

The packed dirt and gravel road leading to Gertie that my mother once dragged me over is a long line of glinting windshield glass.

"Some advice," I tell her. "She helped me make a decision."

"Hey, Uncle Ivan!" Eb shouts at me through cupped hands. "Look at Danny!"

The little boy is holding a big stick and standing on top of a pile of tires with his blanket knotted around his neck and a jagged half of a coffee can balanced on his head.

Eb grins and calls out, "He's the Czar of Coal Run."

My eyes return to the trail of glitter cut into the distant hillside. It leaves Gertie and keeps going, seemingly forever, curving, disappearing and reappearing from behind stands of trees and dips in the land in an unbroken vein of silver.

# EPILOGUE

Dear Deputy Zoschenko,

I wanted to write and thank you again for the kindness you've shown my mother. It was difficult for me to find out about her after all these years and even more difficult to see her. I hope I didn't seem like a jerk by staying for such a short period of time and then leaving so suddenly. I had a hard time being with her, but I hope I'll be able to get used to it and someday I can treat her the way you do.

The other reason I'm writing is that I've decided to come to Centresburg again in May after finals are over and before I start my summer job. I realize you're very busy, but I was wondering if you might be able to find the time to show me around the area. I was also hoping I might be able to meet some of the family you said I have around there.

I know I could come back and just visit my mom, but I feel like I should get to know Coal Run, too. After all, it is where I'm from.

Sincerely,
John Harris (Raynor)

March 22, 2001

Dear John,

I'll look forward to your visit. I'd be happy to show you around and introduce you to your family.

Regards,
Ivan Z

# ACKNOWLEDGMENTS

*Coal Run* almost never saw the light of day because of some personal problems I had to deal with over the past two years, which made finding the time and the concentration to write next to impossible. Now that the book is finished and all that's left is the pleasurable task of thanking the people who helped me, I find that what I'm thanking them for has little to do with the book itself but has everything to do with my own well-being. For me as a writer, my most valuable assistance came not from a team of researchers or access to the experts in their fields, but from people in my life who cared about me.

That said, I'd like to thank my agent, Liza Dawson, who patiently waited for this book, never pushed me yet never forgot me, and was always there for me anytime I needed to vent. Thank you to my editor, the masterful Molly Stern, who once again proved to be my literary alter ego and instinctively knew exactly what needed to be done to make this a better book.

Thank you to Françoise Triffaux at Belfond, whose esteem for my work has meant the world to me.

Thanks to my baby sis, Molly, for being my fiercest fan. To my little sis, Trina, and her husband, Chuck, for keeping me on the family radar. To Roy, for going far above and beyond the basic requirements of stepfathering; thanks for your friendship and that all-important "swoop." To Uncle Butch, for his immense generosity. Thanks, Mikey, for the heavy lifting. Thanks, Fern, for the listening. Thanks, Dad, for your steady faith in me.

To my wonderful kids, Tirzah and Connor: We had to go through some tough times recently but through it all you behaved with a grace and maturity well beyond your years. I'm proud to be your mom.

And speaking of moms, I don't think I would have survived these past few years with my sanity intact without the help of mine. It's very important as a woman to be reminded from time to time that before you were a mother yourself, a wife, an ex-wife, a student, an employee, a lover, a homeowner, a taxpayer, an author, you were someone's little girl and that someone will always see you in that way; you, stripped of all your adult labels and responsibilities; you, just you; the purest sense of yourself. And while you are busy putting everyone else first, she will be putting you first. Thanks, Mom.

To Bernard, the man of my dreams who became the man in my life. Thank you for showing me the world and all the joys of living in it.

# TAWNI O'DELL

**COAL RUN**

# QUESTIONS FOR DISCUSSION

⁘

1. Lost identity is a recurring theme in this book, both locally, in the Pennsylvania boys' forgetting their hometowns, and in a larger sense, in Americans' forgetting their ethnic identities. From tales of Magadan to the portrait of Volodymyr that sits above the Zoschenko dinner table, allusions to Ivan's father's former life in Ukraine and Russia are made throughout the novel. Discuss what Ivan's heritage means to him.

2. The land of Coal Run is inexplicably, irrevocably part of each character, drawing back those who leave it. Discuss each of the very different homecomings of the book—those of Val, Reese Raynor, Ivan, and John Harris. What is it that ties each character to the town?

3. Compare Ivan as a little boy to Ivan as the narrator of the novel. How does his voice change? How are his relationships to Val and Eb similar?

4. Ivan loses his father, uncle, and grandfather in the Gertie mine explosion and Val to the Vietnam War, then denies the existence of his own son. None of Jolene's three sons have any kind of relationship with his father. Discuss the lack of male role models and father figures throughout the book. How does this affect the men of each generation?

5. The loss of Ivan's knee, his heroic self, and his chance to forever leave Coal Run all occur at Gertie. Discuss the significance of his choice to self-destruct at that location.

6. The burning land of Coal Run, with its simmering, unstoppable fires beneath the surface, literally sucks down people, homes, and objects into its fiery depths. The festering rage of each character similarly manifests itself with violence. Discuss how the violence and anger of Bobbie, Reese, and Ivan differ.

7. Discuss the role of women in this town that is defined by mining, a very male profession. Ivan's mother, his sister Jolene, Zo—are they better at coping with tragedy? Are they stronger?

8. In many ways Zo and Dr. Ed mastermind the fates of several of the characters, guiding their fates, yet without reprimand or condemnation. Dr. Ed anonymously sends the clipping to Ivan. Zo leaves her home to Jolene and her grandson, forever tying Randy to Coal Run. Discuss the silent but strong (and effective) techniques of this generation.

9. Ivan's father is able to separate the profession of coal mining from the fact that he learned it while in Siberia at a work camp. Reese, though an abusive husband and a murderer, at one time behaved honorably by marrying Crystal when Ivan would not. But Ivan cannot separate his identity as a football hero and town figure from who he is inside as a person. Discuss how profession and the ability to provide shape male identity. How is male identity tied to duty?

10. The demons of the past haunt several characters, most notably Ivan. How does the past literally and figuratively cripple him and prevent him from embarking on a future of any kind?

# The new psychological thriller from *New York Times* bestselling author Tawni O'Dell

Famed psychologist Dr. Sheridan Doyle uncovers startling truths about his family, his past, and himself when he returns to his hometown in pursuit of a killer.

Pick up or download your copy today.

Printed in the United States
by Baker & Taylor Publisher Services